LEGEND OF THE FIVE RINGS

Rokugan – the Emerald Empire. For centuries, the samurai of the Great Clans have defended and served the Hantei dynasty. But now, danger besets Rokugan from all sides.

Emperor Hantei XXVI is dying, and the courts bristle with opportunity while rebellion stalks the land, and rumors of foul magic threaten to corrupt the Empire from within.

A forgotten evil is at work, and it hungers for power and blood.

With the Great Clans distracted and divided, seven heroes must take up the call and forge their own destiny or risk everything in the pursuit of glory.

T0023107

ALSO AVAILABLE

LEGEND OF THE FIVE RINGS
  Curse of Honor by David Annandale

  The Night Parade of 100 Demons by Marie Brennan
  The Game of 100 Candles by Marie Brennan

  To Chart the Clouds by Evan Dicken
  The Heart of Iuchiban by Evan Dicken

THE DAIDOJI SHIN MYSTERIES
Poison River by Josh Reynolds
Death's Kiss by Josh Reynolds
The Flower Path by Josh Reynolds
Three Oaths by Josh Reynolds

THE GREAT CLANS OF ROKUGAN
The Collected Novellas Vol 1
The Collected Novellas Vol 2

The SOUL
of IUCHIBAN

Evan Dicken

ACONYTE

First published by Aconyte Books in 2023

ISBN 978 1 83908 229 0

Ebook ISBN 978 1 83908 230 6

Copyright © 2023 Fantasy Flight Games

All rights reserved. The Aconyte name and logo and the Asmodee Entertainment name and logo are registered or unregistered trademarks of Asmodee Entertainment Limited. Legend of the Five Rings and the FFG logo are trademarks or registered trademarks of Fantasy Flight Games.

This novel is entirely a work of fiction. Names, characters, places, and incidents are the products of the author's imagination or are used fictitiously. Any resemblance to actual events, locales, organizations or persons, living or dead, is entirely coincidental.

Sales of this book without a front cover may be unauthorized. If this book is coverless, it may have been reported to the publisher as "unsold and destroyed" and neither the author nor the publisher may have received payment for it.

Cover art by Larry Rostant

Rokugan map by Francesca Baerald

Distributed in North America by Simon & Schuster Inc, New York, USA

Printed in the United States of America

9 8 7 6 5 4 3 2 1

ACONYTE BOOKS

An imprint of Asmodee Entertainment Ltd

Mercury House, Shipstones Business Centre

North Gate, Nottingham NG7 7FN, UK

aconytebooks.com // twitter.com/aconytebooks

*To Alana and George, who've journeyed
with me from Heian to Bakumatsu and back
again – one Tuesday at a time.*

PROLOGUE

"Iuchiban lives." Iuchi Qadan felt her lips move, a traitor's voice shaping words not her own.

"Who?" Lord Shinjo Bataar leaned forward, one fist resting on his knee. Although in his eightieth year, the Unicorn Clan Champion still cut an imposing figure – deep purple robes, fringes of bleached lion fur, and jade-scaled sash a testament to the many border skirmishes he had won.

Irritation flickered at the edges of Qadan's awareness, Iuchiban annoyed his name had sparked no recognition. In the weeks since the ancient Bloodspeaker had seized her body, she had noticed a few cracks in the ancient sorcerer's calm façade.

"If you see anything, it is because I wish it."

Iuchiban's words echoed through Qadan's thoughts. That they came in her own voice was a cutting reminder of the power the sorcerer held over her.

"You think me some ancient shade risen to plague the land. But I am human, too."

Perhaps once. Whatever he was now, Iuchiban was more than man or demon.

"In that, you are right." His chuckle was the delighted laugh of a teacher whose student has mastered some esoteric formulation. At the same time, he was speaking to the Unicorn nobles, gesturing like some fireside storyteller set before a rapt audience.

"Iuchiban is a sorcerer of tremendous power, locked away beneath a seal of purest jade," Iuchiban said. "In centuries past, he raised a legion of dead, almost destroying the Scorpion Clan."

"Would that he had succeeded and saved the Empire trouble." Shinjo Bataar slapped his knee, laughter the sharp croak of a startled crow.

"It took the might of all Rokugan to send him back to the grave," Iuchiban continued once the tent was silent. "Even then, he could not be slain, for it is said he removed his heart, hiding it away where none could find the key to his destruction."

A lie, Qadan knew now. She and her erstwhile companions had breached the ancient sorcerer's tomb, braving Iuchiban's traps and deadly tests to reach the center. But there was no heart to be found, if such a thing even existed.

"Very clever, disciple. I knew my faith in you was not misplaced."

As much as it stung to receive praise from a dark sorcerer, Qadan could not quell the blush of satisfaction. Iuchiban could have destroyed her, but he had allowed Qadan to keep her mind if not the body that held it.

"And how do you know this?" Iuchi Arban spoke for the first time. Although decades younger than the Unicorn Champion, the slight, dark-eyed daimyō of the Iuchi family carried himself with a wisdom belying his age. A powerful name keeper, he wore the talismans of his spirits in plain view, clearly proud of the bond they represented. The sight brought a twinge of longing to Qadan. Although Iuchiban had kept her satchel, the talismans within were empty of spirits. All save the bladed one that held one of Iuchiban's names.

Qadan had released her own spirits just before Iuchiban possessed her body. It comforted her to know they had escaped the sorcerer's grasp even when she could not.

"Do you recall my studies, Lord Iuchi?" Iuchiban asked.

Arban tapped his chin with one long finger. "You were researching our clan's history... pre-Exodus, I believe."

"My search took me into the Twilight Mountains, lands administered by the Crab Clan," Iuchiban replied. "I sought the tombs of our Ki-Rin Clan ancestors slain in ancient conflicts. In them, I hoped to find history lost to our clan over the long exodus."

Although Qadan was aware Iuchiban had access to her memories, it was still disconcerting to have the blood sorcerer repeat them. She wished he would do something to give himself away, but there was no hesitation in their voice, Iuchiban's imitation of her posture and cadence almost flawless.

Almost.

"Those are dangerous lands." Bataar grunted. "Even more dangerous now."

There were nods around the tent, hands clenched in unspoken anger. The Unicorn had lost many warriors in the Twilight Mountains, slain along with the rest of the imperial expeditionary force sent to quell a peasant revolt. The rebellion had been but another obfuscation. In truth, the expedition had been stricken by infighting, overwhelmed by a legion of walking corpses animated by a powerful blood sorcerer known as the Shrike.

"The tombs sat at the heart of the revolt." Iuchiban said nothing of the dead. "I lost much in the search – my horse; my wealth; my bodyguard, Jargal."

Another cut. Jargal had been Qadan's closest companion. He had not deserved to be slain by blood magic.

"But my search uncovered more than expected… more, indeed, than I could have dreamed," Iuchiban continued. "We thought the Green Horde lost in the jungles of the south, but I found evidence it returned in secret, its leader possessed of powers like none seen in Rokugan."

"You speak of blood magic?" Arban's lips curled as if he found the very words bitter. Qadan heartily agreed with his assessment, her time with Iuchiban having only reinforced her hatred of blood magic.

"I wish it were not so." Iuchiban gave a very credible sigh of distress. "Among the tombs, I found a terrible place laden with traps and wards. And yet, it also held the key to Iuchiban's destruction."

"His heart," Arban said.

"Indeed," Iuchiban lied. "Amidst the tumult, I discovered others also sought the ancient sorcerer's heart – some to destroy it, some to claim its power. I joined forces with the former, and together we breached the hideous tomb. Many fell along the way, but at last I reached the heart."

"And…?" Bataar leaned in, craggy face alight with interest.

For all his inhuman arrogance, it seemed Iuchiban was a fine storyteller.

"I had not the power to destroy it." Iuchiban shook their

head, shoulders rounding. "I barely escaped. I do not know Iuchiban's plans now that he is free of his tomb. But I *do* know we cannot allow him to succeed, lest his dark designs consume the Empire and the Unicorn along with it. Even now, covens of Bloodspeakers work in secret across Rokugan, attempting to realize their master's vision."

Murmurs rose like spring midges swirling amidst the smoky shadows. Qadan could see concern writ large upon the battle-hardened faces, men and women who would face a hundred enemy samurai unnerved by the prospect of ancient sorceries. There was no question as to whether Qadan spoke the truth – she was a noble, a name keeper, a respected historian. Her lineage was impeccable as her deeds.

"Why reveal your plans to them?" she asked Iuchiban. *"Do Bloodspeakers not work best in secret?"*

"Patience, disciple," he replied.

"This is… troubling news," Bataar said at last, a sigh blowing out the ends of his long, white mustache. "We should inform the Imperial Court."

"Emperor Hantei XXVI is on his deathbed, his heir lost to the plague last winter." Iuchiban wrinkled their nose. "With succession unclear, the court will only make a mess of things – if they respond at all. Meanwhile, our rivals seek to take advantage of the chaos."

Bataar frowned. All knew of whom they spoke. Although pretending neutrality, the Dragon Clan never balked from interfering in politics when it suited them, and the Lion were always looking for a way to reclaim the lands they had administered during the Unicorn's long exodus.

"Then we march," Bataar said.

"To where?" Arban asked. "Iuchiban has escaped his tomb, the rebellion is scattered. Marshaling our forces would only antagonize the other clans."

Bataar sat quietly, lips pursed in thought. It did not matter if the Unicorn Champion had made a decision; to give it voice would be to insult all the others present by denying them the chance to speak. He raised a hand, nodding to one of the nearer nobles.

"What is your advice, Lord Tseren?"

There was more debate as lesser nobles rose to speak, bellicose and anxious by turns, as if by failing to state their opinion, however banal, they might be forgotten. Once, Qadan might have been among them. Now she saw the shallowness in their bearing, voices raised in meaningless discussion, wasting time while Iuchiban's agents continued their dire work.

"Do you see how they cluck and crow? Chickens jostling to be first into the slaughterhouse."

"*You seek to foment chaos?*" she asked Iuchiban.

"*Chaos does not need my aid to flourish,*" came his amused reply.

"Then what?"

"*Patience, disciple.*" Once more came the cryptic reply.

Questions were put to Qadan: What else did she know of Iuchiban? Who were her companions? Had any survived to spread word of the blood sorcerer's return? Where was his tomb? What powers, what assets did he possess?

Iuchiban gave just enough information to stoke the flames of fear and anger. Qadan listened as carefully as the others, sifting the ancient sorcerer's replies for flecks of insight. She was a historian after all, used to seeking the truth in others' words.

"And you, Lord Iuchi?" Bataar turned to Arban.

"Something must be done," Arban said. "But massing forces might be construed as an act of war. Better to move quickly, quietly – as Iuchiban will. A small force of our clan's best samurai."

"Who shall lead this force?" Bataar asked.

The young name keeper drew in a slow breath, gaze flicking to Qadan. Muscles bunched along his sharp jawline, eyes narrowed as if in silent question. It was a look he had given her many times – in court, on the hunt, studying elemental spirits, even playing with stuffed ox hide balls when they were children.

Iuchiban cocked their head, nodding silent agreement, just as she had all those times before. Arban was powerful, but young. He depended upon his family for support, for advice. He could trust Qadan.

They *were* cousins, after all.

"Iuchi Qadan should lead." Arban's voice cut through the torrent of whispers. "She is the only one to have faced the blood sorcerer. More, she is a name keeper with strong spiritual allies."

Bataar fixed Qadan with a squint-eyed stare, as if measuring the worth of a foal at the night market.

"What of it? Can you save Rokugan?" Sharp as the champion himself, Bataar's question cut to the heart of the issue.

"I can," Iuchiban replied, and meant it.

Qadan wanted to tear free of Iuchiban's clutches, invisible chains melted by the blistering heat of her wrath. Iuchiban did not chide her. What concern was Qadan's anger to him? There was nothing to push against, nothing to break. All around her was nothing but darkness – limitless and cold as the grave.

When none objected, Bataar gave a slow nod. "Let it be done."

And there it was. The Unicorn had placed a cadre of their best in the hands of the very creature they sought to destroy.

They bowed low to the assembled Unicorn nobility, Iuchiban's smile hidden as they pressed their forehead to the carpeted earth.

"You shall not regret your faith in me."

With typical Unicorn directness, the meeting dispersed quickly. Iuchiban caught up with Arban just outside the tent.

"Thank you, cousin," Iuchiban said softly.

Arban nodded, dark eyes hooded by shadow.

"Jargal." He swallowed, hands bunching into fists at his side. "How did he die?"

"It is better you not know." Voice rough with false concern, Iuchiban laid a hand upon her cousin's arm. The old Moto samurai had been tutor to them both, teaching them how to ride, to hunt, to laugh.

"This Bloodspeaker has much to answer for." He turned to her, moonlight glinting silver on his cheeks.

"He does," Iuchiban replied. "He will."

"Come, cousin." Arban scrubbed a hand across his eyes. "We have much to discuss."

With a nod, Iuchiban fell in beside the Iuchi daimyō, whispering softly of abominations and blood rituals, of the taking of names and dark sorceries powerful enough to shake the pillars of Heaven.

Qadan could not but listen. Although her rage had cooled, her anger remained, sharp as a fresh blade – one she longed to press to Iuchiban's throat.

Her throat.

Qadan needed to watch, to wait, as if Iuchiban were a sheaf of ancient scrolls she sought to translate. For all she despised the blood sorcerer, he was correct about one thing.

This task required patience.

Fortunately, Qadan had nothing but time.

CHAPTER ONE

"Iuchiban is dead." Doji Masahiro took a sip of tea, offering an appreciative sigh. The blend was mediocre as the surroundings – a rather sparse garden in one of the ancillary villas surrounding the Imperial Palace. Still, courtesy cost nothing. And Masahiro could afford to be generous.

"Who?" Lord Otomo Yasunori raised one thin eyebrow, his face wrinkled as his robes – a rather garish cherry blossom print that had been out of fashion even before Masahiro's erstwhile exile. That Yasunori had been reduced to wearing such dross spoke volumes about the lord's fall from grace.

At least Lord Yasunori lived. Which was more than Masahiro could say about the other members of their failed conspiracy. Even now, memory of his brother's death came sharp as broken pottery – jagged and liable to cut. He and Hiroshige could have selected the next emperor. Instead, Masahiro's brother had fallen to an assassin's blade, his body lost amidst the Twilight Mountains.

That is, if Hiroshige remained dead.

Swallowing, Masahiro pushed down memories of walking corpses, of fire and death and blood-slicked blades.

"Iuchiban is a dark sorcerer, ancient and powerful." As if to echo his dire thoughts, Masahiro's missing hand gave a twinge of pain. It hardly mattered that the wound was long healed, smooth flesh covering the wrist of his sword arm; the spirit of his severed hand seemed bent on reminding him of its loss – severed by Shosuro Gensuke, the same Scorpion Clan assassin who had murdered his brother.

Masahiro's only consolation was that Gensuke had come out far worse in the bargain, hacked to pieces by one of Iuchiban's horrible traps.

Pressing down the phantom pain, Masahiro continued, "We lost several brave companions in the sorcerer's tomb."

"They should be memorialized." Yasunori tapped his chin with one long finger, following the tenor of Masahiro's thoughts. "A large ceremony. Full court honors."

Masahiro shared a smile with the Otomo lord. The old badger had always been quick to seize advantage. For all his modest surroundings, Yasunori was a survivor.

One of the many things they had in common.

"That may be hasty." Kitsuki Naoki shifted beside Masahiro, seemingly uncomfortable in her magisterial robes. Despite her newly exalted rank, the Dragon investigator comported herself with all the delicacy of a rustic tax assessor. If anything, her promotion to full Emerald Magistrate seemed to have magnified her willfulness.

Masahiro offered her a warning look, but as always, Naoki forged ahead with no regard for decorum.

"Lord Yasunori, we cannot know for certain if Iuchiban has been destroyed."

"We slew his disciples, did we not?" Masahiro did not wait

for Naoki's reply. "The Shrike, that murderous monk – two vicious blood sorcerers who will no longer trouble Rokugan."

Like a stray dog with a bit of bone, Naoki would not relent. "We do not know if Qadan and the others succeeded."

"Nor do we know they failed." Masahiro flicked his fingers as if to brush away an errant insect, turning to Yasunori. "If anything, this threat will divide our opposition. With your aid, Prince Tokihito may yet rise to power."

Yasunori's gaze drifted across his sad excuse for a garden. Masahiro could almost see the Otomo lord's hungry calculations – it was not every day one was gifted a chance to select the next emperor.

"There is great opportunity here," Masahiro said.

"*Opportunity*." Naoki spoke the word like a curse. She rose from the sitting pillow with a bow so brusque it verged on insulting. "Apologies, lords, but I have pressing matters to attend to."

Fortunately, Yasunori did not deign to take offense. He dismissed the Emerald Magistrate with a distracted wave. Only when Naoki's footfalls faded did he turn once more to Masahiro.

"Strange company you keep. Can we trust her?"

"We can trust Naoki will do her duty," Masahiro replied.

"Will that be a problem?"

"Not so long as our goals align."

"See to it they do." Yasunori spoke as if he were the senior partner in their endeavor, which, technically, he was.

"Yes, lord." Masahiro returned a low bow. He had long grown accustomed to taking orders from the petulant Otomo lord. It was one of the polite fictions that underpinned their relationship. Yasunori possessed that particular admixture of qualities common in many who inherited high court rank – a lust for power and prestige without the wit to attain them.

What set Lord Yasunori apart was that he recognized this deficiency.

So long as forms were followed, deference paid, and results delivered, Yasunori was content to let Masahiro pull the proverbial strings.

"The magistrate did not touch her tea." Lord Yasunori frowned at the rapidly cooling cup.

"I am sure she meant no insult. Weighty matters, and all…"

"The manners of a rustic magistrate are of little concern to me," Lord Yasunori replied coldly. "So long as Naoki aids our cause."

"She will." Masahiro pushed to his feet. "Speaking of which, I had best be after her."

Yasunori dismissed him with a nod, gaze already slipping across the garden to the Imperial Palace, its high-gabled summit rising like distant mountain peaks, gilded statues bright as flame in the autumn light.

Masahiro did not mind such naked ambition. Such fancies kept Yasunori out of trouble while Masahiro did the real work.

He hurried down the wood-paneled walkway, servants fluttering like startled pigeons as they prepared Masahiro's rented palanquin. As he ducked under the artfully parted curtains, Masahiro reflected on how nice it was to have such base concerns as walking removed from his purview. It was pleasant to be home, even if neither the courts nor the Crane Clan knew quite what to do with him.

The palanquin swayed as the bearers shouldered their

burden. Far from the smooth ride Masahiro was accustomed to, they nonetheless navigated the streets of the Inner Districts competently enough. Although autumn had come, summer had yet to relinquish its grip upon the season.

Servants, bureaucrats, and guards hurried along the edges of the road, taking care to yield the wide thoroughfare for their betters. Most wore the colors of various imperial families, but here and there Masahiro spied clan robes – the tawny gold of Lion, the black and red of Scorpion. The majority, by far, wore the white and blue of Masahiro's own clan, the Crane. The sight of so many of his fellows conjured a strange mix of hopefulness and anxiety in Masahiro's breast.

The last time Masahiro had ridden a palanquin through the Inner Districts, he had been fleeing the city in shame – friendless, unprotected, with assassins on his heels. Now it was pleasurable to imagine the various ways he would avenge himself on those who had sought his ignominious demise.

He had dropped their assassin into a pit of accursed blades. He had faced down rebels, blood sorcerers, and an army of walking dead. What need had Masahiro to fear the machinations of perfumed courtiers?

The Emerald Magistracy sat along one of the wider avenues, a straight jaunt from Lord Yasunori's modest manor. Had it not been for the flash of emerald robes amidst the tapestry of more subdued colors, Masahiro might have missed Naoki entirely.

"What happened back there?" He did not bother with preamble, sweeping aside the bamboo curtain as his palanquin came abreast of the magistrate.

"I could ask you the same," she replied without even looking up.

"We discussed this, Naoki." Masahiro fought to keep his voice level. "Now is not the right time."

"And when will that be?" She turned, hands on hips. "When Iuchiban has risen? When his dead sweep over the land? When Bloodspeakers rule the people of Rokugan?"

Masahiro grit his teeth, forcing a smile as he glanced meaningfully up and down the road. Although no one had stopped, it was clear many noted Naoki's outburst.

Sighing, Masahiro ordered his bearers to lower the palanquin.

"Walk with me, please." He rose, threading his handless arm through Naoki's as if they were out for a midmorning stroll. The magistrate tensed at his touch, but thankfully did not pitch Masahiro onto his backside. Even with two hands, he would not have fancied his chances if it came to blows.

With a regretful wave, Masahiro dismissed his palanquin. They walked for some time, long enough to dispel any lingering curiosity from potential onlookers. Masahiro remarked on various shrines and stately manors, voice light while Naoki positively vibrated at his side, arm tight as a bowstring.

When he was sure they weren't being followed, Masahiro turned to weightier matters.

"Do you know who Lord Yasunori is?"

She shrugged. "A court noble fallen on hard times."

"Not untrue." Masahiro chuckled. For all her brusque mannerisms, he would do well to remember Naoki was a skilled investigator. "He is also the appointed guardian of Tokihito, Emperor Hantei's third son – a strong, handsome lad of eleven winters. Normally, Tokihito would have little chance of inheriting, except that my dear departed brother and I spent *years* working on his behalf. Many remain who support our cause."

"Our cause, or yours?"

"We want the same thing, Naoki." He ignored her rudeness. "The court is grateful for our victory over the rebellion. I have been reinstated, *you* have been promoted. We should not squander such opportunity."

"There's that word again... opportunity." She looked away. "You said we were going to warn the court of Iuchiban's return."

"We do not know *if* he will return."

Her brow furrowed. "We should have taken news of Iuchiban directly to the high courts."

Masahiro drew in a calming breath. Single-mindedness made for a fine magistrate, but it made for a poor coconspirator.

"Emperor Hantei XXVI lingers on death's door, unconscious these long months, his heir lost to the plague. The court is in shambles, half the nobles are lining up behind potential candidates, and the other half are settling old grudges while the rule of law is weak." He spoke softly, but urgently. "This is hardly the time to stagger about spouting nonsense about immortal blood sorcerers no one seems to recall."

"All the more reason to bring Iuchiban's evil to light."

"What evil?" Masahiro asked. "You found no record of him in the Imperial Archives."

"Then I shall look elsewhere." Her jaw pulsed. "The High Histories of the Ikoma."

"I have spent my life in the Imperial City, Naoki. I know this place. If you feel our cause is best served by antagonizing the high nobility, then I will accompany you to court this very moment." He sighed, hoping inwardly she would not get them both laughed out of court. "I can assure you though, *nothing* will be done. Not yet, at least."

"And what would you propose?"

He leaned in as if to share a secret. "Give me time to gather support and you can voice your concerns directly into the ear of the next emperor."

That got her attention.

"How much time?" she asked.

"Three months."

Naoki blew out a long puff of air. "Even that may be too long."

"The healers are saying Emperor Hantei will not last the week, and it is considered inauspicious to hold Winter Court without a sitting emperor."

"Tokihito is a boy."

"Certainly not the youngest to assume the throne," Masahiro replied.

"Sacrilege." Her eyes widened. "You mean to control the next Hantei emperor?"

"I mean to influence him, yes." Masahiro grinned. "Come now, Naoki. *Every* ruler since the first Hantei has had their advisors. What better position to ward Rokugan against the Bloodspeaker threat?"

"Did not schemes like this lead to your exile?" she asked.

"I was not exiled." Masahiro leashed his burgeoning temper. "I *accepted* a distant posting. One, might I add, that allowed me to assist our august company in defeating two powerful Bloodspeakers and breaching Iuchiban's tomb."

"We do not know if–"

Masahiro held up a hand. "Let me remind you, we are still

not sure if Iuchiban even exists. All we know for certain is that a pair of dark sorcerers terrorized the Twilight Mountains, and that we accomplished what an entire imperial expeditionary force could not."

She shook her head. "The tomb remains."

"Where is it? Show me on a map?" Masahiro spread his fingers, mimicking confusion. "Face the truth, Naoki. We have nothing but supposition."

Feeling her tense, Masahiro moderated his tone. "Find evidence – records, stories, reports, *anything*, and I shall see them conveyed into the hands of those with the power to act. Until then, continue your work and let me continue mine."

She shrugged free of his grip, arms crossed in the sleeves of her robe, one foot tapping a jittery staccato on the stone tiles.

Used to Naoki's affectations, Masahiro knew better than to push the issue. He merely waited, patient as age.

"What do you propose?" she asked, voice wary.

"You spoke of the High Histories of the Ikoma," he replied. "I may have some… contacts among the Lion Clan to whom I can make introduction."

"And what do you require of me?"

"Simply speak to your colleagues at the Magistracy on Prince Tokihito's behalf," he said.

She glanced back, expression dark. "I am no courtier."

"And I am no warrior." Masahiro brandished the stump of his right hand. "But alas, these times require sacrifices of us all."

Naoki's lips twitched, a flutter of pain gone quick as a midsummer breeze. Masahiro might have lost his hand, but neither of them had emerged from Iuchiban's tomb unscarred.

She straightened, shoulders firm. "If he lives, I will find him."

"I know you will." Masahiro nodded, unsure if that comforted or unsettled him.

"Three months." Naoki turned away, head high as she made her way back toward the Emerald Magistracy alone.

Masahiro watched her go, unsure if the sweat prickling between his shoulder blades was from concern or the early afternoon heat. Lady Sun had climbed high in the cloudless sky and the day was already growing uncomfortable. The streets had mostly cleared out, empty save for those few servants and officials unlucky enough to have tasks unfinished. They hurried along, heads down, eyes fixed on the middle distance.

All save one.

He stood in the shade of a temple awning, hidden by shadow. At first, Masahiro thought him some curious servant. The Inner Districts were full of such opportunistic spies. But the man was too far away to have heard anything.

Masahiro raised a hand to shield his eyes from the afternoon glare, trying to make out the watcher's face. Although the shadows parted with no secrets, there was something distressingly familiar about the man. Before Masahiro could call out, he turned, disappearing deeper into the temple grounds.

He considered following, but discarded the notion. Such strangeness was far too reminiscent of the horrors he had witnessed in the Twilight Mountains. Almost unconsciously, Masahiro found himself gripping the stump of his severed hand.

He shook his head, grinning at his foolishness. This was the Imperial City, not some demon-haunted backwater.

Alive or dead, Iuchiban could wait.

At the moment, Masahiro's foremost concern was getting to the next audience without sweating through his best robes.

CHAPTER TWO

Kuni Seiji had almost finished overseeing repairs when the bell began to ring. He stood upon the west wall of the ancient Crab hill fort, plans in hand as he directed the workers to shore up the crumbling foundations.

The chime was soft at first, almost inaudible amidst the clatter of pick and shovel. Even so, the ringing seemed to resonate within Seiji's chest, drawing his attention from the fortress walls.

The place was centuries old, one of a score of defenses erected along the Crab Clan's western border. Abandoned generations ago, the forts had fallen into disrepair, becoming a haunt for bandits, spirits, and rebellious villagers.

The lands around were rocky and sparsely populated, hardly worth defending. Whatever threat these forts had warded against was gone. With typical practicality, the Crab had turned their attention to greater dangers.

Now, rebellion in the Twilight Mountains had Seiji's clan shoring up defenses along their western marches. The rebels had annihilated an imperial expeditionary force, and that was worthy of consideration.

Seiji laid a hand upon the battlement, feeling the strikes of pick and hammer resonate through the cool stone. It had always been such with Seiji, more at home with plans and architectural drawings than the tomes of sorcerous lore that were his Kuni birthright.

The hammer blows began to form a rough rhythm, like the cadence of distant war drums. Eyes closed, Seiji found his head nodding along with the strikes.

"Resting already?" Hiruma Izō's rough voice dragged Seiji from his contemplation. "Should I tell the workers to leave off?"

Normally, Seiji would have marked Izō's approach, the uneven thump of the scarred Hiruma foreman's wooden leg providing ample warning.

"No." He turned, mentally chiding himself for letting Izō creep up. "I thought I heard–"

"Heard what?" Although the foreman possessed but one eye, he managed to imbue his glare with a full measure of disdain.

Seiji shook his head, straightening. "Nothing."

Izō looked Seiji up and down as if searching a wall for cracks. The foreman had made no secret of his distaste at shepherding an unblooded scholar fresh from academy. Truthfully, Seiji could not blame him. Before giving two limbs and an eye in service to the clan, Izō had been a Hiruma scout, ranging far into the Shadowlands. Izō did not belong here.

In truth, neither of them did.

As a senior disciple of the Kaiu Architecture School, Seiji

should have been overseeing repairs on the Carpenter Wall. It was an insult to be tasked with shoring up this tumbledown ruin. Although he was the equal of any of his fellow disciples, the masters had always been skeptical of Seiji's lineage.

The Kuni were many things – sorcerers, witch hunters, walkers in shadow.

Seldom architects.

"How go the repairs?" Seiji asked.

"East wall still has gaps, but the west is…" The foreman leaned upon his crutch, remaining arm gesturing toward the workers below.

"And the central keep?"

"Relatively sound, as you suspected." Izō parted with compliments as if doling out precious jade.

Seiji ignored the foreman's tone. "Excellent work on the bell. Although you can tell whoever is ringing it to leave off."

"Ringing?"

"The bell." Seiji thrust his chin at the dilapidated keep. "Can't you hear it?"

Izō frowned. "I hear nothing."

The foreman continued, but Seiji's attention was on the keep. He had heard a bell, could hear it still, but the one in the tower stood silent.

"You well, boy?" Izō's question dragged Seiji back into the moment.

"I'm fine." He drew in a deep breath. "See to the buttresses near the main approach."

"As you say. Just see you don't faint and tumble from the battlements." Izō nodded toward the long drop, smile ugly. "Long way down, and the stone is hungry."

The foreman turned away, his posture betraying not even a hint of deference.

Had they been working the Carpenter Wall, Seiji would have called the old man to task for his insolence. But they were not on the wall, they were repairing a half-forgotten hill fort several days' ride from anywhere of note.

These were dangerous lands – wild and loosely governed. The workers were already unhappy. It would not take much for their grievances to boil over. The harshness of the Crab Clan's unending vigil made little room for ineffectual leaders. Seiji was under no illusions concerning how quickly he could vanish in these unforgiving hills.

He tried to turn his attention back to the plans only to find the paper crumpled in his fists. The ringing grew louder, more insistent. Seiji could discern neither cause nor reason for the chime, and yet it enfolded him, filled him, each chime settling upon his bones with an almost physical weight.

He had spent days upon his architectural drawings, weeks measuring, calculating, until Seiji knew the walls of the old hill fort as well as he knew the lines of his own palms. Now the plans fluttered from his grip, forgotten as he clapped his hands to his ears.

If anything, it intensified the terrible clangor. Faster and faster, as if the chimes came from inside Seiji's skull. He could make out little upon the rocky western approach, earth and boulder blurred to gray sameness by the stinging tears that filled his eyes.

And yet, somehow, he could *hear* them approach.

"Boy?" Genuine concern edged Izō's gravelly call.

Jaw tight against the urge to scream, Seiji glanced back to see the old samurai hobbling up. Not trusting his voice, Seiji raised a trembling hand, one finger extended toward a tear-blurred smudge of cliff.

"What has possessed you?" The foreman made to grasp his arm only to stop short as his gaze tracked Seiji's pointing finger.

"Hida's bones." It was as if the old scout's curse had thrown a blanket over the bell. Blessedly, the chime receded from Seiji's thoughts. He scrubbed a hand across his eyes, drawing in a great hitching breath.

Out in the valley, the cliffs *crawled*.

They moved like ants – progress haphazard, yet driven by singular purpose. At first Seiji thought they were rebels, but although they carried weapons, wore clothes, even stood upright, they did not move like humans.

Streaks of blood marred a mixture of peasant roughspun and battle armor. A panoply of clan colors mixed into the muddy browns of lower classes. The only uniting factor seemed the rusty red of old gore and yellow-white flashes of exposed bone.

Some wore helms, others went bareheaded, but Seiji could not see their faces. All wore a mask of pale porcelain, featureless but for two eyes and a dark slash of a mouth. Some shambled on broken legs, others were still pinioned by the spear that had ended their life. And yet they scrabbled across the broken rock, movements deft as hunting spiders.

"To the walls!" Izō's rough hand dragged Seiji back. "Protect the lord!"

Although the garrison boasted no samurai other than Seiji and Izō, it took but a few breaths for the wall to swarm with armed laborers. Other clans might balk at training peasants in spear and bow, but the Crab had long ago discarded such refined notions. When your foe crawled up from the underworld itself, you needed every hand that could wield a weapon.

Seiji drew his own sword. Straighter than the katanas favored by most samurai, the blade swelled toward the tip, providing the extra weight needed to cleave through foes of a more unnatural aspect. Warding trigrams glittered in the chill afternoon light. Incised along the length of the blade, they were set with precious jade. Although Seiji had never manifested a talent for sorcery, he remained a Kuni, a heritage that conferred certain benefits.

Seeing the blade, Izō gave an appreciative grunt. "Seems I may have misjudged you, lad."

Seiji leaned on the wall in an attempt to hide the tremble in his knees. "What are they?"

"Dead," came Izō's terse reply.

"Have you ever seen anything like it?"

"I've seen shadow-tainted creatures rise after killing wounds." He shook his grizzled head. "But never so many."

"Dark sorcery?"

"You're the Kuni. You tell me." Without waiting for an answer, Izō turned away. "Arrows ready!"

Seiji glanced back at the armed laborers – a few score on the walls, another dozen buttressing the gate. The dead moved too chaotically for him to get a proper count, but there were easily several hundred below.

Fortunately, the Crab were used to such odds.

"Loose!" Izō shouted.

Corpses stumbled as arrows found gaps in armor, sinking into knees, elbows, necks. A few fell, but not enough.

"Fire! Fire scours corrupted flesh." Seiji felt a twinge of pride as Izō echoed his order.

Torches were passed, arrows dipped in the pitch, which had been used to seal cracks in ancient wood.

The next volley reaped more worthwhile results. But ultimately, there was little a score of archers could do against such a relentless advance.

The dead did not bother with the gate, instead leaping onto the wall, their bony fingers finding cracks in the old stone. Seiji pushed down a flash of irritation – another few days and he would have sealed those gaps.

Archers leaned over the walls to aim straight down while others with spears and polearms pushed to the fore. Seiji saw a spearman dragged from the wall, his weapon trapped in the torso of a bloodied Crane samurai. Two broad-shouldered women emptied a bucket of burning pitch over the wall, the dead below flailing like wind-twisted embers.

A one-armed samurai in a Dragon Clan breastplate heaved himself over the battlement. Seiji's enchanted blade cleaved through armor and bone. He dropped a shoulder into the creature, toppling it back over the wall.

Two blood-flecked peasants had clambered up to slash at Izō with curved reaping hooks. The old scout parried the first cut, twisting to put his attacker in the path of second creature's swing.

Seiji stepped up behind him and together they bulled the two mangled corpses over the lip of the wall.

Izō's nod might as well have been an imperial commendation

for the upswell of pride it conjured in Seiji's chest. His satisfaction was short-lived. All along the wall, workers struggled with bloody-handed dead. The Crab might train their peasantry, but laborers were not samurai.

Like a poorly anchored wall, the defenders began to crumble.

Some tried to flee, the dead leaping upon them. Others jumped from the wall, preferring a quick death upon the stones below.

Seiji hacked at the bloodied press, wild overhand strokes like he was chopping through thick bamboo. It was impossible to miss. Behind, he could hear Izō cursing, his stream of invectives punctuated by the thud of steel into flesh. Barely a dozen laborers remained, a sweating, struggling knot that grew smaller by the moment.

"The stables." Izō ground the words out between labored breaths. "You must warn the clan."

"I won't flee."

"Are you some Lion Clan pup drunk on tales of glorious demise?" Izō almost spat the words. "Act like a Crab."

The admonition rocked Seiji like a hurled stone. Other clans might cleave to principles like valor, cleverness, or decorum, but ultimately, the Crab were a practical people. The clan elders would never take the word of a common laborer, and Izō could not ride.

Seiji was the only one who could bear tidings of this slaughter.

Cutting down the corpse of a near-headless Crane samurai, he turned to clap Izō on the shoulder.

The old scout returned the barest of nods, then hurled

himself at the teeming ranks. "Let's show these beasts how the Crab hold a wall!"

Despite the urgency of his task, Seiji could not quell the shame that prickled along his spine. He wormed his way into one of the murder holes that opened into the courtyard below. The fort's dilapidated stables housed the draft horses they used to haul stone up the hill. Seiji selected the one that seemed least likely to throw him – a placid roan mare who trembled as he fastened her tack. The others he freed, wishing them luck as he mounted up.

For the first time in weeks, Seiji was glad the workers hadn't gotten around to patching the east wall.

Several abominations leapt from the battlements as Seiji thundered by, but the dead were unable to keep pace with a galloping horse. At least Seiji did not need to urge the roan on.

The east wall loomed ahead, gaps like missing teeth.

Seiji glanced back. He could not pick Izō from the struggle atop the western battlement, but the old scout's throaty shouts told him he still drew breath.

One more sacrifice in the Crab's endless war.

A scrap of crumpled paper fluttered past Seiji's head. It caught along the edge of the gap, just long enough for him to see carefully inked plans upon the page. Then Seiji was through, his mare skittering down the wide switchback that led down the hillside.

No dead followed, but Seiji knew that would change. There had been clan samurai among the abominations, remains of the slaughtered imperial expedition – hundreds, perhaps even thousands of warriors.

Gradually, the sounds of battle faded, Seiji's flight silent but for the thunder of hooves, the pounding of his heart.

That, and the deep, sonorous toll of a distant bell.

CHAPTER THREE

Isawa Tomiko rubbed tired eyes, trying to make sense of the chaos before her. Scrolls lay spread across the bamboo mats of Master Masatsuge's study, *her* study. Bits of yellowed parchment swam in a sea of outstanding loans. When Tomiko had become master of Heaven's Blaze Dōjō, she had expected debate and study, not bookkeeping. She had seen this role as an end rather than a beginning, a way to prove her family wrong, to show they had been mistaken to shut her out.

Lesser talent, indeed.

Tomiko rubbed at her neck, sore from so many hours bent over her writing desk, begging merchants and petty officials for extensions on the school's debt. Heaven's Blaze was well-regarded in the surrounding lands; Master Masatsuge had taken pains to extend charity to even the meanest peasants. Never mind that the dōjō's meager student dues were hardly enough to pay for anything beyond the most basic repair and upkeep.

Tomiko had known the school's finances were in arrears, but she had not understood the depth of their debt until she found the stacks of unopened scrolls. Tomiko could not even share the letters with her fellow disciples lest they realize the extent of the school's insolvency. For all his ascetic lifestyle, Master Masatsuge had borrowed as if the world were about to end.

Tomiko lifted one of the older missives, a request for the repayment of thirty koku loaned by one Shiba Kenichi, captain of the garrison at Stone Grove, one of the larger trade towns in the valley below Heaven's Blaze. As always, the Shiba name conjured a pang in Tomiko's stomach – irritation or regret, she could never tell.

When her fellow senior disciple, Shiba Irie, had left to seek out Master Masatsuge's killers, Tomiko thought she was getting the better end of the deal. Now, staring at the growing mound of debts, she wondered if it might have been better to tramp off to the Twilight Mountains in search of rebels and rogue sorcerers. Dead or alive, at least Irie had put their master's teachings to real use.

And Tomiko? Well she was only good for bookkeeping.

Paper crumpled in her hands. *That* was the profession Tomiko's parents had selected for her. They had seen to it she received an education in sums and figures, preparation for her humble future. That Tomiko actually had a talent for accounting only compounded the insult.

She would be an elementalist, not some bleary-eyed accountant with ink-stained fingers and a perpetual stoop.

After her Coming-of-Age, Tomiko had all but run from the Phoenix Embassy where her parents served. It had been humiliating, an Isawa of noble birth debasing herself before the masters of lesser schools, although not as much as their refusals – polite, but firm. Tomiko might be a lesser talent, but she was still an Isawa.

Fortunately, Master Masatsuge turned none away.

Like the heroine of some peasant fable, Tomiko had found this blessing soon became a curse. She struggled with what came easily to other initiates. Even the most basic rituals required weeks to master. It was not that Tomiko couldn't perform the rites – her hands were steady, her posture immaculate, every movement precise as a water clock. It was simply that her talent was weak. The voices of other elementalists echoed within the spiritual realm, whereas Tomiko felt like she had to shout just to be heard.

Wincing, she smoothed the old scroll, setting it with the other debts. She mentally added the totals, the rising sum like a stone upon her chest seeming to grow in weight with every koku.

Breathing slowly to calm the nervous flutter of her heart, Tomiko spread a sheet of blank paper upon her writing desk. She inked her brush, held back the sleeve of her robe, and sat, unmoving. She needed to secure another loan, but Masatsuge had borrowed from everyone.

Tomiko squeezed her eyes shut, swallowing against the hollowness in her stomach. Realization came cold and uncomfortable as a fall of running snowmelt.

No, not *everyone*.

Truly, Tomiko must have offended the ancestors in a past life. Why else would they heap such miseries upon her? This should have been her moment of triumph, the wayward scion of a noble line now master of her own school. Instead, she must humble herself yet again.

It was a simple letter, addressed to the Phoenix Embassy in the Imperial City:

Mother, Father,
*   In this season of late summer blossoms, I write to you*
with glad tidings…

Tomiko paused mid-pleasantry, hand jittering as if gripped by a sudden chill. Ink bled across the page, and with a cry of frustration, Tomiko swept it from the writing desk.

Better to lose everything than crawl back to her family.

Papers shifted under her questing fingers, names and figures printed in neat rows in her logbook. It took hours to compile a final accounting. Servants came and went, leaving rice, grilled vegetables, and a salty broth that sat cooling upon the tray as the mistress of Heaven's Blaze worked through the night.

At last, Tomiko sat back, hands pressed into the small of her back. It seemed impossible the school had borrowed so much. Swallowing against a sudden dryness in her throat, Tomiko stared down at the measured columns.

It *was* impossible.

Tired muscles cried out as she stood. Tomiko steadied herself on one of the study beams, turning not to the school's debts, but its expenditures.

The logbooks lay stacked in the rear of the study. Written in Masatsuge's elegant hand, they detailed the many costs of running a small dōjō. Like a child sneaking a pillow book from her parents' chambers, Tomiko sat and laid one across her lap.

"Forty koku for robes, eight for alms, two for candles, twelve for coal…" she muttered under her breath. A less skilled accountant might have overlooked the discrepancy, but as Tomiko examined the ledgers the oversight became clearer and clearer.

Masatsuge was overpaying for *everything*.

"Eighteen koku to house pilgrims bound for Hikari Shrine?" Tomiko shook her head. She had been there when the school entertained those monks. They had requested simple fare and slept on the floor of one of the education halls. Yet Masatsuge had spent enough to host an imperial delegation.

It was laughable to imagine Masatsuge hoarding wealth like some mountain ogre, but as Tomiko dug deeper, the discrepancy became undeniable. Which meant only one thing.

Her master had been cheated.

Comparing the ledgers, one name appeared with distressing frequency: Kosue. Tomiko knew little of the man, save that he owned several warehouses in Stone Grove.

Tomiko pushed to her feet, papers fluttering like windswept leaves. The sudden noise brought a servant rushing to her door, but Tomiko swept the screen aside to tower over the bowing servant, a white-haired man with a face wrinkled as a dried persimmon.

"Ready my horse." Tomiko stepped past him, hurrying down the hall, the morning light bright in her eyes.

Heads turned, students and teachers alike tracking her progress across the school's small courtyard. Tomiko knew she must look a sight, hair loose like some temple ghost, her eyes red from lack of sleep. She did not care. At last, she had found the root of the school's misery, *her* misery.

She all but threw on her formal robes, packing her satchel with such ritual equipment as might be required. It seemed likely this merchant Kosue would bow beneath the weight of her accusation, but cornered men could be dangerous.

"Send a runner to the Stone Grove garrison." Tomiko took the reins from the waiting servant. "Have a patrol sent to the offices of Kosue the merchant."

"Shall I inform them of the reason, mistress?" the white-haired servant asked.

Tomiko mounted, half-turning in her saddle even as she kicked the horse into motion. "I have caught a thief."

A narrow path led from Heaven's Blaze down into the valley. Normally, Tomiko would not have taken the trail at a canter, but the upswell of hot anger had boiled away any reservations.

Merchants were grasping by trade, but to defraud a monastic school went beyond greed. Every moment Kosue remained free was an insult to Masatsuge's memory.

Tomiko kicked her mount into a gallop as the ground leveled off. Smudges of cook-smoke gradually resolved into homes and storefronts, the town of Stone Grove seeming almost to sprout in Tomiko's vision. Nestled around a high river bend, the town sat at the conflux of several trade roads, a steady flow of inland goods shipped down the river to the sea, and from there along the coast to markets in the Imperial City. Tomiko recalled Kosue kept offices along the waterfront and headed in that direction.

Although the impending confrontation sparked another wave of heat along Tomiko's neck, she slowed her mount. She was, after all, mistress of Heaven's Blaze. There were proprieties to be maintained.

Villagers bowed as if she were some visiting dignitary. Heaven's Blaze had long been a source of pride for the valley.

Although there was no sign of the local constables, one of Kosue's guards sat upon a barrel outside the merchant's warehouse – a massive, ramshackle affair that looked to have been cobbled together from several smaller buildings. There were docks beyond, a trade junk vessel sitting high in the water, ready to be loaded down with cargo bound to the Imperial City.

"Mistress Isawa." The guard scratched his bristly scruff of a beard as Tomiko reined up. "To what do we owe the pleasure of–"

"Where is Kosue?" Tomiko slipped from the saddle, tying her mount to a nearby post.

"In back taking inventory." The man's surprise seemed genuine. "I shall summon him, mistress."

"No need." Tomiko stepped into the shadow of the warehouse.

She ignored the guard's further questions, threading stacks of crates and platforms piled with oil barrels. The fact that Kosue's business seemed quite profitable only whetted Tomiko's temper.

She found the thief squatting next to a rack of dried salmon, lips pursed as he inspected the rows of leathery fish, logbook in hand.

Kosue was a tall man, thin-faced and slope-shouldered. His robes were well made, but calculated not to show overt wealth. He stood as Tomiko approached, head cocked like a curious crow as she thrust the expense ledger at his chest.

He glanced down, expression confused.

"Would you care to explain?" Tomiko narrowed her eyes.

"A fine example of record keeping." His gaze flicked to her, then back. "I must commend your dear departed master. Would that all my customers were so assiduous."

"*Fourteen* koku for coal." Tomiko tapped the page. "We could heat the whole valley with that much."

"I am a simple purveyor of goods." His smile was practiced. "Far be it from me to question the needs of my spiritual betters."

"Spare me your excuses." Tomiko drew in a quick breath, leashing her temper. Such emotion would only cloud her judgment. "You took advantage of my master, gouging a wise man for unlawful profit."

Kosue straightened, shoulders high, expression suddenly guarded. "I charged what the market would bear."

"You robbed us." Tomiko kept her voice level. "And I will see it made right."

"The contracts are sealed with your master's chop." Kosue took a tentative step back.

"We shall see what Captain Kenichi has to say about that."

Kosue held his ledger book like a shield, gaze darting about as if searching for escape.

He would not get far. The Phoenix might be pacifists, but Tomiko had many ways of stopping Kosue without violence.

Tomiko held up a hand as if to confront the thief. "I know what you are, merchant."

"Do you, now?" Her words seemed to shift something in Kosue. The anxiety bled from his face, timidity cast aside like a broken sandal.

"Very clever, Phoenix." Kosue's words dripped with cold malice. "Also very foolish of you to come alone."

Confused, Tomiko cocked her head. She had meant to name the merchant a thief, but his reaction held true hatred.

Before she could give voice to her confusion, the merchant hurled the ledger at Tomiko. Reflexively, she snatched it from the air.

Kosue drew a knife from his belt, but rather than strike at Tomiko, the merchant slashed it across his own forearm, dark blood welling in the shadows of the warehouse. His hissed incantations seemed to pierce the space between them.

Tomiko felt the chill of corruption a moment before the spirit struck her. It came like oil welling from some crack in the earth, dark and irresistible. Tomiko was thrown from her feet to crash amidst racks of drying fish.

She scrambled back, already chanting as the corrupt spirit reared back. Her invocation called a gyre of whirling wind, spirits manifesting to shield Tomiko from their twisted brethren.

Surprise bled into terrifying realization. Kosue had used dark sorcery against her, *blood magic*. All thought of passivity fled from Tomiko's thoughts. Phoenix strictures of nonviolence did not apply to such corruption.

Flame lit the dusty shadows as Tomiko rose, fire dripping from her outstretched hands. She cast a blazing arrow at Kosue only to see the erstwhile merchant brush it aside. His return strike shattered Tomiko's shield, wind spirits fading like a high summer breeze. She threw herself to the ground as the blood sorcerer's shadows knifed through barrels and bags. Rice spilled across the warehouse floor, sticking to Tomiko's robes as she rolled behind a stack of crates.

Like all elementalists, she had been trained in arcane combat, but Kosue's power far exceeded hers.

"You would bring me to justice? Me?!" He stalked between

the rows of crates. "Little Phoenix, you have no idea whom you face."

Back pressed to the rough wood, apprehension made a cold fist in her stomach. There was no way the constables would arrive in time to save Tomiko. She would need to act, and act quickly.

Flicking her fingers toward a nearby pile of oil barrels, she conjured a blossom of flame upon the bindings.

"Ah, *there* you are." Kosue rounded the corner, narrow face alight with cruel glee. "Oh, how I have longed to–"

The heavy rope gave way, sending barrels crashing into Kosue's legs. He stumbled, struggling to rise even as the rest of the pile tumbled down upon him. Tendrils of gore-streaked shadow lashed up from the flailing blood mage, smashing barrels to flinders, the air sharp with the smell of cooking oil.

Something flopped from the barrel. At first, Tomiko did not understand what she was seeing – a tangle of cord-bound limbs, desiccated skin glistening with oil. Patchy hair framed slack faces, their eyes and mouths sewn shut with twine.

Bodies. Unburnt and unhallowed, they had been roped together like cordwood and stuffed into the barrels. Tomiko's gaze flicked to the hundreds of barrels stacked along the warehouse's high walls, ready to be delivered to the Imperial City.

"Abomination!" Tomiko surged to her feet, hands raised as she summoned an arc of flame. It was hardly the conflagration true Phoenix masters could command, but she only needed a spark.

The whomp of igniting oil snatched the breath from Tomiko's lungs. One sleeve pressed across her mouth, Tomiko blinked back stinging tears as she stumbled from the burning warehouse, Kosue's screams louder than the crackle of hungry flame.

There were people out front already hurrying to bring water. A wedge of guards pushed through the press, Captain Kenichi at their head.

"By the ancestors." Fire reflected in his wide-eyed stare. "Mistress Isawa, what has happened?"

Tomiko almost told him, but her tongue was stilled by concern. In his merchant guise, Kosue had done brisk business with Heaven's Blaze. It would reflect disastrously on the school that none had sensed the dark sorcerer's taint. She pressed the Bloodspeaker's logbook to her chest as if to shield it from the flames.

"I discovered irregularities in Kosue's dealings with my school." It was the truth, if not the whole of it. "When I confronted him about them, the merchant attacked me. In the struggle, some oil barrels caught fire."

"Foolish to assault a master elementalist." There was no hint of disbelief in Captain Kenichi's broad face. Nor would there be. Tomiko was the mistress of Heaven's Blaze and a Phoenix noble. Her word was unimpeachable.

Flames crackled as they spread along the dock to the ship. Hot as Lady Sun, Tomiko already knew the fire would leave little behind save ashes. Silently, she prayed that the souls of those Kosue defiled would find peace in the pyre.

Better that than whatever the merchant had planned.

Tomiko glanced to the burning ship, apprehension kindling in her chest. The bodies had been bound for the Imperial City, although for what purpose she could not guess.

Peasants hurried to douse nearby buildings, local

elementalists calling upon spirits of water and wind to contain the raging fire. Tomiko moved to assist them only to stop as Captain Kenichi called after her.

"What drove Kosue to it?"

Tomiko's hands tightened on the record of the corrupt merchant's dealings, one that might lead to his contacts in the Imperial City. She should hand it to Kenichi, tell him of Kosue's dark powers, but the knowledge Master Masatsuge unknowingly engaged in commerce with a Bloodspeaker would irrevocably harm her school's reputation.

Tomiko could not even countenance the alternative – that her master *had* known, but done nothing. Such truths would destroy her school, her students, perhaps even her soul. As mistress of Heaven's Blaze, that was not something Tomiko could allow.

"I cannot say." Hands tight on the ledger, she turned toward the elementalists.

"Some would do anything to keep their shame from coming to light."

CHAPTER FOUR

Kitsuki Naoki was fidgeting again – legs jittering, needing to brush back an invisible strand of hair tickling her forehead. The seams on her magisterial robes never seemed to fall right. She glanced at the two Lion Clan guards kneeling near the chamber entrance. They might have been temple statues, eyes fixed on the middle distance, faces wearing the same somber scowls as when Naoki had been escorted into Last Breath Castle over an hour ago.

Naoki tried to echo their composure. Emerald Magistrates were meant to be calm and collected. Unfair as it was, restlessness was often seen as evidence of a disordered mind. Hopefully, Daimyō Matsu Akoya would not see it as such – the Matsu family had always valued action over stillness.

Naoki quashed the urge to take another sip of tea. An overfull bladder would only add to her discomfort. Thin bars of afternoon sun slipped through heavy wooden slats meant to ward against enemy arrows, the air hot and close. Once pleasant, the smell of the heavy cedar beams had become cloying in the early autumn warmth.

The chamber was one of many that honeycombed the interior of Last Breath Castle, a much-abused fortification on the southern edge of Lion territory. Despite its patched walls and arrow-gnawed parapets, Naoki knew it was one of the few citadels in this swath of contested territory that had never changed hands. Quite a feat, given that it sat between Scorpion and Crane – great clans with obvious designs upon the fertile river valley running north of the castle.

Smoothing the creases of her robe for perhaps the dozenth time, Naoki fixed her gaze upon Masahiro's sealed letter of introduction. The Crane might be an ambitious, self-serving peacock, but he was one of the few who knew the true darkness they faced. Which was why she had honored his request not to open the letter.

Naoki wanted to believe that Qadan and the others had dealt with Iuchiban. The sorcerer seemed half a ghost already, what few mentions she could find in the imperial records fragmented and contradictory.

Fortunately, the Grand Histories of the Ikoma offered another source. If only Naoki could obtain access.

"Magistrate."

The word almost sent Naoki to her feet, quick as a startled fox. She had become lost in contemplation, but so it always was – as if her thoughts were a storm-tossed sea, each wave sweeping in to consume the whole of her attention.

Bowing to conceal her flush of surprise, Naoki regarded the Matsu daimyō through lowered eyes.

Lady Matsu Akoya was a tall woman, broad-shouldered and long-limbed. Despite the streaks of gray in her hair and the creases around her eyes and mouth, she moved with the predatory ease of a lifelong warrior. Her armor was unadorned but for a ruff of lion fur around the collar and an emblem signifying her rank as head of the Matsu family.

"Apologies for my tardiness. I was reviewing the garrison." Lady Akoya moved to kneel upon the raised dais before Naoki.

"Of course, Daimyō." Naoki inclined her head. Although the guards had taken pains to hide their numbers, Naoki did not need to be a general to recognize there were far more samurai in Last Breath than a castle of its size warranted.

Akoya frowned, apparently mistaking Naoki's agreement for cynicism. "Hantei XXVI's ascension to the Realm of Waiting threatens the peace. As Rokugan's strong right arm, the Lion Clan must ensure stability."

"More than one war has been waged under the guise of 'ensuring stability.'" Naoki fixed the Matsu lord with a level stare.

Although Akoya's expression did not flicker, something shifted. Like the shimmer of heat above a bonfire, the air around her seemed charged with unstated menace.

"I am not here to pry into your clan's affairs, but neither will I feign ignorance," Naoki said.

"Why *are* you here, magistrate?" Akoya asked.

Naoki handed Masahiro's letter to Akoya.

Akoya took it with the wariness of a woman handling broken glass, eyes narrowing as she beheld the Crane crest. The lord broke the seal, spreading the paper before her. Typical of Masahiro, the letter overflowed with flowery elaborations and poetic references popular in the high courts – as if taking an age to say something made it more important.

Even so, the effect on Akoya was visible. The Matsu lord paled, looking to Naoki, wariness replaced by a conflicting swirl of emotions – surprise, anger, sorrow.

"Is this true?" Akoya held up the letter.

"I was not privy to the contents," Naoki replied.

Akoya thrust the letter away as if to deny its message. "Matsu Chiaki is dead?"

"I am afraid so, lady."

Akoya rocked back on her heels, iron composure moment-arily broken. Naoki pretended to regard the pattern on her empty teacup so as to give the daimyō a moment to compose herself.

"How?" When Akoya spoke again, there was no quaver in her voice.

"She fell holding a pass against a swarm of walking corpses," Naoki replied. "Allowing me and my companions to escape."

"Fitting." The barest hint of a smile nestled at the corner of Akoya's scarred lips. "You knew Chiaki?"

"Only briefly."

"And this…" Akoya glanced at the letter. "Doji Masahiro?"

"They seemed close, lady."

"How close?"

"Masahiro said she was his bodyguard." Seeing Akoya's surprise, Naoki added. "And I have no reason to doubt him."

"Strange times indeed." Akoya set the letter aside. "Tell me what evil delivered my old master to such a storied end."

Naoki could not conceal her surprise. She had suspected a connection between Akoya and Chiaki – commander and soldier, lord and vassal, even war comrades. The bond between master and student was a sacred one, often transcending even familial obligations.

Naoki's reaction seemed to loosen something in Lady Akoya, the heat in her gaze fading.

"It seems we both owe Chiaki a debt," Naoki continued. At last, she understood Masahiro's gambit. The Crane had not revealed the letter's contents so Naoki's reaction would be genuine, her unfeigned sorrow echoing Akoya's.

"You said she was slain by walking dead," Akoya said. "How can this be?"

"What do you know of blood magic, lady?"

Akoya made a reflexive warding gesture. "Only that its practitioners must be destroyed."

Naoki nodded. "There is a reason Rokugani burn our dead."

"I knew the imperial expedition was not slaughtered by mere peasants," Akoya said. "Chiaki was right to seek answers."

"We found them," Naoki replied. "The revolt was merely cover, sowing disorder so that blood sorcerers might raise an army of dead, all in service to their dark master's whim."

"And the imperial expedition?" Akoya asked.

"I fear they too joined the dead."

"My nephew Katamori commanded the expedition." Akoya's words came whetted by anger. "Why was I not informed of this?"

"*That* is what I seek to uncover."

Akoya's jaw pulsed, as if the Matsu lady were working a bit of gristle from her teeth. "Tell me *everything*."

Naoki had little to lose by dissembling, so she related the events as best she could, beginning with her investigation into the murder of several Dragon Clan officials, the search that led her and her companions to the Twilight Mountains, the running battle with the dead, Chiaki's death, and finally Iuchiban's tomb.

Lady Akoya's lip curled as Naoki described vicious chambers filled with traps, wards, and corrupted spirits. The lady nodded in approval as Naoki detailed their battle with the powerful Bloodspeaker who had tormented Rokugan while disguised as a traveling monk, but there her story ended.

"And this Iuchiban?" Akoya asked. "Did Qadan and the others destroy him?"

"I have heard nothing since Masahiro and I escaped." Naoki leaned forward, voice urgent. "But I fear the sorcerer survives."

Akoya drew in a slow breath. "What aid do you require?"

Relieved, Naoki told her.

"You are an Emerald Magistrate," Akoya replied. "You have but to ask and the High Histories will be at your disposal."

"A magistrate's command may not open as many doors as the request of a Lion Clan noble." Seeing Akoya's expression harden at the insinuation her clan scholars might not perform their duties, Naoki gave an apologetic bob of her head. "And it was important to us the Matsu learn of Chiaki's sacrifice. If not for her, we might never have reached Iuchiban's tomb."

Akoya considered Naoki's words for a long moment. Abruptly, she rose, hands fluttering down to brush imaginary dust from her breastplate. "Walk with me, magistrate."

Without waiting for a reply, the Matsu lord swept past Naoki, who rose to follow.

At a nod from their lord, the guards fell back, following at a discreet distance as Akoya led Naoki through the maze-like interior passages of the fortress. She had once read the Lion designed their fortresses to be purposely obtuse to frustrate attackers. After a half-dozen turns, she acknowledged the rumors' truth.

A heavy ironbound door opened into a columned hall. In keeping with the Lion's penchant for utility, the room was sparsely decorated – a few alcoves held scrolls extolling some of the Akodo's finer military maxims, the bamboo mats bare but for a large table and several sitting pillows.

The wood of the table was etched with hills and rivers, Last Breath Castle and its surrounding villages represented by small carvings, replete with tawny flags bearing the Matsu family crest – a Lion's paw gripping a blade. To the east, the Crane holdings were denoted with light blue stones, a line of red and black markers to the west showing Scorpion lands. Akoya's domain seemed little more than a blade thrust into a sea of blue and crimson.

"She sat here." Akoya paused near the foot of the table, gaze distant as if snared by memory.

"Chiaki?" Naoki asked.

Akoya thrust her chin at a place near the head of the table. "Katamori, there."

Slowly, she rounded the table, words measured as if she read from a prayer scroll. "Kazuya Wolfhound, Emi, Motoharu, Kaori One-Eye. All stolen from me." Reaching the head of the war table, Akoya spun, arms spread. "My hall is full of ghosts."

"I am sorry," Naoki replied.

"And you tell me their bodies have been defiled, their spirits enslaved by blood sorcery." The Matsu lord's face tightened – with rage or sorrow, Naoki could not tell.

"You were right, magistrate." Akoya's laugh was rough as rusted steel. "The Clan Champion bid the Lion gather our forces. With imperial succession murky, he felt it best we make a show of strength."

Akoya turned, pushing through a door at the rear of the chamber. Naoki followed her out onto a tower overlook, the castle spread around them like a game board. Samurai swarmed along the gardens and nested courtyards, some armed and armored in Lion gold, others stockpiling enough supplies to withstand a siege.

Or wage a war.

The Matsu lord looked beyond the walls, to the river valley spread beyond the castle. It was as the map in the war room, towns and villages marked by thin streamers of smoke rather than embroidered flags.

"That was Chiaki's dōjō." Akoya nodded at the cluster of buildings in the shadow of an enormous camphor tree. "I thought I could preserve her like an ancestral blade, but my master was a sword forged for battle. It is good she found an end there."

They stood for a long while, breaths lost against the cool mountain wind. Naoki wanted to speak, but could think of no words equal to the task.

At last, Akoya glanced over, as if remembering Naoki was there.

"You have my full support, magistrate." She nodded. "On one condition."

"Name it," Naoki said.

Akoya's hands tightened on the battlement, gripping the stone with white-knuckled fury. "That you do not stand in my way when the time comes to avenge Chiaki and Katamori."

It was as if there had been a rope drawn tight around Naoki's chest, suddenly severed by a sharp pang of relief. She drew in a deep breath, baring her teeth as the chilled mountain air tingled in her lungs.

"Nothing would please me more."

CHAPTER FIVE

Masahiro despised waiting. In his long tenure in the Imperial Court, he had never found a more telling measure of individual worth. It was not the enforced contemplation that irritated him – Masahiro had never lacked for ways to occupy his mind – but rather, the implication.

Waiting was a way to chastise the inferior by reminding them that *their* time was not as valuable as *your* time.

Vassals waited. Servants waited. *Peasants* waited.

Once, high lords had waited upon Masahiro's pleasure, a gaggle of clucking nobles, thin-faced and pompous, borne on palanquins from dusty manors. People of note. People of substance.

Now Masahiro's time had no value. Although reinstated for defeating what the commoners had taken to calling "the Twilight Rebellion," public acclaim did not translate to courtly approval. Masahiro's favored status had returned neither his family's wealth nor rank. It simply meant his enemies must be more circumspect.

Rather than call upon his coterie from the safety of his family's manor, Masahiro had been reduced to squatting in one of the outbuildings of the Crane Embassy – a rather dingy suite of rooms usually occupied by youths from backwater provinces come to tour the Imperial Capital. Masahiro's stipend was barely enough to rent a palanquin, let alone hire servants or bodyguards.

With a sigh, he cast about the garden for something to occupy his attention. One of the smaller courtyards in Lady Doji Otose's manor, it was barely a dozen paces across, but tastefully arranged. A pruned wisteria shaded a small pond, the single stone bench overlooking a rambling patch of white valerian and pale blue bellflowers. Pleasant enough, except for the ruff of red spider lilies near the southwestern corner.

The lilies were out of season, a streak of garish crimson insulting the more subdued blues and whites of the garden. If Otose thought such ostentation would impress Masahiro, she was mistaken.

He pushed down the swell of irritation, remaining perfectly still lest any of the lady's servants be watching. It would have been insulting had Otose not posted at least a few discreet observers.

Again, his gaze drifted back to the spider lilies. Doji Otose had been a friend for many years and his sister-in-law after she had married Hiroshige. Otose had returned to her family after Masahiro's brother had met his end, but he liked to think they were still friends. A patron of arts and literature with valuable estates in the south, Otose's wealth had been invaluable in their attempt to seat Prince Tokihito upon the imperial throne.

Hopefully it would be again.

Masahiro considered the out-of-place blooms. Otose had never been given to overt displays of wealth. She must have known Masahiro would notice the lilies, which meant they were placed with intent.

Spider lilies symbolized death, their thin curling petals and bright color reminiscent of fresh blood. More, they had been arranged along the southwestern corner of the garden – the direction of the Twilight Mountains. Masahiro had lost both a brother and a hand amidst those unlovely peaks.

His scalp prickled with understanding. Otose had not made him wait to underscore his diminished status, but to ensure he observed the garden.

A flutter of soft-soled sandals presaged the appearance of a servant. The woman was already bowing by the time Masahiro turned, her hands forming a careful triangle, forehead pressed to the wood.

"Lady Otose requests your presence in the Peony Blossom Chamber." The servant rose without Masahiro's leave. Once, he might have taken the woman to task, but recent travails had somewhat punctured his views of such propriety. One could not crawl through the bloody filth of an ancient sorcerer's tomb without leaving a bit of pride behind.

A pair of Daidoji guards awaited outside the Peony Chamber. Bowing as Masahiro approached, they accompanied him inside, taking up position on either side of the entrance.

Little had changed in the Peony Chamber. Beams of pale rosewood accented spreading blossoms inked upon the vases and wall screens. A symbol of luck, devotion, and beauty, it would have been easy to give in to the peony's vibrant colors; but the forest of painted trees was subdued, subtle pinks and whites accenting rich browns, limbs twisting as if caught by a sudden gust.

One of the last known works of the reclusive Crane artist Kakita Tsutomu Masahiro had once been enamored with the mural, spending hours tracing the branches with his eyes. Now he knew the truth of the artist's vision, the blossoms seemed sharp as razors, the careful weave of limbs like blood seeping across the canvas.

The last time Masahiro had seen Lady Otose, she had been dressed like a peasant, fleeing the capital after their conspiracy had unraveled. Now she knelt upon a silk pillow, tastefully embroidered robes in careful array, her long hair held back by a jade comb carved to resemble a diving cormorant.

"Forgive me for the delay." Otose delivered the perfunctory expression with the proper amount of regret.

As was expected of him, Masahiro waved away her apology. No lord was ever *truly* sorry to make their guests wait.

"I have been in meetings all morning," she continued with a bit more warmth. "But I can always find time for an old friend."

"I am grateful for your attention." Masahiro kept the edge from his voice. Old friend, indeed. The insinuation was clear enough; Otose was consorting with individuals of note – no doubt eager to secure her financial backing for their schemes. By naming Masahiro friend, Otose had delivered an implicit rebuke, namely that she had no desire to discuss politics.

Fair enough. Masahiro had come to Otose's manor, he must play by her rules.

He turned to appreciate the flowering peony tree painted upon a nearby vase. It had been shattered when Masahiro found it. Now jagged lines of gold crisscrossed the image where the vase had been painstakingly reassembled. Known as *Kintsugi*, the golden fractures highlighted the vase's flaws, treating the breakage as part of the piece's history rather than something to be concealed.

"You have always had an eye for art," Masahiro said, not mentioning it had been *he* who purchased the vase for Otose.

"I am but a collector. Kakita Tsutomu is the true master." Otose's smile was not feigned. They had spent many afternoons in the Peony Room together with Hiroshige admiring Tsutomu's careful lines.

"So delicate." Masahiro leaned forward.

"If only Tsutomu passed down his techniques," Otose said, as Masahiro had known she would. She and Hiroshige had oft lamented the famous artist's disappearance. "Or found a patron worthy of his talents."

Masahiro sighed. "Unfortunately, he did."

Otose frowned, no doubt expecting Masahiro to continue the well-worn exchange of pleasantries. But he would not be patted on the head and shuffled off like some shoeless petitioner.

"You have heard of my journey to the Twilight Mountains?"

"I have." Her response was wary. "They say you defeated a blood sorcerer."

"Two, actually," Masahiro replied. He hadn't been involved with destroying the Shrike, but such distinctions were trivial.

"The Empire is grateful for your service." It was a deflection, but Masahiro would not be so easily put off.

"Tsutomu." He inclined his head toward the screens. "We found a veritable gallery of his art in the sorcerer's tomb. I would have brought some home, but unfortunately they were all cursed."

"To discuss such dark things is to invite ill fortune." Although Otose's eyes narrowed, her expression held something else. Had they not been in the center of her manor, surrounded by guards and servants, Masahiro would have thought her afraid.

"Luck is the least of our concerns." He chose his next words carefully. "The Empire faces more than a succession crisis."

Otose's gaze flicked over Masahiro's shoulder toward the chamber's entrance, almost as if she expected someone.

He forged on, undaunted. "What Rokugan needs is a peaceful transition of power, an emperor who can act to forestall the shadow that even now stretches ragged fingers across our land." He edged toward her, voice sharp. "Even now, my allies seek the truth of the Bloodspeaker conspiracy. If Prince Tokihito is not the next emperor, I worry what fate may befall the Empire. If we act quickly–"

"We?" She shook her head, expression clouded. "I have always been envious of your ability to weave ambition and necessity."

"Lord Otomo Yasunori has given his blessing."

"Yasunori would back an ogre if he thought the beast might free him from exile."

"I have made discreet inquiries." Masahiro did not let his temper rise. "We still have allies in court."

"Allies who fell over one another trying to distance themselves from us after Hiroshige's death."

"Such has always been the way of court." Now Masahiro let real emotion color his tone. "My brother is gone, but that need not be the end of our dream."

"And why would Lady Otose support such a wild gamble?"

The reply came from behind Masahiro.

No servant announced the Scorpion courtier, for he needed no introduction. All knew Bayushi Terumoto. Swathed in flowing red and black robes, the lower half of his face concealed by a silken mask bearing a scorpion in gold embroidery, the man seemed almost to exude confidence.

With a bow to Otose, Terumoto entered the chamber accompanied by two black-clad samurai, faces hidden by masks of lacquered wood carved to resemble fearsome ogres. Masahiro could not but be reminded of the featureless porcelain masks worn by the walking dead.

"Apologies for my lateness, lady." At Terumoto's nod, one of the Scorpion samurai withdrew a small bundle from his robes. Placing it delicately before the dais, he unwrapped the silken bindings to reveal a peony flower carved of pale rose quartz.

"I hope this small memento will smooth my inconsiderate tardiness." Terumoto's voice was rich and warm, his eyes seeming almost to glitter with hidden mirth.

"How could I hold anything against someone with such fine taste?" Otose turned the quartz blossom to catch the light, obviously pleased by the artistry. Only when Masahiro shifted did the slightest of blushes rise up her neck.

"Lord Bayushi, please allow me to introduce Lord Doji Masahiro."

"We have met." It was all Masahiro could do to keep the venom from his voice.

"Forgive me, Lord Doji." Terumoto turned his dark eyes upon Masahiro. "I did not know you had returned from your posting... abroad."

A lie, of course, but one that propriety bid Masahiro stomach.

"It is well and proper to put down rebellions against the divine order." He returned a tepid smile. "But I was called home by matters of state."

The Scorpion lord chuckled. "I must chastise you for not allowing me to prepare a proper welcome."

"Next time I will send a runner." Masahiro shuddered to think of the "welcome" Terumoto would concoct, especially given he had almost certainly been the one to dispatch Shosuro Gensuke. The Scorpion's cabal had backed a rival claimant for the throne; he stood to gain more than any from Hiroshige's death, not to mention Gensuke was a Scorpion Clan assassin, at least until Masahiro had tossed him into a bladed pit.

"You must forgive me," Terumoto continued smoothly. "I have come to meet with Lady Otose."

"Please, do not concern yourself with my presence." Masahiro feigned ignorance of Terumoto's desire to see him gone.

The slightest tic of anger flashed across Terumoto's face, quickly smoothed by cold courtesy. "I am afraid the matter is of some delicacy."

"Surely nothing that can stand between family," Masahiro said with a meaningful glance to Otose. Although not bound by bonds of kinship, they remained Doji. It would do good to remind her she was conspiring with a Scorpion against the interests of her own clan.

Otose made no reply, her gaze fixed upon the carved peony.

"So be it," Terumoto said airily. "I had hoped to spare you

embarrassment, Lord Masahiro, but one cannot turn aside a diving hawk."

He removed a gilded scroll from his robes, unrolling it so the imperial seal was in full view.

"An invitation to Prince Takamochi's moon viewing." Terumoto inclined his head as if he were a priest doling out benedictions.

Masahiro did not let his surprise show. Such events were usually reserved for high nobility. More, Takamochi was the strongest contender for the imperial throne, being the emperor's second child. That Terumoto had managed to secure invitations to such an event spoke highly of his connections to the prince – and his connection to Lady Otose.

Masahiro looked to his erstwhile sister, but she would not meet his eyes.

Terumoto handed the scroll to Otose's guards, who accepted it with barely concealed disdain. It seemed Masahiro was not the only one concerned by how freely the Scorpion came and went.

"Apologies, lady, but business calls me elsewhere." Terumoto offered another gracious bow. "I hope to see you at the viewing."

"I will be in attendance." Only someone who knew Otose well would have recognized the strain in her smile.

Flicking back his long sleeves, Terumoto departed, his guards silent shadows in his wake.

"There's one Scorpion who should have his stinger pulled." With a shake of his head, Masahiro turned to regard Otose. He was surprised when she rose, her tone dismissive.

"You should go."

"Otose, I–"

"It isn't safe here." Otose spoke in a whisper, words hidden beneath the swish of robes. She paused at the door, half-turning. "It is always a pleasure to see old friends."

And with that, Otose left Masahiro alone, the cruel branches inked upon the screens like the bars of a cage. It stung to be dismissed so coolly by one he considered a friend. Only a few months had passed since Masahiro fled the Imperial City, but so much had changed.

This time no servant appeared to guide him to the main gate. It was as if the manor had been abandoned, the distant hiss of sandals on wood like wind through dry branches.

Terumoto was waiting for him outside.

"I must confess surprise at your return." He cocked his head as Masahiro stepped into the lengthening afternoon shadows. "But I suppose you never could take a hint."

"I see you wasted no time consolidating your power," Masahiro replied, more than a little relieved they had dispensed with the veneer of courtesy.

Terumoto shrugged. "*Someone* needed to hold the court together."

"Fortunate you were there to pick up the pieces." Masahiro made as if to finger the hem of Terumoto's fine robes. "Prince Takamochi seems to be a clear favorite to ascend the Emerald Throne. Quite a rise in status for you and your little coterie."

"To think I would live to be lectured on ambition by Doji Masahiro." He clucked his tongue. "Now I have truly heard it all."

"Not quite."

"Come to frighten me with tales of walking dead?" Terumoto

stepped close. "If not for the word of that Emerald Magistrate, you would have been laughed out of court."

Masahiro's only reply was an icy glare, somewhat spoiled by the fact Terumoto was a head taller than him.

"Your lies change nothing." He chuckled. "Prince Takamochi will be the next emperor, and when he ascends you will be alone once again."

Like a distant tower coming into focus, Otose's message came clear. The red spider lilies symbolized not only death but danger, their color crimson as Scorpion robes. A man who hired assassins to dispose of his political opponents would not balk at espionage and threats of violence. Terumoto's control of the courts meant the man could literally get away with murder.

Otose had told him everything without speaking a word. Masahiro had simply been too self-absorbed to notice.

"Nothing to say, Crane?" Terumoto stepped back, brushing at the front of his robes as if soiled by proximity to Masahiro. "Do you know why Lady Otose supports me?"

"I have an inkling." Masahiro glanced toward the two black-clad guards.

Terumoto ignored the insinuation. "She has accepted a role in the inevitable." He spread his hands. "Do you think I accomplished all this *alone*? I count allies among not only the high court, but the Crane as well."

It was as if Terumoto had driven a fist into Masahiro's gut. That realization made Otose's forced acquiescence more understandable. If the Crane would not protect one of their own, then Masahiro's hope of swaying the succession had become vanishingly small.

"You did not know?" Terumoto's laugh pierced Masahiro

like a spear. "Not all of your fellow Crane are so..." He sucked air through his teeth. "Shortsighted."

Masahiro fought to keep his breath steady. He had survived Iuchiban's vile tomb only to find crueler fiends waiting for him back home.

"You have given me much to consider." Masahiro fell back on cool courtesy. "I hope the skies are clear and the evening air pleasant."

Terumoto frowned, seemingly taken aback by the sudden change.

"For Prince Takamochi's moon viewing." Masahiro made to move past Terumoto, heading for where his palanquin waited, bored bearers lounging in the shade of the manor wall.

One of Terumoto's guards moved to block Masahiro's path.

"Where are you going?" the Scorpion asked.

"Home."

"Oh, not that way." Terumoto swept past him in a flutter of robes. "My palanquin is in need of repairs, so I took the liberty of renting yours."

"I paid them for the day." Masahiro glared at the bearers, who had the courtesy to at least look abashed.

"And I offered them triple." Terumoto ducked into the palanquin. "Lady Otose is not the only one who can recognize a good deal."

Masahiro could only watch as Terumoto settled himself upon the cushions. As the bearers lifted the palanquin, he fixed Masahiro with a look of false concern.

"My condolences about your brother."

The barest wave, and the bearers started off down the street. One of Terumoto's guards lingered, reaching into his breastplate. Masahiro took a step back, expecting the samurai to brandish a blade.

Instead he dropped a coin pouch at Masahiro's feet.

"A day's wages." The guard jogged away, leaving Masahiro to stare at the small leather pouch.

He waited until they were out of sight before kicking it into the gutter. Terumoto may have outmaneuvered him, but Masahiro would curse the souls of his ancestors before he accepted anything from Bayushi Terumoto.

Masahiro steeled himself for another long walk back to his disappointing accommodations. Still smarting from his encounter with Terumoto, he resolved to stick to the less traveled streets that webbed the Inner Districts. Usually frequented by servants, the shadowed alleys would be balm for his wounded pride.

He might have forgiven Terumoto's arrogance, but the man was petty as well. Unsurprising from someone who would employ a creature like Gensuke to dispose of his political opponents. If only Masahiro could remove the Scorpion so decisively, but blades and poison had always seemed the last resort of the truly desperate.

Was Masahiro *truly* desperate?

He discarded the idea. Even were Masahiro to lower himself to employing killers, he could not afford competent ones.

He must outthink Terumoto. A man that petty must have made enemies in court. With a bit of cajoling, Masahiro might undermine Terumoto's conspiracy, perhaps even supplant the Scorpion.

There were meetings to arrange, favors to call in, a thousand strings of obligation and enmity Masahiro could tug upon.

Immortal sorcerers be damned, *here* was a foe Masahiro understood.

Wrapped in courtly minutiae, Masahiro did not notice the dagger until it thudded into his shoulder. Frowning, he regarded the spreading blot of crimson staining his best robe. A pair of shadows detached from the darkness of the alley ahead, the whisper of sandals on stone telling Masahiro more were closing in behind.

He drew his sword – not to fight, but because it seemed appropriate he should die with blade in hand.

The assassins closed the circle, moving like consummate professionals. Bayushi Terumoto's coffers were apparently deep enough to afford the best.

Back against the wall, blade held awkwardly in his left hand, Masahiro was surprised to find the thought of his impending demise filled him not with fear or regret, but a strange species of irritation.

He *really* should have seen this coming.

CHAPTER SIX

A week after the attack, a patrol found Seiji wandering the broken foothills north of Razor of Dawn Castle. A dozen Hiruma scouts, faces scarred as teahouse tables. They might have been the Divine Siblings for the relief their appearance conjured in Seiji's chest. He collapsed into the arms of a sharp-jawed woman, her callused hands seeming as soft as silk.

"He's a Kuni." The scout turned Seiji so the others could inspect him for corruption. Lone travelers, even ones in Crab armor, were treated with caution. Apparently satisfied, she raised a gourd to Seiji's lips. The water was warm and tasted of limestone, but to Seiji it seemed fresh from a temple spring.

"Easy, easy." The woman guided him to a nearby flat stone. "Are you alone?"

Seiji nodded, not yet willing to trust his voice. He had abandoned his horse when the ground became too treacherous.

"What happened?"

"Dead." Seiji spoke through gritted teeth, jaw clenched against the ringing in his thoughts.

"Who is dead, boy?" the woman asked. "Was your party ambushed?"

"From the northwest." It was all Seiji could do not to moan every time the bell rang. "Walking dead. Hundreds. They scaled the cliffs, the walls, killed my laborers."

"How close?" With typical Crab practicality, the Hiruma scout dispensed with superfluous inquiries.

"I have seen none since the attack." Seiji shook his head. "But they move fast."

"Can you walk?"

Seiji tried to push upright only to fall back on legs like rotten pine.

The scout commander gave two sharp whistles, two of her companions seeming to emerge from the stone of the cliffs.

She thrust her chin at Seiji. "See he makes it back to Razor of Dawn."

The two scouts lifted him, half-dragging him across the uneven stone. It was not a pleasant experience, but better than moving under his own power. Although the chimes came slower, the bell seemed only to grow more strident, each ring dragging a soft moan from Seiji.

Fortunately, the scouts seemed to mistake his distress for exhaustion. Seiji did not trust himself to explain the terrible ringing in his head. Such things often spoke of deep corruption. Should the scouts learn of his condition, all Seiji was likely to receive would be a swift end.

Pain blurred Seiji's vision. Even his heart seemed to throb in time with the bell. He must have lost consciousness, because the scouts were carrying him.

He heard the creak of heavy gates, then the clatter of

winches. The leftmost must have been missing several teeth, as the chain skipped every few heartbeats, causing one of the doors to open more slowly than the other.

It would need to be replaced, Seiji thought. A mistimed opening could spoil a sally or doom a retreat.

Someone was talking, voices lost amidst the ringing. Seiji smelled smoke, oil. Something cool touched his forehead, not the comfort of a damp cloth, but wet ink as warding symbols were painted across Seiji's face.

Blessedly, the bell's chime receded, not wholly gone, but also not drowning Seiji's every thought. More water. Then a bowl full of salty broth fed to him in delicate sips. At last his heartbeat slowed, tired muscles relaxing as Seiji slipped into exhausted slumber. Even unconsciousness offered no respite from the bell. Seiji dreamed of shadows and tangled chains. A vast web of snarled links stretching in all directions, seeming to shiver with every dire chime.

Seiji tried to untangle the rusty knots, but every twist seemed only to draw him deeper. Although he could not see it, Seiji knew he was not alone. Something crawled upon the web, a huge and terrible shadow, its movements only evident by the shifting of chains drawn taut by its hideous passage.

"Seiji." A voice echoed in the darkness.

He opened his eyes to see the craggy features of his aunt Chiyo. Evidently roused from sleep, she wore only a light robe, gray hair drawn back by an onyx band. Her expression was severe as the cliffs that warded Razor of Dawn Castle, a wide scar tracing a puckered line down Chiyo's cheek, the hollow of her missing eye filled with an orb of polished jade. Although Seiji knew the false eye was wholly mundane, he still could not dispel the feeling it let Chiyo peer right to the root of his soul.

"They tell me everyone is dead." As usual, Chiyo did not bother with preamble.

It was a rather harsh way to sum up the slaughter, but Seiji could only return a glum nod.

"Pity." She sucked air through her teeth, filed to points and etched with warding trigrams. "Even that old boar Izō couldn't keep you safe."

"He held back the dead while I carried warning," Seiji replied, trying very hard to make it sound like an act of foresight rather than cowardice.

Chiyo was unmoved, her glare sharp enough to flense skin. "Walking dead, they say. Shadowlands creatures?"

Seiji frowned, considering. "Dark magic, certainly."

"Is that your expert opinion, architect?" Chiyo jabbed Seiji with a bony finger.

"I fought them, not you." Seiji glanced over Chiyo's shoulder to where his sheathed blade leaned against the wall.

She followed his gaze, lip curling. "You would've done more than fight if you were a true witch hunter."

Seiji's cheeks grew hot, old anger welling up from deep inside. "We discussed this, aunt."

"A discussion, was it?" She cocked her head, voice a mocking rasp. "I don't seem to recall being consulted when you turned your back on our family."

"I didn't–" Seiji bit back his rejoinder, forcing his breath to calm. Now was not the time to refight old battles.

"There was a bell," he said.

"In the castle tower?" She raised an eyebrow.

"No. Invisible." He tapped his forehead. "It rings in here."

Chiyo leaned close, her jade eye seeming almost to glow in the candlelight. Passing gnarled hands over him, she muttered under her breath, a croaking chant that tugged at the shadows in the small chamber, causing the light to flutter.

"There's something calling within you." She gave a low whistle. "Powerful."

"Corruption?" Although he dreaded the answer, Seiji could not but ask.

She pressed her palm to his chest, head tilted back as if testing the air. "No."

Seiji let out the breath he had been holding. There may yet be hope.

"Have you ever heard of anything like this?"

"No." She stood. "We should consult Elder Nakame."

Seiji could not hold back a wince. His last meeting with the head of the Kuni family had not been one he cared to repeat, but if anyone could provide insight into Seiji's condition, it would be Nakame.

He pushed up, legs unsteady but at least able to support his weight. He did not ask for assistance, nor did Chiyo offer any. She merely snatched up her walking stick, an old twist of slash pine cut with a pattern of interlocking prayers, its knobby ball perfect for crushing skulls.

Chiyo moved quickly despite her age, seeming more spider than woman as she navigated the branching halls of Razor of Dawn. Although there were many ways to the Kuni suites, Seiji's aunt took the one through the central courtyard. It was the most direct route, but it also took them by the high, gabled roof of the Kaiu Architecture School. Far smaller than those boasted by other castles, Seiji had dreamed of adding his designs to the archives, of earning the right to work upon the Carpenter Wall itself. Now he could not even bring himself to look at the place.

Around the school castle walls rose like sea cliffs. Razor of Dawn was old, and yet should Seiji wish, he could find its plans within the architectural archives. The Kaiu were meticulous about preservation, especially those castles that had stood the test of time.

Unlike Seiji's ambitions.

Rootless dread welled up within him at the thought of having to explain how he had lost not only his plans, but his laborers, and the castle he was trying to rebuild. As if to echo his dire thoughts, the bell gave a muffled chime, low but insistent – a reminder that Seiji had larger concerns than the shame of failure.

Head down, he continued after Chiyo, fleeing the judging shadow of the architecture school.

Although the Kuni maintained a small presence in the castle, they were nonetheless accorded a rather large suite of rooms in the eastern donjon. Ostensibly, this was a testament to the high regard in which the Kuni were held by the clan, but Seiji had always suspected the remoteness of his family's chambers had more to do with apprehension than respect. The Crab Clan might depend upon the witch hunters, but the Kuni walked close to darkness.

Kaiu guards in full battle armor stood at attention outside the thrice-warded door. Although they were quick to step aside, shouldering their heavy tetsubo clubs, Seiji could not but notice the careful way they regarded him and Chiyo, nor could he ignore that, unlike other doors in Razor of Dawn, the Kuni door bore protective jade sigils on *both* sides. Other more prickly families might have seen this as insult, but the Kuni accepted it with a strange sense of pride.

Just one of the many things Seiji disliked about his family.

Inside, two witch hunters waited, making a show of not watching the Kaiu guards. Faces painted with holy sigils, they wore nothing but simple robes, unadorned but for the crossed crab claws that were the Kuni sigil.

A far cry from the spirit-haunted halls the other families feared, the interior of the Kuni suites was clean and well lit, pale screens framed by heavy cedar beams polished to mirror sheen by a legion of gray-robed acolytes.

They stepped from Chiyo's path, heads bowed. Seiji's aunt affected not to notice, but Seiji could not help but offer his younger kin a sympathetic wince. Well did he remember the long hours spent scrubbing the floorboards. Such painful perfection was meant to instill a sense of exactness, one that would serve the acolytes as witch hunters – where the slightest misstep could lead to corruption.

A series of small rock gardens circled the central manor. Like islands in a misty sea, the stones were arranged in geomantic formations, the waves of sand raked into protective mandalas.

"Wait here." Chiyo thrust her chin at the door of the central audience chamber before ducking through the low entry door.

Seiji knelt as the screen slid shut, seeking to compose himself – an impossibility given the irregular chimes that sent ripples through his calm.

"Come." The call came as a whisper, more felt than heard.

Bowing low, Seiji slid the screen aside and entered.

The chamber was unadorned, its walls barren save for a few prayer scrolls and a small alcove boasting a jade carving of the Kuni manor in miniature. The sparseness served to draw the eyes toward the raised platform at the rear of the hall.

Chiyo knelt facing the rear dais, her good eye like a chip of flint. The central platform was taken up by a carved wooden screen, gnarled scrollwork and embellishments concealing the shape of the person behind. Seiji had met Elder Nakame on several occasions, although never seen her. Rumors abounded – that she was ancient, or hideously scarred, or twisted by shadow. Some whispered she was inhuman, half-specter, that to even look upon her would leave the viewer a twitching husk. Seiji had his own theories, but was wise enough not to test them.

"I have informed the elder of your failure." Chiyo's voice came flat as a frozen pond.

"And of your discovery." Although barely a whisper, Elder Nakame's voice seemed to come from all around. "A bell?"

"Yes, elder," Seiji replied. "It began before the dead arrived."

"And it rings even now? Even here?" Nakame asked.

Seiji nodded.

Chiyo regarded him, scarred face betraying nothing. "I sensed no corruption, but the shadow can be subtle. It may be best to hold my nephew for interrogation."

"You would burn a scroll before even glancing at the contents?" Nakame asked.

"If it came accompanied by a legion of dead, yes." Chiyo crossed her arms. "*Something* destroyed the imperial expedition. The high courts claim the threat has been dealt with, but we should mount an expedition of our own."

"I recall… a bell." Nakame's words came like wind skittering through fallen leaves. "A monastery in the northern hinterlands, deep within the shadow of the Twilight Mountains."

"I have heard of no such place," Chiyo said.

"Old, very old." Elder Nakame moved, a hint of many limbs folding and unfolding behind the latticed wood of her screen. "An order formed to oppose an evil long forgotten."

Seiji drew in a shaky breath. "If this curse has its roots in our family history, we should seek it out."

"Is it curse or warning?" Chiyo asked.

"Yes," Nakame replied, apparently unwilling to elaborate.

Chiyo turned her gaze upon Seiji, jade eye glittering in the light.

Even without the bell dragging at his thoughts, the last thing Seiji wished was to travel north again. He blinked back memories of corpses clambering over the jagged battlements, masked faces expressionless as they tore his workers limb from limb.

He had abandoned his birthright, but it seemed the Kuni were not finished with him.

"The Twilight Mountains cover many miles. Elder Nakame, do you recall where this bell was located?" Chiyo glanced to the carved screen, but if Nakame had any more wisdom to impart, she did not share it.

"We can start at the hill fort my nephew lost." Disdain whetted Chiyo's words. As usual, she did not consult Seiji, treating him like a dagger – something to be drawn or sheathed as the situation dictated. "I require a few days to gather enough samurai, a few more for the necessary provisions. We'll need horses, scouts, witch hunters…"

Seiji lost the thread of Chiyo's speech. Like floodwater trickling through cracks in an ancient foundation, the bell undermined the structure of his thoughts. Wards weakened, its call growing more insistent, each slow chime louder than the last. It was all Seiji could do not to leap to his feet and run from the chamber.

Through the rising clangor, Seiji was struck with a strange feeling of being watched. He glanced around the chamber, but Chiyo was still embroiled in expeditionary preparations.

Then his gaze fell upon the screen.

Geometric patterns shifted upon the lattice, scrollwork twisting to form a vague impression of faces.

Go.

A chorus filled his thoughts, louder than even the bell.

"I don't know where it is." Seiji mouthed the words.

The truth dwells within your shame, face it.

He hesitated, unsure.

GO.

The call propelled Seiji to his feet. Chiyo seemed not to notice, the whole of the chamber strange and liquid, like light reflected through water. He moved as if in a dream, seeming almost to flow down the hall and out into the tepid sunlight. Only when Seiji drew in a shaky breath of cool evening air did the feeling fade, replaced by the bell's unrelenting call. It seemed to emanate from Seiji himself, overpowering yet directionless.

He did not know where to turn. Nakame had bid him face his shame, but if that was not here, in the house of the family he had turned his back on, Seiji did not know where it could be.

He wandered through the stone garden and into the outer halls, every footfall in time with the terrible chime. Seiji might not be able to parse Nakame's cryptic wishes, but he knew he could not wait for his kin to gather. The bell's call would drive him mad long before then. He thought of following the chime, but that would only lead to the dead.

The witch hunters opened the gate, Kaiu guards turning as Seiji drifted past.

Almost by instinct, he found himself heading back toward the central courtyard, feet treading familiar paths to the place that had once brought him such fulfillment. He traced a hand along the castle wall as if to draw strength from its immovable weight. His clan had laid these stones, hundreds of laborers straining to fulfill the vision of some ancient architect whose work had sheltered and protected the Crab for generations.

How arrogant of Seiji to believe he could do the same.

And there it was – his shame.

He stood before the Kaiu school, the place that had accepted him, but where he never belonged. Classes were done, students retiring to quarters deeper within the castle. All that remained were servants, lanterns bobbing like distant fireflies.

Like Lady Sun's rising, the light seemed to penetrate Seiji's churning thoughts. He swallowed against a throat gone suddenly dry, the bell's sharp chime seeming to fade as if to acknowledge Seiji's realization.

The Crab had built Razor of Dawn, just as they had built the mysterious monastery. Pushing aside his discomfort, he strode toward the school, legs steady for the first time in days. There might be no maps of the Twilight Mountains, no guides to the ancient and terrible place Seiji sought.

But if the Crab had built it, there would be plans.
And that would be enough.

CHAPTER SEVEN

"Iuchiban?" Lady Ikoma Kiyomi, Senior Archivist of the High Histories, glanced to her record book. "I seem to remember *The Spring and Autumn Annals* mentions an oni by that name. It was during the reign of Hantei XXI. The demon had corrupted a young noble and ravaged several towns along the Twilight Mountains before Falcon and Scorpion Clan spiritualists were able to banish the beast."

"Iuchiban is a blood sorcerer, not an oni." Naoki struggled to keep her voice level. She had explained as much to the last four archivists, but it seemed they would have to start over once again.

"We have been in these stacks for the better part of a week." Lady Matsu Akoya paced between the scroll racks like a caged treecat. "I had hoped a senior archivist could provide deeper insights."

"The High Histories are vast." Kiyomi spoke as if reading from a scroll. "Thousands of books, tens of thousands of scrolls – even I cannot fathom the breadth of our collection."

"I am daimyō of the Matsu family," Akoya replied. "I am not in the habit of having requests shuffled off onto underlings."

"Alas, recent uncertainty in the imperial succession has seen many requests of the High Histories." Kiyomi's gaze flicked to Naoki, then back to Akoya, one brow arched as if in question. Naoki understood her concern. She and Akoya had arrived to find Sacred Watch Castle crawling with Lion samurai. Ostensibly, the Clan Champion had scheduled several large military exercises concurrently, but it did not take a master investigator to see through such a flimsy pretext.

The Lion were marshaling forces.

Even the most upright clans did not appreciate Emerald Magistrates prying into their affairs, especially at a time like this.

"I personally vouch for the magistrate," Lady Akoya replied without hesitation. The senior archivist seemed to weigh the response, expression cold. "Kiyomi, please." Although Akoya spoke softly, her voice was roughened by emotion. Something passed between the two women, as soundless and quick as distant lightning.

"Of course." The stiffness bled from the senior archivist's bearing. "Why did you not come to me first?"

The Matsu daimyō shifted as if the archivist's question were a blow to be parried. In the few weeks Naoki had spent with Akoya, she had never seen the woman display such unease.

"I did not want to disturb your–"

"Did not want to be in my debt, you mean?" Kiyomi straightened, her expression turning imperious. "Do not trouble yourself with such concerns, Lady Matsu. Our accounts were settled long ago."

Akoya seemed about to reply, but before she could speak, Kiyomi gestured to one of the scribes kneeling at the rear of the record chamber, who brought forward a pair of yellowed scrolls.

"You mentioned the seal at Five-Dragon Gate. I was able to track the substantial outlay of jade bound for the Twilight Mountains." Kiyomi unrolled the scrolls upon the low table. Naoki noted the old script, a flowing style popular in court documents several centuries ago.

"A Record of the Fallen from just before the seal was laid." Kiyomi ran a finger down the list of archaic names. "It includes many clans. This speaks to a large battle, but there are no records of deeds, nor do any histories make reference to the conflict."

"Could they have been destroyed?" Naoki asked.

Kiyomi spared her a cold glance. "Every archivist here would die before allowing harm to befall the histories."

"Magistrate Naoki meant no insult." Akoya said. "But surely even you cannot hold back the ravages of time."

"Records are copied in exacting detail, even down to mistakes and stray brush strokes," Kiyomi replied. "Once housed within the archives, nothing short of an imperial edict can remove them from these walls. If we have no record of your blood sorcerer, it means either no one wrote of him, or the documents never reached us."

Naoki's hopes crumpled like a burning lantern.

"Two of my companions knew of him," she continued, hating the plaintive note that threaded her voice. "A Kuni samurai and a Shiba elementalist; perhaps there are more esoteric references?"

"That was my first assumption." Kiyomi's nod was almost pleased. "While our collection focuses primarily on historical matters, we do possess many records of a more arcane nature."

"I expect you found nothing there as well." Akoya frowned.

"Quite the contrary." At Kiyomi's wave, several attendants piled books and scrolls upon the table. "We found *far* too much."

"This is excellent." Naoki felt her optimism rekindle.

"Alas, they present a different problem." Kiyomi paged through one of the books so Naoki and Akoya could see the fearsome demon inked upon the page. "Here is record of the oni I mentioned earlier." She opened another book, setting it beside the first. "And here is one of an underworld spirit sent to torment the living."

Almost apologetically, she paged through another. "And here, a mountain witch who raised an army of goblin spiders." She ran a finger along the stack of tomes. "There are easily forty different creatures spoken of in these arcane records, all named Iuchiban. And these are only those from the period surrounding the laying of Five-Dragon Gate. We found literally hundreds of scrolls chronicling Bloodspeaker cults, each claiming to worship some ancient spirit of evil."

"We defeated two such sorcerers in the Twilight Mountains." Uncomfortable trepidation blossomed in Naoki's chest, cold and prickly. "Could they *all* follow Iuchiban?"

"A hundred cults with a hundred names for darkness?" Kiyomi shook her head. "It makes no sense. Even an initiate elementalist can tell you spirits have but one name."

Akoya blew out a long, frustrated breath. "Is Iuchiban sorcerer or shade?"

Kiyomi shook her head. "According to these scrolls, he is both and a dozen more things beside."

Naoki realized she was picking at the sleeves of her robe again and folded her hands in her lap. Like a swimmer struggling against a strong current, she was expending time and energy to no good cause. Both the Shrike and the murderous monk had been secretive to the point of paranoia.

But those had not been the only Bloodspeakers Naoki had encountered.

"What of Shosuro Akifumi?" She frowned, trying to recall the name of the other ancient builders of Iuchiban's tomb. "Or Kakita Tsutomu? Do the histories hold any records of them?"

"I have heard of Tsutomu," Kiyomi replied. "He was an artist, yes? Late seventh century?"

"We found a room full of his works in the tomb." Naoki replied. "They were cruel, beautiful things, portraits painted with blood, scenes so real you could lose yourself in them."

"That is... troubling." Kiyomi looked to Akoya again, as if to question Naoki's sanity.

Thankfully, Akoya waved away Kiyomi's doubts. "The magistrate speaks true."

"There is little to condemn Tsutomu." Kiyomi's tone was clipped. "The man was prickly and self-important even for a Crane, but there is no hint of corrupt leanings before his disappearance from court."

"Even so, I would like to see the records," Naoki said.

Thankfully, Kiyomi did not seem offended by the request. She nodded to her attendants, who departed with a bow, leaving the three of them alone.

"And Shosuro Akifumi?" Akoya asked.

"Of him, I must claim ignorance," Kiyomi replied. "The Shosuro are an enigmatic family, even among the Scorpion. May I ask how you came to know of this man?"

"From an assassin sent to kill one of my companions," Naoki replied. "He was also Shosuro, but was quick to discard his mission when he discovered Akifumi was one of Iuchiban's disciples."

"And this assassin, where is he now?" Kiyomi asked.

"Dead." Naoki blinked back memories of flashing blades, a grinding, cutting hell of knives down in the hungry dark. "Murdered by one of Akifumi's cruel tests."

Kiyomi leaned forward, curiosity writ upon her thin face; even Akoya seemed interested. Although Naoki had told her all she knew of Iuchiban, she had been reticent to share details of the tomb itself – as if by not speaking of them, she might erase all memory of that horrible place.

"Magistrate, are you well?" Akoya grasped Naoki's hands. Naoki flinched from the sudden touch, a mix of anger and surprise hardening her scowl. Then she saw the bloody marks where her fingernails had dug into her palms.

"My apologies. It is difficult to speak of the tomb." She nodded to Akoya, who released her hands.

"Anything you can tell me of Akifumi will aid in the search," Kiyomi said.

Naoki found herself hesitating, tongue stilled not by fear, but wariness. The High Histories were the greatest repository of knowledge in Rokugan; it was impossible they held no mention of a dark sorcerer so powerful it had taken the entire Empire to put him down.

She glanced at Kiyomi. The archivist had said she would die before allowing any harm to come to the records, but there was an obvious hole in the histories, one Kiyomi could neither explain nor justify.

Akoya must have sensed Naoki's reluctance, because she gave a slow nod. "I have known Kiyomi for many years. She was a friend of Chiaki's... and of mine."

It was not the Matsu daimyō's words that convinced Naoki, but the small smile she gave Kiyomi, a shy, almost tentative expression that seemed strange on Akoya's scarred face.

Squeezing her eyes shut as if to blind herself to the memory, Naoki told Akoya and Kiyomi of the tomb. They were silent as she spoke of the cruel traps that had borne Akifumi's symbol, of the statues of murdered clan nobles, the Chamber of Even Blades. Whatever the Shosuro noble had once been, what emerged was a picture of a callous scholar, a man who sought to test the bounds of choice without regard for morality or suffering.

When she had finished, both of the Lion nobles sat silently for a time, their expressions troubled.

"Now I understand why Chiaki gave her life," Akoya said softly.

"If any hint of Akifumi survives in the records, I will winnow it out." Real concern threaded Kiyomi's voice.

"You have my gratitude, archivist." Naoki bowed. For the first time since they had begun the audience, Kiyomi's answering nod came tinged with true respect.

"How long do you require?" Akoya asked.

"The histories are vast." She frowned, considering. "I suspect any records of Akifumi will be fragmentary at best. Even were I to devote my full attention to the task, it would be a matter of weeks, perhaps months."

Akoya sucked air through her teeth. "A long time for Bloodspeakers to work their evil upon Rokugan."

"Do we have another choice?" Naoki asked.

"Perhaps." Akoya tapped a finger upon her knee. "If the past holds no answers, then we must look to the present. This tomb – could you find it again?"

"I could guide you to Five-Dragon Pass, but the tomb itself... I cannot say." Naoki shook her head. "Masahiro and I entered in the Twilight Mountains, but we emerged within Shinomen Forest a hundred miles north. I suspect the tomb is not bound to a single place, or at least its entrances are not."

"Even so, the search may provide new opportunities." Akoya nodded as if to herself. "If the mountains are haunted by walking dead, perhaps Bloodspeakers remain as well. I would bet my ancestor's blade we could drag truth from them."

Naoki stiffened against the unsettling tremor that ran down her back. Akoya's logic was inescapable. Deep down, Naoki had always known her path would take her back to those cruel peaks, back to the dead. Like a cloistered scholar, she had hoped to find truth in archives and histories, all the while dreading that the answers she sought were not hidden amidst crackling parchments, but buried beneath a mountain of blood.

She gave a tight-lipped nod, not trusting her voice to speak her assent.

"And what do you plan, Akoya? To lead an army into Crab lands?" Kiyomi's question was an arrow fired from cover, unexpected and sharp. "Even if the Crab do not see it as an act of war, the Scorpion and Crane are already on edge."

"An army? No." Akoya smiled. "But my personal guard, certainly."

Kiyomi shook her head. "No one would believe a Matsu daimyō has left her castle to chase down rumors of dark sorcery. You would be hounded."

Akoya's eyes glittered in the lamplight. "A Matsu daimyō, perhaps, but not the entourage of an Emerald Magistrate."

Naoki could not but stare wide-eyed. Many magistrates maintained networks of guards and agents, some numbering in the dozens, even hundreds. Even so, the thought of gathering an entourage seemed foreign to her.

"You would serve Naoki?" Kiyomi's tone echoed Naoki's incredulity.

"Until this is done, yes." Akoya nodded as if the matter were already decided.

"This is not a matter of a samurai swearing to an Emerald Magistrate." Kiyomi threw up her hands. "You are the Matsu *daimyō*, Akoya. A lord cannot serve two masters. This would mean giving up your castle, your title. You might as well take holy vows and become a monk!"

"I have heirs." Akoya shrugged. "Trained and blooded warriors. I would trust any with my estates."

Kiyomi shook her head. "You would cast everything aside to seek vengeance for Chiaki and Katamori?"

"For justice, yes."

Kiyomi crossed her arms. "Stubborn Matsu samurai."

"Hidebound Ikoma scholar." Akoya's response had the well-worn feeling of an exchange the two had shared many times.

"I have served the Lion all my life. Now let me serve the Empire." Akoya seemed to catch herself, turning to Naoki. "If you will have me, magistrate."

"I would be a fool not to." Naoki swallowed against the knot in her throat. It was humbling to have such a storied warrior aid Naoki's search. Truly the lord must have shared a strong bond with her nephew and master.

"Then it is decided." Akoya slapped her knee.

"For you perhaps, but what about the others?" Kiyomi asked.

"I was not the only one who lost kin to the Bloodspeakers," Akoya replied. "We shall have volunteers aplenty."

Kiyomi shook her head, rendered speechless for the first time since their audience had begun.

"I am in your debt." Naoki settled for a bow, even though Akoya would soon be her retainer. "Both of you."

"Do not trouble yourself with such concerns, magistrate. The only debt owed is to Iuchiban." Akoya's grin was almost feral. "And it shall be paid in steel."

CHAPTER EIGHT

There were six killers. Two in front, two behind, and two that idiot Crane had yet to notice.

Shosuro Gensuke killed them first.

They were dressed as court messengers, a common enough sight on the backstreets of the Inner Districts. Even in his prime, Gensuke would never have faced six trained assassins in a place of their choosing. If anything, he would have much preferred to bury his blade in the neck of that insufferable Crane, but Shosuro Akifumi's orders left no room for interpretation.

Gensuke slipped behind the nearest one, a woman leant against the corner of one of the rows of buildings that hemmed the thin alley. Clearly the lookout, and therefore the first to die.

It was quick, a hand pressed to her mouth, one unmarked blade tracing a thin line across her throat. Even dying, she tried to alert her companions, twisting like an eel in Gensuke's grip, a concealed dagger slashing toward his stomach. Had he been but a man, the woman might have succeeded in gutting him, but Gensuke was more than a man.

More, and less.

Swaying away from the slash, he twisted to pin the assassin to the wall, slipping his own blade between her ribs.

Gensuke had never taken pleasure in killing – no true professional did. He gently guided her to the ground then turned back to the fight.

Masahiro flailed about like a wounded boar, his katana more a danger to himself than the circling killers. Fortunately, the Crane possessed the foresight to put his back against the wall, a move that kept him from being surrounded, but also blinded him to the killer on the roof above lowering a wire noose.

Gensuke's hurled dagger took the attempted strangler in the eye, a throw that would have been impossible before Akifumi plucked Gensuke from the Chamber of Even Blades. The ancient Bloodspeaker had done more than heal Gensuke; he had changed him, bones steeped in arcane unguents, flesh inscribed with cruel sigils, a mask of bone and bloodstained cedar affixed to his face.

Death would have been kinder.

The assassin tumbled from the roof, soundless until he struck the cobbles with a wet thud. A dagger hissed toward Gensuke's face, its spin almost lazy in the dappled shadows of the alley. He plucked it from the air, hurling it back at the assassin almost as an afterthought.

As if the noise had broken some unspoken agreement between killers and victim, Masahiro began to shout for the guards. As usual, the Crane acted far too late to save himself, but succeeded in making things more difficult for Gensuke. No doubt the assassins had believed the Crane an easy target as well.

Gensuke could not blame them. He had once made the same mistake.

Already he could hear the answering calls, the slap of sandals on stone echoed by the rough shouts of samurai. Gensuke would have scowled had Akifumi's accursed mask not robbed him of all expression.

Spurred by the guards' calls, the remaining assassins closed on Masahiro. Gensuke dove between them, quick as a lunging heron, his twin short swords slashing tendons. Even as the first killers crumpled, he was among the rest like a winter storm, blades slipping past their parries like wind through a threadbare cloak.

One assassin stumbled back, spitting blood from slashed mouth. Gensuke followed him, close as a shadow, his other blade diving in for the kill stroke. Something struck him from behind. One of the hamstrung killers had hurled himself at Gensuke.

He might as well have tackled a temple pillar. Gensuke brought an elbow down, feeling the man's spine snap, then cast the body aside like a broken sandal.

He expected to find Masahiro pinioned by the remaining assassin. Instead, he saw the Crane standing over a crumpled body. Masahiro's robe was daubed with crimson, his hair pulled loose from its queue to haze his head in a pale tangle. He held a bloodied hilt in his one remaining hand, the blade of his broken sword jutting from the assassin's ribs.

Alone, essentially unarmed, it would be easy for Gensuke to slip over and slit the Crane's throat. He took a faltering step toward Masahiro, muscles unconsciously tensing against the pain that came whenever he disobeyed Akifumi. As part of his Shosuro instruction, Gensuke had been trained to resist torture – he had been burnt, beaten, frozen, cut, and almost drowned on several occasions. But this was different. The agony was more than physical. No matter how he steeled himself, it seemed to carve to the root of him every time.

At least he didn't scream this time. It was as if he were burnt from the inside out, muscles crackling with pain, his bones like steel drawn fresh from the forge.

Even so, the desire to end the Crane carried him forward. It hardly mattered that Masahiro had been justified in dropping Gensuke into that pit of blades. He had killed the Crane's brother, true, but Hiroshige's soul had ascended to the Realm of Waiting.

Gensuke's had been cast into hell.

The alley was wreathed in shadow, Gensuke's face hidden behind Akifumi's cruel mask, his inscribed flesh swathed in bandages and robes.

Somehow, Masahiro still recognized him.

"How?" It came not as a question, but an accusation, a strangled gasp wrung from the lips of a condemned man.

Gensuke could not reply, but he did not need to.

Masahiro knew. He had *always* known.

With a flutter of robes, Gensuke leapt. Clearing Masahiro's head by an arm's length he kicked off the wall above the startled Crane, stretching to catch the downspout of the building across the alley and clamber up onto the roof.

Behind, Gensuke could hear the city guard, but he was already out of sight, Masahiro's shouts little more than wind. It was blustery above the rooftops, cold perhaps, but Gensuke could no longer feel such things as he skipped across the tiled roofs of the Imperial City.

It was good the Crane had recognized him. Akifumi's orders may prevent Gensuke from killing Masahiro, but they had said nothing of terrifying the courtier. More than a threat, it was a warning – dark powers, dark plans, even Gensuke knew little of his new master's goals.

Hate was an unfamiliar feeling for Gensuke. He had killed before, many times, but he had never hated his targets, even the cruel or immoral ones. How could an assassin pass judgment upon others? But Gensuke *hated* Akifumi, not only for what the withered sorcerer had done, but who he was – a traitor to the Shosuro.

Now Masahiro would know their companions had failed, that Bloodspeakers yet worked their will upon Rokugan. Gensuke might be a pawn in Akifumi's schemes, but only a fool thought he could cage a scorpion without being stung.

Gensuke had seen to it that Masahiro would turn his admittedly formidable talents toward tracking him down. When he did, he would discover Akifumi, and then one of them would die.

Or perhaps both.

But satisfaction would have to wait. For the moment, Gensuke had work to do.

For all his myriad cruelties, Akifumi was no fool. Since they had come to the Imperial City, the ancient Bloodspeaker had kept Gensuke busy. The ascension of a new emperor always ushered in a rash of untimely deaths. It would have been easy for Gensuke to add his tally to the bloody-handed work, but he was no back-alley knife man.

Anyone could kill, but only professionals could make it look natural – an elderly priest passing in her sleep, a mid-rank bureaucrat thrown from his horse, an imperial guard captain dying from an infected dueling wound. Gensuke's true masterstroke had been the deaths of half a dozen elder officials in the Ministry of Rites. Even with his newfound abilities, it had been difficult to slip into their poetry reading and taint the sweet bean cakes with a poison that mimicked all the symptoms of the wasting sickness that had stricken Emperor Hantei XXVI.

This time however, Akifumi had ordered a far less eloquent demise.

To reach Bayushi Terumoto, Gensuke had to cross half the district. Had the Bayushi noble ridden in his own palanquin, he might have been safely ensconced in the Scorpion Embassy – far beyond even Gensuke's reach. Fortunately, the bearers of Masahiro's rented litter were of a rougher sort, their progress marked by jostling and frequent stops. No doubt the uncomfortable ride had Terumoto regretting his vindictive act.

Night cloaked the District of Fortitude, tepid pools of lantern light illuminating the occasional guard stationed outside manor gates or on rambling patrol, breath fogging in the autumn air. A thin sliver of Lady Moon peeked through the clouds like a heavy-lidded eye.

In perhaps a minute, Terumoto's laborious progress would bring him abreast of a multi-tiered shrine to the Fortune of Luck. Gensuke took up position on one of the rooftops with a clear view of the empty street. He considered offering up a prayer only to discard the notion as foolish. Professionals made their own luck.

Gensuke knew Bayushi Terumoto only by reputation. One of the clan's most powerful courtiers, he had spent the better part of his life deep in the vagaries and vicissitudes of court. Perhaps Gensuke had worked for him, perhaps not. It was not good practice for a Shosuro assassin to know the names of his employers.

With a clatter, Terumoto's palanquin rounded the corner perhaps thirty paces beyond where Gensuke crouched, daggers in hand. Two guards jogged alongside, relaxed but alert.

Gensuke reversed his blades, counting steps. If it were up to him, he would have leapt from the shrine roof, charging with daggers bared in the hopes Terumoto's guards would end his suffering. But Akifumi's orders allowed for no such foolishness. Gensuke had been bidden to kill with stealth and efficiency. Although it burned him to murder a member of his own clan, there was nothing Gensuke could do.

His first dagger struck the nearest bearer hilt-first, rebounding from the man's head. It would have been easier to kill the man, but only amateurs left unnecessary bodies. Akifumi had only ordered Terumoto's death.

Gensuke might be a killer, but he would not let Akifumi make him a monster.

With a cry, the bearer clapped a hand to his head, dropping to one knee. The sudden departure of one of the palanquin's front supports caused the rickety conveyance to list, Terumoto cursing as he was flung forward.

The guards reacted with laudable quickness. One stepped in to shoulder the abandoned bearer pole, working to right the palanquin even as his companion rushed to shield their lord.

Gensuke struck before the man's blade could even clear its scabbard. Like a darting sparrow, his knife threaded the tiny gap in the palanquin's woven screen to bury itself, hilt-deep, in Bayushi Terumoto's throat.

Knowing the Scorpion lord would be dead in moments, Gensuke rose from his crouch, ready to slip around the corner of the shrine. Something struck him in the leg and Gensuke looked down to see a knife jutting from his calf. A glance back saw one Scorpion guard charging across the street, already drawing another throwing blade from the sleeve of his robes.

Gensuke could not help but feel a swell of painful pride at how quickly his clan mates had reacted to the ambush. Had Gensuke been a normal assassin, the leg wound would have incapacitated him, but his cold flesh felt no pain.

He plucked the knife from his leg, slipping it into his robes as he dodged around the corner of the shrine, then leapt to catch the roof. By the time the guard sprinted into the alley, Gensuke was already running along the wall that circumscribed the shrine's meager gardens.

Another knife spun toward him. Gensuke swayed from its path, letting it rattle down among the weeds as he vaulted over an intervening balcony and onto the flat roof of a rice storehouse.

Just as before, only shouts pursued him. This time however, there was shame as well.

He had murdered a lord of his clan, of *their* clan. Whatever he had become, Akifumi still bore the Shosuro name. It mattered little that Gensuke could not resist the Bloodspeaker's orders. He was a traitor, not only to the Empire, but his clan, too.

As if to outrun his disgrace, Gensuke sprinted across the shadowed rooftops. Even this provided no solace. He had no hammering heart to thunder in his ears, no gasping breath. His muscles did not tire, and whatever filled his veins was blood no longer.

Akifumi's orders required he take a circuitous route back to the District of Fortitude, skirting the vast, jagged crevasse locals called the Oni's Smile. As befitted a district largely dominated by the dour shadow of the Crab Clan Embassy, its streets were sparsely traveled, its collection of dilapidated manors inhabited by court exiles and a scattering of low-rank nobles. Recently the Crane had established markets in the district, no doubt hoping to capitalize on the Imperial Museum of Antiquities to draw potential customers, but they were small affairs, virtually abandoned now night had fallen.

Fewer to witness Gensuke's shame.

Darkness reigned in the tumbledown manor Akifumi had claimed as his own. Ostensibly the residence of a minor court official, it was an unassuming structure, easily lost amidst the scores of others crowding the curved streets around the Oni's Smile.

The first indication that the manor was more than it seemed came past the entrance room, down the creaking hall to where the beams took on a darker hue. Easily mistaken for cherry or red walnut, Gensuke knew the wood's rich crimson color came from the blood in which it had been steeped.

Beneath a secret door hidden below the dais in the sitting room, a curved set of stairs led down. They bore no indication of tool or joint, almost as if each stair had been gnawed from the rock. Smooth walls held no sconces for lantern or torch – none who trod this path had need of light.

Akifumi was working. Akifumi was *always* working.

Beyond a rusted steel door, its face carved with cruel

sigils, Akifumi's workshop sprawled across a dozen or more sepulchral chambers. Like Iuchiban's tomb in miniature, they were filled with the vicious tests that seemed to obsess the ancient Bloodspeaker. Walking corpses shuffled in the sputtering half-light carrying stones, and logs, and oddly shaped bits of metal. Unlike Gensuke, they were faded, hollow things, souls carved from mortal flesh and replaced with corrupt spirits. At the moment they were constructing a large tree, its trunk composed of twisted iron, a wealth of obsidian blades hanging from bent and clutching limbs. There would be blood involved as well.

There was always blood.

"Is it done?" Akifumi bent low over the roots of the tree, hands deep in the snarled nest of iron. He was a small man, stooped and ancient, with skin like salt-scarred driftwood, a few wispy hairs ringing his age-spotted scalp. Robes of faded black cloth were spattered with all manner of unsavory effluvium, the twining ivy crest of the Shosuro barely visible. This had been Gensuke's cruelest revelation.

Akifumi still believed himself part of the family.

"Masahiro lives," Gensuke replied. "Terumoto does not."

Akifumi straightened, absently rubbing gnarled hands upon the front of his robe. Something dark smeared across the Shosuro symbol, but the sorcerer seemed not to notice. Turning, he hobbled around the tree, craning his neck to peer into the lower branches.

"Not right." He clucked his tongue. "The trapdoor is off balance."

When Gensuke did not reply, Akifumi thrust his chin at the tree. "Go adjust the upper branches."

"I am not your servant."

"You are what I made you to be, little nephew." It was Akifumi's name for Gensuke, a painful reminder of their shared blood. "Now, up."

Gensuke climbed amidst dangling razors. Not just blades, he saw now, but mirrors, curved surfaces bending light and shadow.

"That one. To the left." Akifumi raised a gnarled finger. Like many things about the ancient sorcerer, his venerable form was misleading. Gensuke had seen Akifumi casually bend steel.

Gensuke grasped the branch, pulling it into place. Usually, Akifumi was blunt to the point of rudeness, but Gensuke had had some success in getting the sorcerer to talk when he was occupied with one of his projects.

"A bit to the right," came Akifumi's terse order. In the months that Gensuke had been with Akifumi, he had witnessed little emotion from the ancient Bloodspeaker save varying degrees of irritation.

"I understand Terumoto's death will weaken the Scorpion Clan, but why protect Masahiro?"

"You think I am *protecting* the Crane?" Akifumi wrinkled his nose, the closest Gensuke had ever seen him to amusement. "He is a subject, a lesson, carefully tested and prepared – like yourself."

"To what end?"

"End?" Akifumi sniffed. "It is a *beginning*."

"Is that why you built all…" Gensuke gestured vaguely around the workshop. "This?"

"What is moral and right?" Akifumi absently reached down to fiddle with a lever near the snarled base of the tree.

"To serve one's clan, to seek perfection and enlighten–"

"Not that Shinseist rubbish." Akifumi waved a liver-spotted hand. "What is *moral and right*?"

Gensuke twisted to glare at the sorcerer. "To oppose evil."

"And what is evil?"

Gensuke did not have a ready answer for that. Even before Akifumi had remade his torn flesh, there were many who would have considered Gensuke a villain.

Akifumi tugged the lever, frowned, then pushed it the other way. A trapdoor opened beside the wizened sorcerer, spilling into some room below. Akifumi wiped wrinkled hands upon the front of his robe.

"Wipe away the veneer of class, of culture and society, of family. Loosen the stifling bonds of Divine Order. What is moral, then?"

Gensuke paused, considering. "I cannot say."

"Exactly." Akifumi tottered a few steps back as the trapdoor snapped shut. "Now come down from there."

"So Masahiro will push the bounds of morality?" Gensuke hopped down.

"Hardly." Akifumi inspected the tree. "Flawed conditions produce flawed results. I require a clean workspace."

Gensuke narrowed his eyes, following the sorcerer's train of logic. "And Iuchiban will somehow bring this about?"

"Enough questions." Akifumi removed a bottle of blood from his robes, emptying it upon the twisting roots.

Slowly, terribly, the tree began to move. Like a constellation of pale stars, the mirrors shifted and spun. Almost unconsciously, Gensuke's eyes were drawn to glittering reflections, but what he saw in the distorted field of mirrors made him turn away with a shudder.

"Close, but we yet need the thread," he heard Akifumi mutter.

Rather than watch the mirrored tree, Gensuke imagined slitting Akifumi's throat. Gensuke's encounter with Masahiro proved there were perhaps some limits to the Bloodspeaker's control. Gensuke could not resist, but he might circumvent. Akifumi had caged a scorpion, but not for long. Somehow, some way, Gensuke would destroy the ancient sorcerer.

Even if it killed him.

Again.

CHAPTER NINE

Cold salt spray flecked Tomiko's cheeks as the Phoenix trade ship knifed through a rising wave. They could have made better progress in open water, but the captain, a gnarled old trader by the name of Gōhei, had hugged the coast as if it were his mother. Unfortunately, *The Autumn Dragon* had been the fastest available after Kosue's vessel had burnt along with its accursed master. So Tomiko had booked passage.

And waited.

"Can I get you anything, mistress?" Gōhei edged closer, head lowered. Although permitted to wear Phoenix colors, he was but a merchant.

"Better wind." She glanced at the sails.

Gōhei winced. "Any more would swamp us."

"Then this is sufficient."

Ostensibly, Tomiko traveled to seek funding for Heaven's Blaze. It was also her hope to unearth Kosue's unsavory contacts. She had no intention of facing a coven of Bloodspeakers alone, but the more evidence she could present to the Phoenix Elders, the more likely they would be to overlook any indiscretions on the part of her former master.

Little remained in Stone Grove. The warehouse fire left nothing save oily soot. Kosue's associates had conveniently fled during the chaos, and although Captain Kenichi sent word to other garrisons, the Bloodspeakers had been clever enough to smuggle hundreds of corpses through Stone Grove. They would not be apprehended by provincial authorities.

Tomiko suppressed a flicker of shame at the thought of not telling Captain Kenichi about the Bloodspeakers. A few days would make little difference, especially if she could use Kosue's logbook to locate the merchant's contacts. The Phoenix could round them up and Tomiko would be a hero rather than a failure.

Almost unconsciously, her fingers crept to the small, oilcloth-wrapped bundle that contained the Bloodspeaker's logbook. Kosue had hidden his tracks well, but in masquerading as an honest merchant, he had bared his dealings to the imperial bureaucracy. Little business was transacted in the capital outside the gaze of assessors and trade officials. There might be no record of corpses and dark magic, but there *would* be documents of oil barrels.

As if conjured by her desire, the next wave crested to reveal the towers and vaulted temples of the Imperial City. High quays lined the northern docks, shielding the rickety collection of wharves that reached into the bay like skeletal fingers. A veritable forest of structures had sprung up along the northern bank of the River of Gold, thin runnels of smoke from a thousand, thousand cookfires merging into a wispy haze.

Tomiko detected the slightest hint of resentment in the captain's tone as he bid her farewell. No doubt he would have preferred a paying passenger to a clan priest, but such was the duty of lessers. Once matters were settled, Tomiko would see all debts were paid.

First however, she must swallow her pride.

A rented palanquin carried her from the salt-rimed shacks of the northern docks and through the harbor districts. Once they reached the massive shadow of the Enchanted Wall that girded the inner districts, Tomiko dismissed her ragged bearers and hired a palanquin more suited to the Imperial Precincts. It pained her to waste what remained of her school's meager funds, but even the Phoenix must keep up appearances.

Normally a high-ranking noble like Tomiko would enter through the vast crystal arch that spanned the Road Most High, but as she was coming from the north, Tomiko resigned herself to the more mundane gate used by servants and messengers.

The imperial guards were quick to wave Tomiko's palanquin to the front of the line of dust-streaked couriers, accepting her travel papers with brusque nods. Their manner became more respectful at the sight of her parents' names and rank, and Tomiko was ushered past with refreshing alacrity.

Although the air was cleaner in the Inner Districts, the streets less crowded, Tomiko found it harder to breathe, nerves and apprehension conspiring to constrict her ribs in their chill grip.

As befitted a clan more interested in spiritual matters, the Phoenix Embassy was relatively modest, far overshadowed by the high walls of the eastern Lion Embassy. Only a fool would mistake size for power. Like the clan itself, the Phoenix Embassy exercised outsized sway upon the surrounds.

Tomiko was met at the gate by a shaven-headed initiate, who ushered her into a sitting room overlooking one of the embassy's small stone gardens. After cleaning the dust of the road from her face, tea and plain rice cakes were brought. Tomiko ate sparingly, not trusting her stomach to keep down even the smallest morsels.

It was late afternoon by the time her parents deigned to arrive, both attired in the gold and orange robes of high priests. Although their clothes were bare of embellishments save for the Isawa family sigil and the five-feathered crest that marked them as clan ambassadors, they were accompanied by a veritable flock of initiates.

Gathering herself, Tomiko offered respectful bows to both her parents – filial, but not deferential. She *was* the mistress of a school. However few its disciples, Heaven's Blaze still commanded respect.

Her mother, Kuwashi, had the broad shoulders of a laborer, muscles toned as any samurai's by a daily regimen of training. By contrast, Tomiko's father, Kōrei, was thin as a sapling, preferring physical deprivation and fasting to his partner's more active meditations. Although different in build and manner, her parents' solemn expressions might have been cast from mirrored bronze.

"We are glad you have returned, daughter." Despite the kindness of her father's greeting, even the most banal pleasantries came laden with the crushing weight of unfulfilled expectation.

"Autumn winds bear thoughts of home." Tomiko nodded toward a small stand of maple in the garden, their leaves a mix of brilliant orange and gold. "One cannot look at the foliage without being reminded of family."

"Indeed." Her mother shifted to regard the trees, meditative calm more damning than any recrimination.

So it was to be silence, then.

Tomiko pressed down the roil of unkind emotions churning in her thoughts.

Her parents were powerful nobles, second only to the Elemental Masters in knowledge and prestige. They might have been the head of one of the great Isawa schools; instead they had chosen to dedicate themselves to representing the Phoenix in matters of state. By neither word nor deed did they condemn Tomiko's choices, and yet their very lives set rule to her existence.

Although Tomiko gave no sign, she felt her insides curdle, as if her presence had somehow profaned the beauty of this moment. If she did not speak soon, Tomiko feared she might scream.

"My school is deeply in debt."

"Troubling." Sympathy creased her mother's face, cutting deeper than recrimination. "Such dire tidings weigh heavily upon us all."

"A good bookkeeper is worth their weight in jade." Her father's tone was absent, as if he were recalling a bit of Shinseist wisdom. "We shall provide one."

Tomiko kept her voice level, her posture relaxed. "The problem is not one of accounting."

"What, then?" her mother asked.

Tomiko drew in a slow breath. Her parents seemed to have a knack for placing her in impossible situations – either Tomiko could admit Masatsuge was a fool, or confess to frittering away her school's wealth.

"Heaven's Blaze was... ill-used by an unscrupulous merchant." Tomiko bowed her head, regret only partially feigned.

"So do the immoral always seek to bind enlightenment in chains of the material world." Her father offered a reassuring nod. "Do not let such dishonesties sully your thoughts."

Her mother leaned forward, voice solemn. "Do you require money, daughter?"

"No." Tomiko felt her jaw clench, her parents' perfection filling the room like smoke – blinding, choking, impossible to breathe.

"Our stipends are generous, but we have little use for such wealth," her mother continued, every word striking Tomiko like a thrown stone.

"It is not that," Tomiko replied. "The merchant–"

"Was he brought to justice?" her mother asked.

"He is dead." Tomiko kept her head low. "Burned along with his warehouse, his ship, everything."

"Then the Fortunes have already delivered penance." Her father nodded.

"No trader acts alone." Her mother clucked her tongue. "Surely this man has partners, investors, others to share his profits and bear his losses."

"He frequently traded in the Imperial City," Tomiko replied softly. "I rescued one of the merchant's logbooks from the fire." She withdrew the small bundle. Carefully unwrapping the book, she spread it to show her notes. "The entries were difficult to decipher, but I believe I have documented some dates and amounts."

Her parents shared a look, eyes sharp as hawks spying fresh prey.

The Phoenix might eschew violence, but they craved justice.

"You have done well to bring this to us, daughter," her mother said.

"Truth is a coin that multiplies in the spending," her father added. "Thus does a true sage prosper in honesty and the wicked find themselves bereft."

Tomiko could but smile, her own lies seeming to press against her bared teeth, jostling to come out. She had tried to live by Shinsei's teachings, struggled with every fiber of her being, only to fail and fail again.

It would not be truth that redeemed Tomiko in her parents' eyes, but deeds. If they knew she sought a cabal of Bloodspeakers, they would take this from her just as they had taken everything else.

"I did not return for money," she said. "But to track the merchants' associates. Anyone so unscrupulous as to cheat a respected school would surely not balk at robbing others."

"Well reasoned, daughter." Her mother's compliment conjured no warmth in Tomiko's chest. "We shall make inquiries of the Imperial Assessors."

"I had hoped to be of some assistance in the search," Tomiko said, daring to raise her head a fraction. "The code is complex."

"You can explain it to our scribes," her mother replied.

And there it was. Her parents might love their daughter, but they did not *respect* her. Why should they? Tomiko had brought them nothing but disappointment.

"I fear there is little time." Tomiko steeled herself. She had resolved not to lie to her parents, but neither did she need to share the whole story. "The merchant's associates fled after the fire. If any reached the Imperial City before me…"

Her parents shared a glance. Tomiko knew they would much rather entrust this matter to someone more skilled. But now their scrupulousness worked against them. They could not risk letting criminals harm others.

Tomiko had placed an impossible choice before them, one she knew they would decide in her favor.

She had learned from the best, after all.

Her parents shared another look. Time seemed to stretch in the tiny room, drawn out thin as a strand of gossamer, all of Tomiko's hopes balanced upon that slender thread.

"So be it." Her father shook his head as if to deny his words. "I shall pen letters to the assessors, but imperial bureaucracy is a tortoise, slow and well-armored."

"How long?" Tomiko asked.

"A few days." He gave a noncommittal tilt of his head. "I shall endeavor to speed their progress."

"And what of your school?" her mother asked off-handedly.

"I had hoped Heaven's Blaze would be made whole once the associates were apprehended," Tomiko said, resigning herself to the role she must play.

"The merchant's goods burned along with his warehouse," her mother replied. "Nothing remains to return."

"But the others–"

"Have no doubt robbed *other* victims." Although soft, her mother's tone brooked no concession. "You would deny them recompense?"

"Forgive me." It was as if Tomiko's stomach had become a river rock, hard and cold.

"You are forgiven." Her mother nodded with the satisfaction of a priest doling out benedictions. "How much is required?"

Tomiko told them.

Although none of the initiates moved, she could almost sense a tightening in their bearing, eyes sharp as bared blades.

Her father gave a thoughtful sigh. "So much…"

Although the statement was carefully chosen not to give offense, it was the words he did not say that echoed in Tomiko's thoughts.

Foolish. Profligate. Wasteful.

Not trusting her voice, Tomiko drew in a slow breath. She could not defend her choices, nor could she throw herself on her parents' mercy without embarrassing all present.

So she simply waited.

After an eternity, her mother nodded.

"We shall consider your request."

Her parents stood, movements so precise it was as if they had practiced the motion. They looked down at Tomiko like dragons perched upon a mountain, perfect in their exalted role.

Tomiko met their impossible gaze, muscles clenched as if she pressed against the weight of her parents' stifling regard. It was petty not to show gratitude, but after the humbling she had endured, Tomiko reckoned she was due a small measure of pettiness.

"And what will you do now?" her mother asked.

"I have other matters to attend to." Tomiko worked to imbue

her words with the calm that seemed to come so easily to her parents.

"Perhaps we can help," her mother said.

"The library at Heaven's Blaze is small. I would like the opportunity to consult the Imperial Archives on some points of interest."

"No one was ever harmed by a surfeit of knowledge." Her father spoke as if reciting from a wall scroll.

Tomiko returned his vague smile, not deigning to elaborate. If her parents knew she planned to comb the histories for Bloodspeaker lore they might disown Tomiko on the spot.

Contrary to her father's platitudes, some knowledge *did* harm.

As if sensing her anxiety, her mother leaned forward. "All will be well, so long as you learn from this."

"I will." Tomiko swallowed. "I have."

"We know your path has been hard, daughter." Her father folded his hands in the sleeves of his robe. "But remember, buds must break to blossom, flowers shatter to bloom."

The tranquility with which he delivered even consolation sent a spike of hot anger along Tomiko's spine. Criticism masquerading as wisdom. Even after she had humbled herself before them, it was too much for her parents to show even a flicker of humanity.

Without another word, her parents departed, the whisper of robes across bamboo matting echoed by a soft chorus of slippered feet as their initiates hurried after. Tomiko sat, unmoving, until the last footfalls faded, alone but for her troubled thoughts.

She rose, calling for the servants to summon a litter to bear her to the archives, her face still flushed from the meeting with her parents. For all his vague proverbs, her father had been right about one thing.

Tomiko had broken.

It was high time she bloomed.

CHAPTER TEN

The sorcerer died screaming. He writhed amidst Iuchi Arban's summoned flames, blood magic boiled away by the elemental conflagration. At Iuchiban's nod, a Unicorn samurai put an arrow in the sorcerer's throat, ending his suffering.

It was better than the fiend deserved. They had found the cult masquerading as performers, traveling between the herding villages and trade towns that dotted the grassy plains of the southern Iuchi family holdings. Such troupes often collected the wayward and overlooked. The cult had picked through the slums and orphan houses for children, promising to teach them a trade. In reality, they had sacrificed their pupils, believing innocent blood best for communing with a being they knew only as "the Young Master."

Qadan would have gladly watched every Bloodspeaker burn.

Iuchiban insisted on *kindness*.

"That is the last of them, I think." Arban glanced around the circle of scorched wagons. Although hunting Bloodspeakers was a task far below the Iuchi daimyō's exalted rank, Qadan's cousin had insisted on accompanying her, offended that such cults could operate under his rule.

"Not quite," Qadan felt herself say. Iuchiban guided them toward a wagon, a bevy of costume chests still smoking upon its back. A woman crouched in the shadows beneath, teeth bared as she pressed a brush knife to the neck of a child. The poor thing was rigid with fear, eyes squeezed shut as if to blind herself to the threat of death.

Qadan heard the creak of drawn bows.

"Put it down." Iuchiban spoke in two voices. Arban and the veteran Unicorn samurai tasked to the mission heard Qadan's voice.

The cultist heard the voice of her Young Master.

Trembling, she let the child slide to the ground, arms spread as if to embrace Qadan.

"M- m- mast–"

Qadan's fist snapped the woman's head back. Her second blow shattered the wretch's jaw. Iuchiban let her feel the pain of the blows, skinned knuckles heightening Qadan's satisfaction at dealing such rough justice to a murderer of children.

"Search the surrounds." Iuchiban nodded toward the tall grass on either side of the road.

With an efficiency born of long practice, the Unicorn vaulted into their saddles to search the perimeter for any wayward cultists.

None remained, but Iuchiban needed to keep up appearances.

"See the little one is cared for." Arban gestured for one of the samurai to gather up the shaking child. He gazed down at the bleeding cultist, voice hard. "Shall we question her?"

"If that is your wish, daimyō." Iuchiban glanced at her cousin. Although she had no control over her body, her voice, even her gaze, Qadan willed Arban to recognize the dark spirit that dwelt within her. From experience, she knew it to be a hopeless wish, but could not quiet her desire to be *seen*.

"Damn my rank." Arban shook his head angrily. "What do *you* think, cousin?"

"I think you are lord of these lands." Iuchiban let the smallest amount of hurt creep into Qadan's voice.

"Apologies for my outburst." Almost unconsciously, her cousin's hands felt for the comfort of his talismans. Qadan understood the need. Once, she would have done much the same. But now the talismans in her satchel were empty and could bring no comfort. Qadan took solace in the fact her spirits had been spared the corruption of Iuchiban.

At least she prayed they had.

Arban drew in a slow breath, shoulders rounding. "These were my people. If not for you I would be blind to this atrocity."

"All of Rokugan is blind." Iuchiban laid a reassuring hand on Arban's shoulder. "But we shall make them see."

"Lords!" a samurai shouted from the far side of the camp.

Arban strode toward the call. Iuchiban was quick to follow, but not before sparing a moment for his erstwhile follower. With barely a glance the woman's life guttered and died. There was hardly any sorcery involved. She had given her soul to Iuchiban, his to preserve or destroy.

"*It is better this way.*" The sorcerer's voice slipped through Qadan's thoughts.

"*Why hunt your own followers?*" she asked, curious despite herself. Over the past weeks they had destroyed three

Bloodspeaker cults. Although composed mostly of peasants and disaffected samurai, one of the cults had infested a monastery, the corrupt abbot perverting Shinseist doctrine to bend entire villages toward profane beliefs.

"You believe I patronize murderers of children?" Amusement threaded the ancient sorcerer's reply.

"Everything they did, they did for you." Qadan did not bother to hide her disgust.

"And no atrocities have been committed in the name of the Divine Siblings? The Fortunes? Would you hold Shinsei responsible for all who claim to follow him?"

Not for the first time, Qadan wished she could snort. *"It is not the same."*

"Is it not?" he asked. "Even the purest teachings can be corrupted by impure motives. These poor folk were victims of a broken system, condemned by birth to suffer at the hands of their supposed betters. Tell me, is it not understandable that they sought justice?"

"What they did was not justice."

"On that, we agree." Iuchiban's reply came threaded with something akin to regret. *"And thus the need to root them out."*

There was no time for rejoinder as they had reached the samurai.

He knelt next to an overturned chest, a spray of muddied fabrics spread across the soot-streaked ground. On first look they appeared to be just another collection of actors' robes. Dyed a uniform rusty red, they were embroidered with thread the dark, almost purplish color of an old scab.

The samurai fingered the fabric, glancing to Arban and Qadan. "These are far too fine for mere actors."

"Mulberry silk, full brocade. And look at the embroidery." Arban prodded the robes with the toe of his riding boot. "These would not be out of place in the Winter Court."

"No insult to our clan's weavers, but such finery was not made in Khanbulak," Iuchiban agreed. Qadan suspected the ancient sorcerer was well aware of the robes' provenance, but he could not be seen to know *too* much.

"Look at the sigils. Dark sorcery," Arban said. As if emboldened by Qadan's cousin's words, the robes began to shift, symbols wavering like a heat mirage, seeming to tug at the eye.

The Unicorn samurai surged to his feet, stumbling back.

"Your hand," Arban said.

The man glanced down to see his fingers stained the same reddish brown as the robes.

"This is… blood." He wiped them on a fall of soot-stained drapery on a nearby wagon.

"*Corrupted spirits* are bound within the robes!" Arban grasped the carved pumice talisman that was home to his fire spirit.

"Wait!" Qadan wanted to shy away from the cursed fabric, but Iuchiban made her kneel. Drawing her dagger she cut a swatch from the sleeve of a robe, the fabric warm and almost oily to the touch. "If we find the source, we may find other Bloodspeakers."

Arban gave a thin-lipped nod, waiting for Qadan to step back before unleashing the full fury of his allied spirits.

The robes screamed, like the panicked shrieks of animals.

Qadan added her own flames to her cousin's blaze. Eruar was lost to her, but Iuchiban had a host of arcane forces to draw upon, many of which could pass for elemental spirits. Had Arban turned his full attention upon Iuchiban's summoning, he might have been able to discern the spirits were slaves rather than allies, but her cousin's attentions were wholly consumed with banishing the corrupted spirits bound within the tainted robes.

With a final cry, the last of the corrupted spirits fled to whatever realm lay claim to pitiable entities.

"Are you well?" Breathing hard, Arban turned to Qadan.

Iuchiban returned the slightest of nods, Qadan's face filled with feigned concern. "This fabric. It is like the corrupt abbot's vestment."

Arban glanced over, mouth curling as if he'd tasted something bitter. Qadan well knew his revulsion; the Bloodspeaker monastery had been a terrible place, holy spaces profaned by unspeakable rituals. The abbot had laid a trap for them, filling the air with soporific incense that muddied their thoughts. He and his followers might have overwhelmed them all if not for Iuchiban's dark knowledge.

They had left the monstrous abbot in a pool of his own blood. Upon the corrupted altar had been a panoply of profane relics, but Iuchiban had taken care to draw attention to the fabric draped across the tiered shrine.

Now Qadan knew why.

Arban ran a cautious finger over the fabric. "It *is* the same."

"Only a master could have created such fine weave," Iuchiban replied. "And only with the proper equipment. Who might possess such resources?"

Arban sucked air through his teeth. "The Crane?"

"Scorpion, more likely," the Unicorn samurai replied.

"Perhaps." Iuchiban pretended to suppress a shudder. As much as Qadan despised the sorcerer, his acting would have put any of the corrupt troupe to shame. "But the cults we have discovered thus far have been isolated. Apart from the abbot they seem largely confined to the lower classes."

"The City of the Rich Frog boasts many weavers," Arban said. "And the merchants who call it home are certainly wealthy enough to afford such robes."

Qadan could tell it was not the answer Iuchiban desired, but the ancient sorcerer was nothing if not patient.

"A good place to start," he replied.

"It has been too long since I visited our kin in Rich Frog." Arban nodded. Although ostensibly ruled by an imperial governor, control of the city was split between the Lion, Dragonfly, and Unicorn – a testament to its position astride the lands of all three clans.

"Do you not have duties elsewhere?" Iuchiban asked.

"My advisors can manage for a little while longer." Arban waved his hand at the scattered bodies of the cultists. "What duty is more pressing than eradicating such evil?"

"Will Lord Bataar not think something amiss?" Iuchiban asked.

"The Clan Champion knows the importance of our mission."

Our mission.

Qadan would have wept had Iuchiban allowed it. While it was comforting to have her cousin nearby, Arban's presence only offered Iuchiban another soul to corrupt.

"As you wish." Iuchiban returned the slightest of bows.

Several scouts came cantering back into camp, breath

steaming in the cool autumn air as they spoke of tracks leading away from the wagons. While Arban went to converse with the samurai, Iuchiban made a slow circle of camp, pretending to look for more evidence of taint.

Sensing the sorcerer was in a contemplative mood, Qadan sought to press him further.

"*Young Master.*" Qadan spoke the title like an insult. "*Another one of your names?*"

Iuchiban gave a soft chuckle. "Truth be told, even I can hardly remember them all."

"Do you claim so many?"

"*There was a time when I hungered for such power. But I was far younger, then. Younger and more foolish.*" His tone held the patience of a Shinseist monk, calm woven with the slightest thread of regret. "*History is a desert. The winds of the present constantly reshape the past. All who seek immortality must be prepared for change.*"

"*And are you immortal?*" she asked.

"I have never died, if that is what you mean."

Iuchiban was seldom so forthcoming.

"*And this Young Master,*" she asked. "*They used the name to summon you?*"

"*A part of me, yes,*" he replied.

"How is that possible?" she asked. "You are… were mortal, not some elemental spirit."

"Come now, Qadan, do not play the fool. You know the power names hold." He knelt to regard one of the dead Bloodspeakers. "Her name was Kao, born to sharecroppers at the height of the Nightbloom Famine. Indentured to pay off her mother's debts before she even came of age." Iuchiban stood. "I wonder how different her life might have been had she been born with the name Iuchi... or Hantei?"

"The Divine Order ensures souls are placed where they belong," Qadan said.

"Order?" Iuchiban scoffed. "Hardly. The Fortunes give or withhold favor as they see fit. How can you look at the suffering their 'order' has wrought and not hunger for something better?"

If anyone other than Iuchiban had spoken those words, Qadan would have named them a fool. Even the emperor was bound by the will of Heaven. And yet, somehow the sorcerer's claims filled her with apprehension.

If anyone had the power to shake the pillars of creation, it was Iuchiban.

Sensing her hesitation, the ancient sorcerer pushed deeper. *"The world is controlled by names, bound by them – noble and commoner, god and mortal, spirt and demon. Definition is shaped by name, signifier by sign."* He nodded toward the knot of Unicorn samurai. *"They follow you because of your name... kill for it, die for it. The only difference between the mortal and spirit is that we can change, we can grow, whereas spirits can never become more. Shinjo understood this."*

"Do not profane her holy name!" Qadan's shout echoed within the confines of her skull.

"And why not?" he asked sharply. "I knew her better than most. Shinjo was my teacher, after all."

Qadan had always known, and yet to hear it stated so bluntly could not but give her pause.

"You are as a frog in a well, gazing at a fleck of sky and thinking it encompasses all existence," Iuchiban continued, his tone calm once more. "But worry not, together we shall sweep aside this Empire's old and wretched names."

The sorcerer's voice was a rising tide that drowned her arguments in chilling rhetoric. As much as Qadan wished to cast down Iuchiban's assertions, she could not deny their terrible logic. She had sought to learn more about the creature that held her body, but all she had found were more doubts.

"Cousin!" Arban's call brought their head around.

Qadan jogged down to find her cousin regarding the Bloodspeaker Iuchiban had slain.

"She is dead."

Iuchiban feigned surprise. "I didn't hit her *that* hard."

Her cousin gave a frustrated grunt, a little bit of the boy she knew peeping through the mask of Iuchi daimyō.

"She could have shed light upon the origins of the robes."

"We have interrogated Bloodspeakers before," Iuchiban replied. "They cannot even agree on a single name for their master."

He sighed. "Even so, it pains me to lose the opportunity."

"Fear not, cousin. We shall follow this trail to its end," Iuchiban said, smiling. "You have my word as an Iuchi."

CHAPTER ELEVEN

The dead moved like locusts, sudden and swift, their jerky limbs imbued with terrible purpose. Kuni Seiji pressed his back against the boulder as if he might merge with the rough stone. He could hear them scrabbling across the slope above. Since he had left Razor of Dawn, the bell had grown more muted, its chime the barest of flickers on the edges of Seiji's perceptions.

He regretted fleeing the castle like a thief in the night, satchel stuffed with stolen architectural drawings. Hopefully Chiyo would find the note Seiji had left, paper spattered with ink as each chime of the horrible bell set him shaking. A few more would have driven Seiji mad.

If it did not kill him.

If anything, the chime had grown more bearable as he journeyed toward the Twilight Mountains, the incessant call quieting to the point Seiji had even been able to steal a few hours' sleep, wedged into a rocky crevasse like a mountain goblin.

Something scraped across the far side of the boulder, vibration felt as much as heard. Seiji considered drawing his blade, but feared the noise would alert the dead.

A shadow flitted across the ground, hunched form picked out against the cool afternoon light as it squatted less than an arm's length above Seiji's head. He was struck by the urge to shut his eyes, like a small child believing it might make him invisible.

A moment, and the shadow was gone, its descent marked by a trickle of pebbles upon Seiji's head and shoulders. As if to mark the passing of the dead, the bell's chime began to slow – still loud, but nothing like the grating peal it inflicted upon Seiji back in Razor of Dawn.

He waited for the sounds of the dead to fade, only belatedly realizing he was measuring their progress by the urgency of the bell. Its chime had risen and fallen over the last several days, but never by such a degree. Then again, Seiji had never drawn close enough to actually *see* the dead.

A foolish thought came to mind. Frowning, Seiji sought to sweep it away, but like the chiming from which it sprang, the idea would not give him peace. Finally he rose, shaking his head at the rashness of this wild supposition but unable not to test it.

Drawing in a shaky breath, he followed the dead.

Seiji picked his way up the slope, whispering prayers that his boots did not dislodge any loose stone. The ancestors must have been listening, because no walking corpse leapt from the shadows. Even so, it took an act of singular will to approach the gap through which the dead had skittered.

After a hundred paces, he made out shadows on the canyon

wall – some still pierced by the weapons that had ended their life. Although the bell's chime quickened, it remained bearable.

Seiji had been right.

A flash of pale skin caused him to freeze. Although the creatures' masks had no eyeholes, no features at all apart from two dark spots and a mouth, Seiji knew the creatures could see well. He held still, listening.

Blessedly, the bell slowed. The dead were moving off.

He let out his held breath, feeling as if he could collapse upon the stone. Seiji had been too caught up in the moment to mark the strength of the bell's chime when the dead had assaulted his partially repaired keep, but now he had found a means of avoiding the creatures.

Heartened by this new discovery, Seiji wasted no time in putting some distance between himself and the nearest corpses. As expected, the bell calmed even more. Now he need only find the ancient Kuni temple.

When the chimes came far apart enough to ensure no dead might come upon him, Seiji drew forth the sheaf of documents from his satchel, carefully spreading them upon the ground.

He murmured a prayer of thanks to the thoroughness of ancient Crab architects. Although hampered by archaic forms and techniques, the plans contained enough detail for Seiji to determine the rough shape of the mountain on which the temple sat. The architect had even included several nearby peaks for reference, noting both the path and river that ran along the base of the slope. While maps of the Twilight Mountains were famously poor, Seiji had discovered a number of fortifications constructed at roughly the same time as the temple, the most notable being the one he had been originally tasked to repair.

His plan had been to reach the area and use the plans to find the specific mountain. Now, as he sat upon the broken hillside, stony slopes seeming to stretch in every direction, Seiji began to suspect he would need more than a general idea of the temple's location.

Fortunately, the bell saved him once again.

Even at its loudest, Seiji would have been hard pressed to determine the chime's direction. Like booming thunder, it had seemed to echo from all around. But as he frowned down at the plans spread before him, Seiji realized the bell was louder in one ear than the other.

Like a wolf scenting prey, he raised his head and executed a slow spin. It was not an exact process compared to the sharp measures that had first drawn Seiji to the study of architecture. Even so, by pacing up and down the slope he was able to get a general sense of direction. Despite the excited flutter of his heart, Seiji took time to carefully fold and store the drawings. He did plan to return them, after all.

That is, if he made it back to Razor of Dawn alive.

Even guided by the bell, the ascent was punishing. More than once, Seiji was forced to his hands and knees, scrabbling up the ragged shale cliffs like one of the hungry dead. Already cold, the autumn air grew talons as he climbed, the pain in his fingers fading to a troubling numbness. The wind seemed to find the gaps in his thick robes, every gust like a frost-rimed blade dragged across Seiji's flesh.

As if to compound his misery, it began to rain – a thin,

almost oily mist that clung to Seiji's face and seeped through his clothes.

He almost cracked his skull on the monastery wall – almost invisible in the mist.

The wall was smooth to the touch and almost seamless, stones fitted together with only the barest hint of joint and mortar. Although Seiji craned his neck, he could not spy the top. It rose, cold and implacable as the artisans who had hacked it from these inhospitable mountains.

Seiji followed the base of the wall, one hand trailing on the stone for fear he might stumble off a cliff. The wall seemed to vibrate with every chime of the bell, slight tremors like the beat of some distant heart, as if the monastery itself were alive.

The gate was black iron, etched with all manner of warding sigils. There were names carved amidst the protective trigrams. Although Seiji was unclear on the pronunciation of such archaic characters, he recognized a surname repeated over and over.

Kuni.

They were his ancestors, bound by blood if not by purpose, but such was always the way of family. Not for the first time, Seiji wondered why the bell had chosen him over Chiyo, or really *any* other Kuni.

He pressed against the cold iron, straining already overtaxed muscles until his vision swam. Although the gate bore the names of Seiji's kin, it seemed to hold no familial affection.

Something fluttered at the edge of his vision – a man's shadow, tall and severe, clothed in monk's robes, a heavy staff held in one callused hand. It extended the staff to touch one of the sigils. Seiji drew in a long breath, swaying as he inspected the ward. Not fast enough, apparently, as the shade pivoted to smack its staff across Seiji's shoulders, driving him to his knees.

He looked up, more surprised than hurt, only to see the shade point at the sigil again, then raise its staff threateningly.

Seiji wasted no time in laying his hand upon the symbol and was rewarded by a grinding vibration as something within the door shifted. A moment and all was silent, and yet the door remained firmly shut. Seiji glanced back, shoulders hunched in expectation of another ghostly strike, but the small plateau was empty save for swirling mist.

Not knowing what else to do, he touched the sigil again. Nothing. Eyes narrowed, Seiji touched another symbol. More silence. He could still hear the bell, but it did not echo through the iron. Like a man feeling his way across a darkened room, Seiji's fingers ghosted over the carved metal. He found another sigil that vibrated with the bell's chime and upon pressing it was rewarded with the creak of metal on metal. After a moment, he found another, and another.

At last, the gate swung open.

Seiji was struck by the sudden feeling of being watched, a prickling between his shoulder blades that caused him to half turn.

A score of shades stood in the twisting half-light, men and women with matching robes, united in severe aspect. There was no acknowledgment of Seiji's success, only pitiless scrutiny, as if he were some cracked pot or tarnished blade that would have to suffice. Without a word, they vanished amidst a swirl of misty rain.

Seiji wasted no time hurrying inside, lest the spirits felt compelled to return. Unlike more aesthetically minded clans, the Crab seldom employed architectural embellishments – finding beauty in perfection of purpose. The walls were carefully angled. Only the occasional buttress marred the precise lines of the fortifications. Although as Seiji studied the stonework, he realized the supports were unnecessary, added only to reinforce the stone in the case of assault – as if the builders expected the walls to resist some massive, crushing weight.

The courtyard was covered with bodies. Most were little more than yellowing bones, but some looked more recent. Seiji was no judge of death and so wasted little time with the corpses save to ensure that none still moved.

Even among the most literal-minded of the Kaiu architects, architectural plans were mostly aspirational. One could ensure angles and distances were measured, stones carefully fit together, but ultimately construction was at the mercy of a thousand uncontrollable factors – topography, weather, the quality of materials, even the temperament of one's workers.

And yet somehow, the Kuni monastery was *exactly* as promised.

More than once, Seiji felt the need to take out the plans, comparing the angle of a joist or column to the drawings. In all cases, they matched perfectly. If not for the imminent threat of walking dead, Seiji would have hurried back to the Kaiu school to tell his teachers of this place. Even masters could learn much from the elegant severity of this wayward monastery. Despite the call of the bell, Seiji felt compelled to sketch some particularly noteworthy lintels and rib vaults. Only when the chime became almost unbearable did he move on with a regretful sigh.

Sound filled the inner temple. It was as if Seiji moved among storm clouds, every sonorous ring the crack of nearby thunder. He was tempted to cover his ears, but knew it would do no good.

Perhaps thirty skeletons lay tangled upon the broken tile of the nave. Limbs intertwined, they were positioned in a spreading arch, feet pointed toward the bell like worshippers struck down mid-prayer. As Seiji approached, he noted the bones were cracked – not broken, but covered in a fine patina of lines, delicate as glazed porcelain. He knew without wondering that proximity to the bell had boiled away their flesh, every chime vibrating through tooth and bone. Soon, it would leave nothing but dust.

The bell was huge, surpassed only by some of the great temple bells in Rokugan's most important shrines. Seiji had expected more arcane scripture, but the bell was unadorned – dark iron beautiful in its simplicity. It rang again, the sound seeming to enfold Seiji, to draw him closer, closer.

Gingerly, he reached out a hand, surprised to find the metal warm to the touch. After the chill of the monastery, the heat was welcome, and Seiji pressed his palms to the bell, feeling its warm tone resonate within him. It was as if Seiji were a still pond, every tone sending ripples through his blood.

He closed his eyes, images rising from the darkness like woodblock pictures laid in sequence. He saw an army of dead so vast it seemed to swallow the land.

Rokugan spread before him, as if Seiji sat at the right hand of Lady Sun. Veins of darkness colored the map, inky capillaries spreading to web the land in shadow. Battle scenes filled his mind, samurai in archaic armor struggling with masked dead. He recognized clan colors amidst the flashing steel and spilled blood – not only the Imperial Legions, but an allied force of clan samurai larger than any Seiji could imagine. He had known risen dead betokened dark magic, but had not suspected the threat extended beyond Crab lands.

The battles dissolved into smoke, and a thousand, thousand funeral pyres consumed the bodies of the righteous dead and their unliving foes. Ancient tombs were desecrated, hard-eyed warriors ripping bodies from their sacred rest to toss upon banked blazes. The cries of priests rose to the heavens, dispersing like smoke in the uncaring sky. Such shameful acts were necessary, imperative, lest the dead be once more turned to dire purpose.

The scenes came faster – a man in imperial robes, his eyes red from crying; a line of Crab samurai, their faces painted with holy sigils; masked men slipping through the dark; a great edifice cut into the weeping stone; a clawed hand pawing at the emperor's crest.

Seiji swayed backward, overwhelmed by the flood of images but unable to remove his hands from the bell. Strange memories flowed into him, lost amidst the churning gulf of his subconscious, scattered recollections buried like so many unquiet dead, waiting to claw their way back into Seiji's thoughts. All the while his mind echoed with the terrible chime. No longer simply sound, it gained in clarity, a word. No. A name repeated over and over.

Iuchiban

Seiji opened his mouth to scream, but all that emerged was the name, ancient, powerful and cruel. A hundred faces laid over one another, a hundred names spreading like the branches of a great gallows tree.

He shook his head, unable to comprehend the images.

Bound in blood, bound in soul, bound in name. Find him. Destroy him.

"I don't know how." Tears traced hot tracks down Seiji's cheeks. "Please, choose someone else."

But the bell was merciless. He felt a presence, more than one. They crowded in, armored bodies close as the press of battle. Seiji felt the weight of their expectations, their *need*, and he knew them to be his ancestors, unable to rest until Iuchiban was driven from Rokugan.

They laid hands upon him, rough and callused, strong in purpose, harsh in judgment. Seiji knew they would not hesitate to rip the very soul from his body and cast it into the torments of the underworld. Their shared blood betokened no kindness, no familiarity, nothing save duty.

"Yes." He gasped out the word, grasping at anything to end the agony of their shared consciousness. "I will hunt Iuchiban."

Like blowing out a lantern, the spirits withdrew. Seiji could still feel them within the bell, within his mind, watching for any hesitation. He fell back amidst the scattered bones, racked by coughs like a diver too long beneath the waves.

It was some time before he could breathe without gagging, even longer before he could push to his knees, the first trembling flicker of consciousness rising above the murky babble of memories that were not his own.

It was painful to swallow, but the hurt seemed distant, removed, as did Seiji's exhaustion. He had inherited not only the spirits' duty, but some measure of their fortitude.

If only he had their determination as well.

The bell still rang within his thoughts, but it no longer

overwhelmed them. Seiji knew it would guide him to the dead, just as it would their dark master. What he did not know was why, or how, or even what he was meant to do with the haze of disjointed memories that slipped along the edges of his thoughts.

Go.

The order came as it had with Elder Nakame, a chorus of voices raised in pitiless command.

Seiji found himself lingering beneath the high-arched door of the nave, one hand upon the frame as if to draw strength from the stone. He knew the ancestor spirits had shared all they could, but one question lingered, impossible to ignore.

"There are hundreds of Kuni better suited to this task," Seiji said plaintively. "Why choose me?"

The ancestors' reply came as a terse whisper.

"Because you were closest."

CHAPTER TWELVE

Doji Masahiro should have been enjoying himself. While he had always reveled in the push and pull of politics, it was in planning parties he truly excelled. The perfect gathering required not only an understanding of the space, but of the attendees themselves. A wall scroll featuring the poetry of a shared ancestor; flowers and clippings arranged to complement a high official's robes; music to set the mood and ease conversation. Even the selection of courses required near intimate knowledge of those who would be consuming them. In Masahiro's experience, a truly successful party could do more to advance one's cause than a battlefield victory, with the added benefit that none need die.

Usually.

Servants fluttered around Otose's manor like nervous starlings, arms full of draperies and pine cuttings, lacquered boxes and stacked pillows. Once Masahiro had reveled in such petty things, thrilled by the understanding that this event might shape the fate of the Empire itself. Although the gathering was yet a week away, already Otose's gatehouse had been flooded with messengers bearing word from their noble masters. If all went well, Masahiro would secure the support he needed to see young prince Tokihito named Emperor Hantei XXVII.

Bayushi Terumoto's assassination had sent ripples through the court, factions reforming like windswept clouds. Half the court believed Masahiro had the Scorpion courtier killed; the other half that he was the real target. The assassin *had* struck at Masahiro's palanquin, after all. Either way, the death of his most powerful rival had further burnished Masahiro's reputation. He stood poised to sit at the right hand of the emperor, and yet it had cost him almost everything.

"Are you well, Masa?" Otose's soft question was like a dipper of cold water splashed across Masahiro's face.

"Of course." He turned, false smile like a theater mask. "It is only... I wish Hiroshige could see this."

It was not a lie. Although Masahiro's thoughts were troubled by more pressing anxieties, his brother's death would always hang like a stone around his neck. They had planned to rise together.

As he had known it would, mention of her former husband caused Otose's shoulders to round. Masahiro felt a pang of regret for invoking Hiroshige, but it was better than raving to her about undead assassins.

She gave a sad smile. "Wherever he is, Hiroshige is proud of us."

Masahiro turned as if to take in the garden. In truth, he was unsure as to how his brother might respond to learning his murderer yet lived. Masahiro had thrown Gensuke into a pit of blades, had sacrificed his sword hand to ensure the assassin did not survive. And yet, even masked and swathed in bandages, Masahiro would have recognized the killer anywhere.

Somehow Gensuke had returned.

Masahiro glanced around the manor garden, as if the wisteria and pine boughs might conceal the masked murderer. They were empty, the paths patrolled by a veritable army of Daidoji guards. Although their loyalty lay with the Crane Clan, he had no doubt any of the stone-faced sentinels would step between Masahiro and Gensuke's knives.

As if they could stop such an inhuman killer.

Masahiro's scalp prickled at the memory of those flashing blades, Gensuke quick as a swooping hawk and just as deadly. Four skilled assassins dead in as many heartbeats. Whatever Gensuke was, he was no longer human. And yet he stayed his hand when Masahiro had been at his mercy, then fled into the darkness to fall upon Bayushi Terumoto – Masahiro was sure of it.

That monster is toying with me.

"Who?" Otose asked.

Masahiro hadn't realized he'd spoke aloud.

"A bad dream, nothing more." If only it were so. Masahiro turned away to conceal the flush that had colored his cheeks, pretending to inspect a stand of fresh-cut bamboo.

"My sleep is troubled as well." She stepped to his side, close enough even the servants could not overhear. "This all feels… wrong."

Masahiro could not agree more. Unfortunately, the truth could only compound Otose's concerns, and Masahiro needed her fortune to ensure Prince Tokihito became emperor.

"It is not uncommon to feel trepidation before such a momentous undertaking." He gave Otose a reassuring nod. Once the pomp and pageantry was over and Hantei XXVII firmly ensconced upon the Emerald Throne, Masahiro would see to it Gensuke was destroyed.

"You are right." Otose blew out a soft sigh. "I never enjoyed politics the same way you and Hiroshige did."

"Do not understate your talents." Masahiro nudged her, grinning. "Who was it who first convinced that old crow Otomo Yasunori to throw his weight behind us?"

"Five hours tortured by bad poetry." Otose rolled her eyes. "Would that I could have drowned in my teacup."

"A heroic sacrifice." Masahiro gave a low bow.

"Stand up." She cuffed him softly on the shoulder. "The servants are watching."

"Let them." He shrugged. "We have nothing to hide."

Otose's smile became something strange.

Masahiro spread his hands. "Lady, if I have given offense–"

"No." She shook her head, a mix of emotions Masahiro could not name flitting across her face. Before he could inquire further, Otose straightened. "Lord Yasunori is coming this afternoon to review the preparations."

"I would expect nothing less." Masahiro stepped back to give Otose space. If such topics made the lady uncomfortable, he would not press the issue. Masahiro needed her more than she needed him.

"I have ordered a dozen winter melons." She sniffed. "Out of season, I know, but there is a Dragon merchant who brings them down from the high peaks months early."

"Well done." Masahiro's enthusiasm was not feigned. "It will be good to put our guests in mind of the Winter Court and just who shall preside over it."

"It is a bit late in the season for bush clover, but I've planted the beds with arrowroot and silver grass." In true court fashion, Otose deflected the compliment. Masahiro acquiesced, happy to lose himself in the discussion of organizational minutiae.

Even so, he could not but glance over his shoulder, seeing Gensuke in every shadow. The fact that the darkness birthed nothing more than a parade of flustered servants did nothing to put Masahiro's mind at ease. He even found himself wishing Naoki were here. For all her frustrating qualities, the magistrate was one of the few alive who understood the true peril of their situation.

In the wake of his encounter with Gensuke, Masahiro had sent a hurried missive to Sacred Watch Castle, but had yet to receive a response. Perhaps the assassin had found Naoki first. Masahiro swallowed against a mouth gone suddenly sour, unsettled by the realization that he might be well and truly alone.

Normally he would have spent hours deciding which drapery would best accent the garden pines, but his thoughts kept drifting back to images of blood and unquiet dead. Masahiro was no scholar, no priest, and certainly no warrior – even before he lost his hand. There was little he could do, and no one he could tell lest he puncture the fiction that he and his companions had put an end to the troubles in the Twilight Mountains. He was unaccustomed to feeling so helpless.

"You're staring again." Otose nudged him.

Dimly Masahiro realized he held a pair of cloth swatches, each an almost imperceptibly different shade of green.

"My apologies." Finding his palms suddenly sweaty, Masahiro set them down. "Sometimes I cannot help but be back in that sorcerer's dungeon."

"Perhaps you should consult a priest?" Otose gave a sympathetic frown.

"Perhaps." Masahiro returned a tepid smile. There was little a priest could do unless they specialized in hunting corrupt assassins. And yet Otose's suggestion kindled the spark of an idea in Masahiro's thoughts.

The city was full of those with the skill to track down rumors of Gensuke and the wit not to ask too many questions. Unlike before, Masahiro had the status to arrange meetings and the wealth to ensure the proper enticements were applied. If anything, it would be far easier than his normal subterfuges. He would, in essence, be bribing officials to do their jobs. That, and inform Masahiro if anyone breathed a word about blood magic within the city limits.

He stood. "I must depart."

Otose frowned. "But Lord Yasunori will arrive any moment."

"You are familiar with the preparations." Masahiro waved away her concerns. "And this *is* your manor, after all."

But Otose would not be put off so easily. "What could call you away so suddenly?"

"A meeting with the new Master of Rites, Miya Katagiri." Masahiro pressed a hand to his forehead, feigning shame. Lying to his sister-in-law was distasteful, but necessary.

"Yasunori can bring the Otomo, but other imperial families must be wooed as well." Masahiro gave a helpless shrug, already waving for the servants to ready his palanquin. "It would not do to keep Lord Katagiri waiting."

Otose regarded him through wary eyes.

He gave a companionable nod. "You will do just fine."

"I know." She scowled. "There is no meeting. Why are you lying to me?"

"We shall speak upon my return."

"We shall speak now," she replied, implacable as winter. "Or you can find somewhere else to hold Tokihito's gala."

Masahiro considered his former sister-in-law. Otose had inherited a substantial fortune, using it to establish herself as a preeminent patron of art and literature. She had always disliked the dangers of politics, had gone along with his and Hiroshige's plans only with protest. Masahiro could only imagine how she would react upon learning he was the target of blood sorcerers and undead assassins.

And yet, Otose was one of his oldest friends. If he continued to keep her in the dark, any harm that befell her would be upon Masahiro's head.

Ultimately, that might be more than he could bear.

"Gensuke." He sighed.

"The Shosuro assassin Terumoto sent after you and Hiroshige." Otose's brows knit. "I thought you disposed of him in the sorcerer's tomb?"

"I did." Masahiro gripped the stump of his missing hand. "He is back."

"How is that possible?"

"I may have been… mistaken about Iuchiban's death." Masahiro glanced away, as nervous as if he stood before a court inquisition.

There was nothing for it but to forge ahead, so he did, laying the whole sordid affair at Otose's feet. Through it all, his former sister-in-law stood quietly, back straight, expression unreadable. When he was done, she closed her eyes.

"I thought you freed me from Terumoto." Her voice was as tight as her shoulders. "But you have merely delivered me from one monster into the hands of another."

"I am sorry." He reached toward her. "If I had known–"

Eyes snapping open, Otose stepped away. "Known what? That my husband's murderer had returned from the grave to seek revenge? That you may have released an immortal sorcerer into the world?" She shook her head. "I am not like Hiroshige, not like you. I looked for none of this."

"And yet it has found us nonetheless," Masahiro said.

"There is no us, Masa." Genuine regret colored Otose's words. She turned, walking away down the garden path.

"Where are you going?" he called after her.

"Away." Otose half-turned, voice soft but urgent. "This place is no longer safe, if it ever was."

Masahiro wilted, crestfallen. "No, I will depart."

"To where?" Anger colored her cheeks. "Back to your apartments at the embassy? Out on the street where Gensuke can finish the job?"

Masahiro swallowed, no answer forthcoming.

She took a step toward him, fury seemingly diminished by the sight of his helplessness. "Take this manor, I have others. My guards will keep you safe."

Now it was Masahiro who reddened. "I could not possibly accept such largesse."

"Another lie." Her smile was sharp. "You really can't help yourself, can you?"

Masahiro could see the words that would bridge the gap

between them. Clear as gold embroidery, they glittered in his mind – threads of obligation and friendship with which he could twist Otose's misgivings and bind her close.

With a wince, Masahiro pushed it all away. Otose deserved better than this. Better than him.

"I am grateful for the use of your manor. Can Prince Tokihito count on your continued financial support?" The question was calculated to wound.

Several emotions flashed across Otose's face – disbelief, hurt, and finally, anger.

Masahiro made himself hold her gaze, expression bland as a palace servant's. Let Otose hate him, so long as it kept her safe.

Relationships could be restored, lives could not.

At least in any way that mattered.

Otose drew in a slow breath, emotions disappearing behind a veneer of cold courtesy.

"I will see to it Prince Tokihito's coffers are adequately filled." She spoke like a merchant discussing the price of fish. Somehow, a sharper rebuke than if she had slapped Masahiro.

"And Yasunori?" He might as well add one final cruelty to the litany he had heaped upon her.

"Do not trouble yourself," she replied. "I can find time to meet with Lord Yasunori before I depart the capital."

"I am in your debt, as is Prince Tokihito." Masahiro bowed. "We shall see you rewarded for this support."

Otose regarded him like he had taken a hammer to her finest vase. "I am sure you will."

Without another word, she spun on her heel, all but fleeing the garden.

Eyes stinging, Masahiro turned away, waving for the servants to ready his palanquin. A complement of Daidoji guards fell in on either side as he ducked behind the litter's woven bamboo curtain before any could note his obvious distress.

"Where are we bound, lord?"

Head in his hand, Masahiro frowned, unsure – the courts, the ministries, the Crane Embassy? If only Naoki were here. What would that damnable magistrate have done?

And like that, Masahiro knew.

"The Imperial Archives," he replied, hoping they did not note the hoarseness in his voice. The archives might not contain much on Iuchiban, but the scholars who curated the vast collection were privy to a surprising amount of secrets. Also, they would be the cheapest to bribe. Some kind words and a few koku in the right hand would ensure that Masahiro was informed of any who searched the archives for knowledge of Bloodspeakers.

Iuchiban was not the only one who could spin webs.

CHAPTER THIRTEEN

If anything, the Twilight Mountains seemed more foreboding than when Naoki and Irie had traveled south in search of the blood sorcerer who had slain so many Dragon Clan officials. It felt as if an age had passed between now and then. The myriad cruelties of Iuchiban's tomb had marked Naoki's life as surely as her Coming-of Age Ceremony, her past self like some distant land mentioned only in vague stories.

The high peaks seemed to press down upon her, their sharp unlovely crags like talons clutching at the slate-gray sky. At least this journey had been more comfortable. Lady Akoya may have retired, but her name remained sufficient to see herself, Naoki, and the score of Lion samurai who accompanied them ferried south by one of the clan's smaller warships. They had traveled down Three Sides River under a flag of parley, the captain informing all who questioned that his ship bore Lion representatives bound to speak with Crab elders. The ruse was sufficient to see them past the various towers and watchforts that lined the much-contested river.

The ride west had been more difficult. They had skirted the rough hinterlands between Crab, Crane, and Scorpion. Those few patrols who accosted them were deflected by Naoki's magisterial credentials. Akoya and her followers might be Lion samurai, but their armor was empty of crest or distinguishing mark, the steel lacquered a pale, unobtrusive green that reminded Naoki of old moss.

The ground grew more broken as they passed from the Shinomen Forest into the northern foothills of the Twilight Mountains, the path dwindling to little more than a suggestion. Akoya called for her warriors to dismount lest their horses break a leg on the uneven ground, and Naoki followed suit.

As if to mark the edge of the mountains, they passed a leafless maple, crooked limbs bare but for a tattered kimono hanging high in the branches. Although the crest was ruined, the color faded by sun and rain, the fabric looked to be of good quality, perhaps belonging to a wealthy merchant.

Naoki suppressed a shudder as it billowed in the chill breeze, ghostlike as the limbs twisted and swayed.

"How long to Five-Dragon Pass?" Akoya squinted at the jagged horizon.

"A few days, perhaps longer depending on the weather." Naoki nodded at an ominous line of clouds that seemed to be headed in their direction.

"These are Crab lands?" Akoya asked.

"Yes," Naoki replied. "Although if experience serves, their attentions are focused elsewhere."

"As they should be." Akoya gave a brusque nod. "The Empire depends upon them."

"Such respect for another clan?" Naoki regarded the former

Matsu daimyō. The Lion and Crab were not open rivals, but neither were their relations cordial.

"I ruled over a contested border for near twenty years." Her grin was sharp as the distant peaks. "I respect anyone who can take a place and hold it."

"Let us hope the Crab feel the same way about you. If we encounter any alive, that is." Naoki swallowed against the sudden tightness in her throat. She would have happily lived out her life a thousand miles from this accursed place.

Naoki shook her head. Barely a few months as a full magistrate and she was already thinking about retirement.

They walked in silence, hands close to their weapons. Although the rough hills were silent but for the bird calls and the occasional whicker from one of their mounts, the cold air held a close, almost violent energy, as if any moment the mountains themselves might crack open to disgorge a horde of hungry dead.

The ruins of a Crab hill fort shadowed the deep valley, its ragged battlements like a mouth full of broken teeth.

"Someone has repaired those walls." Akoya thrust her chin at the castle. "Recently, by the look of it."

Naoki craned her neck to peer up the jagged switchback. "How can you tell?"

"Fresh stone along the south face." Akoya pointed at the wall high above them. "Not discolored like the others. The Crab do not waste effort rebuilding useless fortifications. *Something* has them concerned."

"The dead." Naoki spared the cliffs an uncomfortable glance. As much as the surroundings unsettled her, Naoki much preferred barren slopes to ones crawling with corpses.

"Let us pray they do not find us."

"Save your prayers, magistrate." Akoya's response was little more than a grunt. "Those creatures have much to answer for."

Naoki stopped, causing the samurai behind her to bunch up along the sad excuse for a trail. "You will find no justice amidst these peaks."

Anger flickered across Akoya's hard features, a brief flash of temper that settled into something colder and harder. "I care nothing for corpses. But do not forget your promise. If Iuchiban lives, he is mine."

"I have forgotten nothing," Naoki replied coolly. "But I must know that you will obey my orders."

"We swore to follow you." Akoya glanced back along the line. "Do not mock our oaths with such questions."

"My apologies," Naoki said, and meant it. "This place unsettles me."

"You are not the only one." Akoya's smile was thin, but reassuring. "Lead on, magistrate."

It began to rain, fat oily droplets that bled through Naoki's robes to trace icy fingers across her skin. The wind clutched at her robes even as thunder rumbled overhead.

They trudged along, heads down, shoulders tight as the occasional flash of lightning cast the rocks in jagged relief. Naoki found herself glancing up as if to somehow anticipate the chest-rattling peal of thunder. Even so, it surprised her every time.

It also saved her life.

Her nervous gaze caught a flicker of movement on the cliffs above. Although the shadow it cast was human, its movements were quick and insectile as it leapt from the cliff, long limbs spread as if to catch the wind.

"Beware above!" Naoki shouted too late as the creature slammed into one of Akoya's priests like a falling boulder. The elementalist did not even have time to scream as he was smashed to the ground with bone-crushing force.

"Form ranks!" Akoya shouted as more dead hurled themselves from the cliffs.

"No! Spread out!" Naoki flung out a hand, desperate to be heard over the tumult. Most of the dead missed their targets, bodies splayed upon the jagged rock, still endeavoring to move despite shattered limbs and twisted spines.

To her credit, Akoya followed order, calling for her guard to find cover. Eyes rolling, Naoki's horse bucked, almost dislocating her arm before she could release the reins. Although the horses were battle trained, the sense of wrongness was almost palpable, dark spirits and walking corpses combining to conjure panic in even the most hardened mounts.

More dead came rushing down the path ahead, clambering over one another in their haste to reach the living. They were met by arrows and storms of cutting stone as the surviving Lion mediums drew upon the hard-edged spirits of the mountains.

Naoki drew her jitte, the heavy, unsharpened short swords held like shields against the onrushing foe. Blinking against the rain, she ducked the clutching hands of what was once a Crane samurai, pivoting to hammer her jitte against the creature's elbow. Although the joint broke with a satisfying crack, it did not stop the Crane from lunging at her, bloodied mouth open.

A sword removed the creature's head, Akoya shouldering the corpse aside. A wedge of Lion samurai followed their lord, swords in front, spears stabbing behind, the occasional arc of elemental fire illuminating scarred faces. Akoya fought at the head, a blade in each hand. Wherever her steel touched, a walking corpse fell and did not rise again.

Naoki had known Matsu Chiaki for only a short time, but if her student was so formidable, the old Lion master must have been a true terror on the battlefield. Soon the stone ahead of the Lion phalanx was piled with twitching corpses.

A reflected glimmer caught Naoki's eye and she looked up to see a one-armed Crab samurai leap from the cliff above. Although half the corpse's skull was gone, his aim was true. Realizing the Crab would crash down amidst the Lion formation, Naoki hurled herself at the rear ranks, shouting as she dragged warriors from the path.

She earned an elbow to the face for her trouble, but when the Crab came crashing down, he found only hard stone waiting.

"We cannot hold." There was no fear in Akoya's voice. "Not with these demons raining down on us."

Naoki scanned the heights. A flash of lightning revealed more crabbed shadows scuttling across the rock. If only they could get above the dead, find a cave or plateau, somewhere they could hold until the storm passed.

She bared her teeth as realization struck.

"The Crab fort." She had to lean in to be heard over the din of battle.

With a grim nod, Akoya turned back to her surviving warriors.

"Withdraw to the Crab fort." Her command cut through the tumult like a peal of thunder. She nodded to the half-dozen samurai at the front of the formation. "Hold. The rest with us."

Without a word, the rear ranks turned upon their heel, hurrying back down the rocky path as their six companions hacked at the vicious press of corpses.

Even as she jogged alongside Akoya, Naoki could not but spare a glance at the doomed warriors. She had always been taught that samurai did not fear death, but the callous ease with which the Matsu warriors accepted their fate sat like a cold stone in her stomach.

Naoki had never been good at hiding her emotions, a poor trait in a magistrate, but one she could not seem to shake. Akoya must have noticed her discomfort, for the Lion daimyō caught Naoki's shoulder, propelling her forward.

"We shall celebrate them later. To linger would only belittle their sacrifice."

Naoki nodded. Akoya's justification held a harsh and bloody logic, and yet Naoki could not help but notice that the Lion's eyes glittered silver as she led them up the narrow switchback.

It might have been the rain, though.

Despite the recent attempt at repairs, the Crab fortress had seen better days. The gate hung from its hinges, a few scattered logs evidence of a desperate attempt to buttress the door. Although the fortress stone was spattered with old blood, the courtyard was distressingly empty of bodies. Naoki shuddered to think they might have joined the horde outside.

Akoya led them through the small courtyard, making for the blocky stone bell tower that looked to be the fort's central keep. At its top, Naoki picked out the shadow of an old bell.

"Thank the ancestors for Crab stubbornness." Akoya breathed a relieved sigh as they pushed through the iron-shod gate and into the bell tower. It was a small affair, a short tunnel opening into a wide, rectangular hall, a single staircase at the back leading up to the old bell. There were no other doors and no windows save for a number of thin slits carved into the walls.

"Spears and bows to the arrow loops." Akoya spoke with an almost preternatural calm. "The rest of you brace the door with whatever you can find."

"Can we hold them?" Naoki asked.

Akoya checked her blades. Apparently satisfied, she slipped them back into their sheaths.

"No."

Naoki glanced to the tower stairs. "Do you think there are any Crab nearby?"

Akoya sucked her teeth. "Perhaps."

"The bell looked old," Naoki continued. "But it may yet sound."

Akoya frowned. "It may also summon every walking corpse in the mountains."

"I think we already have." Naoki winced at the snap of rotting wood from out in the courtyard.

"Fair point." Akoya's nod was that of a duelist conceding a victory.

"I shall see to it." Naoki made for the stairs.

It was a hard climb to the top of the tower, made more difficult by steps that seemed intentionally cut to break Naoki's stride – most likely another Crab defensive measure. She could only imagine how difficult it would be to assault the staircase.

The bronze bell had been hung with fresh rope, a wooden

clapper positioned to strike the worn surface. Once, its surface had been covered in reliefs, now rendered unintelligible by scabs of bright green verdigris. Despite being rusted through in several places, the bell still made a loud chime when Naoki struck it with the clapper.

Satisfied, she rang it again and again, not daring to look below for fear of what she might see below the tower. The Lion had trained together, fought together; Naoki would only get in the way. But this, *this* she could do.

She rang the bell until her hands were chapped and raw from the rope, until the clouds rolled back to reveal a flat, gray sky, until Lady Sun sank below the horizon and Lady Moon's pale light wreathed the bell tower in tepid shadows. It became a sort of mantra, a means for Naoki to quiet her racing thoughts. Her mind had always been a jumble, a sea of disconnected plans and ideas. Occasionally something would rise from the depths to consume her attention, distraction resolving into razor focus.

The bell was one such thing.

She lost herself in the sound, each chime vibrating down her arms, her perceptions circumscribed, her body bent to singular purpose. Dimly, Naoki heard fighting, screams and the clash of steel on steel, but it was like the wind – always present, seldom noticed.

Somehow, it was day again. Naoki's arms ached, her head swam, her tongue seeming to fill the whole of her mouth, but there was simply nothing else to do.

Nothing else but die.

Like a swimmer surfacing after a deep dive, Naoki drew in a ragged breath, stumbling back from the bell to leave bloody smears upon the low stone walls. Almost as an afterthought, she drew her jitte, their cord-wrapped handles uncomfortable in hands rubbed raw by rope.

What came up the stairs was not a corpse, but Akoya. Her face was drawn, eyes and cheeks shaded by exhausted shadows. Even so, the Lion daimyō's face held no resignation, no fear. If anything, she looked pleased.

"The dead are gone." Akoya spoke softly.

"Gone?" Naoki's voice came ragged as her palms.

"Destroyed."

"You... defeated them?"

"Not I." The Lion Daimyō thrust her chin at the lip of stone. "Them."

Naoki stumbled over to the low wall.

Gray-armored samurai filled the courtyard, their flags and breastplates emblazoned with the crossed claws of the Kuni.

"They came." Naoki's words were almost a whisper.

"You summoned them, magistrate." Akoya gave a grateful nod.

A woman elbowed her way through the jostling press to glare up at them – one eye dark beneath lowered brows, the other the pale green of polished jade.

"I am Kuni Chiyo, commander of this expedition." Her voice carried through the thin air. "And you are trespassing upon these lands."

"I am Kitsuki Naoki, Emerald Magistrate and servant of the Empire," Naoki croaked back. "We seek information on the Bloodspeaker Iuchiban."

That seemed to catch Chiyo's attention. She crossed her arms, jaw tight as she regarded the two of them, but whatever hope the Crab's arrival had kindled in Naoki faded as the woman spoke again.

"All I see is a band of trespassers. Come out and surrender your weapons." She chopped a hand through the air. "Or we shall come in and take them."

CHAPTER FOURTEEN

Tomiko rubbed tired eyes. Leaning away from the small table, she pressed a hand into the small of her back, muscles tight as the bound scrolls stacked about the room. She had been through dozens of records already, stooped over the table, her vision swimming with archaic text. She had come to the Imperial Archives to learn more about the Bloodspeakers, but found little more than rumors.

Even the war records were sparse. Although descriptions of the Battles of Stolen Graves and Sleeping River made reference to an "ancient evil," they included no other detail. Likewise, while chronicles of courtly appointments spoke of a Jade Champion responsible for rooting out spiritual corruption, the position had remained vacant for more than a century due to a conflict with the Phoenix Clan's Asako Inquisitors.

Tomiko had been reduced to combing through fragmented letters and musty appointment scrolls in the hopes of stumbling across something, *anything* that would provide insight into the Bloodspeakers' goals.

"And this is all of it?" Tomiko tried to keep the frustration from her voice. Although her rank was enough to compel the junior archivist's compliance, the gulf between obedience and cheerful assistance loomed large.

"Yes, Mistress Isawa," the small man replied. "Everything from the period surrounding the battles."

Tomiko worked her tongue around her mouth, sour from so long amidst these dusty racks. It seemed no matter how far she traveled, she could not outdistance paperwork.

"I am grateful for your assistance." With a sigh, she turned back to the mountain of letters, expecting the junior archivist to scuttle away.

Instead, the man remained.

"Mistress, if I may be so bold…" He fidgeted, glancing at the door.

Tomiko favored him with what she hoped was a reassuring smile. "You may."

"Our collection largely concerns the mundane." He bobbed his head, appearing like nothing so much as a pigeon picking at crumbs. "While I do not wish to pry into your research, I cannot help but suspect you are searching for more… esoteric knowledge?"

Tomiko had been loath to reveal the object of her search, asking for historical records dealing with investigations into the dark arts without specifically mentioning Bloodspeakers. Like every imperial organization, the archives were awash in politics. Word would reach her parents, perhaps even the courts. There would be uncomfortable questions, questions for which Tomiko did not possess answers.

Yet.

"Would your own clan's records be better suited to such research?"

"A fine idea." Tomiko nodded as if she had not considered his suggestion. "But alas, I have not the time to journey back to the Isawa Elemental Academies."

In truth, the Phoenix records almost certainly contained a wealth of information on Bloodspeakers; but such inquiry would bring her to the attention of the Asako. If Tomiko was apprehensive about revealing the truth to her parents, she absolutely dreaded being interrogated by one of her clan's feared inquisitors.

"I see." The archivist looked to his hands. "Perhaps if you could provide more information on the object of your research…"

Tomiko regarded the little gray-haired man. She was reluctant to give tinder to rumors and speculation, but there was also expediency to consider. The Imperial Bursar's logbooks might reveal the details of Kosue's business within the city, but no ledgers would provide her with the means to face the other Bloodspeakers. Although it burned Tomiko to admit as much, the encounter with Kosue had almost killed her.

"I am searching for an esoteric order," Tomiko said at last. "One that has arisen to periodically threaten Rokugan."

"History holds many such dangers," the archivist replied.

"Not like this." Tomiko drew in a slow breath. "They practice dark sorcery, blood magic, and necromancy."

She had expected the archivist to show surprise. Instead, the little man gave a quiet nod. "Bloodspeakers."

"How do you know of this?" Tomiko asked.

"You are not the first to make such inquiries, mistress." The archivist gave a sly smile.

Tomiko's first reaction was unease. Kosue had seemed but

an unscrupulous merchant right up until he unleashed his blood magic; could the archivist be a similar creature?

"An Emerald Magistrate." He nodded. "A month or so back, she came looking for these selfsame records."

Tomiko leaned in, interested. "This magistrate, what was her name?"

The archivist tapped his chin, frowning. "My memory is not what it used to be."

And there it was. Tomiko's parents had furnished her with sufficient money to keep up appearances, but certainly not enough to bribe an imperial official, even a low-ranking one.

Fortunately, there were other currencies than coin.

She studied the man for a moment. Perhaps sixty winters, his robes were fine if somewhat threadbare – most likely the only formal wear the man possessed. Despite his age, the man remained a junior archivist, which spoke to a lack of ambition, wealth, or connections. Tomiko could not help with the first two, but she had a remedy for the last.

"I understand." She drew forth a blank sheet of paper, gently setting aside several scrolls so she might spread it on the table and begin to write.

"What is that?" The archivist leaned in.

"A letter to your superiors." Tomiko's brush moved quickly over the page. "You have been of great assistance, junior archivist. I would have others know of your diligent service."

The little man gave a start, eyes widening. "That is... most kind, mistress."

"The least I can do." Tomiko blew on the ink, then added her personal seal. Such a letter cost her nothing, but it might give wings to the man's languishing career.

"My apologies." Tomiko pulled the letter back before the archivist's trembling hands could close upon it. "Your memory is not the only one that has failed this day. I seem to have forgotten your name." Tomiko smiled her sweetest smile. "Without that, this letter could be about almost anyone."

"Ichiro, mistress. Satoshi Ichiro." The man gave an expectant nod, almost vibrating with excitement.

"Your family are vassals of the Miya?"

"Yes, mistress." He swallowed, gaze darting from Tomiko to the letter.

Tomiko sat unmoving, attempting to mimic her parents' disconcerting calm.

At last, the little archivist seemed to grasp her meaning.

"The magistrate's name was Kitsuki Naoki," he said. "She left the Imperial City shortly after consulting the archives."

"Where was this Naoki bound?"

"I do not know." Ichiro sounded almost pained. His hands worked the front of his robe, twisting the fabric into nervous bunches. Then he raised a finger. "But there was another – a companion, or patron, perhaps – Doji Masahiro."

"A Crane?" Tomiko asked. Although Masahiro was not familiar to her, the Doji were always inserting themselves into imperial politics. With a flourish, she added the archivist's name. "Thank you, Satoshi Ichiro."

The little man prostrated himself before her. "If there is anything else I can do, mistress."

"Thank you." Tomiko rose with only the slightest wince, the muscles of her legs complaining after kneeling for so long. "But I believe only one man can help me now."

Normally Tomiko's rank would entitle her to guards and a

palanquin, but her lack of funds and her parents' distaste for ostentation had left her bereft. She did however possess the funds to employ one of the archives' bonded messengers.

"Please deliver a message to Lord Doji Masahiro," she addressed the wiry courier. "I would speak at his earliest convenience."

With a bow, the man was off, the slap of his sandals already fading before Tomiko had reached the high wall that warded the archive garden.

A thin man wearing messenger bells stepped from the shadows of the gate.

"Lady Isawa Tomiko?"

At first Tomiko thought it was the courier she had recently dispatched, but he moved into the light to reveal a lined face and graying hair.

At her nod, the man gave a perfunctory bow.

"I bear a message from your father. The assessors' ledgers have been prepared. They await you at the Imperial Treasury's southwestern annex."

"Excellent." Tomiko paused, frowning. She had expected to review the ledgers in the Treasury's main offices. "Although I am unfamiliar with the southwestern annex."

"It is in the District of Fortitude, lady. Several streets north of the Museum of Antiquities."

"My thanks." Smiling to conceal her exasperation, Tomiko pressed several coins into the man's hand and sent him on his way. Although part of the Inner City, the District of Fortitude was largely considered to be one of the least savory. A haunt for actors, traders, and low-rank samurai, it was nominally administered by the Crab Clan, who paid about as much attention to its care and governance as they did anything not pertaining to the Kaiu Wall.

With a sigh, she began the long walk. It made sense the Treasury would have many annexes dotting the Imperial City. Her father could have easily had the ledgers delivered somewhere closer. Likely he thought the walk would do Tomiko good.

That, and keep her humble.

If such were her parents' intentions, they were only marginally successful. The autumn chill was refreshing after so long in the dusty confines of the Imperial Archives, but Tomiko's feet ached and her eyes felt as if someone had cast a handful of sand into them.

It took the better part of an hour to wend across the inner districts. Tomiko would have made better time if not for the profusion of palanquins. The fact she outranked many of the puffed-up courtiers who rode in such luxury only rankled a bit. Petulance would make enemies, so Tomiko endeavored to be patient.

Lady Sun was low in the west when she finally found the wretched building that called itself the Treasury's southwestern annex – little more than a half-dozen storerooms stuffed with racks of dusty logbooks. After some vague pleasantries, Tomiko was ushered into the assessor's cramped office, several large stacks of ledger books surrounding another low table.

Tomiko suppressed a sigh as she drifted to the table, the junior assessor at her elbow. Unlike Ichiro, the man was young – red-cheeked and smiling, his chin framed by a carefully trimmed beard. Thankfully he was also more circumspect than the aging archivist.

"Your father's missive said this was a matter of some delicacy, so I will not inquire as to your purpose. Merely know these represent the total documented receipts of all tithes, tariffs, and assessments paid by the merchant Kosue of Stone Grove." He stood, expression flawlessly shifting from a welcoming grin to one of thoughtful conciliation. "Should you require anything, please send for me."

"I will, thank you." Tomiko regarded the man, surprised by his discretion.

That one would go far.

Although she much preferred romances and pillow books to stuffy ledgers, Tomiko had always had a distressing faculty for bookkeeping. Once she had grasped the rudiments of the assessors' recording method, it was easy to compare the imperial accounts with Kosue's logbook.

She had thought him a wealthy river trader, but the merchant had connections across Rokugan, with transactions stretching from Earthquake Fish Bay in the far southeast to the City of the Rich Frog to the west. Tomiko's stomach tightened as she marked numerous shipments of fabric and oil to the Imperial City. Memory of barrel-bound corpses surfaced like some half-remembered nightmare. Flicking from page to page, she did some quick calculations and sat back, wide-eyed.

If every barrel had held several bodies, Kosue might have delivered hundreds, perhaps even thousands to the Imperial City. But where had he gotten so many? And why bring them here?

Tomiko dug into the dire accounting. Although Kosue owned warehouses in Stone Grove, he seemed only to rent space in the Imperial City. A barn here, a storehouse there, several large houses along the waterfront. Such was standard practice for smaller merchants, or larger ones who wished to obfuscate their dealings.

Tomiko had expected Kosue to be smuggling goods. What she did not expect was the scale of his enterprise. At first she thought she had miscalculated. Even taking into account the corrupt merchant's wealth, it seemed impossible Kosue could have mustered such resources. There were no loans in his name, nor outstanding debts. Kosue's costs far exceeded his income and yet the merchant spent seemingly without regard.

Afternoon gave way to evening as Tomiko paged through the various ledgers, comparing long columns of figures. The simple answer was that Kosue had cheated others as he had Master Masatsuge, but Tomiko could not find evidence of complaints. It was as if the merchant's wealth appeared by magic, a vast hoard conjured from empty earth. Either the man was a financial prodigy or he had a patron.

Fingers ink-stained as any scribe's, Tomiko jotted down figures, double and triple-checking her calculations. No matter how she compared the accounts, the numbers did not lie. There were gaps in the imperial record, vast sums unaccounted for by tithes, but temples and schools remained outside the purview of secular authorities. Only when Tomiko added in the figures from Heaven's Blaze did the records achieve parity.

It seemed impossible, but all paths led back to Masatsuge.

Tomiko's trembling hands left ink blotted along the margins of her logbook, her tears blurring the careful columns of figures.

Masatsuge had not been cheated. Rather, he had beggared his dōjō to fund the merchant's vile trade, using his status as a priest to conceal the transactions from the imperial authorities.

Tomiko had thought the imperial ledgers would be the key, but she had possessed it all along.

She stood, one hand pressed to her mouth as she steadied herself on the door beam, her thoughts like insects scuttling from beneath an overturned rock.

Masatsuge was dead, as was Kosue. The only thing that linked Heaven's Blaze to the Bloodspeakers was the logbook resting on the table before her. With a whispered prayer, she could set it aflame, scouring the evidence of her school's corruption. It was as if someone had filled Tomiko's throat with ashes, her joints tight as boiled leather. Slowly, she raised a hand, one finger outstretched, a chant building behind her clenched jaw.

What emerged was a ragged breath, hard and voiceless. With a shake of her head, Tomiko lowered her hand. Those who concealed corruption could not but embrace it.

Truth is a coin that multiplies in the spending.

The admonition came in her father's voice, heavy with judgment. Although Tomiko doubted this truth would be a boon, she could not bring herself to perpetuate such a vulgar lie. Someone must be told, and quickly, before Kosue's allies could put the mountain of corpses to use.

Unless they already had.

Tomiko gathered up the logbooks only to pause as the office door slid open. She half-turned, expecting the junior assessor, only to flinch back as something terrible stepped into the room.

The dim light of the office lamps glittered on bared blades, the robes of a ministerial servant at odds with the man's hideous mask. Crafted of darkly lacquered wood, its features were vaguely human but possessed of a strange geometry – eyes too large and too far apart, the wide, leering mouth full of teeth like broken glass. She could not look away, but neither could her eyes focus upon the mask.

The man darted forward. Swift as a changing breeze, his swords slashed down. If Tomiko had not already had a prayer on her lips, the killer's blade would have found her. Instead, she gasped out the invocation she had once intended for the ledgers, a bright smear of fire blistering the air between them.

Although the assassin ducked, Tomiko's invocation raked along his back, setting robes and hair aflame. Apparently untroubled by the burning clothes, the killer straightened, angling an impossibly quick cut at her throat.

She stumbled back, almost falling in her haste to avoid the burning man's slash. He came on like a vengeful demon limned by the fires of the underworld.

This time Tomiko did fall, crashing into the table as the masked killer lunged. She set another burst of flame spearing out. This one struck the man full in the chest, sending him crashing back into the office door. He was on his feet in a heartbeat, surrounded by spreading fire.

"Lady Isawa, what is–?" The assessor rounded the corner only to receive a slashed throat for his concern. He fell back in a spray of blood, feet drumming a ragged staccato upon the floor as Tomiko backed away. Voice rough with smoke, she unleashed a burst of cutting wind. Not only did it spoil the assassin's strike, the sudden gust fanned the flames between them.

The masked killer regarded her for a moment, then retreated into the smoky shadows.

Tomiko drew a gasping breath, gaze flicking down to the ruins of the table, ledger books already blackening in the spreading flames. A groan seemed to rise within her, coiling up her raw throat like a twist of smoke.

Before she could give voice to her frustration, the wall of the tiny office exploded. Tomiko was showered with bits of burning wood as the killer kicked through the boards. Reflexively, she raised a hand to shield her face, and the masked assassin's blade traced a line of cold fire across her forearm.

Surprise gave way to fear. The killer seemed unstoppable.

Tomiko unleashed her flames upon the outer wall of the office. Wood blackened and charred, peeling away to reveal an arc of evening shadow. Without hesitation, Tomiko hurled herself at the crackling boards, exhorting the fire spirits to spare her flesh.

She crashed through and into the night, blessedly cool after the heat of the burning office. Through stinging eyes, she saw the killer step from the burning building.

His robes were little more than soot-smeared tatters, his pallid skin pocked with scorch marks, his blades black with soot. But the mask was untouched. Its eyes seemed to bore into Tomiko, thoughts of escape withering beneath the cold heat of its gaze.

Something flickered in the corner of her vision. At first Tomiko thought it one of the killer's blades. She tensed, expecting to feel the cold bite of steel, only to see the masked man reel back, chest cut to the bone by the slash of a katana.

Blue and white swam in Tomiko's blurred vision as armored samurai charged from the swirling smoke. She recognized Crane colors. A tornado of slashing blades surrounded the masked killer, bright with reflected firelight. Rather than defend himself, the man dove back into the burning office, disappearing into the smoke like the demon he was.

Unable to give chase, the Crane samurai spread out. Tomiko's limbs felt loose and liquid, her thoughts blurred as if by smoke. It was as if she watched from far away, spectator to some cruel theater performance.

"Lady Isawa, are you injured?" A cultured voice seemed to drag her back to the moment.

Slowly, she turned to regard the speaker, a one-handed Crane noble in courtly robes, his pale hair pulled back in a loose queue. Although there was a sword belted at his waist, the man had not drawn it, no doubt trusting in the pair of hard-eyed Daidoji samurai who trailed behind him like a loose cloak.

Tomiko could have told him two guards were not enough.

A hundred questions jostled behind Tomiko's chapped lips, but what emerged was the most simple.

"Who are you?"

"Doji Masahiro, at your service." He sketched a grinning bow.

"Isawa Tomiko." Her reply was reflexive.

"I know." He cocked his head. "I know much about you, in fact."

"Ichiro." Clearly Tomiko was not the only one who had thought to bribe an imperial archivist.

"Do not think too poorly of him." Masahiro threw a conciliatory arm around her shoulders – a very forward gesture, but Tomiko raised no complaint as her vision swam once more.

"We should hurry." He guided her toward a waiting palanquin. "Fire will bring everyone running."

Tomiko allowed herself to be led to the palanquin, well-appointed and big enough for several riders. Masahiro settled himself in the seat across from her with a grateful sigh.

"Where are you taking me?"

"Somewhere safe." He gestured to the bearers. "As safe as anywhere can be."

Tomiko gave a pained swallow. Her mouth tasted of blood and ash. "What was that creature? And how did it slip into the Inner City?"

"Very good questions." Although Masahiro's smile did not falter, his eyes glittered with something cold and hard. "I was very much hoping you could tell me."

CHAPTER FIFTEEN

"You have no authority here, Unicorn." The Lion captain gripped the cord-wrapped hilt of his katana, truculent scowl on his narrow face.

"A tiny emperor, lording over an insignificant fief."

Qadan could not tell if the thought was her own or Iuchiban's. Such confusion was happening with distressing regularity, a symptom of the sorcerer's control or a gradual weakening of Qadan's resistance. Either way, it was not reassuring.

"I am Arban, daimyō of the Iuchi family," her cousin replied. From his expression, Qadan could tell Arban was struggling to retain his composure in the face of Lion belligerence.

"Welcome to the East Canal Gate, Lord Iuchi. I am Akodo Kanbei, Senior Warden of Lion District." The captain's bow stretched the limits of courtesy. "Would that we had received news of your coming."

"There was no time," Arban replied.

"Why such haste?" Captain Kanbei spoke the question like an accusation.

Arban cast a questioning glance at Qadan. Relations between the Lion and Unicorn were far from cordial. During the long exodus that transformed the Ki-Rin Clan into the Unicorn, the Lion had administered their old fiefs. Although they had returned the Unicorn's lands, a current of resentment yet remained. Along with the Dragonfly, both clans shared administration of Rich Frog. In practice, Qadan knew each guarded their territory like ancestral relics.

Fortunately or unfortunately, Iuchiban seemed to care little for clan politics.

"We are tracking a group of thieves." The sorcerer spoke softly, leaning in as if to bring the Lion into his confidence. "Brigands posing as honest merchants, they robbed several of our traders, making off with much fine fabric."

The Lion captain's scowl seemed cut from granite. "You think we harbor outlaws?"

"Absolutely not," Iuchiban replied. "Which is why we sought to bring the matter to your attention."

"And now you have." Kanbei crossed his arms.

Iuchiban gave an uncomfortable tilt of their head. "The brigands have been remarkably adept at avoiding detection."

"We have little problem with thieves," he responded coolly. "Perhaps the Lion are made of sterner stuff, lady."

"Perhaps." Iuchiban ignored the insult. "It is only... if they flee Rich Frog, I fear we shall never find them again."

"And how did you discover they were here in the first place?"

Iuchiban feigned discomfort. In truth, they had made discreet inquiries of local merchants. The weaving of such fine silk required specialized equipment, equipment neither the Unicorn nor the Dragonfly possessed. Although the Lion's territory comprised a third of the city, Iuchiban had winnowed out his followers' lair, the search aided by the fact that he knew exactly where it was.

"We do not seek glory, only justice." Iuchiban let a note of pleading creep into their voice. "Let us assist in the apprehension. To you will go the credit, the praise, and not least the gratitude of a Unicorn daimyō."

Iuchiban glanced at Arban, who returned a munificent nod. "I would be in your debt, Captain Kanbei."

Qadan could see the rough calculation behind the captain's eyes, suspicion warring with ambition. The capture of wanted thieves would burnish his reputation. It was not as if they were asking Kanbei to betray his clan, only to accept aid.

At last he gave a quick nod. "Follow my lead. You may be lords among your people, but these are Lion lands."

"You have our word." Iuchiban fixed Arban with a quick glance and the Iuchi daimyō acquiesced with only the slightest flicker of irritation.

"Ambition and avarice. See how easily mortals are swayed? It is the same now as it was centuries ago. Such base desires remain inherent. Only by a rectification of names may we free ourselves of the shackles of history."

"You have spoken of this rectification before. What does it mean?" Qadan asked as they followed the Lion samurai down the canal to the high-gabled guard station. *"How can it change our very nature?"*

"When a child comes of age, they take a new name, one that sweeps aside their youthful past." Iuchiban's reply filled Qadan's thoughts. "It is the same when a samurai sets aside their blade and becomes a monk – a litany of bloody-handed cruelties replaced by a life of peaceful contemplation. They are no longer what they were, they are only what they are, what they will become. The individual remains the same. Only the name, the spirit has changed, becoming something wiser, something better. I would do that for all of Rokugan."

Qadan would have pursued the sorcerer's reasoning, but the Lion captain was inquiring about the Bloodspeakers' whereabouts.

Iuchiban told them without hesitation.

"I know of this place," Kanbei replied. "Weaver's Row – near the southern wharf, just beyond the clan storerooms. Most of the finished work travels east along Drowned Merchant River, bound for the courts."

"The perfect place for thieves to dispose of stolen goods," Iuchiban replied. "With dye and a bit of tailoring, we would never recognize the missing fabric."

"Allow me a few moments to prepare." Kanbei waved his guards into the post.

"Of course," Iuchiban said.

"Lord Shinjo bade us keep this matter private," Arban whispered as Kanbei's guards exchanged their spears and brightly lacquered plate for less conspicuous arms.

"You have seen what the Bloodspeakers are capable of, cousin." The calmness of Iuchiban's reply could not but unnerve Qadan. "We need all the allies we can muster."

"But... Lion?" he asked. "They have been jealous of our lands for centuries. This could hurt our cause in court, especially with the imperial succession in doubt."

"I am not worried about the next emperor," Iuchiban said. "I am worried about the people of Rokugan."

It was exactly what Qadan would have said, which only unsettled her more.

Chastened, Arban looked away, shoulders high, palms flat on his thighs. It was the same as when Master Erhi had caught the two of them trying to sneak into the Foaling Festival. They had waited until the old name keeper was asleep, then slipped from the yurt to steal across the tall grass toward the distant glow of celebration.

Erhi had been waiting amidst the sward, her hands hard as knotty pine as she marched the two of them back, her voice so sharp Qadan still could not believe the old woman's tongue had not drawn blood. Back then, it had seemed the end of their little world. Now it was one of the many invisible threads that bound their lives together.

"My apologies, cousin." Iuchiban laid a hand on Arban's arm. "That came harsher than I intended."

"We have all been stretched as of late." His smile was tentative but honest. "I should be less thin-skinned."

Iuchiban mirrored his grin. "And I less sharp-tongued."

He nodded, glancing toward the Lion. "Should we reveal we are name keepers?"

"Best not to test our new allies' trust," Iuchiban replied.

"Agreed." Arban gave a thoughtful nod. Although the last two centuries had done much to normalize their clan's idiosyncratic sorceries in Rokugan, there were still those who looked askance at name keepers.

"Let us be about it then." Qadan could not but be amazed at how easily Iuchiban had manipulated her cousin, tugging on threads of shared memory to bind him tight. Ambition and avarice were not the only qualities inherent in mortals.

"*At last you begin to understand.*" Iuchiban spoke within her thoughts.

Qadan was not sure she did, but further questions were quickly silenced as Lion guards fanned out before them.

"Lord Arban." Kanbei's bow was far more respectful. "I know of a route to Weaver's Row that will avoid unwanted eyes."

"Lead on, captain." Arban glanced back to Qadan, offering a nod as if to congratulate her for recognizing the value of local guards.

Captain Kanbei led them deep into the warren of storehouses crowding Rich Frog's southern canals.

"These streets are a maze." Arban blew out a wondering sigh, looking to Kanbei. "How do you find your way?"

"Practice." The Lion's grin was toothy as his clan's namesake.

"This would be difficult to patrol," Arban said.

Kanbei gave an amused sniff. "It is also difficult to assault."

The Lion's comment seemed to alter their surroundings. Instead of a haphazard jumble of buildings, Qadan saw a series of blinds and choke points. A fewscore warriors familiar with the local layout could hold the district against a small army.

They rounded some sharp curves, moving single file down an alley where the buildings almost touched overhead, a thin trickle of light filtering between balconies. Qadan could not but picture a squad of Lion archers upon the heights. Fortunately, the galleries were empty save for an old man taking in his laundry. Although he affected to pay little attention to the passing samurai, Qadan noted the furtive glances, as if he were scouting enemy numbers before a battle.

Iuchiban chuckled. "*He's not one of mine.*"

Qadan ignored the sorcerer, irritated he was privy to even her offhand thoughts.

She smelled Weaver's Row long before they reached the first storefront. Although possessed of a far better odor than the Unicorn Clan tanneries they had sailed past on their entrance to Rich Frog, the sharp tang of dyes and bleaches was impossible to ignore. Looms clacked and creaked behind windows thrown open despite the autumn chill. Steam billowed from dying vats, filling the air with acrid fog.

Kanbei paused in the shadow of a mossy stone wall, the lichens dyed all manner of bright colors by runoff from the vats above.

"The place we seek lies just beyond this alley," he said softly. "One of the larger operations – perhaps thirty or forty weavers."

"Assume all are hostile," Iuchiban said.

"They are also merchants operating within Lion Clan jurisdiction," Captain Kanbei replied. "I will not have it said we harmed our people without good cause."

Iuchiban smiled. "And here I thought the Lion cared only for blood and battle."

Kanbei stiffened, crossing his arms. "Swords cost money."

"Very practical of you, captain." Iuchiban's playful tone took all sting from the rebuke. Qadan would have thought such banter could only antagonize the prickly Lion, but to her surprise, Kanbei actually smiled.

"Thank you, Lady Qadan."

"How did you know he had a sense of humor?" she asked.

"Look to his warriors," Iuchiban directed their attention to the dozen Lion samurai arrayed along the wall. "See how amiably they follow orders? There is more than duty at work. Captain Kanbei has made friends of his warriors."

"Harm no one unless necessary." Kanbei regarded them all, smile gone. "We desire prisoners, not corpses."

"Of course, captain," Arban replied without hesitation. "We only wish to put an end to this."

Regret threaded Qadan's thoughts. If only her cousin knew the truth. This was no end, only a beginning.

Kanbei drew his blade. Raising a fist for silence, he moved to the end of the alley to glance upon the street beyond.

"Several ox carts passing on the left." He nodded to the two Lion samurai behind them. "Stop the carts. Block the road on both sides. We don't want anyone blundering into this." Kanbei drew in a steadying breath. "The rest of you follow me."

They stepped from the steam of the alley, crossing the cobbled road beyond with long strides. The Lion were quick about their work, drivers quickly silenced by the sight of so many samurai.

The Bloodspeakers' weaving house was a large wooden building no different from a score of similar storefronts that lined the street. The only differences Qadan noted were that the windows were barred and there were no guards upon the street. If anything, it appeared the workers had packed up for the day.

After gesturing for several of his guards to circle around back, Kanbei led them quickly toward the shuttered storefront. A pair of burly Lion samurai made short work of the barred door and Qadan followed the others inside.

Various textile displays filled the interior of the large front room. Robes of silk and cotton hung upon rough armatures, various patterns arranged to complement one another. The fabric was embroidered with autumn scenes – reds and golds of leaves offset by cool evergreens and the occasional flash of arrowroot blossoms. As with the outside, the front room also seemed deserted.

Kanbei thrust his chin at the various alcoves, Unicorn and Lion samurai spreading out to search the front room while he led Qadan and the others toward the back.

Vacant looms crowded the shadows. Although abandoned, many of the wooden armatures bore partially completed fabric, a riot of colors at odds with the dusty surrounds. Samurai moved among latticed shadows, blades at the ready, but if any cultists crouched in the gloom, they were yet biding their time.

"It appears the weavers were suddenly called away," Kanbei said.

"Do you think they learned of our approach?" Arban asked.

"Not from us." Kanbei's reply was curt.

"Perhaps they left something behind," Iuchiban said.

"We shall see." The Lion captain waved them toward the back room.

A pair of double doors opened into a large warehouse space. Bales of raw cloth filled the room, stacked almost to the ceiling in some places. High slatted windows let bars of light, dust motes the only thing moving in the wide room.

Frustration edged Kanbei's movements as he directed his warriors to search the warehouse. Qadan could understand the captain's irritation – the seizure of stolen goods was no substitute for apprehending the thieves themselves.

"It appears your bandits have fled."

"Perhaps not." Iuchiban thrust their chin at a smear of blood upon one of the bales.

Kanbei hissed to catch the guards' attention; they rounded

the stack to find a score of bodies laid out upon the earthen floor.

They were arranged in a loose circle, feet pointed toward the center, heads away, their arms crossed over their chests as if in peaceful repose. The seeming calmness of the scene was at odds with the blood surrounding each corpse. Each looked to have slit their throat then lain back, dagger still in hand.

"What manner of foulness is this?" The captain looked to Arban.

Arban ignored the captain, glancing over as Iuchiban joined him. "Can you feel it, cousin?"

Iuchiban nodded. All the dead were clothed in robes woven from corrupt fabric, waves of taint rising like smoke from a roaring fire.

"What have you not told me?" Kanbei asked, his voice rough with anger.

Iuchiban heaved a false sigh. "Tell him. I will examine the dead."

Arban gave a grim nod, turning back to the red-faced Lion. Despite Kanbei's emotion, their conversation seemed muted, fading in Qadan's perceptions as if she listened from the end of a long hall.

"You... had your followers kill themselves?"

"Weavers, tailors, seamstresses the equal of any master in Rokugan. All would have languished in poverty if not for my intervention." Iuchiban seemed genuinely regretful. "Did you think me bound within your tawdry flesh? I am many things to many people. Often am I called upon to offer wisdom. These followers served me well, but I was left no other choice."

"You could have bid them flee."

"And have Lion brutes hound them to the ends of the Empire?" Iuchiban replied. "No. This is quicker, kinder. They are in a better place."

"How can you know that?" Qadan asked.

"Because I sent them there myself." Iuchiban's reply was soft.

Qadan regarded the bloody tableau, still trying to parse what lay before her. *"Enough theology. You murdered these people."*

"Do not lecture me on morals." Real anger colored Iuchiban's tone. "They died for what they believed. How many warriors have the Unicorn sacrificed? How many have fallen for this hollow Empire?"

"It is not the same."

"Is it not?" he asked.

Dimly, Qadan could hear Arban and Kanbei arguing, voices raised, but their words flowed around her like water.

"I did not wish to come here," Iuchiban continued. "But this charade must be maintained, if only for a little longer."

They rounded the bodies, taking a moment to study each bloodless face. To any who watched, it must have seemed as if Qadan were looking for arcane evidence. Only she knew that Iuchiban mourned the dead.

At last they stood, returning to where Arban and Kanbei waited. Although the Lion captain practically vibrated with anger, the fact he had not ordered his guards to apprehend the lot of them spoke well of Arban's explanation.

"We suspected dark sorcery," her cousin lied, fixing Qadan with a warning glance. "But could not be sure. Not until now."

"The robes are steeped in corruption," Iuchiban said. "They should be destroyed."

"I will summon Lion priests," Kanbei said.

"And how long will that take?" Iuchiban asked. "Every moment we delay, the darkness of this place bleeds into your district, captain."

"Very convenient." Kanbei's grimace was almost a snarl. "As you wish, Unicorn, but I will watch you destroy them."

"Of course." Iuchiban nodded for Arban to step forward. Her cousin's flame spirit made short work of the corrupt fabric. Soon only a circle of gray ash remained.

Iuchiban did not stay to watch. Instead, the ancient sorcerer walked the perimeter of the warehouse, two Unicorn samurai close behind. Amidst the stacks and tightly bound bolts of cloth, they found an empty space, several dusty squares upon the floor showing where a number of crates had rested.

Iuchiban knelt, one hand hovering over the earth. After a moment, he glanced up. "Bring Arban and the captain."

A few moments, and they arrived, staring down at the empty dirt.

"Something corrupt was stored here." Iuchiban glanced at Arban. "Can you feel it?"

Qadan's cousin returned a somber nod.

"What could it be?" Kanbei asked.

"More cursed fabric, no doubt." Iuchiban sucked air through their teeth. "But bound for where?"

Qadan knew the answer before Kanbei replied. Somehow she had always known. Rich Frog had been an unwelcome detour. Their true path ran east, beyond the lands of Unicorn and Lion to the place where all roads eventually led.

"The Imperial City," Kanbei replied.

"Then that is where we are headed." Arban looked to Qadan, the earnestness of his gaze seeming to carve to the very root of her. Arban might not know it, but he did the dark sorcerer's bidding as surely as if Iuchiban held his mind in thrall.

Hopelessness welled up within Qadan, a flood of darkness that seemed to eclipse even the memory of freedom. Like insects struggling in a great invisible web, those who opposed Iuchiban only grew more enmeshed.

Unbidden, the image of the dead weavers filled Qadan's mind. She had thought all Bloodspeakers like the Shrike or the Monk, lured by promises of dark power. But most seemed little more than peasants mistreated and ignored by their supposed betters. Only Iuchiban had looked beyond such false distinctions as status and clan. The ancient sorcerer had lifted them up and they worshiped him for it. Qadan did not know what terrified her more.

That the weavers had been willing to die for their master.

Or that she was beginning to understand why they had.

CHAPTER SIXTEEN

Seiji felt better than he had in weeks – physically, at least. The ancestors had freed him from hunger, exhaustion, and the pain of overtaxed muscles. He was stronger too; faster, tougher, crossing the broken foothills of the Twilight Mountains at a brisk jog, breath easy as if he strolled along a country road. The wind did not bite, the cold did not settle in his bones. Seiji's hands seemed harder than the stone itself.

Time was without meaning, day and night little more than flickers on the edges of Seiji's perception. Like some mountain oni from the old fables, he saw almost as well in the dark as he did in the light. It would have been unsettling had Seiji not known the gift was rooted in his own ancestors. Willing or not, he had become their emissary.

Their blade.

The bell remained in his thoughts. Far from the ever-consuming chime that had harrowed his mind, its sonorous toll seemed almost a part of Seiji, familiar as his heartbeat. While the chime yet warned Seiji of nearby dead, its purpose was different.

Memories not his own trickled through the cracks of Seiji's

thoughts. He had but to close his eyes to see images of ancient battlefields, armies riven by terrible sorcery, piles of burning dead. While he had not the understanding to make sense of the scenes, Seiji knew the cause.

Blood magic.

That was where the bell drew him. Toward the abomination sat at the heart of this twisted web. Seiji would find Iuchiban and face whatever it was. He knew that surely as he understood Lady Sun would rise in the east.

And it terrified him.

Seiji had tried to resist the call. Once, only once.

It had been the first night after the Temple of the Bell. He had come upon the ruins of an old Crab mining complex, the remains of a small fort warding the entrance. Seiji had walked amidst the partially fallen walls, one hand trailing across the wind-scoured stone as if to strike some spark of familiarity amidst his troubled thoughts.

Nothing came.

He understood the wall, could name every stone from foundation to cope. And yet something was missing. There was no joy in his knowledge, no buttress of interest to support his regard. Seiji knew the realization should fill him with sorrow, but the ancestors had planed away the undesirable parts of him like a carpenter smoothing a rough log.

He had halted then, sat amidst the fallen stones like some indigent vagabond, head down, hands around his knees as he rocked back and forth. Even this held no comfort. The ancestors had swept away Seiji's self-deception as well. Even as he sought to resist their will, he could not but recognize his sorrow for what it was.

Petulant.

Shameful.

Who was Seiji to put himself above the needs of his family, his clan, his Empire?

It had been all he could do not to run from the fortification, the shades of its ancient builders like wolves at Seiji's back. The bell had him now, and like the Crab, it would *never* let go.

He traveled northeast, avoiding packs of roving dead. They were nothing to the bell now, distractions better left for others to deal with. Without the need to eat or rest, the cliffs took on a rugged sameness, a palette of angry gray broken by the occasional goblin pine or patch of moss.

So it was he almost missed the curls of smoke rising from a nearby peak. Seiji was far enough away to detect only the slightest odor, but judging by the smoke it was either a large fire or a number of smaller ones.

Ascending a ragged cliff, Seiji spied the remains of a heavy stone curtain wall, a high tower rising behind. The stone looked to have been recently patched, clean lines and near-invisible joints speaking of careful work.

Only belatedly did Seiji realize it was his own.

The sight of the ruined hill fort should have unsettled him, or at least conjured some pang of anxious regret. It was the site of Seiji's shame, the place where he had first heard the bell's call. Instead he felt only vague curiosity.

The fortress was inhabited, flashes of gray and dark blue armor visible as samurai patrolled the outer wall, their bulky silhouettes backlit by the glow of flames from within. Seiji counted a score or more on the gatehouse and more upon the walls, all Crab Clan judging from their arms and armor.

Although Seiji was not close enough to make out individual crests, he had no doubt they were Kuni.

Chiyo had led her expedition west.

Without even considering, Seiji understood the pall of smoke.

His kin were not burning wood. They were burning bodies.

Seiji scaled the cliff below the fortress, almost receiving an arrow in the eye for his troubles. It glinted off the stone just to the left of Seiji's head, sending flecks of rock bouncing from his cheek. For a moment he did not understand why his kin had loosed their bows, only to realize his quick ascent resembled that of a living corpse.

"I am Kuni Seiji!" His call echoed back from the walls above. "Returned from the Temple of the Bell."

Although the Crab guards gave no answering call, neither did they send any more arrows slashing down. A few minutes of climbing saw Seiji before the fort's ruined gate.

A half-dozen Crab samurai waited in the shadows, spears leveled.

Seiji spread his arms, straightening so they might get a good look at his face.

"It is him," the lead guard grunted, turning away without preamble. "Follow me. Lady Chiyo will want to see you."

Although the other guards lowered their spears, they did not relax. Seiji could not blame them.

The interior of the fort showed signs of struggle, not only the remains of several crackling pyres but scars upon the stone, the occasional smear of blood or ash marking the walls like battle paint. The keep itself was still ringed with bodies. Crab samurai worked along the footing. Stripped to the waist, their breath fogging in the cool air, they dragged tangled corpses from beneath the wall accompanied by a pair of hard-eyed spearmen, weapons ready lest any of the dead rise once more.

The keep doors had been ripped from their moorings, the wood gnawed upon. Well did Seiji remember hauling the door up the mountain, Izō's rough call exhorting the workers as they sweated and strained. At the time, Seiji had agonized over whether to join their labors or remain aloof lest the workers grow too familiar.

What a fool he had been.

Still, Seiji could not but wonder how long the door had held.

A dozen Kuni were arrayed in a loose semicircle in the keep's central hall. As Seiji approached, he saw the object of their interest. Two prisoners knelt upon the hard stone, arms and legs bound, gags fitted in their mouths.

Chiyo sat upon a camp chair, scarred chin resting in her palm as she regarded the foremost prisoners. One was a samurai, her armor slightly more ornate than the others, although without crest or sigil. The other wore the robes of an Emerald Magistrate, if somewhat tattered.

"Quite convenient." Suspicion threaded Chiyo's rough voice. "We heard rumors the Lion were gathering forces, and now we find samurai in our land, with an Emerald Magistrate, no less?"

"We follow the trail of a dark sorcerer," the magistrate replied. "The one responsible for these unquiet dead."

"I have heard of no investigation." Chiyo gave a skeptical frown, jade eye glittering in the shadows. "If you are who you claim, where are your travel papers? Why did you not speak to the local lord?"

"There *is* no local lord," the Lion commander gritted through clenched teeth.

"This is Crab land. And it is the Crab who defend it… from *all* threats." Chiyo spoke like an official passing sentence. "You may be who you say, you may be spies, you may be dark sorcerers masquerading as officials. Whatever you are, we have ways of finding the truth."

"I am an Emerald Magistrate, bound to enforce the Empire's laws."

"And bound *by* them," Chiyo replied coolly. "If you have nothing to hide, why travel in secret accompanied by a small army?"

The magistrate spoke quickly, words almost tumbling out. "There was not time to introduce ourselves. If Iuchiban lives, we must–"

"Take them away. Find me answers." Chiyo nodded to the surrounding Kuni, who quickly dragged the prisoners to their feet.

"Stop." Seiji didn't realize he had spoken until the others turned. *Iuchiban.* The name conjured a fire within the ashes of Seiji's heart, a blaze of righteous anger that scoured doubt and trepidation. Seiji knew that name.

And he *hated* it.

"Oh, you're back." Chiyo regarded Seiji for a long moment, then glanced back at the prisoners. "You know these spies?"

"Never seen them before in my life," Seiji replied. "But I know the one they seek."

His aunt gave a wry toss of her head, as if she wished to spit at his feet. "And why would I trust the word of a coward and traitor?"

Once, Chiyo's admonition would have torn the heart from
his chest. Now her words were as a handful of snow cast into
a fire.

"Because I found the bell." There was no mirth in Seiji's
smile. "And it showed me *everything*."

Chiyo took a step back. Surprise bleeding into suspicion, she
whispered a few words, fingers moving in ritual formulations.
After a moment she cocked her head.

"You do not walk alone."

"Our ancestors guide my path," Seiji replied.

"The Kuni chose you? Why?" Chiyo scoffed.

Seiji did not answer. No explanation he could offer would
quiet his aunt's misgivings.

After a moment Chiyo blew out a frustrated sigh. "You
should not have left."

"I had no choice."

"So I see." She sucked air through her teeth, then thrust her
chin at the prisoners. "And what would the ancestors have me
do with these spies?"

"Release them," Seiji replied. "They seek the same evil I do."

Although Chiyo's glare could have etched steel, she drew a
short blade and cut the ropes binding the magistrate and Lion
commander.

"Take them." She nodded for the others to be set free. "But
you had best find me answers, nephew."

"I would like nothing more," Seiji said, and meant it.

"Who are you, Crab?" The Lion commander regarded him
through narrowed eyes.

"He's the man who just saved your lives." Chiyo's smile was
cold. "Might want to show a bit more respect."

"We are grateful for your consideration," the magistrate said. "I am Kitsuki Naoki and my companion is Lady Matsu Akoya."

The latter name sent mutters through the assembled samurai. Even Seiji had heard of Akoya. Daimyō of the Matsu and one of the Lion's fiercest march wardens, she had protected the clan's southernmost territories for decades, resisting threats from Crane, Scorpion, and bandits with equal tenacity.

"What brings a Lion lord to these accursed lands?" Chiyo asked.

"As I said, we seek information about the dark sorcerer Iuchiban," Naoki replied.

"The necromancer?" Chiyo gave a doubting snort. "He is many centuries dead."

"If only that were true." Although Naoki spoke softly, there was a sharp curiosity in her expression, a flicker of something approaching recognition. Stepping closer, she peered up at Seiji for an uncomfortable moment.

"Do you know of a Kuni called Tetsuo?"

Somehow, Seiji *did* know despite never having met the man.

"I know he is dead." His reply seemed to shake the magistrate.

Paling, she glanced back at Akoya. "It is worse than I feared."

"I think it might be best if you tell me everything." Chiyo settled back into her camp chair. Arms crossed, she nodded at Seiji. "You first."

Seiji could think of no reason to lie. He told them of the battle with the dead, how he had hurried back to Razor of Dawn Castle pursued by the terrible ringing, how it had drawn him to the ancient Crab monastery only to bombard him with disjointed images of the past. Scenes he now realized were gleaned from Iuchiban's last assault upon Rokugan.

Through the whole explanation, Naoki watched with eyes almost fever bright, her hands nervously picking at the hem of her robe. By the end, even Akoya and Chiyo were leaning forward, their expressions similarly troubled.

"Tetsuo too followed this bell," Naoki said when, at last, Seiji had finished. "It led us to Iuchiban's tomb, just as it must have led Tetsuo to the dark sorcerer himself."

Naoki told them of rebellion west of the Twilight Mountains, of the destruction of the imperial expedition by an army of dead, and how she had tracked a murderous Bloodspeaker across the breadth of Rokugan only to find a far darker threat hidden beneath the ancient peaks.

"If Tetsuo is dead, then Qadan and Irie must have fallen as well." Naoki's voice held sorrow and fear in equal measure. "Iuchiban walks free, or perhaps one of his disciples. Either way, Rokugan is in grave danger."

It was only when Naoki took a half-step back that Seiji realized he had clenched his fists as if to strike. With effort, he pushed the tension down. Surely even the ancestors must realize Naoki and Akoya were allies.

"Is that why you returned to the Twilight Peaks?" Seiji asked.

"We came because there was nowhere else to go," Naoki replied. "The Imperial Archives make no mention of Iuchiban – even the High Histories of the Ikoma seem blind to his existence."

"Would the Crab have some record of him?" Akoya asked.

"The Kuni deal in things best not recorded," Chiyo added.

"But I shall send a message back to Razor of Dawn. Perhaps one of our kin knows more."

"How long will that take?" Naoki asked.

"Several days to reach the castle, longer to spread the word." Chiyo gave a thoughtful frown. "A few weeks. That is if the snows don't come early this year. Once the passes close we will be on our own."

The thought of waiting weeks for a reply filled Seiji with a sense of rootless dread. As if he were being stalked by a pack of wolves drawing closer with every ragged heartbeat.

"There is little time to spare," he said.

"How do you know this?" Akoya asked.

"I cannot say." Seiji shook his head, eyes screwed shut. "I only know that whatever slipped from that tomb works toward some terrible goal, one that fast approaches."

Naoki ran a hand through her hair, frustration almost palpable. "Hints and rumors, old tales and muddied visions. How can we oppose an evil we cannot even *find*."

"I can find it." Although Seiji's words had been soft, they caught the attention of all within the hall. "The bell guides my path."

"Ancestors be praised." Chiyo breathed a whispered prayer.

"And where is the bell telling you to go now?" Akoya asked.

"That way." Seiji thrust his chin at the northeastern corner of the hall. His vision blurred, the stones seeming to unweave as dark visions of the past jostled within his perceptions. He saw a gleaming city, a vast metropolis curled around the bay like a protective hand, its towers and palaces familiar even to one who had never set foot upon its wide thoroughfares.

"The Imperial City." He spoke as if reciting Shinseist scripture. "He is there."

Naoki gave a strangled moan. "I should have remained, should have looked *harder*."

"You would have found nothing," Seiji replied. "We tread upon the strands of a web woven centuries before our birth."

"Then let us cut this spider from its perch." Akoya slapped a thigh to punctuate her words.

"I shall travel north with the magistrate." Seiji turned to Chiyo. "Aunt, can you hold back the dead?"

"I am a Kuni." Her reply was curt. Chiyo looked Naoki and Akoya up and down as if sizing them up, then gave a quick nod to the nearby Crab samurai. "Return their weapons. I shall write up some travel papers." Her grin was somehow more threatening than her scowl. "We wouldn't want another... misunderstanding."

Although Naoki's bow was respectful, Seiji could tell the magistrate's thoughts were moving quickly as his own. A long road stood before them, its end uncertain, and all Seiji had to study were fragmented visions of a time centuries past and the callous call of the bell singing in his blood. At least he had companions, ones who had faced Iuchiban's minions before.

And lost.

It did not matter to the Kuni ancestors. If Seiji failed, they would find another, and another. All that mattered was blood. Seiji did not know if the realization comforted or unsettled him. All he knew was that the Kuni had set his path.

And Seiji had no choice but to follow.

CHAPTER SEVENTEEN

"And that is everything I know of Bloodspeakers." Masahiro reached for his teacup. To be fair, it wasn't *all* he knew, but it was all Tomiko needed to know. Despite the finery of the surroundings, the Phoenix appeared as something recently washed up after a storm.

"And Iuchiban is... dead?" Tomiko's question was soft, hopeful.

Masahiro favored her with his warmest smile. "As far as I am aware."

It was not a lie, not quite.

"Then what of the assassin?" Tomiko asked.

"Iuchiban has many disciples." Masahiro returned a sober nod, considering his next words carefully. Already the guests were arriving for Prince Tokihito's moon viewing, and Masahiro very much did not need an overexcited Phoenix priest babbling about supernatural assassins.

Tomiko shifted uncomfortably. "Why has the Emerald Magistracy not been informed?"

"They have," Masahiro said. "Even now my comrade, Senior Magistrate Kitsuki Naoki, searches the High Histories for records of blood magic. She entrusted me to search for corruption in the Imperial City."

Well, Naoki probably *would* have entrusted Masahiro had she known of the situation.

Tomiko frowned. "So we are to act as if nothing occurred?"

"I am convinced this goes deeper than a single assassin." Masahiro leaned in as if to draw the Phoenix priest into his confidence. "How could they strike a clan noble so precisely? Such killings require more than dark sorcery. I suspect the Bloodspeakers have connections in the Inner Districts, perhaps even at court."

Masahiro noted the twitch of discomfort that flickered across Tomiko's face. The Phoenix was definitely concealing something.

He offered a thin smile. "Were we to make our knowledge public, it would send the whole vicious conspiracy scuttling back into the shadows."

"So what would you have me do?" Skepticism colored Tomiko's tone.

"Find allies, gather knowledge and strength." Masahiro let his smile broaden. "If there is one thing I have learned in my tenure at court, the best way to uproot a conspiracy is to form a better one." He nodded toward the distant garden, strains of flute and biwa just audible through the manor halls. "Our foes may possess dark magic and shadowy killers, but we shall have an advantage of which they cannot even dream."

Tomiko narrowed her eyes. "And what is that?"

"Why, the next Hantei emperor, of course."

"And where do I fit in?" Tomiko looked dubious.

"A very good question," Masahiro replied. "What did you do to earn the Bloodspeakers' ire, Lady Isawa?"

Tomiko looked away, hands bunching the elegantly embroidered silk of her robe.

"I have shared my secrets with you." Not entirely true, but Masahiro felt little guilt at the deception. "What would cause a dead assassin to target a Phoenix elementalist?" He studied the young priest for a long moment. "You are clearly noble, but I don't recall seeing you at court."

"I have not been at court." She looked at her hands. "Not for many years."

"Back with your clan then?"

"Yes." The Phoenix priest looked up. "I am mistress of Heaven's Blaze."

Masahiro could not help the grunt of surprise that slipped from his lips. "That was Irie's dōjō."

Tomiko reacted as if Masahiro had drawn a blade. "What do you know of Irie?"

"Little, I'm afraid." He shrugged. "She accompanied us into Iuchiban's tomb and helped battle the corruption within. If you are her colleague, you should be proud."

"What became of Irie?" Tomiko's question was almost a gasp.

"I cannot say. Naoki and I were too wounded to continue, but Irie and the others traveled deeper into the tomb." Masahiro sighed. "I have heard nothing since."

"You did not see Iuchiban destroyed?" Tomiko asked.

"Nor did I see him triumph." Masahiro deflected the

question. "Irie sought to avenge her master… Asako Masatake, I believe?"

"Masatsuge." Tomiko's correction was almost unconscious.

"A wise man." Masahiro favored her with a sympathetic nod. "He fell with the imperial expedition, as did my brother."

"My condolences." Tomiko's reply was distant, her expression troubled.

Masahiro hid his irritation at the priest's evasion. Otose would have been able to dispel Tomiko's reticence with a few kind words, but his sister-in-law had fled the capital for her family's estates in the south.

Remembering their last encounter only served to sharpen Masahiro's temper. There was no time to coddle Tomiko, not when Gensuke may be even now hunting them both.

"I saved your life, Lady Isawa, and now your silence endangers mine." Masahiro squared his shoulders. "I think it is time you told me the truth."

For a moment, Masahiro was worried Tomiko would flee the room. Although there were guards nearby, forcibly restraining a Phoenix noble would not mark an auspicious beginning to tonight's festivities.

Fortunately, the priest seemed to gather herself, drawing in a meditative breath.

"I did not travel to the Imperial City to avenge my master." When Tomiko spoke again, her voice was soft but firm. "If anything, I came to ensure he was truly dead."

"I don't understand." Masahiro could not conceal his surprise.

"My master, Irie's master…" Tomiko shook her head, tears glittering like flecks of pale jade. "He was a Bloodspeaker."

"An Asako?" Masahiro asked. "How is that possible?"

"I cannot say." Tomiko made as if to draw a paper from her robes only to belatedly realize they contained nothing. "My school owed great debts. At first I thought Masatsuge had been cheated by unscrupulous merchants, but when I confronted one, he unleashed dark sorcery. I followed the web of contacts here only to find Masatsuge at its heart. My master beggared our dōjō to supply cults in the Imperial City, perhaps across the whole of Rokugan."

Masahiro could not blame the Phoenix for her discomfort. If one of the Empire's most respected priests could be corrupted by Iuchiban, then none were safe from the ancient sorcerer's machinations. More troubling was the fact Irie had not shared this information with any of them.

Did his former companion's secrecy spring from shame or corruption? Masahiro could understand Irie wanting to protect her school and clan from such dire revelations, but her silence in the tomb itself hinted at far more troubling motives.

"I would understand if you summoned your guards," Tomiko said. "I should be brought before the Magistracy."

Silence stretched between them, tight as a wind-caught sail.

Masahiro tapped his chin, considering. "*Are* you corrupted, Lady Isawa?"

Tomiko spoke like a woman awaiting execution. "I concealed my suspicions, sought to uproot the Bloodspeakers on my own."

"So you are guilty of ambition." Masahiro shrugged. "If that warranted an inquisition, most of court would be in an Asako cell."

Tomiko's eyes widened as if she recalled something troubling. "I must inform my parents."

"And they are?" Masahiro asked casually, reaching for his cooling tea.

"Lady Isawa Kuwashi and Lord Isawa Kōrei."

"You're the Phoenix ambassadors' daughter?" Masahiro almost fumbled his cup. Although Kuwashi and Kōrei did often deign to directly influence political matters, for years they had involved themselves in court while pretending to stand apart from it. Masahiro had all but given up on attempting to win the Phoenix ambassadors' backing for Prince Tokihito, and now their only daughter sat before him.

Old courtly instincts came to the fore, Masahiro's thoughts churning with possibilities.

"Perhaps it might be best to shield your parents from these... uncomfortable revelations." He spoke quickly. "While I have no doubt such esteemed nobles as Kuwashi and Kōrei remain pure of spirit, the same might not be said for the rest of your clan." He held up a hand to forestall Tomiko's response. "If even one such as Asako Masatsuge might fall to darkness, we cannot be sure there are not others."

Although Tomiko narrowed her eyes at the implication, she did not argue.

"The ancestors brought us together for a reason." Masahiro spread his arms as if to draw Tomiko closer. "And on this auspicious day, no less."

Ignoring her dubious expression, Masahiro forged onward. "Even as we speak, nobles and courtiers gather in this manor's gardens, drawn here at the invitation of Prince Tokihito. Amidst the poetry and music, we discuss the matter of imperial succession free from the stifling propriety of court."

Normally Masahiro would have spent hours finessing such an entreaty, but needs will as needs must, and he had little enough time as it was. "The Fortunes have put us in the perfect position to oppose the ancient darkness that threatens our empire."

Fortunately, Tomiko did not laugh in his face. "How so?"

"We gather to celebrate the slaying of Iuchiban. The court shall reward the heroes responsible." Masahiro inclined his head, smiling. "An imperial commendation along with a not insignificant gift of silver. Since Irie is not with us, it is only right you should accept on behalf of your dōjō."

Although Tomiko seemed taken aback, there was something in her bearing Masahiro recognized, a subtle tightening around the eyes as the Phoenix leaned forward, her posture excited, almost *hungry*. Masahiro knew the look well, for he saw it often enough in the mirror.

"The reward might not erase your school's burden," he continued. "But it will give you time to breathe."

"And what must I do for this unexpected largesse?" Tomiko asked, causing Masahiro to silently reassess his evaluation of her. The Phoenix might have spent her life in a remote dōjō, but she had courtly instincts.

"Your parents will be in attendance tonight. Speak with them on Tokihito's behalf," he said. "The support of the Phoenix Embassy would go a long way toward smoothing the young prince's path to the throne."

Tomiko shook her head, expression clouded. "They will not listen to me."

"They do not need to listen," Masahiro replied. "They only need to be *seen* to listen. If you ask for support publicly, other nobles will mark it, and that will work in our favor."

Tomiko regarded him, her expression guarded. "I see your ambition, Crane."

"Am I that obvious?" Masahiro chuckled.

"As my father says: 'Truth is the foundation of trust,'" Tomiko continued solemnly. "You have told me truth this night. I do not yet trust you, but should your deeds match your words…"

Masahiro pressed his remaining hand to his heart. "We can all but strive for harmony."

"I will need new robes." Tomiko rubbed a smudge of soot upon the back of one hand. "And a bath."

"You shall have that and more, Lady Isawa." Masahiro stood. "If you will excuse me, the guests are arriving. Lower court bureaucrats – but when trying to start an avalanche, one must pay attention to pebbles first."

"You may wish to consider a bath as well, Lord Masahiro." She glanced up at him, wrinkling her nose. "Your robes reek of woodsmoke and desperation."

Masahiro could not help but laugh.

His good humor melted as he stepped into the long hall. Although he could hear the soft strains of flute and drum from the garden, the night felt only more precarious. He turned, half expecting Gensuke, but the long hall was empty save for a pair of guards kneeling by the garden door.

Masahiro ran his remaining hand through his hair, surprised to find it trembling.

He chuckled at the sight, giving a rueful shake of his head.

Somehow he needed to winnow consensus from a gaggle of fractious courtiers while avoiding the knives of an undead killer, all while working to topple a millennia-old cabal of sorcerers.

Truly, nerves were the least of Masahiro's concerns.

CHAPTER EIGHTEEN

Kitsuki Naoki was glad to leave mountains behind, an irony given how much of her life had been spent among the high peaks of the Dragon Clan's northern frontier. Any relief Naoki might have felt departing the Twilight Mountains was eclipsed by a growing trepidation at what awaited back at the capital.

She, Akoya, and Seiji had been hurried through Crab lands, Lady Chiyo's seal sufficient to see them through the numerous watchforts that studded the slate-gray hills the Crab called home.

Naoki's mind was awhirl with possibilities, thoughts bitter as windblown snow. Her search for Iuchiban had taken her from the Imperial City exactly when she was most needed. At least Masahiro remained, although the Crane was likely more preoccupied with court intrigues than ancient sorcerers. Still, Naoki could not believe Masahiro would sit idle as Iuchiban's servants worked their master's vile will.

That is, if the Crane was even aware of the Bloodspeakers' machinations.

Although her search had flung Naoki across the breadth of

Rokugan, it had not been a total failure. Contrary to the vague accounts and wild descriptions in the High Histories, Kuni Seiji held a wealth of information on Iuchiban and his followers. The knowledge of scores of Kuni ancestors roiled within the young Crab's mind, a maze of disjointed recollections Naoki was compelled to navigate.

If she could only find the right questions.

"Can you recall any weaknesses?" Akoya asked. Legs crossed, elbows on knees, the former Matsu lord sat half in shadow, her expression that of a general sizing up an opposing force. "What weapons were used to defeat him? Blades? Sorcery? Some manner of holy relic? How was Iuchiban destroyed?"

"His body was burned." Seiji pressed a hand to his forehead as if remembering caused him physical pain. "But the sorcerer's spirit survived."

Akoya made an irritated sound in the back of her throat. Since most of her guard had fallen in the Twilight Mountains, the Matsu lord had been sharper than usual, her scarred face haggard and hollow-cheeked.

They sat in a small guard post in Maemikake, waiting for the ship that would carry them to the coast, then up to the Imperial City. One of the Crab Clan's few trade towns, Maemikake stretched along the southern shore of the Lake of Cherry Blossom Snow – named for the many cherry trees that lined its shores. Naoki had read poems about the lake's beauty, how every autumn when the trees shed so many blossoms the water seemed dusted with delicate pink frost. Now however, the trees stood barren and leafless, the whole town shaded in tones of dusky gray, as if winter had leached the color from the land.

"Can Iuchiban's spirit be captured? Destroyed?" Akoya pressed further.

Seiji bared his teeth, youthful features twisted in concentration. "I cannot say."

"What *can* you say, boy?" Akoya pushed to her feet, fists clenched. For a moment, Naoki thought the Lion would strike Seiji, but she only spun on her heel, ducking from the small room.

Naoki watched her go, then looked to Seiji. The Kuni seemed crestfallen, head bowed, shoulders low, his eyes staring from shadowed hollows.

"I am sorry, magistrate." He struck his temple as if to dislodge something. "The memories are… hazy."

Naoki could empathize with Seiji's frustration. She had experienced such scattered thoughts often enough herself. They had been at the young Kuni for days, but it was like Seiji consulted an ancient manuscript, ink faded by time, its pages so delicate the very act of reading caused them to fray.

"Exhaustion is no goad to memory," Naoki said. "You should rest."

"I cannot."

"The road ahead is long," she replied. "Even if you do not sleep, it might be good to–"

"You don't understand." He shook his head. "I do not sleep anymore. Not after the bell."

Naoki studied him for a long moment. "It was the same with Tetsuo, I think."

"You knew him?"

"Only briefly." Naoki shrugged.

Seiji edged forward. "What was he like?"

"An avalanche." Naoki returned a thin smile.

Her reply seemed to unsettle the Crab. Seiji scrubbed a hand across his face, drawing in a shaky breath. The reaction surprised Naoki. She had thought the Kuni another witch hunter, albeit a young one, but Seiji looked like nothing so much as a scholar who had somehow wandered into a pitched battle.

She cocked her head. "You are not like him."

"To my shame."

"Falling stones are powerful, but little use when one wishes to thread a needle." Naoki chuckled. "Tetsuo faced Iuchiban like a charging ox and it destroyed him. Perhaps that was why the ancestors chose you to carry on his work?"

Seiji turned away. "It was not."

Seeing the Crab tense, Naoki took a different path. "What were you before... this?"

"An architect." Seiji gave a jagged laugh. "A fool."

Naoki studied the Crab for a long moment. So very different from Tetsuo's single-minded confidence, she found his uncertainty endearing – perhaps because it echoed her own.

"The Empire needs builders more than it needs warriors."

"That is kind of you to say." Seiji gave a helpless shrug.

"Please, call me Naoki," she said. "In my experience, rank frustrates cooperation."

He gave a wan smile. "In my experience, it is blood."

Naoki could not but laugh at the Crab's jest, doubly amused as she imagined the words in Tetsuo's gravelly baritone.

"True," she said. "But I would gladly take family troubles over blood sorcery."

"Blood is means to an end." Seiji's voice was distant. "The true power is in naming."

Naoki frowned. "I'm afraid I don't follow."

"I am Kuni." He straightened. "Were I Kaiu, even now I would be upon the Carpenter Wall, shoring up my clan's defenses." He nodded at her. "You are Kitsuki, and our esteemed comrade is Matsu. We can resist the call of our blood, but it is like moving upriver, always walking against the current. That is why Iuchiban has taken many names."

It was more than Seiji had spoken since they had first met. Naoki was tempted to probe further, but knew better than to interrupt a confession.

"Laughing Turtle, Tomebreaker, Truthseeker, He Who Walks Above, the Young Master, Grandfather, the Empty Flame – many names bent to singular purpose." The Crab rocked back on his heels, words seeming to slip from his lips. "Neither spirit nor mortal, he walks in twilight, ageless malevolence disguising noble goals. Once he sought to rule us, but found the conqueror's draft too bitter. Now the goal is more subtle, a shifting not of politics, but foundational precepts." Seiji sketched a rough curve in the air before him, hands meeting at the apex. "Rokugan is like an arch – all the pieces matter, but it is the keystone that holds everything in balance."

"The Imperial City." Naoki drew in a quick breath. "But how does one fight a name?"

Her question seemed to startle Seiji from his half-trance. Blinking, the Crab ran a shaky hand through his hair.

"I am sorry." He shut his eyes, jaw tight. "The past is like mist."

Naoki swallowed her frustration, leaning in to pat Seiji on the arm. "You have given us more than the High Histories of the Ikoma. For that, you should be proud."

"Of course." He gave a tired smile, lips tight. "Perhaps I *should* try to rest after all."

"Yes, of course." Naoki stood, unconsciously smoothing the creases from her robe. If anything, the Kuni's words had left her with more questions, but she could see that pressing further would yield nothing but frustration. She ducked from the small guardhouse, sliding the screen shut behind her.

Matsu Akoya stood just outside the door. The Lion lord's perennial scowl was gone, replaced by a thoughtful look, her arms folded across her broad chest.

"How much did you overhear?" Naoki asked.

"Enough." Akoya thrust her chin toward the docks. "Walk with me."

Drawing her robes tighter to ward off the afternoon chill, Naoki followed Akoya across the heavy boards.

"What do you make of all this dark sorcery?" The Matsu lord's breath steamed in the air.

"I am no priest." Naoki chose her next words carefully. "But one of my companions, Iuchi Qadan, was a name keeper."

"I have crossed paths with such spiritualists, although seldom in friendly circumstances. They are . . ." Akoya wrinkled her nose. "Powerful."

Naoki could well imagine the many border skirmishes in which Akoya had fought. The Lion and Unicorn were like siblings forced to share a room. Always tense, occasionally respectful, their relationship marked by frequent scuffles.

"One of their earth spirits almost buried me at Singing Vale." Akoya spoke like Naoki would recognize the name of the battle. "I would have been crushed had Chiaki not bulled me from the path of the avalanche. Old boar broke three of my ribs saving my life." Akoya pressed a hand to her side. "But I paid her back. Many times over."

Naoki offered a sympathetic nod. "I am sorry I did not have the chance to know her better."

"You would not have liked Chiaki, magistrate." Akoya's smile was raw as a fresh wound. "She was stubborn, sharp-tempered, inflexible. Her thoughts moved like a spear thrust. She would have had little patience for..." Akoya flicked her fingers at the guard post, the bobbing ships, the flat waters of the lake. "*This.*"

"And you do?" Naoki asked.

"Chiaki and I won many battles together," Akoya replied. "But that does not mean we learned the same lessons. She was always more comfortable in the barracks than a council hall. The Lion Clan treasures such warriors, but there is more to life than battle, more to victory than blades. I tried to teach Katamori that." She blew out a slow breath. "Now my nephew is with the dead."

"We shall see them avenged – Chiaki, Katamori, *all* of them." It seemed like the right thing to say, but Akoya only turned to fix Naoki with a narrow-eyed look.

"You think I do this for vengeance?" She sniffed, shaking her head. "I *loved* my master, my nephew, just as I loved the guards who fell defending that pitiful Crab castle. I have drunk deep from the cup of revenge, magistrate, many times, and it is a bitter, hollow draft – one without end. I will destroy Iuchiban, of that you can be sure, but his end will be a gift to the future, not the past."

Naoki swallowed her surprise. She had thought Akoya cut from the Lion banner, but the Matsu lord appeared to possess a more philosophical bent. The mischaracterization brought a flush of shame. She too had often felt confined by expectations of family and clan, trying to force herself into the mold of a Kitsuki investigator only to find her thoughts did not travel such rigid paths. Naoki had only begun to succeed when she set aside the belief there was but *one* correct method.

"I misjudged you." She offered Akoya a low bow. "Apologies, Lady Matsu."

"Matsu." Akoya echoed the name with a rueful chuckle. "I suppose I still am, aren't I? Names are difficult to resist."

"And Iuchiban's names?" Naoki was happy to change the topic.

"I am no priest." Akoya echoed Naoki's earlier words. "But I have had several names, as have you, I assume?"

Naoki nodded. Children were expected to take a new name during their Coming-of-Age Ceremony, as were those who left worldly concerns behind to become monks. Names could be taken to reflect new social status, or title, even intent. Naoki had taken her current name when she dedicated herself to the magistracy, combining the characters for "straight" and "tree" to reflect her dedication to justice.

"But we do not take them at the same time," she replied. "And I have certainly never derived any sorcerous power from them."

"You are not a Bloodspeaker," Akoya replied. "Nor are you a name keeper."

Not for the first time, Naoki wished Qadan were here. The Unicorn had been prickly and suspicious, but her dedication had never wavered. Qadan and the others had given their lives to stop Iuchiban's return; Naoki could do no less.

"Both the Imperial Archives and High Histories mention

Bloodspeakers, but there seemed no central authority. Even their connection to Iuchiban was tenuous." Naoki cast a glance to the gray sky as if it might piece together the disparate understanding. "I thought each cult worshipped a different fiend, now I see they were all facets of Iuchiban."

Akoya sucked air through her teeth. "How do you kill a name?"

"I cannot say." Naoki rested a hand upon one of the pier's mooring beams, the wood rough beneath her fingers. "But we must find out."

CHAPTER NINETEEN

Isawa Tomiko had taken many baths in her life – from bracing plunges into spring meltwater to leisurely soaks in the hot springs that bubbled up in the valley below Heaven's Blaze. All Rokugani prized cleanliness, and the Phoenix more than most. Any temple of even moderate note was equipped with a modest bathhouse for monks and pilgrims, and Tomiko had visited more than her share.

Until this day however, she had never truly *bathed*.

The pool was larger than any Tomiko had ever seen, its tiles adorned with pleasing flower mosaics, the lacquered cedar walls painted with forest scenes. Lilac scented steam rose from a pile of heated rocks upon which servants poured dippers of perfumed water. Others waited nearby with a profusion of oils and soaps, ready to attend to Tomiko's every need. Thus far she had resisted the temptation to call upon their services – she was still a Phoenix after all – but nothing could stop Tomiko from luxuriating in the warm water.

She leaned back, eyes closed, feeling the tension bleed

from her shoulders. The last few days had been filled with old manuscripts and punctuated by wild danger.

The hours since her rescue seemed a blur and Tomiko's memories were tangled. Masahiro had spoken all the right words, but such was always the way with the Crane.

Despite his protestations to the contrary, Tomiko knew Masahiro had not shared all he knew. Their relationship was new, untested; it would be suspicious if he brought Tomiko into his full confidence. In the end, Tomiko had not been swayed by honeyed promises. She had peered behind Masahiro's veneer of civility, marking his pauses, his sideways glances, the way his lips tightened as he spoke of Bloodspeakers.

Masahiro was *afraid*. And that, more than anything, had made Tomiko believe him.

Although she would have dearly loved to spend the night soaking in the well-appointed bath, Tomiko marked the distant murmur of conversation from the gardens.

With a regretful sigh, she stepped from the bath, nodding her thanks as servants rushed forward with towels. They moved to dry her, but Tomiko waved them off.

"Lady Isawa, your formal robes have been acquired." A thin-faced woman in the robes of a senior servant seemed to materialize from the haze. She offered Tomiko a scandalously soft robe, then gestured toward the rear door. "They await you in the Peony Blossom Chamber."

Tomiko allowed herself to be led down several back halls, trying not to stare at the elegant murals and arrangements that graced the alcoves. Even the manor's staff corridors seemed arranged with an eye toward artistry.

She could not but gawk at the Peony Chamber. It was as if Tomiko had stepped into a spring garden, the brushwork so delicate and color so vibrant she was surprised that the limbs did not sway in the breeze. Lines of glittering kintsugi gold webbed cracks in the mosaics and pottery, celebrating rather than attempting to disguise their flaws. This seemed to resonate within Tomiko, painfully appropriate to her situation.

The senior servant bowed, her smile one of quiet pride. "It will be an hour or so before your presence is requested in the main garden. Shall I summon body servants for your hair and makeup?"

"That will not be necessary," Tomiko replied. "A few hair pins shall suffice. We Phoenix pride ourselves on simplicity."

"As you wish." Amusement flickered across the servant's lined face, so quickly Tomiko could almost believe she had imagined it. "Lord Masahiro has requested you be given privacy, so you may take your leisure in this wing. Should you require anything, call out and I shall be close at hand."

"Thank you." Propriety forbade Tomiko from returning the servant's bow, but she favored the woman with a grateful smile. "The hospitality of the Crane cannot be overstated."

Once the servant had departed, Tomiko changed into her formal robes, then spent time admiring the art. The artists of her clan tended toward more understated representations. Although the mosaics embodied the Crane predilection for more flowery depictions, it possessed a quality of immediacy Tomiko found fascinating.

She wandered the chamber until she came to a wooden door, the edges carved to resemble intertwined branches.

Sliding it aside, Tomiko found another hall, this one hung with poetry scrolls, each featuring an ode to early winter. Beyond, another door opened into what looked to be a library.

The chamber was perhaps ten paces square, boasting several large bookcases. Although small compared to the rambling stacks of the Imperial Archives, that the Crane could fill even a few shelves spoke well of their commitment to the written word.

Stepping in to study the nearest books, Tomiko was surprised to discover not history or theology, but literature – *The Pillow Book of Kiyohara Nagiko, Collections of Thirty-Six Poets, The Summer and Winter Annals, The Tale of the Shining Prince*. Tomiko ran her fingers along the spines, unable to restrain a smile.

Her parents had no time for historical romances, believing that a well-ordered mind did not engage in such frivolous pastimes, but Tomiko had always found time for pillow books. Reading behind closed doors by candlelight, she had delighted in the poetry of Izumi Shikibu, the romance of Lady Shion's shining prince, unable to resist the salacious details of Lady Kiyohara's courtly dramas.

A departure from the dry philosophical treatises the masters pressed upon her, the novels seemed to awaken something in Tomiko, a freedom unconstrained by expectation. In them she could be more or less than she was – and that was precious.

With a sigh, she drew forth one of Shion's romances, thumbing to her favorite section almost by reflex. The Shining Prince found himself pursued by two high noblewomen, unable to return the affections of one without grievously offending the other. In any other romance, this would have resulted in a profusion of overwrought protestations, a duel, perhaps several, and a final confession as one or the other lay bleeding upon the snow. But Shion's prince was too clever for such a trite outcome, cleverly manipulating his two would-be paramours into a relationship with one another.

"Oh, apologies." A voice caused Tomiko to jump. "I was not aware anyone else was here."

Pressing Shion's historical romance to her chest, she looked to the speaker – a young man of perhaps twelve winters, round-cheeked and scholar-pale, with wide, long-lashed eyes the color of burnished oak. Although his robes bore no crest or clan color, they were of fine make, and trimmed in gold and green. Two guards stood nearby, faces stern, eyes alert. Their robes were similarly nondescript, but the blades thrust through their sashes looked well made.

Tomiko hesitated. Judging by his dress and attendants, the young man was obviously someone of rank, either the child of a high court official or scion of one of the imperial families – perhaps Seppun or Otomo. Whatever his parentage, he outranked Tomiko, except that the lad clearly did not want to be recognized.

As if sensing her indecision the young man reddened, glancing at the book in her hands.

"Is that Shion?" Craning his neck for a better look, he grinned. "*Tale of Three Seasons*. Oh, I *love* that one."

Tomiko let out her held breath. By dispensing with protocol, the lad had sidestepped any need for formality.

"One of my favorites." She held it out. The boy took it, gaze intent as he rifled through the pages. "Lady Otose has one of the best collections of pillow books in the Imperial City."

"This is not Lord Masahiro's manor?"

"Oh, it is. For the moment, at least." He favored her with a knowing smile. "Although we have Otose to thank for the literature and décor."

Tomiko tried and failed to hide her surprise. Although the boy did not seem to notice, the guards continued to watch with the coiled focus of hunting hawks.

"Do you prefer Lady Spring or Lady Winter?" The young noble flipped to the same passage Tomiko had been recently reading.

"Lady Spring seems to be everyone's favorite." Tomiko ventured a smile. "But I've always preferred Winter."

"I as well." The lad bobbed his head. "Spring is a time of growth and renewal. Winter is harsh, unforgiving, but more is accomplished during Winter Court than the other seasons combined."

Tomiko could not but agree.

"Oh, she has *The Thirty-Six Poets*!" He drew another book from the stacks and recited one of the verses in the musical dialect of the high courts.

The young noble's enthusiasm was infectious. Tomiko found herself reciting the answering verse, to the lad's obvious delight. He began another, which she also finished. Such was the structure of the collection, a lyrical conversation between two friends separated by time and distance. Soon they had worked through the whole poem, her young companion positively glowing.

"They do not often let me read things like this," he said.

Again, Tomiko could not but return a sympathetic nod.

"That is why I wanted to come early." He glanced back at his guards as if afraid they might drag him from the room.

They remained still.

"What brings you to this manor?" He glanced at the crest on her robes. "Lady Isawa."

Tomiko hesitated. "I am a... friend of Lord Masahiro."

"What do you think of him?"

The forwardness of the young noble's question took Tomiko by surprise. She took a slow breath, considering.

"Masahiro is ambitious, perhaps dangerously so," she replied at last. "But I believe he cares about the Empire."

"Can he be trusted?"

Tomiko frowned. "I have been asking myself the same question."

"And?" Although the young noble's expression was earnest, there was a sharpness in his eyes – not calculation, but concern. If Tomiko had felt a kinship with the lad, it now blossomed into open regard.

She gave a thoughtful nod. "I think so."

"Good." His smile returned, brighter than ever. "Now I want to hear what you think of Lady Kiyohara's pillow book. The chrysanthemum chapter has some cutting insights on–"

"Prince." One of the guards stepped forward, voice soft but firm. "We must prepare."

Tomiko took an unconscious step back, breath catching in her throat. She had thought the lad a noble scion who had snuck off before the more stuffy formalities began. Never in her wildest imaginings did Tomiko consider she had been talking of romances with the next Hantei emperor.

"Thank you for the conversation." He did not bow, but his gaze was warm. "I enjoyed it very much."

"Prince Tokihito." She dropped to her knees, would have

pressed her forehead to the floor if not for the look of vague disappointment that shaded the prince's expression.

"This evening will burst with bows." He shook his head. "No need to start early."

"Yes, prince."

"It has been a pleasure, Lady Isawa…" he paused.

"Tomiko," she replied softly.

"I am glad we crossed paths." With that, he turned, ushered from the library by careful guards.

As if to echo the prince's departure, the door behind Tomiko slid open, revealing the senior servant.

Tomiko turned, an uncomfortable flush coloring her cheeks. If she had offended Tokihito, or worse, *insulted* him, Tomiko's life might have very well been forfeit. By the ancestor's grace she had somehow managed to ingratiate herself to the young prince.

"Why did you not warn me?" she asked the servant.

"Lord Masahiro bid me follow the prince's commands as his own." The servant gave a helpless shrug. "And *he* ordered me to tell no one."

Tomiko could only shake her head.

"Lady, it is time we made our way to the garden."

Tomiko had hoped to steal a moment to center herself before the confrontation with her parents, but the last encounter had left her heart fluttering like a caged bird. Drawing in a steadying breath, she nodded.

"Lead the way."

The garden was beautiful, but Tomiko would have expected nothing else. Nobles in quilted robes mingled along the stone-lined paths, drifting between the pools of lamplight like wayward spirits. Although the night was bracing, braziers had been arranged around the edges of the enclosure. Aromatic woods and incense filled the air with pleasant smells even as the fires warded off the evening chill. Soft chords on koto and biwa threaded the sweet sound of bamboo flute, the occasional hand drum serving to accentuate rather than overwhelm the melody.

It was a scene plucked from some courtly romance. Tomiko half expected Lady Winter to stride from beneath the shadowed eaves, her beauty like a burst of icy wind snatching the breath from all.

But Tomiko was unable to appreciate the surroundings. Hands bunched in the sleeves of her robe, she scanned the scattered groups. Masahiro was easy to spot. The Crane sat amidst a flock of Otomo officials in richly embroidered robes. Around them milled Seppun officers in parade armor, even a small knot of Miya, bright smiles at odds with the subdued browns and greens of their courtly attire. If the Crane noticed Tomiko he gave no sign, but she had barely stepped onto the garden path before a servant hurried to her elbow.

"Lady Kuwashi and Lord Kōrei are outside Pavilion of Eighteen Pines." The woman spoke softly.

Throat tight, Tomiko followed the servant across the low, arcing bridge and around a stand of carefully cultivated pines. Beyond lay a modest pavilion painted in imperial greens and golds, its eaves hung with banners bearing the Hantei crest. All the clans seemed to have sent representatives, but Tomiko's eyes drifted over the mottled sea of color, drawn to the orange and yellow that marked the Phoenix.

Her parents were accompanied by a handful of initiates and

guards. Such a small presence would have been perceived as insult had it come from Scorpion or Crane, but the Phoenix had always cultivated a sense of distance. The fact that Kuwashi and Kōrei had come at all was proof of their interest in the young prince.

"The ceremony is about to begin." Like a specter from some peasant fable, Masahiro appeared from the shadows. "Shall we, lady?"

Jaw tight, Tomiko nodded.

Conversation quieted as the ceremonial wood block sounded once, twice, the high drone of priestly chant filling the night. Unable to match Masahiro's easy confidence, Tomiko settled for what she hoped was an air of outward calm. To either side stood some of the most powerful people in Rokugan, their collective regard seeming to squeeze the air from her. It was a battle not to glance at her parents not only for propriety's sake, but out of fear of what she might see upon their faces.

She barely recognized Tokihito. Gone was the red-cheeked boy, his face concealed by a curtain of dangling beads, his gangly limbs lost amidst a sea of embroidered silk. He looked every inch a prince of the Empire, just as Masahiro and his supporters intended.

A line of imperial guards stood at the base of the villa, more arrayed on each of the four broad steps that led to the central platform. The prince was almost alone on the dais, the wide expanse empty but for a pair of imperial heralds, their foreheads pressed to the polished floorboards.

Following Masahiro's lead, Tomiko knelt upon a bamboo mat thoughtfully arranged so she need not dirty her robes.

They bowed low once, twice.

Prince Tokihito was speaking, but Tomiko could barely make out the words over her hammering heart. Dimly, she realized Masahiro had stood, was graciously accepting a calligraphed scroll from one of the Miya heralds. The ceremonial chant seemed a garbled buzz, as if Tomiko listened through rushing water.

"...*representing Heaven's Blaze*." The words cut through the murky babble. With a start, Tomiko looked up to see a young Miya noble attired as Master of Rites standing before her, a large scroll in his hands.

"Lady Isawa Tomiko, we bid you accept this commendation on behalf of your fellow disciple, Shiba Irie, who fell defeating the sorcerous rebellion in the Twilight Mountains." Prince Tokihito spoke as if reciting from a text, his voice planed to smoothness by the demands of court and custom.

Lips buzzing, Tomiko took the scroll – surprised by its lightness. It seemed silly, but somehow she expected an imperial commendation to be *heavier*.

"...with all the rights and honors accorded to such an august title."

And with that the ceremony was over. Bamboo screens were drawn across the front of the pavilion, a processional melody ushering all from the viewing area and back into the garden proper.

"Congratulations," Masahiro whispered as they walked back toward the pines. "You can now claim courtly title, albeit a minor one – Shōsoige, lesser initial rank, lower grade. Still, it is more than most achieve."

Tomiko was spared from having to reply by the appearance

of her parents. They stood along the banks of the wide pond as if admiring the play of moonlight upon the mirrored water. Like everything her parents did, the move was carefully calculated. There was but one way from the viewing pavilion back into the garden.

Even now, they made Tomiko come to them.

"Ambassadors." Masahiro's bow was precise, his greeting warm. "Your presence enlightens this humble evening."

"We were grateful for the invitation," Lady Kuwashi responded smoothly. "Although I would hardly call this occasion humble. Not often do we see a Hantei this far from the Forbidden City."

"I would hardly call it far." Masahiro glanced to the garden's northern wall, over which the towers of the Imperial Palace were clearly visible. "More of a pleasant stroll."

Although Lady Kuwashi's expression did not change, Tomiko knew her mother well enough to sense the mounting coolness in her regard. She glanced at Masahiro, surprised to see the Crane smiling as if he actually *enjoyed* the verbal sparring.

"I must congratulate you on your commendation," Kuwashi continued. "Although I must confess surprise at the company you keep."

"Shiba Irie was instrumental in defeating the dark sorcerers," Masahiro replied. "It is only right that her service to the Empire be recognized."

"I was not speaking to you, Lord Masahiro." Kuwashi turned her pitiless gaze upon Tomiko.

"Apologies, mother." She bowed to hide her flush, taking refuge in civility. "I received the notice just this evening. There was no time to convey a message."

"I'm afraid that is my fault, ambassadors," Masahiro added smoothly. "I only just learned Lady Tomiko was in the city. Irie was… a friend, and I wanted to ensure her dōjō received recognition."

"We are grateful for your diligence." Lady Kuwashi's tone was anything but. "I am sure you have much to attend to, lord. Please, do not let us detain you further."

"Of course." Masahiro inclined his head. Unable to remain without giving offense, he cast a reassuring glance at Tomiko, then continued on down the path, leaving her to the tender mercies of her parents.

"Flame reflected upon gold may shed light, but it offers no warmth." Kōrei spoke for the first time. Although he did not deign to look at Tomiko, her father's rebuke was clear enough.

"We thought you were conducting research," Kuwashi said.

"I was. I am." Tomiko held the gilded scroll before her like a shield. "But one does not refuse an imperial commendation."

Her father sighed. "When accepting a reward, one must look not only at the gift, but the giver."

"You have been away from the capital for many years, daughter." Kuwashi's smile did not reach her eyes. "There are plans in motion, things you do not understand."

"Then *tell* me." Tomiko drew herself up. "I am mistress of Heaven's Blaze and a noble of the Phoenix Clan."

"Exactly." Her mother folded her arms. "Your presence here will cause ripples, lead many to believe our clan supports the child."

Tomiko remembered the prince's shining eyes, his obvious delight as they discussed pillow books and historical romances.

Like a bird imprisoned by propriety, he had been set free to stretch his wings only to find a silver chain of expectation still looped about his leg.

One tug and they were dragged back to the cage.

"And why should we not?" Tomiko's question provoked a genuine blink of surprise from her mother. "Yes, he is young, but there is time to grow into the throne."

"Rokugan requires an oak, not a bonsai, carefully pruned and twisted," her father said.

"You would prefer a tree cultivated by the Phoenix," Tomiko replied.

"I would not have put it so bluntly, but yes," her mother said. "Doji Masahiro is a political opportunist, all smoke and silks." She waved a hand at the gardens. "This is but an illusion. Do not be taken in, child."

And there it was. Her mother had called Tokihito a child, but in truth it was Tomiko she spoke of. No matter what she did, her parents would never trust her, never see her as anything but a disappointment to be managed, guided, hidden away. Tomiko had failed them long ago; that the fault lay in her blood rather than her deeds hardly mattered.

The realization seemed to loosen something within her, the knot that bound her heart all these long years slashed by a single stroke of understanding. She had placed her parents upon a temple dais, her every act calculated to exalt an illusion, an image of Lord Kōrei and Lady Kuwashi that had never truly existed.

For all their power, their wisdom, Tomiko's parents were ultimately human. How could she expect perfection when even the gods were not without flaw?

"It is not that you believe Prince Tokihito beyond our influence," Tomiko said softly. "It is that you believe *I* cannot influence him."

Her parents' silence was rebuke enough.

Although Tomiko drew in a deep breath, the act seemed different, as if she had never truly filled her lungs before.

"I misjudged you both. And for that, I am deeply sorry." She met and held her parents' gazes. "I hope that one day you can forgive me."

Her mother's lips parted, uncharacteristic confusion creasing her brow. She glanced to Tomiko's father, who stood, head cocked, eyes narrowed as if he sought to parse some Shinseist koan.

Whatever reply they might have mustered was preempted by the sound of processional drums. As one, Tomiko and her parents turned to see the imperial palanquin borne from the pavilion. Flanked by Seppun guards in armor of brightly lacquered jade, it progressed down the central garden path, trailed by a small army of attendants and courtiers.

All made way before Prince Tokihito.

Tomiko knelt next to her parents, hands upon her knees, eyes downcast as was proper. Each boom of the drum was echoed by the crunch of sandals on gravel, the guards' steps so precisely timed it seemed as if but one warrior passed rather than scores.

Cymbals rang, all sound seeming to fade along with the echo of their crash. Dimly, Tomiko realized the procession had halted. She stole a glance up only to see the palanquin had halted directly in front of her.

A hand extended from the beaded curtain, beckoning for

her to rise. Tomiko stood on legs that seemed insubstantial as clouds.

"Lady Tomiko, I had hoped to see you again before we departed." Tokihito's voice was somewhere between the lad in the library and the presumptive emperor upon the dais. "I applaud your school's meritorious service and much enjoyed our conversation." The shadow behind the curtain shifted uncomfortably. "Perhaps we might continue the discussion at a later date?"

Tomiko felt as if she might float from the earth. "I would enjoy that very much, prince."

"Excellent." He clapped his hands and the procession continued on.

Tomiko knelt once more, the heat of her parents' curiosity bonfire bright at either side. Almost by reflex, her gaze found Masahiro. The Crane knelt near the mansion gate next to a pinch-faced noble in Otomo green. Tradition bid that they ritually thank the prince for his presence. Even so, Masahiro spared a glance for Tomiko, his expression one of distinct bemusement as he mouthed a single word.

"*How*?"

No doubt the same question was foremost in Lord Kōrei's and Lady Kuwashi's thoughts.

Tomiko returned little more than an enigmatic smile. Her friends and family might be powerful, clever, well-connected.

But they did not need to know *everything*.

CHAPTER TWENTY

The Imperial City teemed. Compared to the mountain towns of the Dragon Clan, Naoki had always found Rokugan's capital noisy and crowded, but the impending imperial succession had filled the city to bursting. The outer districts swarmed with merchants, traders, and entertainers of every stripe. While Naoki's magisterial credentials could see her, Seiji, and Akoya through the high crystal arch of the Enchanted Wall's southern gate, it did nothing to part the sea of high nobility that swamped the wide streets of the Inner City.

Naoki's first hope was to find Masahiro, a search that proved more difficult than expected. Prickly nobles refused to yield the road, leading to more than a few scuffles and no doubt several duels. At Akoya's suggestion they left their horses at an imperial guard post, as it proved quicker to walk.

Naoki and her companions spent the better part of the afternoon navigating the garden-lined avenues of the District of Sagacity only to be informed by a harried Crane majordomo that Doji Masahiro had vacated his embassy suite in favor of a manor on the *other* side of the Inner City.

Lady Akoya received this news with the thin-lipped grimace of a soldier marching through a torrential downpour. For his part, Seiji seemed hardly to notice, his gaze fixed upon the wealth of elegant manors and shrines that were spread around. When they had first entered the city, Naoki asked about the bell, but the Crab architect had only shaken his head.

"Close, but muffled. I cannot seem to find my bearings."

Distinctly unsettled, Naoki had bid Seiji keep at it, but the Crab seemed more interested in walls and spires than tracking the location of dark sorcerers. Recalling a similar sense of awe from her first visit to the capital, Naoki resolved to let Seiji enjoy the moment. There would be time enough for trouble once they had found Masahiro.

The Inner City became more overwhelming by the moment, sights, sounds, and smells of countless people combining into a jagged tumult that set Naoki on edge. More than once she was forced to duck into a side street, eyes squeezed shut, hands on knees as she forced her breathing to slow. She could tell the stops frustrated Akoya, but thankfully the Lion noble held her tongue.

At last, they reached the elegantly carved gates of the manor. Situated near the walls of the Forbidden City, it was a testament to Masahiro's wealth and connections that he held such a large residence. Two somber Daidoji warded the main entrance. Spears in hand, their blue lacquered armor gleaming in the late afternoon sun, they could have been a mosaic.

Memory of Kakita Tsutomu's accursed artworks sent an unconscious prickle up Naoki's neck. Fortunately, the guards were more welcoming than Iuchiban's tomb. Once she had made introductions and presented her magisterial seal, they were ushered into one of the many villas that dotted the manor's prodigious gardens. Naoki could not but be surprised by the décor – a profusion of Hantei green and the imperial chrysanthemum crest. Apparently Masahiro remained hard at work pressing Prince Tokihito's claim to the Emerald Throne.

The servants had barely arrived with tea and cakes when the Crane himself came hurrying from the central manor, a pair of well-armed guards close behind. Underneath the robes and carefully applied makeup, Masahiro looked positively haggard, sleepless shadows beneath his eyes.

"Naoki!" In defiance of all propriety Masahiro embraced her, a move that surprised none so much as Naoki herself. After extricating herself from the Crane's grip she took a quick step back, regarding Masahiro.

"You've been busy." She nodded at the drapery dangling from the villa's eaves.

"You have *no* idea." Masahiro drifted to his knees. With a wave, he dismissed the servants, then arched an eyebrow at Naoki's companions.

"Lady Matsu Akoya I know by reputation." He gave a solemn bow. "My sincerest condolences concerning your family members. I did not have the pleasure of meeting Katamori, but if Chiaki was any indication, he must have been truly formidable."

Although Akoya acknowledged the Crane's sympathy, her wary expression did not waver.

Masahiro seemed unperturbed by the Lion's scrutiny, turning to Seiji. "And who is this fine young fellow?"

"Kuni Seiji." Naoki gave the Crab an encouraging smile.

"A witch hunter?" Masahiro sounded distinctly relieved.

Seiji glanced away. "Actually, I am an architect."

"But he is guided by the bell," Naoki said. "Just as Tetsuo was."

The smile fell from Masahiro's face. "Then Tetsuo is…"

"Gone," Seiji replied.

"I had rather hoped he and the others might have actually succeeded." Masahiro turned to catch the nearest guard's attention. "Bring Lady Tomiko. She will want to hear this."

"Tomiko?" Naoki frowned, trying to place the name. "Where have I heard that before?"

"A disciple of Heaven's Blaze, like Shiba Irie." Masahiro nodded. "She also seeks Bloodspeakers. A fine elementalist in her own right, and *far* more reasonable than our dear departed friend – no insult to the dead."

Akoya gave an angry grunt, her tone one of barely restrained anger. "*You* were the one my master died to save?"

"To be fair, Chiaki saved our dear magistrate's life as well."

The Lion lord's scowl only deepened, but rather than be irritated by Akoya's apparent disdain, Masahiro seemed to soften, his mask of conceited courtesy replaced by a flicker of genuine sorrow.

"Apologies for my uncharitable response. Chiaki was…" He shook his head, then sighed. "An example I can only hope to match. I owe her more than my life."

Akoya seemed surprised, not by Masahiro's words, but by the honest emotion with which they were delivered. She seemed about to reply, but the arrival of Isawa Tomiko preempted further discussion.

The Phoenix priest was dressed in courtly robes of

understated, if obvious quality. Although Tomiko carried herself like the mistress of a dōjō, there was a tightness in her bearing, a nervous desperation in her eyes that Naoki remembered well. Shiba Irie had looked much the same. As if she had gazed upon true darkness and found her heart a mirror.

Tomiko's arrival necessitated introductions, terse bows exchanged all around.

"She can be trusted," Masahiro said, nodding at Naoki's companions. "Am I to assume the same of them?"

"Yes," she answered without hesitation.

"Have you told them of the tomb and of…" Masahiro drew in a shaky breath. "*Him.*"

Naoki nodded. "They know all I do."

"Then I welcome you to our doomed fellowship." Masahiro favored them with a thin smile before turning back to Naoki. "What have you learned?"

"Little enough." She sighed. "The High Histories held almost nothing. There were records, but they had been picked through, all reference to Iuchiban removed."

"Could Bloodspeakers have stolen the documents?" Tomiko asked.

"All are sealed behind guards and wards," Akoya said. "Only the emperor or someone bearing his personal seal can order records purged."

"Why would the Hantei protect a creature like Iuchiban?" Masahiro asked.

"That is the question," Naoki replied. "We sought answers in the Twilight Mountains, hoping to find some lingering evidence of Iuchiban's plans." She swallowed. "What we found was an army of dead."

"My family will deal with them," Seiji said. "But the ancestors tell me their source lies here."

"On that we agree." Masahiro drew in a shaky breath, meeting Naoki's gaze. "Shosuro Gensuke lives. Well, actually, it might be more accurate to say he walks – a purely semantic distinction. What's important is that he *kills*." He winced. "At least one high noble I'm aware of, and certainly others. Both Tomiko and I barely survived his attentions."

Naoki did not try to conceal her surprise. "I saw him chopped to pieces in the Chamber of Even Blades."

Masahiro made a face. "We face sorcerers who excel in raising the dead and your first question is how one of our companions is up and about?"

Naoki ignored the barb. "What of the others? Could Tetsuo, Irie, and Qadan be among our foes?"

"Tetsuo will not rise again." It was Seiji who answered.

"And you know this how?" Masahiro asked.

The Crab shrugged. "The same way I know this city reeks of dark magic."

"Fair point." Masahiro nodded. "So I expect you can lead us right to the sorcerer?"

Seiji looked to his hands. "It's not that simple."

"For once, I was truly hoping it would be." Masahiro ran a hand through his pale hair.

"If Irie survived the tomb, she may be corrupted," Tomiko said softly. Seemingly discomfited by the others' attention, she glanced at Masahiro, who returned a quick nod.

"What aren't you telling us?" Akoya asked.

"My former master, Asako Masatsuge, was a Bloodspeaker. I fear Irie was as well." Although Tomiko's confession was calm, almost resigned, its effect on the others was anything but.

Akoya was on her feet in an eye blink, Seiji close behind. The Crab's youthful features twisted in a look of intense concentration as if he might peer into the Phoenix priest's heart. Even Naoki found herself reaching for her jitte, surprise giving way to disbelief. Shiba Irie had traveled with them, *fought* with them. Her powers had been instrumental in breaching Iuchiban's tomb. It seemed impossible she was corrupt.

And yet Naoki could not but recall how Irie had changed as they delved deeper into the corrupt maze. She had thought the Phoenix's hollow eyes merely the result of strain. Except Irie had behaved differently as well – guarded, almost furtive. At the time Naoki had suspected nothing, but Tomiko's revelation raised a host of doubts.

"Explain, priest." Naoki glanced at her companions. "And quickly."

"Why should we trust anything she says?" Akoya asked.

"I trust her," Masahiro said.

"Not a ringing endorsement," Akoya replied.

"She is... not corrupt." Seiji seemed surprised by his admission. "I sense no blood sorcery in Tomiko."

"The Bloodspeakers are adept at hiding their influence," Naoki replied, her thoughts still churning. "Kuni Tetsuo also possessed your abilities and he sensed no corruption in Irie."

At that, Tomiko let out a relieved sigh. "I hoped as much, but Irie and Masatsuge were very close."

"And just how close were *you* to Masatsuge?" Akoya asked.

"I possess not even a shadow of Irie's ability." The Phoenix gave a sad shake of her head. "If not for my family name, I would have never risen beyond the rank of initiate." She looked away, seemingly embarrassed by the admission. "I do not know how far Masatsuge's corruption spread, but as mistress of *Heaven's Blaze*, it is my duty to root it out."

"Fine words, Phoenix. I would very much like to believe them," Akoya said. "But words are like silk – they can conceal as well as reveal."

"You sound like my father." Tomiko's smile was not at all amused.

Masahiro cleared his throat. "Before we start flinging accusations, let us not forget that Gensuke tried his best to murder Tomiko. I find it hard to believe even the Bloodspeakers could arrange such a fortuitous coincidence."

"I believe Masahiro," Naoki said, glancing at Seiji, who returned a slow nod.

"So do I."

Naoki regarded the Akoya. "A wise woman once told me there is more to battle than blades."

Although Akoya's scowl did not waver, her fists did. With a shake of her head, she sat, legs crossed, hands resting on her knees.

"It seems you are an ally, Lady Tomiko," the Lion General said. "For the moment, at least."

Tomiko gave a graceful bow. "I shall do all I can to earn your trust."

Akoya returned the Phoenix's genuflection, if a bit stiffly. "I hope you do."

"So." Naoki raised a hand, fingers spread as she ticked off points. "We still know nothing new concerning Iuchiban's plans, nor of the sorcerer himself. There are Bloodspeakers in the Imperial City led by an undead assassin. The very fact they entered the Inner Districts speaks to corruption in the imperial bureaucracy, perhaps the clans as well. And one of Rokugan's most famous Asako priests was a Bloodspeaker." Glancing at her closed fist, Naoki winced. "Do you have any *good* news?"

"Prince Tokihito's ascension is proceeding as planned," Masahiro said. "We made many allies at the party a few days ago. Emperor Hantei XXVI does not seem likely to regain consciousness. The healers give him days, weeks at most." He glanced at Tomiko. "Our Phoenix friend made quite an impression on the young prince. We need but persevere, and soon every hand in Rokugan will turn against Iuchiban."

"I just wish we knew what he planned." Naoki massaged the back of her neck, wincing. "Or why all mention of Iuchiban has been removed from every official record."

"One of my old friends is a senior archivist of the High Histories," Akoya said. "Even now she searches Rokugan for more records – diaries, letters, perhaps even personal accounts."

"They would be two centuries old, at least," Masahiro said. "Very little survives that is not preserved in the archives. We might find a letter or two in some daimyō's collection, but without knowing where to look, your friend is searching blind."

The room drifted to sullen silence as Naoki's companions considered their next step. Naoki could not blame them for such brooding contemplation; she was a magistrate, one of two survivors of Iuchiban's tomb – and even she could see no clear path forward.

"What about pillow books?" Tomiko asked.

"Romances and adventure tales?" Akoya frowned. "Such fables cannot be trusted."

"Many were written by noblewomen and based on personal experience." Although Tomiko's cheeks reddened, the Phoenix persisted. "It's widely believed Lady Shion was an Otomo noble, perhaps even a minister. Her novels display an insider's perspective on court."

Masahiro sucked air through his teeth. "Courtly romances are a far cry from historical record."

"It cannot hurt to look," Tomiko said. "There is a large collection in this very manor."

"The Peony Chamber." Masahiro gave a sad smile. "A relic of better times, certainly, but I doubt it holds the answers we seek."

"I agree with Tomiko," Naoki said, surprising even herself. "The official records have been scrubbed clean, but if the imperial censors held pillow books in similar low regard, they might not have even thought to look."

"Let us look then." At Masahiro's call, the villa's outer screen slid aside, a kneeling Daidoji guard just beyond.

"Inform the servants we shall be taking dinner in the Peony Chamber." Brushing a bit of dust from his robe with the stump of his missing hand, Masahiro turned to Naoki and the others. "We might be sprinting toward a bloody end, but I'll be damned if I die on an empty stomach."

CHAPTER TWENTY-ONE

Kuni Seiji had always wanted to visit the Imperial City, but not like this, never like this. The outer districts favored form over function, wood and stucco, slate shingles and thatch, the occasional roof of glazed tiles standing out amidst the wild riot of structures. Streets crossed and doubled back with little regard for balance, the whole ramshackle sprawl seeming to have sprung up like spring grass.

The Crab had cities and castle towns all designed with an eye toward defense. The buildings there were sturdy and stolid, mostly stone or reinforced wood with small windows and heavy bolted doors. Seiji had learned to find beauty in sharp angles and thick stone walls, his clan's aesthetic shaped by their long, lonely struggle to ward the Empire's southern borders against the steady creep of shadow.

Even so, the outer districts seemed almost to invite assault, not a wall or choke point to be seen, some buildings so rickety it looked as if a strong breeze might topple them. Like a forest though, fallen trees merely opened the way for new growth.

Despite the numerous flaws in its construction, the outer districts had a lively, colorful aspect that Seiji wished he could appreciate beyond how difficult it would be to defend.

By contrast, the Inner City seemed plucked from an architectural primer. Seiji had read of the Enchanted Wall and pored over architectural sketches of the great crystal arch that warded the southern gate, but even the most talented artists could not do the structure justice. The broad curve of crystal refracted Lady Sun's light into a panoply of colors so vibrant that for a moment, Seiji was able to claw back some small measure of wonder from his ancestors' clutches.

Beyond, the Inner Districts spread like the petals of a chrysanthemum, nested spires, offices, and manors rendered in a hundred different styles. Seiji glanced past a row of passing palanquins to see a nearby temple sporting a ninth century Miko school façade on what appeared to be a stepped pavilion designed in the Falling Water style. Further on sat a sprawling manor, its walls clearly of Crab design, the columned portico and sharply canted roof reminiscent of a Dragon Clan mountain temple.

Even confronted by such brilliant architectural juxtaposition, Seiji felt nothing. He could respect the designers' cleverness, the skill of wood joinery so precise the beams fit together like interlaced fingers, but he could never again exalt in it as he once did.

The bell had faded to a low tone, the slow, steady rhythm seeming to echo from all around, as if muffled by heavy fabric. Although the sound was soothing, almost pleasant, Seiji had little doubt the ancestors would not hesitate to castigate him should he falter in his search.

The Kuni had many admirable qualities, but mercy was not among them.

"Find anything?" Naoki glanced up from the novel spread upon her lap, one of perhaps a score they had pulled from the collection. Despite her severe bearing, the Phoenix elementalist seemed to possess a surprisingly extensive knowledge of literature, selecting tomes by authors alive the last time Iuchiban inflicted his vile attentions upon Rokugan.

"Not yet." Seiji tried to focus upon the novel once more, but the prose was simply too flowery. Where once he might have enjoyed allusions to ancient poems and artistic assignations, now they flitted through his thoughts like a tepid breeze – fleeting and impossible to grasp. None of the characters acted as real people would, enmeshed in a web of romance, rivalry, and duels.

Seiji might have enjoyed the absurdity of it all, but the ancestors had no time for frivolity.

"I think I have found something." Tomiko raised a book, displaying an elegantly calligraphed page. "In *The Thousand Springs of Lady Wisteria*, there's mention of a dark sorcerer called 'the Gatherer' stealing an accursed ruby from the Imperial Treasury and using it to collect the souls of the dead."

"And…?" Doji Masahiro set his scroll aside.

Tomiko rifled through the pages. "That is all."

"Wait." Naoki turned to the books spread around her. "One of these mentioned a ruby." Frowning, she selected a crimson-bound book of poetry and quickly searched its pages.

Falling maple leaves,

Hearts' blood shed upon cold stone.
Souls in ruby chains.

Masahiro gave a dubious frown. "It does mention blood, I suppose."

"It is part of an exchange between a courtesan and the minister seeking to impress her. The style is…" Naoki winced. "Unrefined. But there might be more of import, listen."

Deeds that blister tongues
Gathered names like crimson plague
Purged by stricken page

"And here." She turned the page, voice almost a whisper.

Ignorance is shield
Horrors twisting in bright pyres
Not only dead burn

Masahiro looked distinctly uncomfortable. "Does that mean what I think it does?"

"I thought it the bragging of a self-important noble. But if the author speaks of Iuchiban…" Naoki looked to Akoya. "Your archivist friend said only the emperor could order records destroyed. Perhaps he did."

"But why?" Akoya rested a hand upon the pommel of her blade, as if to steady herself.

Naoki shook her head. "The poems do not say."

"There was a 'Gatherer' mentioned in one of Kakita Kibyōshi's satires." Tomiko looked through the stacks, selecting a thin, yellow-backed book – little more than a woodblock pamphlet, its print faded with age.

"Here." She spread the pages carefully to reveal a rather unsettling figure. Attired in a monk's dark robes, its face wreathed in shadow but for a wide, jagged smile, it leered up at the towers of the Imperial Palace.

"'With cavernous grin, the Gatherer exhumes a moonlight revel,'" she read. "'We nameless actors but play our part.'"

Staring at the pages, Seiji realized what he had thought were shadows was a horde of creatures. They crawled from below, as if the underworld had opened beneath the city. Neither demons nor hook-nosed goblins, their outline was the gangly, long-limbed shapes of hungry ghosts, but rather than the traditional red-tongued maw, they wore leering theater masks.

"Dark sorcery, armies of walking dead." Masahiro drew in a breath, eyes wide as silver coins as he pointed at the grinning sorcerer upon the page. "If that isn't Iuchiban, it is as close as we shall ever find. That demon must have emptied every crypt in the Imperial City."

Akoya gave a low grunt. "Luckily we burn our dead now."

"Not all of them." Tomiko spoke as if the words could cut. Quiet as it was, the admission seemed to suck the air from the Peony Chamber.

Akoya shifted with a creak of leather harness. "What do you know, Phoenix?"

"There may be bodies in the city. Smuggled by the Bloodspeakers who worked with my old master." Her hands bunched the fabric of her robes. "Hidden in crates and oil barrels – hundreds at least, perhaps more. I tracked the transactions to the docks, but all I found were empty warehouses and abandoned stores."

"I sensed nothing." Seiji could not hide his frustration. The bell had led him to the capital surely enough only to fade to a muffled, directionless chime once he was finally here. Perhaps its grip on him weakened the farther they were from the Crab's ancestral lands? The thought was both heartening and disconcerting.

"Why didn't you think to mention the horde of masked abominations festering under our feet?" Masahiro asked.

"I would have spoken, but I could not be sure any remained." Tomiko looked down. "And your trust in me was already tenuous."

Masahiro seemed about to say more, but Naoki raised a hand. "Now is not the time for recriminations. If there are corpses in the city, we must find them."

"We should inform the Imperial Guard," Akoya said.

"Oh, that will certainly help matters." Masahiro threw up his arms. "Patrols tromping around the streets searching for walking corpses and dark sorcerers. How will the clans react to that? How will the people? You've seen the mood out there. This city is a pile of oil-soaked tinder; one wrong word will set the whole place alight."

"I have to agree." Naoki blew out a long sigh. "If we knew where the dead were, I wouldn't hesitate. But too many questions remain."

Seiji looked around to see troubled faces; silence seemed to press in all around as his companions turned to their own dire considerations.

The bell chimed, distant, unfocused, as if the echo

rebounded from the high buildings. Seiji wished with all his might for the ancestors to pierce the clinging murk, but either they could not or would not.

"If I could get closer." He spoke more from the need to break the silence than any real solution.

"The capital is vast." Masahiro made a broad gesture with his remaining hand. "It would take weeks to search even without the crowds."

"But where might hundreds of corpses hide?" Naoki asked.

"Anywhere." The Crane shrugged. "Everywhere."

"The Crystal Arch would prevent such foulness from entering the Inner City," Seiji said.

"If they came from the south," Masahiro replied. "The northern gate along the Road of Fast Hopes is somewhat less rigorously warded. All it takes is a well-placed bribe or a well-placed friend. Walking corpses would raise alarms, oil barrels on a rich and connected merchant's cart..." He gave a low whistle. "Unlikely to be searched."

"What of the arcane protections?" Tomiko asked. "Surely they would warn of dark sorcery."

"If the dead were animated, certainly," Naoki said. "But corpses are neither good nor evil. If the wards reacted to dead flesh, guards would be searching every fish delivery and side of pork."

A pall seemed to descend upon the assembled group, as if the bleakness of their predicament had suddenly snapped into sharp focus.

Seiji found his gaze drawn to the yellow-backed book, the hair prickling along his arms as he regarded the ancient satirist's depiction of Iuchiban. Its jagged smile reminded him of the Shadowlands, ragged chasms carved by the fallen god's horrifying rage.

"Is there a rift in the city?" Seiji asked. "A crater or crevasse, perhaps?"

"There are several sinkholes in the outer city," Masahiro said. "Near the docks where the ground is softer. The autumn rains can swallow entire houses. In the Inner City..." He tapped his chin, considering. "There is Oni's Smile in the District of Fortitude. A rather ill-favored place if I do recall, and not only because it hosts the Crab Embassy."

Seiji's excitement overwhelmed any irritation over the Crane's casual insult. "Take me there."

"At this hour?" Masahiro asked.

"Yes." Seiji pushed to his feet, confidence buttressed by duty. "At this hour."

"Of course." Masahiro's smile did not reach his eyes. "I'll summon my guards."

"The last thing we need is a squad of Daidoji martinets stamping across the city." Akoya spoke in clipped tones. "Their squawking would announce our presence more surely than war drums."

"You wound me, Lady Matsu." Masahiro pressed a hand to his chest, feigning hurt feelings.

"Better sharp words than a sharp blade," she replied.

The Crane raised his right arm, displaying the smooth skin where his right hand had once been. "I lost this fighting in Iuchiban's tomb. It is not blades that concern me."

Any other Matsu might have bristled at the rebuke, but Akoya merely nodded. "Apologies. I should not have questioned your courage."

The admission seemed to take even Masahiro aback. His throat bobbed. "It seems I misjudged you, lady."

"I take no insult," Akoya replied with a shrug. "In absence of experience, we privilege names. Matsu, Doji, Lion, Crane – they carry weight, for good and ill."

Before Masahiro could reply, Akoya turned away, her eyes bright now that she had something to plan. "We travel quickly, quietly. The goal is only to gather information, not engage."

"And if they wish to engage us?" Tomiko asked.

"*Then* we summon the guards." Akoya chuckled.

Naoki touched Seiji's arm. "Can you sense the Bloodspeakers if we get closer?"

"I think so, yes." He nodded to hide the tremor in his voice. While Seiji was sure the ancestors would not fail him, he was not as confident of living up to their expectations.

"Then let us go," Naoki said.

The magistrate's approval seemed to decide the issue. Masahiro dismissed his guards, then called servants to re-shelve the books.

Rather than depart through the front gate, they slipped from a back entrance like thieves, hurrying along the alleys that threaded between the manors of the high and mighty. Although not as crowded as during the day, the streets of the Inner City were far from deserted – servants, couriers, and even the occasional lord's palanquin all went about their business.

Traffic tapered off as they approached the District of Fortitude, shadows growing as the lamps grew farther and farther apart. Seiji knew the district housed his clan's embassy, but while the high stone walls of that austere structure shone with lantern light, his kin seemed less concerned about the surroundings. Here and there a theater or teahouse blazed like torches, the darkness around seeming somehow deeper by comparison.

Seiji heard the Oni's Smile long before he saw it. The hollow chime of the bell grew clearer, as if it echoed from the depths of the wide abyss. Bamboo fences warded either side of the crevasse, no doubt erected to stop drunks and sightseers from stumbling too close.

He cocked his head, trying to parse the bell's loudness and direction.

Masahiro made a small, disgusted noise in the back of his throat. "I suppose we're going down there, aren't we?"

"Afraid you'll dirty your robes, Crane?" Akoya's tone was almost playful.

Masahiro's expression was a study of wounded dignity. "Actually, yes."

That dragged an actual chuckle from the Lion.

"Quiet," Naoki said, gesturing to Seiji. "Can you hear anything?"

Drawing in a deep breath, he closed his eyes, arms outstretched as if feeling along in the dark. The bell rang – once, twice, again – every chime echoed by Seiji's quiet footfalls. He had expected it to lead him down, but instead he rounded the lip of the crevasse, trailing fingers along the smooth boards of the rail.

At last he stopped. Turning his back to the Oni's Smile, Seiji opened his eyes to see the walls of a large, if somewhat dilapidated, manor. Plaster peeled from the stone, beams savaged by wind and rain. Even in the dark, Seiji could see a half-dozen places where a solid kick would bring a wall tumbling down. No lanterns burned in its windows, not even a candle glimmered in shadowed alcoves.

"Do you know who dwells here?" Seiji looked to Masahiro.

He pursed his lips. "No one of rank."

Akoya craned her neck, eyes canny. "I don't see any guards."

"There are no wards," Tomiko said. "At least on the outer walls."

"Then let us see what lays inside." Naoki drew her jitte. Approaching the manor gate, she gathered herself as if to put a shoulder to it. Seiji and Akoya hastened to add their strength only to find the rickety wooden door unbarred.

The creak of rusty hinges announced their entrance into an overgrown garden. The remains of stone paths were barely visible under the thicket of autumn-browned weeds, the whole reeking of rotting vegetation. They picked their way across the garden, Akoya taking the lead, Seiji and Naoki close behind.

The portico was missing steps, its boards warped and bowed. Seiji held up a hand, inspecting the columns. Despite the manor's shabby state, it seemed remarkably solid. Satisfied that the roof would not collapse on them, he nodded for the others to continue.

Inside, the odors of dust and mildew were almost overpowering, a sharp stench that made every breath a chore. Their lanterns revealed torn screens and tattered mats, the remains of a child's doll lying carelessly in a scroll alcove. If not for the ringing of the bell, Seiji would have guessed the manor unoccupied for years, but the Kuni ancestors did not equivocate. There was dark magic here, Seiji was sure of it.

They drifted through a score of empty rooms, silent as stalking cats. But the manor seemed reluctant to give up its secrets.

"That's the whole of it." Akoya shook her head, rebuke implicit in her frustrated tone. She looked to Seiji, but he could only shake his head. The bell rang in his thoughts, urgent but directionless.

He clenched his jaw against the useless clamor. Whatever darkness lurked within this manor had been concealed from the ancestors as well. Perhaps the Kuni were not as all-knowing as they appeared. Force and tenacity would avail them nothing. The manor's structural secrets would not be revealed by samurai or spiritualist.

But an architect...

Seiji lifted his lantern, squinting as if to winnow secrets from the peeling walls. But the manor seemed relentlessly mundane; even its construction was devoid of the artistic flourishes Seiji expected from the Inner City. Every notable aspect of the structure had been worn smooth by the succession of years and owners.

That, or it had been made to *appear* commonplace.

Seiji studied the place – beams and joists at regular angles, its creaking floorboards braced by latticed supports. Like many Rokugani manors it was raised above the ground to allow for air to flow beneath, combatting high summer heat and humidity.

Seiji knelt to lay a hand against the floor and found the wood wet with condensation – something that should not have occurred with adequate ventilation. Conscious of his companions' gazes, he frowned at the support beams, seeking places where they should have sunk through the floor. With the tip of his blade, he dug a bit of the rotted board away only to find that the support beam did not continue through the floor, but only appeared to.

It was as if the whole manor were a façade erected to hide the shabbiness of a small storefront. Only this structure was meant to direct attention *away*.

Standing, he stomped upon the floor. Instead of a hollow thump, his boot made a muffled thud as if the floor rested directly upon stone and earth.

"There is something below." Seiji turned to his companions. "A passage, maybe a stair. Search the floor for a hollow space."

They spread out, poking at the rotting wood with blades and boots.

"Here!" Tomiko's call brought everyone hurrying over. She stood upon a raised dais in what would have been the lord's sitting room. Grinning, the Phoenix priest brought a foot down, the boards giving a hollow thump.

Chest tight with apprehension, Seiji joined Akoya in tearing up the moldering wood to reveal a stone stair beneath. He could almost feel the ancestors' grip on him shift. Not approval, *never* approval, but recognition that perhaps Seiji's studies might not have been wholly useless.

Wrinkling his nose, Masahiro peered down the darkened stairwell. "Looks like we're going down after all."

The stair was broad enough for two, so Seiji and Akoya took the lead, blades at the ready. They found nothing but more steps, perhaps two hundred leading down to a rusty iron door etched with a curling web of arcane symbols Seiji did not recognize. Dark magic seemed to infect the very air, the bell loud but distorted, as if it echoed through murky water.

"Those wards are steeped in blood." Tomiko confirmed everyone's suspicions.

"Can you bypass them?" Naoki asked.

"I can try." The Phoenix pushed back her sleeves. Stepping forward to lay a hand upon the door, she whispered prayers and exhortations, breath steaming in air gone suddenly chill. Sweat beaded on Tomiko's forehead, her face screwed up as if the chant was causing physical pain. Abruptly she gasped, swaying as if drunk, her legs loose as old rope. Seiji stepped forward to catch the priest before she fell and found Tomiko's skin clammy as a plague victim's.

"It's all right. We can find someone else to–" He began, only to be silenced by the aggrieved squeal of iron as the door swung open.

"Thank you." Tomiko smiled at Seiji as she extricated herself from his arms. "The weakness has passed."

They gazed into the darkened chamber beyond, nothing more than a bare expanse of stone visible in the small pool of lantern light.

Seiji looked to the others, receiving grim nods in return.

Carefully they entered the chamber, a tight knot bristling with blades, ready for something to leap from the shadows.

The chamber was empty. Perhaps twenty paces on a side, it appeared to be carved from bedrock, the walls barren but for a darkened hall at the rear. Above the opening a circular symbol was carved into the stone.

Lifting his lantern, Seiji saw a lattice of intertwining lines, like a web or crawling ivy, threads circling and overlapping in a pattern both beautiful and unsettling.

"That's the sigil of the Shosuro family," Akoya said. "What would the Scorpion be doing down here?"

"Not *the* Scorpion, *a* Scorpion." Naoki's voice was grim.

"Akifumi." Masahiro spoke the name like a curse, already backing toward the stairs. "Not again. Not again."

"What does this mean?" Akoya's question was drowned by a threatening rumble. A slab of heavy stone detached from the ceiling, sealing the entrance behind several tons of rock. It happened too quickly for Seiji to do more than dive away from the crashing stone, a surprised cry sharp on his lips.

Although none were hit, the resulting cloud of dust was such that the chamber was filled with coughing and curses for several long moments. Fortunately, the stone slab seemed to mark the extent of the entry chamber's malignancy.

"Only one way out." Akoya glanced around the chamber once the dust had settled. "Sealed in this damned vault."

"This is no vault." Naoki's tone sent an icy prickle along Seiji's neck. Her gaze crawled to the Shosuro crest above the tunnel entrance.

"It is a tomb."

CHAPTER TWENTY-TWO

Gensuke thought he would enjoy watching the man who killed him suffer, but now that Doji Masahiro and the others were finally trapped in Akifumi's workshop, the only emotion he felt was a vague sense of disappointment.

"Why not end it? They're at your mercy." He kept his voice flat, like he was reading from a tax record. Gensuke had found it was the best way to keep his corrupted ancestor's attention.

"Mercy. Yes, exactly." Akifumi leaned over the polished obsidian bowl, his withered face unreadable as he studied the image in the rippling blood.

Gensuke glanced down to see Masahiro slap the slab blocking the exit, as if he could shatter the stone through sheer force of pique.

"Anger." Akifumi's bloodless lips twitched. "Resignation."

The Crane slumped to the ground, arms around his legs, forehead resting upon his knees. They were all speaking at once, but unfortunately the sorcerer's bloody divination conveyed only images.

"Acceptance." Although barely a whisper, Akifumi's pronouncement seemed to summon Naoki from the murky shadows. The magistrate was speaking, hands waving to punctuate her point. The Lion samurai stepped to her side, followed soon by Crab and Phoenix. They made a loose semicircle around Masahiro.

Despite his lofty ambitions, Masahiro had always seemed a practical sort. So Gensuke was not surprised when the Crane eventually stood, following his companions down the long hall and into Akifumi's workshop.

The first chamber was tiled in black and white squares, its walls speckled with holes from which darts could fire. They studied the swirl of ceramic tiles for a pattern – exactly what Gensuke would have done had he not known there was none. The white and black squares were placed at random, stepping on either would cause a dart to fire, unpleasant but far from deadly.

Gensuke had spent days rigging the bellows, pressure plates, and tubes that would propel the small razor-tipped arrows. It had not been hard to guess Akifumi's goal. Black and white, good and evil, interchangeable depending on one's perspective.

The trick was to step on *both*.

The young Crab samurai took a dart in the arm and Naoki barely avoided one in her cheek before they figured out the pattern. They crossed the chamber, hopping like toads as they sought to tread upon both sets of tiles.

Quite humorous, had Gensuke been in the mood for jokes.

He peered into the blood, hoping the others took a moment to examine the darts. Gensuke's unbeating heart shriveled as the Crab tossed his aside.

Then Naoki bent to retrieve it, frowning down at the tiny words Gensuke had etched onto the wooden shaft.

Like any good assassin, he had spent weeks searching for holes in Akifumi's defenses, discovering that while the ancient sorcerer's commands could not be disobeyed, they could be subverted.

Gensuke had known Akifumi would be watching Masahiro and the others. What he had *not* known was how closely. His gaze flicked to the ancient Bloodspeaker, but Akifumi appeared more interested in the series of levers and pulleys on the wall beside the scrying bowl.

Naoki showed the dart to the others, their conversation blessedly inaudible. Gensuke prayed they would finish before Akifumi's attention returned to the crimson image.

Akifumi pulled one of several wooden levers. With a rattle of invisible chains, the whole workshop began to vibrate, dust trickling from the ceiling. The effect on Masahiro and the others was almost instantaneous. Once the last rumble of stone had faded, they set to arguing.

Gensuke could well understand his former companions' concerns. Such sounds were reminiscent of Iuchiban's tomb, where grinding had presaged a rearrangement of the cruel labyrinth. Of course, the rooms in Akifumi's workshop were not capable of such movement, but its potential victims did not know that.

A series of branching corridors created a similar illusion. Designed to disorient and confuse, no matter which was chosen, all led to the same destination. The twisting halls might have been meant to represent the inevitability of death, or perhaps the meaninglessness of life. Gensuke didn't much care.

Hundreds of heavy chains hung from the ceiling of the chamber beyond, each fitted with a set of manacles. Although several barred doors led from the room, the halls beyond each were packed with masked dead. The face of each door was carved to resemble one of the Celestial Realms, the dead behind attired in theater costumes, dressed as spirits, demons, even high divinities.

Of course, none of the doors led to salvation.

After some discussion, Naoki opened the door leading to the Realm of Waiting. In poured a flood of dead in funerary robes, their masks painted to resemble slack and bloodless faces.

Although individually the walking corpses were no match for even Masahiro's off-handed slashes, there were simply too many. The Lion and Crab samurai formed a tight bulwark against the sea of clutching hands, the Phoenix priest stepping up to unleash a fan of flame that set robes burning and skin crackling. Although less powerful than the conflagrations Gensuke had seen Shiba Irie unleash in Iuchiban's tomb, it was sufficient to clear a path for Naoki and Masahiro to dart forward and shoulder the door shut, slamming the bar back into place one-handed.

Dubiously, they studied the other doors.

"*Chains. Look at the chains.*" Gensuke mouthed the words, lips hidden behind the cruel mask.

Akifumi leaned over the bowl like a child entranced by a shadow play, the bowl's crimson-hued glow casting his aged features in bloody relief.

After brief discussion, they approached the door leading to the underworld. Gensuke could not help it as his hands tightened on the lip of the bowl.

Then Masahiro called out, holding up one of the manacles. The others gathered around, studying not only the shackle, but the message Gensuke had painstakingly scratched on the inside of each one.

Again he swallowed a sigh of relief. The image in the bloody obsidian bowl was too hazy to distinguish any symbols upon the iron.

Akifumi gave a suspicious frown as Naoki drew the inscribed dart from her sash, but the sorcerer said nothing as, after an animated discussion, the group fastened the manacles upon their wrists. The ceiling withdrew into the walls, revealing that the chains continued up into the vaulted darkness.

To ascend, one must submit.

At the pull of another of Akifumi's levers, invisible winches turned, winding the chains and the individuals locked to them up into shadow.

Perhaps forty feet above the false ceiling, grinding gears promised a slow and gruesome death. However, a stone balcony extended into the vertical tunnel. Masahiro was the first to swing toward it, benefitting from being able to slip his handless right arm from the manacles. The shackles were quick to open, the pin that locked easy to withdraw using hands or teeth. Soon enough all had gathered upon the balcony, gazing into the hall beyond.

It was another trap, of course, the walls studded with mosaics of various emperors and imperial champions caught in heroic scenes, all but their faces, which were blank. Several low alcoves lined the far wall, on which hung a number of theater masks – features recognizable to any with knowledge of Rokugani history. Upon the floor lay a dozen corpses, limbs spread like unstringed puppets, their faces concealed by featureless masks.

After ensuring the dead would not rise, Naoki and the others carefully picked their way across the hall to study the masks on the far wall. Any scholar worth their brush could have matched faces to bodies, but that was not the goal. The frescoes were imbued with corrupt spirits and would spring to violent life should any of the theater masks be placed upon them.

Gingerly, the young Crab removed one of the masks from the wall, turning it over in his hands. Gensuke had tried to conceal the writing on the inside, but no matter how small he wrote, dark ink would stand out against the pale, unvarnished wood.

"What's that there?" Akifumi squinted down at the bowl, but the others were already moving. Quickly, they stripped the featureless masks from the corpses and placed them upon the frescoes.

Gensuke remained still despite the nervous tension building within him. Although he had no heart left to beat, he could well imagine its caged-bird flutter as Akifumi watched Gensuke's former companions solve yet another of his brutal tests.

The Bloodspeaker's "lesson" had been that the Empire's heroes were faceless, interchangeable grist for a broken and bloody wheel. Puzzle solved, the alcove split down the middle, opening into a cavern of glowing gems.

Searching for Gensuke's warning among the glittering gems, the others quickly discovered the hollowness of wealth, shattering certain gems while avoiding the ones filled with poison gases. Similarly, they bypassed the Riddle of Thrones in the next chamber, and the Noble's Bargain in the one beyond.

With each success Akifumi's scowl grew deeper, his gaze more suspicious.

"Not a one has fallen. Not a one." He shook his age-spotted head as they slipped between the tainted pools of the Gyre of Sorrows, crawling like worms to avoid the smiling caress of the laughing tree, and on down the Oni's Throat.

"As I suspected." Akifumi bared yellowed teeth in a rictus grin, but before he could say another word, a distant boom resounded through the chamber. The Bloodspeaker looked up as another sounded, followed by a rattling crash.

Clucking his tongue, Akifumi swiped a hand over the bowl, the image shifting to show the workshop entrance.

The iron door had been blown off its hinges, the stone slab shattered. Armored samurai poured through the gap, the image hazy with smoke and flame. At first Gensuke thought the Imperial Guard had finally come, but the attackers' attire was different, the outline of their armor and helms unfamiliar.

"I shall deal with these unwelcome guests." Dismissing the image with an irritated flick of his wrist, Akifumi glanced to Gensuke. "See to the others, nephew."

Gensuke bowed to hide his surprise at the sorcerer's broadly worded order. The sudden arrival of unknown assailants must have flustered the usually imperturbable Bloodspeaker. Although he wondered about their provenance, Gensuke was far too practical not to seize such an opportunity.

He hurried off before Akifumi could clarify his command. The Oni's Throat would have taken the others down into the hallucinatory incense of the Bier of Final Regrets. Gensuke would need to arrive before his former companions lost their grip on reality. He slid down a ladder, sprinting down the narrow hall to take the stairs two by two. For the first time, Gensuke was grateful for his unnatural agility as he navigated the latticed scaffolding that led to the Bier and kicked over the poisonous incense pots blazing merrily beneath the floor grates.

He could hear the others overhead, nervous but thankfully un-stupefied. Gensuke considered his options. While it might be possible to lead them from the Bier without revealing himself, even the most direct route to Akifumi's sanctum led through a dozen chambers. He did not know how long the attackers would distract Akifumi. The Bloodspeaker's return would disperse Gensuke's momentary freedom like morning mist.

Ultimately, Gensuke was a practical man, and practicality offered but one choice, risky though was.

Although his lungs no longer required air, Gensuke drew in a slow breath. Throwing open the grate, he vaulted up into the chamber.

His erstwhile comrades turned, eyes wide, weapons already arcing toward his throat.

Gensuke spread his arms as if to welcome the blows, his gaze finding Masahiro's. "If you desire to live, listen carefully."

Gensuke did not know if his words would pierce the haze of impending violence. Even if the others listened, they might not be able to destroy Akifumi.

Fortunately, Gensuke did not need certainty, for he possessed one blessed truth.

One way or another, it was almost over.

CHAPTER TWENTY-THREE

Masahiro had been expecting to die for quite some time. Ever since they had stumbled into this accursed labyrinth he foresaw doom in every twisted shadow. Akifumi's chambers opened like a poisonous blossom, every petal laced with the promise of some new and most likely agonizing demise. It was enough to drive anyone mad.

Which might have been the point all along.

When Gensuke popped up from that rusty grate like a villain in a shadow play, Masahiro's first reaction was, understandably, surprise, followed by an uncomfortable flush of relief. Whatever abomination Akifumi's blood sorcery had made of Gensuke, he was still a killer. Knife or dagger, venom or garrote, it hardly mattered; Masahiro knew at last his end was at hand.

Then the assassin spoke. Although muffled by the hideous mask nailed to the assassin's face, it was undoubtedly Gensuke's voice. Even so, Masahiro could not seem to grasp the individual words. They slipped through his thoughts like a forgotten name, just at the edge of understanding.

Seiji moved first, his heavy blade arcing down to carve deep into the angle where neck met shoulder. There was no blood, no scream, no reaction from Gensuke save a slight stumble as Seiji withdrew the sword.

Akoya was next, two quick slashes that would have covered them all in arterial blood if the assassin's heart yet beat. Again Gensuke ignored the blows, corrupt flesh flowing like thick mud. A few heartbeats and he was whole, unscarred but for three new rents in his already tattered robe.

"Destroy me if you must," he said as Akoya and Seiji circled, blades angled for another assault. "But listen first."

"Let us see if fire fares better than steel." Embers swirled from Tomiko's twisting hands, her voice the soft hiss of ash on the wind.

"Wait." Naoki held up a hand.

"Why should we?" Akoya shook her head. "This is clearly another trap."

"Of *course* it's another trap." Masahiro found his tongue at last. "But what manner of trap?"

"Let me remove this creature's head," she replied. "*Then* we can discuss the subtleties of necromancy."

"For all we know, he might be like an earthworm." Masahiro studied the Scorpion assassin through narrowed eyes. "Splitting him may only make more."

"No, removing my head would do it." The assassin shrugged – a strangely human gesture for one so obviously corrupted.

"Then let us be about it," Akoya said.

In response, Gensuke dropped to his knees, neck bent like a man awaiting execution – or benediction.

Akoya raised her blade.

"Stop," Masahiro said.

"What now?" Akoya's question was almost a snarl.

Masahiro glanced to Naoki, receiving a nod of support from the magistrate. "The very fact Gensuke wishes us to kill him is a strong argument against it."

He thought he would have to convince the bellicose Lion, but Akoya gave an amused snort, stepping back.

"Well reasoned."

Seiji did not lower his blade. "That mask reeks of corruption."

"And Gensuke?" Naoki asked.

The Crab frowned. "A shadow at night, I cannot see for that cursed relic's darkness."

"You do not have much time." Gensuke's rasp cut through the debate. "Akifumi is distracted, but when he returns even I will not be able to save you."

"*Save* us?" Masahiro's laugh had a hysterical edge. "Look at yourself."

"I spared you on the street, Crane," Gensuke replied, words seeming to tumble out. "Just as it was I who left the notes that led you through Akifumi's chambers. If you let me, I can take you to him – but we must *hurry*."

"And if this is another trick?" Akoya asked.

The assassin gestured at their surroundings. "Then you are no worse off."

"The monster makes a fair point," Masahiro said. After so long expecting Gensuke to crawl from every shadow, the assassin's disheveled appearance was almost a disappointment. It was as if Masahiro had moved beyond fear, his dread replaced by a cold pall of resignation. Oddly, he thought of the old warrior tales Hiroshige used to read him when they were children.

Masahiro had always envied the heroes' unflagging courage. Now he wondered if they had simply accepted their fates.

Naoki pointed a jitte at Gensuke. "If we are to trust you–"

"Oh, don't trust me." The assassin cut her off, tapping the mask with one pallid finger. "I am Akifumi's creature, bound to follow the sorcerer's commands. At the moment I have wrestled back a bit of control, but if that withered demon orders me to cut you all down, I must obey."

Akoya glanced to Masahiro. "Not a strong argument for sparing him."

"If we are to follow you," Naoki continued, "then you must answer our questions truthfully."

"Ask quickly."

"What is this place?" she asked.

"A test."

"To what end?"

He gave a muffled sigh. "That, I cannot say."

"What of the corpses?" Tomiko asked. "The register recorded scores of Bloodspeaker shipments funded by Heaven's Blaze."

"Perhaps a hundred dead reside in this labyrinth," Gensuke replied. "Most of the deliveries were actual merchandise. It takes a lot of equipment and material to secretly build a house of traps in the heart of the Imperial City."

The assassin's response seemed to relieve the Phoenix priest. Tomiko blew out a ragged sigh, lips moving in a whispered prayer of gratitude. "So he does not plan to sow discord in the capital?"

"Oh, he does." Gensuke's mask turned toward Tomiko, eyes like chips of obsidian behind the twisted wood. "Just not with walking corpses."

Naoki gave a disgusted wave at the stone walls. "Then what *is* Akifumi's plan?"

"Again, I cannot say." Gensuke shook his head. "The sorcerer himself is rather uncommunicative. He has been sending me after courtiers and nobles, although I have yet to discern a pattern in the killings."

Seiji gave a frustrated grunt. "Do you know if Iuchiban yet lives?"

The assassin shook his head. "If Akifumi communicated with his master, I did not overhear."

Masahiro gave a wry chuckle. "Perhaps Qadan and the others actually managed to destroy the old demon."

Naoki fixed him with a level glare. "Until we have definitive proof, we must assume they did not."

"All beside the point," Akoya said. "Whatever Iuchiban's fate, we know Akifumi is *here*."

"Well reasoned." Masahiro echoed the Lion's earlier compliment, receiving a suspicious nod from Akoya. "The question remains: Does Gensuke speak the truth?"

"Follow and find out. Or you can take your chances in there." The assassin nodded at the gilded door leading to the next of Akifumi's accursed chambers. "Either way, you are running out of time. I can take you to him, all I ask is that you promise to end my suffering."

"I killed you once," Masahiro said, voice cold. "It didn't take."

"So you *did* drop him into the blades," Naoki said.

"He murdered my brother and would have killed me too if not for Chiaki." Outrage colored Masahiro's words. "If anything, I should be lauded for ridding Rokugan of a Shosuro assassin!"

Although Naoki's frown was sharp enough to etch glass, for once, the magistrate did not belabor the issue.

"If it is any comfort, I have been punished. This is…" Gensuke spread his arms, ravaged flesh visible through the tears in his robe. "Excruciating."

Masahiro thought he would be gratified to hear of Gensuke's suffering, but the emptiness of Hiroshige's passing remained a dark hollow within his breast.

If anything, it grew deeper.

He glanced at the door to the next chamber, its surface covered with gilded fish offset with truly massive pearls. "I've never turned my nose up at gold. But there is a first time for everything."

"Gensuke *may* attempt to kill us." Naoki stepped to his side. "But whatever lies beyond that door definitely will."

Surprisingly, Akoya looked to Seiji. "What say your ancestors, Crab?"

He gave a very Tetsuo-like grunt. "This whole rotten dungeon needs to be carved from the earth."

"Then let us be about it." Akoya nodded, stepping to Masahiro's side.

He regarded her for a long moment, unable to restrain a smile.

"What?" the Lion asked.

"Nothing." He shook his head. "It's only… sometimes you remind me of Chiaki."

"I shall take that as a compliment."

"Good," he replied. "Because I certainly meant it as one."

Seeming to take assurance from the Lion's grim confidence, Seiji joined their little group, leaving only Tomiko standing alone.

"There is one thing yet to consider." Her expression flickered between pensive and unsettled. "Are we actually capable of defeating Akifumi?"

"You doubt your abilities, Phoenix?" Akoya asked.

She lowered her gaze. "Always."

Masahiro arched an eyebrow at his would-be killer. "Well, Scorpion, *are* we?"

"Akifumi's form is decrepit, but appearance is meaningless among dark sorcerers." Gensuke stood, dusting off the knees of his shabby pants. "You may not fight alone, though. Others assault this place. Samurai, elemental priests – their attack allowed me to slip Akifumi's yoke."

"And you thought to hold this tidbit until just now?" Masahiro asked.

"Until just now, I wasn't sure if you were going to kill me or not."

"Who are they?" Tomiko asked.

"I did not recognize their armor and they bore no insignia." Gensuke knelt beside the broken grate, then slipped inside. "Follow me and hazard your own guess."

Masahiro peered into the shadowed hole. "I've crawled through worse."

Tomiko raised a hand, flame glimmering on the end of one outstretched finger. "Better to fall opposing evil than stand idle and watch it flourish."

"Fine words," Akoya said. "Is that Shinsei?"

Tomiko returned a sad smile. "Masatsuge."

With that heartening reminder, they descended into the bowels of the sorcerer's labyrinth. While the chambers had been spacious, the tunnels and scaffolded machinery that manipulated the various traps were not designed for ease of movement. If anything, it reminded Masahiro of the time he and Hiroshige had been invited on a tour of the Mariko Theater. Given the theater's prestige and opulent seating, Masahiro had expected a well-appointed backstage only to find a veritable warren of props and disjointed sets.

Strangely, he found himself heartened by Akifumi's clutter. Until now, Masahiro had been working under the impression that Akifumi just snapped his liver-spotted fingers and the whole nasty dungeon assembled from the ether. The gears and chains and rotating shafts were a reassuring reminder that even ancient necromancers must occasionally bow to material needs.

Gensuke moved through the jumble like a man in his own home. Despite the mask's cruel countenance, Masahiro could not mistake the glitter of unease in Gensuke's eyes every time the assassin glanced back. It was a dread the Crane had felt often enough, one he recognized in the wild flutter of his own heart – the cold realization that death was only the beginning.

A distant boom caused everyone to flinch. Not the clank and rattle of Akifumi's dire mechanisms, but the sound of something heavy hitting something hard. Although Masahiro could see no smoke, his nose caught the sharp odor of burning oil.

"This way." Gensuke vaulted up a thin ladder.

Akoya paused at the bottom, glancing to Seiji. "Anything?"

"Yes." He swallowed. "All bad."

"It will be worse if you don't hurry," Gensuke hissed from above.

Face grim, Akoya sheathed her blade and set to climbing,

Seiji and Naoki close behind. Tomiko waited at the bottom, fingers crooked to unleash elemental devastation should anything lunge from the shadows above.

Masahiro stood at the bottom, feeling like an uninvited guest. One-handed, he would need to sheathe his blade to climb. Not much of a loss. Never more than a competent swordsman, it had always been Masahiro's belief that any situation necessitating personal violence was one he had already lost.

"Safe," Akoya called down.

Masahiro highly doubted her judgment, but climbed anyway.

The chamber beyond was easily thirty paces on a side with high ceilings. The walls were studded with alcoves, each boasting a giant iron spindle. Strands of dark thread crisscrossed the intervening space, thin as silk but with a glassy glimmer Masahiro misliked. They stretched from a strange metal tree in the center of the chamber. Perhaps twenty feet high, its spreading limbs seemed fashioned from braided iron, each fitted with dozens of polished obsidian mirrors, a long strand emanating from the center of each.

Several bodies were impaled on the lower branches. Some wore court robes, others dressed in the colors of minor clan nobility. A circle of stage lamps ringed the tree, their directional light casting twisted shadows upon the walls and ceiling.

"Wait. This isn't right." Gensuke spoke as if recalling a dream.

Tomiko took a halting step forward, her expression one of mounting horror. "They... they have no shadows."

A chill prickled up the back of Masahiro's neck as he understood the Phoenix's words. While the tree was picked out in dark relief upon the ceiling, the bodies upon it might as well have been made of glass.

"The spindles." Seiji studied the massive iron rods, his gaze crawling to the strands of dark thread that filled the air. "Akifumi has *unraveled* their souls."

"The Bloodspeaker isn't here." Akoya cast an accusing glare at Gensuke.

"I led you to the scrying room." He shook his head as if to shake free of an illusion. "But this is not it. This is–"

"Do you think so little of me, assassin?" A new voice filled the chamber, thin and high like an elder's but possessed of a dispassionate sharpness, as if they were nothing more than bits of broken pottery to be swept away.

"Quickly." Gensuke fell to his knees, leaning forward to expose his neck. "Destroy me before Akifumi asserts control."

Akoya stepped forward, blade sweeping down. Before it could remove Gensuke's head, the tree began to move. Like wriggling worms, the branches twisted and swayed, the strands connected to each mirror threading the air like a patterned loom, but instead of a robe or cloak, they wove death.

One of the threads crossed the path of Akoya's descending sword and with a sharp screech, sheared through the metal. A dark strand struck one of the Lion's pauldrons, lacquered steel parting like grass before a scythe. Akoya threw herself down before the strand could carve flesh, but her pauldron clattered to the ground.

"Above!" Seiji shouted.

Masahiro glanced up, his stomach like a clenched fist as he beheld several shadows descend from the high ceiling. The dead wore dark robes, their faces concealed by porcelain masks. But unlike the other animated corpses Masahiro had faced, their limbs were strange, twisted things, multi-jointed like an insect's, ending in hooked obsidian claws rather than hands and feet. They skittered down the shifting ebon web, seemingly unconcerned by its razored strands.

"Kill them." Akifumi's command held no anger, no joy, delivered as if he were reciting from a list.

One of the dead leapt for Seiji. The Crab cut it from the air only to hiss in pain as his arm grazed one of the threads. Blood dribbled from the slash in Seiji's armor, but fortunately the Crab seemed imbued with the same unnatural toughness as his predecessor.

At Tomiko's shouted entreaty, a spear of windborne flame transfixed another of the skittering abominations, which fell twitching to the ground. The Phoenix turned, arms raised, only to stumble, her chant becoming a choking gasp as Gensuke snaked an arm around her throat.

"I warned you." The words were almost a sob as he drove a dagger into Tomiko's ribs. The Phoenix crumpled like a courtier's promise. Gensuke let her fall.

Masahiro gave a strangled cry, anger and recrimination hot within his chest. He took a step toward Tomiko only to hesitate, unsure. Even at his best Masahiro could not match Gensuke – better to wait for opportunity than throw his life away.

Leaning to avoid the sweep of an obsidian thread, Gensuke advanced on Akoya. The Lion raised her broken sword, barely four fingers of steel visible above the guard.

Glancing about, Masahiro saw Seiji menaced by four of the crawling corpses, Naoki hurrying to his aid. With Tomiko down and Gensuke in Akifumi's grip once more, it left only Masahiro.

His sword work might be useless. Fortunately, his blade was not.

"Akoya! Catch!" He sent the sword spinning through a gap in the threads. Almost reflexively, the Lion snatched it from the air just in time to parry a pair of looping strikes from Gensuke.

Masahiro picked his way toward them, ducking and flinching as obsidian threads cut the air around him. He was under no illusions about his ability to alter the outcome of the battle, but he could not just sit by and allow Gensuke to cut down his comrades one by one.

The assassin struck again and again, knives like falling stars.

Akoya's blocks seemed slow by comparison, as if she moved through water rather than air. And yet somehow the Lion weathered the assault, shifting to take the slashes and stabs on her armor. She dropped a shoulder into the assassin, knocking him back a pace. Her face a snarl of triumph, Akoya kicked him in the knee, blade coming up for a heavy overhand chop.

It would have taken Gensuke's head had not one of the crawling dead dropped upon her from above. They went down in a tangle of thrashing limbs.

Masahiro struggled to reach the combat. A thread hissed by his ear, almost invisible in the gloom. Cursing, he flinched away, although not in time to stop the accursed strand from carving off a hank of his hair. More threads filled the air in front of him. Although he was but a few paces away, Masahiro might as well have been a district away for all he could do to help.

Fortunately, Akoya seemed to be getting the better of the

exchange with her undead assailant. Gensuke hopped to his feet, dagger held in a reverse grip as he lunged toward the Lion's unprotected shoulder.

The strike faltered, caught in the crook of one of Naoki's jitte. Somehow the magistrate had navigated the chamber to block the assassin's blow. She twisted the blunt iron short sword, a move that would have disarmed any mortal attacker. Gensuke only gripped the blade tighter.

His other dagger darted toward Naoki's eye only to be intercepted by the magistrate's other jitte. She shifted to lock the blade in place, but Gensuke increased the pressure. Arms trembling, Naoki tried to hold back the dagger only to have the tip inch toward her face.

Throwing caution to the wind, Masahiro dove through a gap in the obsidian web. He hit the ground hard, tucking into an awkward roll before stumbling unsteadily to his feet.

There was no time for finesse, so he simply threw himself at the assassin hoping to hook a leg or arm. A shadow in the corner of his eye provided the only warning of a sweeping strand. He stumbled to the side, charge becoming an undignified tumble. The thread grazed his cheek, cool as meltwater. There was no pain, only the hot trickle of blood as it sliced a bit of his cheek and ear away.

Masahiro struck Gensuke's back, arms reflexively wrapping around his midriff. Although Masahiro had no leverage and had lost much of his momentum, the impact still made Gensuke stumble. Naoki jerked her weapons free, bringing them down upon the assassin's wrists.

Daggers clattered to the ground, but Masahiro did not relent, legs pumping as he drove Gensuke back. The assassin caught his balance only to stagger as Naoki hammered a jitte into his skull. It was too much to hope the strike would incapacitate Gensuke, but it bought time for them to press him back toward the tree and the sharpened iron limbs that ringed the lower trunk.

There was a brief feeling of resistance as a jagged spear of metal pierced Gensuke's back. Masahiro released the assassin, planning to drive him onto the stake with a kick only to have Gensuke lash out, cold fingers wrapping around Masahiro's throat.

Naoki's jitte hammered into the assassin's elbow, but Gensuke's flesh might as well have been tempered steel. He caught the magistrate's wrist with his free hand, slamming her against the iron trunk.

Masahiro pawed at the fingers constricting his throat, but could find no purchase. His vision began to darken, the edges crinkling like old paper. Soon it was all he could do to keep his gaze upon the assassin, his arms like clubs of driftwood.

Behind the prison of his mask, Gensuke's eyes mirrored Masahiro's despair. They held his gaze for a moment, then flicked down – as if the assassin were trying to tell him something.

Blood pounding in his ears, Masahiro directed his fading vision toward where Gensuke was looking. From amidst the twining roots a steel bar protruded. Thrust up like an accusatory finger, it was neither sharpened nor twisted, distinctly out of place among the other stakes. Masahiro aimed a kick at it only to find the bar out of reach.

Fingers still locked around Masahiro's throat, Gensuke moved his arm so the next kick would hit the bar.

Not knowing what else to do, Masahiro obliged.

With a clatter of invisible gears, the side of the tree trunk fell inward, taking a small circle of floor with it into the pit below.

Masahiro, Gensuke, and Naoki tumbled down in a fall of stone. The impact knocked what remained of Masahiro's breath from his lungs; fortunately, it also jarred him free of the assassin's grip.

He drew in a great whooping breath, rolling free of the debris. The chamber was clearly Akifumi's workshop. Levers and pull ropes studded the far wall, a profusion of tools hanging from the others. Several workbenches were scattered with scrolls and notebooks.

A rattle of stone drew his attention back to the pile of debris. Naoki had worked herself free, crawling to put her back against the wall, one arm cradled to her chest.

By the Fortunes' grace, it seemed Gensuke had been pinned by the fall, a slab of stone crushing his torso and legs. Masahiro's brief hope that the assassin had been killed died as Gensuke shifted, hands scrabbling at the stone that trapped his lower body.

Blinking against the throbbing in his head, Masahiro knelt to grab a fist sized stone, taking care to remain beyond Gensuke's reach as he approached. The assassin grabbed for him, but behind the mask, Gensuke's eyes were serene, almost grateful.

Masahiro looked down at his brother's murderer, the man who had almost taken his life as well, only to save it again and again. First he had hated Gensuke, then feared him. Now, standing above the assassin, the only emotion Masahiro could summon was pity.

He brought the rock down, aiming not for Gensuke's head, but the mask. It tore free with a wet crack, skittering across the workshop floor.

Apart from the scarring and stitches, the assassin's face was surprisingly mundane – the broad, rounded features Masahiro might expect from a fish merchant or teahouse cook, hardly the hawkish look of a professional killer.

Masahiro raised the rock again only to pause as Gensuke went still.

The assassin gazed up at him, scarred brows arching in surprise, then disbelief. He raised a hand, turning it as if inspecting the limb for the first time.

"It's mine." Wonder edged Gensuke's voice. "I can move. I can *move.*"

"How did you know it was the mask?" Naoki stepped to Masahiro's side, her voice a low croak.

"A guess." He shrugged. "Seiji said the thing was evil, so I figured it couldn't hurt to smash it first. If it truly was Gensuke who left the notes that allowed us to bypass Akifumi's traps, then I owed him this much."

"*Mercy.*" A dreadfully familiar voice echoed from the chamber walls. "Very interesting."

Masahiro looked up to see an old man beside one of the workbenches, cane in hand. Shosuro Akifumi was bent almost double, his limbs like sticks, his features shriveled as a dried persimmon. Despite his enervated appearance, the Bloodspeaker's movements were spry as he bent to retrieve the cursed mask.

"Free me." Gensuke spoke through gritted teeth. "So that I may deliver this creature the end it deserves."

"More violence, little nephew?" Akifumi clucked his tongue. "I thought you had learned a lesson."

"We've had enough of your tests, Bloodspeaker," Naoki said.

"You thought *this* was my test?" Akifumi gestured at the chamber, his laugh the skitter of dry leaves on stone. "No, my friends. The test is you, all of you."

"We're wasting time," Gensuke said. "Quickly, before he summons his powers."

Masahiro frowned down at Gensuke. Despite the assassin's protestations of control, he was loath to release Gensuke, especially before Seiji had given him a thorough inspection.

"All of us?" he asked. "What does that mean?"

"How often do you think I get the chance to study two individuals who survived Iuchiban's tomb?" Akifumi turned the mask in his hands as if to inspect it for damage. Apparently satisfied, he tucked the cursed relic into his sash. "You are clay shaped by the hand of a master. A rare opportunity indeed."

"What of Qadan, Irie, and Tetsuo?" Naoki asked.

Akifumi turned to his workbench, rummaging through the detritus. "Dead, victorious, I care not."

"And Iuchiban's heart?" she asked.

"Ah, now *that* is an interesting question." He looked up. "A statue is the reflection of the mason who carved it, a blade that of the smith. A scroll is empty until a scribe writes upon it, a child nothing until they are taught." Akifumi arranged several of the journals in a neat pile. "What is stronger, then? Steel, stone, ink, flesh, or the name that gives them shape?"

"I'm guessing the name," Masahiro said.

"Indeed." Akifumi gave a brusque nod. "Iuchiban's heart is not–"

The wall behind the ancient sorcerer exploded inward in a spray of dust and stone. Flame gouted into the chamber, setting alight tables and scrolls alike. For a moment, Akifumi's withered form was limned by its red-orange glow, then the Bloodspeaker vanished amidst the inferno.

The sudden heat blistered Masahiro's face. He raised an arm to shield his face, lungs burning as he drew in a gasp of heated air.

He saw Naoki dart forward. She snatched the piled books off the workbench, hair smoking, then flung herself back, beating at the flames.

A heartbeat, and the fire vanished, the tables nearest the opening reduced to little more than ash. Of Akifumi, Masahiro saw no sign but a darkened outline upon the wall.

Probably better than the Bloodspeaker deserved, but enough to satisfy Masahiro.

He looked to where Gensuke had lain only to find him gone. It was too much to hope he had lingered to thank Masahiro for saving him, but such was to be expected from assassins. Ancestors willing, if the destruction of the cursed mask had not freed Gensuke, Akifumi's death had done the trick.

Masahiro's consideration was cut short as samurai poured through the ragged opening. Their armor was a dull gray, absent of crest or distinguishing mark. Even so, Masahiro could not but recognize the woman who ducked through the hole, eyes hard as she surveyed the wreckage of Akifumi's workshop. Masahiro was surprised, but he supposed he shouldn't have been.

Iuchi Qadan had always known how to make an entrance.

CHAPTER TWENTY-FOUR

They were happy to see Qadan. She recognized genuine delight in Naoki's soot-streaked face. Even Masahiro's surprise contained a note of relief. As if Qadan's sudden appearance heralded a change in their fortunes rather than Rokugan's doom.

"Your comrades will suffer, but in the end, they shall be better for it. Just as you are now, disciple."

For the first months of her possession, Qadan had tried to winnow secrets from the ancient sorcerer only to find him maddeningly vague. The irony was, now she had accepted the inevitability of his cruel dominion, Iuchiban had become almost sanguine.

"Return to your studies, old friend. You have played your part." Although the words slipped through Qadan's thoughts, they were meant not for her, but Shosuro Akifumi – who, rather than being consumed by their summoned flames, had been granted a quick escape from his burning house of horrors, scuttling away from the Imperial City to inflict more cruelties on the world.

"Stay close." Arban stepped to Qadan's side, wariness evident in his every movement. They had torn through a dozen of Akifumi's trap rooms. Although far less threatening with a score of Unicorn veterans at their back, there had been enough close calls to keep everyone alert.

"Qadan? How did you–?" Naoki took a step forward only to stop short as a Unicorn blade pressed into the hollow of her throat.

"Peace." Iuchiban waved the samurai back. "They are old comrades."

"Did you destroy the heart?" Masahiro's concern apparently overwhelmed his surprise at seeing Qadan back from the dead.

"No." Frowning, Iuchiban shook their head. "But we destroyed the dark sorcerer's physical form. It will take some time for him to reform."

"Then what is *this*?" The Crane flicked his fingers at Akifumi's workshop.

"Iuchiban had many disciples," they replied, nodding toward Arban and the others. "I have been hunting them down."

"And you didn't think to send us a letter?" Incredulity threaded Masahiro's tone.

"I am sorry, truly." Iuchiban glanced down as if ashamed. "But this was the only way to be sure."

"Were we bait?" he asked.

"No. Never." It wasn't a lie. Although Akifumi had been ordered not to kill them, Iuchiban had been quite liberal with regards to bodily and spiritual harm. "We only discovered Akifumi's location recently."

Masahiro looked about to ask more questions, only to have

Naoki speak. "Our friends are… up there." She glanced at the ragged hole in the stone ceiling. "Lion, Crab, and Phoenix. We must help."

Iuchiban nodded to Arban. "Go. All of you."

He hesitated. "Are you safe alone?"

"Akifumi is gone." Iuchiban returned a comforting smile. "And I am not alone."

Although Arban seemed torn, he called upon his earth spirit to raise a stair of rough stone leading to the upper level. When the last Unicorn samurai had disappeared into the darkness above, Iuchiban turned back to Qadan's former companions.

"I am sure you have questions."

Masahiro shrugged. "Questions, comments, accusations. Take your pick."

Naoki waved the Crane to silence. "We know Tetsuo is gone, but what of Irie?"

Iuchiban gave a sad shake of their head. "Only I made it out."

"How?"

"After the battle, there was a tunnel leading from Iuchiban's chambers." They winced as if the memory were painful. "It emerged somewhere in the Shinomen Forest. My spirits healed the physical damage, but my wounds went deeper. I must have wandered the forest for days, delirious and soul sick, my memories little more than fragments. Thank the Fortunes I was found by some traveling monks, else I might be there still. Even so, it took months for me to piece together what happened, even longer to convince my clan to take action."

"And *that* was when you decided to reach out to old comrades," Masahiro said.

"I did not know you survived," Iuchiban lied.

"You could have asked around," came the Crane's sharp reply.

Normally Masahiro's prodding would have irritated Qadan, but Iuchiban took it in stride. "The Bloodspeakers believed me dead. Anonymity was my sword and armor. Even a coded letter might have given warning to Akifumi and the others. It was not worth the risk."

Masahiro crossed his arms. "As someone who just crawled through a Bloodspeaker labyrinth for the *second* time, allow me to disagree."

"Now is not the time for recriminations." Always the peacemaker, Naoki stepped between them. "Are there more Bloodspeakers in the capital?"

"Perhaps," Iuchiban replied. "Although without Akifumi, they will be disorganized, broken. My comrades and I will root out any who do not flee."

"We did it." Naoki blew out a ragged sigh. "What of the sorcerer's heart?"

"It was not in the tomb," Iuchiban replied. "The fight was… terrible. Even now I cannot recall the whole of it."

"So we braved those horrors for nothing?" Masahiro asked.

"Not nothing." Iuchiban favored the Crane with a warm smile. "The dark sorcerer was beaten, if not defeated. It will be some time before he troubles Rokugan again."

"Thank the ancestors," Naoki said. "We had little luck finding any mention of Iuchiban in the histories."

The Dragon Magistrate's admission conjured a strange emotion in their shared thought, one Qadan had yet to feel from the ancient sorcerer.

Irritation.

Could Iuchiban's arrogance be so great that he was annoyed his name and deeds were not recorded in the High Histories? Such petulance seemed unbecoming of the Bloodspeaker. If her time as Iuchiban's prisoner had taught her anything, it was that the sorcerer had planned for every eventuality. Even now, Qadan watched helpless as he dragged her erstwhile comrades deeper into his web. Despair kindled in her thoughts. It had been Qadan's hope they would notice the change in her, but she should have known better. If Arban could travel with her for weeks and sense nothing, what hope did others have?

"Now that I am here we shall erase Iuchiban's remaining cults from the present as well as the past." Iuchiban spoke as if from the heart. Only Qadan knew he did not possess one.

"It is not as if we have been sitting on our hands," Masahiro said. "Naoki led an expedition to the Twilight Mountains, and I have been working to enthrone an emperor who will give this matter his full attention."

"I did not mean to imply you had been idle." Iuchiban gave a quick bow. "Your presence in this deathtrap is evidence enough."

The apology seemed to surprise Masahiro, who cocked his head. "Your time in the tomb seems to have improved your manners."

Iuchiban returned a thin smile. "It transformed us all."

Masahiro and Naoki glanced away, gazing into the middle distance.

"*Your companions have accomplished more than I dared hope.*" Iuchiban spoke in Qadan's mind. "*After so long, our future is close enough to grasp.*"

"Your *future*," Qadan replied.

"*Perhaps.*" He chuckled. "*But you have seen enough to understand.*"

As much as she wished it were not true, the sorcerer was right. The world was broken, existence steeped in needless suffering, wars fought over land, gold, pride, while those least able to defend themselves suffered at the hands of their so-called betters.

Things must change. It was the pernicious truth underpinning the ancient Bloodspeaker's every act, the one that ate at Qadan's resolve. She had no answer, no solution. She was but one samurai. At least, she had been.

Now she was more, and less.

Iuchiban smiled as the rattle of armor heralded Arban's return. They were carrying a Phoenix priest, face pale and bloodless, her yellow-orange robes wet with splotches of deeper crimson. A woman in battered Lion plate had her arm around a thin-faced man in Crab colors.

"Tomiko!" Naoki took a step toward the supine Phoenix, only to pause as Arban raised a calming hand.

"I was able to close her wounds," he said. "But it will take rest to recover fully."

Awkward introductions were exchanged, smoothed over by Iuchiban's easy manner. With a few words he quieted mistrust, navigating through the shoals of shared history with venomous ease. There was a moment of hope as the Crab, Kuni Seiji, fixed them with a narrow-eyed stare, as if he might part the curtains of Qadan's traitor flesh to reveal the ancient terror that squatted within her soul.

"*You and he have much in common,*" Iuchiban said.

"*Unfortunately, any insights the young Kuni might possess are blunted by my power. Still, we must be careful lest he bring unnecessary harm upon himself.*"

Meaning, of course, Seiji would be killed should he discern Iuchiban's presence. For one so concerned about improving all of existence, the sorcerer was remarkably callous with individual lives.

"*Death means nothing.*"

Another point buttressed by the ancient Bloodspeaker's very existence.

"What now, cousin?" Arban asked.

"We burn this awful place," Iuchiban replied.

"Might Akifumi's lair hold some hints as to other Bloodspeakers?" Naoki asked. "Or even Iuchiban?"

"It holds nothing but corruption," Iuchiban replied. "To explore is to risk your very soul. Perhaps that is why the ancients removed all mention of Bloodspeakers."

Although the Dragon magistrate did not seem pleased, she raised no argument as Iuchiban gestured for Arban and the others to begin the destruction.

"You are welcome to assist," Iuchiban said.

"I would prefer a bath and a strong drink," Masahiro replied.

"I must remain to see the corruption purged," Seiji said.

"As will I." Akoya looked to Naoki and Masahiro in turn. "See Tomiko is taken care of."

"Gladly." The Crane gave a companionable nod, turning to Qadan. "If I might borrow one or two of your warriors to bear the Phoenix? At least until I can summon my own."

Iuchiban acquiesced with a thin smile, addressing the Crane and Dragon. "Is there anything else I should know?"

They shared the slightest of glances, barely more than a flicker of the eye, but Iuchiban noted it – which meant Qadan did as well. Her former companions did not wholly trust them.

"*Nor should they,*" Iuchiban said. "*I seem to recall you parting on less than amiable terms.*"

"*Just let them go, please,*" Qadan said, thinking not only of Naoki and the others, but Arban as well.

"*They still have a part to play,*" came the undying Bloodspeaker's reply.

"*Destroying Akifumi's workshop?*"

"*This place is merely a tool,*" he said.

Qadan had grown used to Iuchiban's vagaries and so could not conceal her surprise as the sorcerer continued.

"*The utility was threefold. First, it was a means to bind us to them, and them to us. Your companions trust us more than they would have had we merely appeared in the city. Second, it serves to allay suspicion – they sought to destroy a powerful Bloodspeaker. I have given them one.*" Iuchiban paused, as if to let the revelations settle. "*And finally, it moves events. Despite Masahiro and Naoki's tales of my tomb, there are still many in court who doubt my existence. Their denials shall wither as you and your companions are lauded as true heroes.*"

The cold calculation of the sorcerer's plan settled upon Qadan like late winter snow, her burgeoning hopes buried beneath a sea of uncaring ice. By uprooting Akifumi, Iuchiban had deftly inserted himself back into her companions' confidence and earned the court's gratitude in the bargain.

So it was with the Bloodspeaker, his machinations like poisonous blossoms. Peel away an outer layer only to find another nested within. The very fact Iuchiban had revealed this scheme to Qadan meant there was nothing she or the others could do to stop it.

And yet there was one aspect she did not quite grasp.

"Why make heroes of us?"

His laugh was that of a parent delighting in their child's precocity.

"Why to help me raise a new emperor, of course."

CHAPTER TWENTY-FIVE

Hantei XXVI was dead, and Masahiro couldn't be more pleased. For months the emperor's personal healers had predicted his imminent passing, and yet the stricken Hantei clung to life with a tenacity never applied to any other aspect of his lackluster rule.

Masahiro played the part of a grieving courtier – face downcast as he sat through days of interminable ritual and prayer. Even so, it was a true test of willpower to observe the traditional week-long mourning period before diving back into the roiling political storm that gripped the capital.

Their destruction of Akifumi's cult had made heroes of Masahiro and the others. Where once the Crane had turned their powdered noses up at Masahiro, now they jostled like hungry geese to enter his good graces. As Prince Tokihito's guardian, Lord Otomo Yasunori had reclaimed his palace residence, working to secure the support of the three imperial families.

Meanwhile, Masahiro fought to bring the clans into line,

or at least defang the various coteries arrayed against Prince Tokihito. Not an easy task – made more difficult by the preoccupation of Masahiro's comrades. Despite Qadan's reassurances and their destruction of Akifumi, Naoki seemed convinced there were Bloodspeakers lurking around every corner. Not that Masahiro could blame her for such squeamishness.

Nonetheless, his gentle exhortations were as seeds cast upon stone. The Dragon magistrate and her young Kuni friend had sequestered themselves in the Imperial Archives, bent on deciphering the fistful of documents they had snatched from Akifumi's workshop before Qadan had burned the wretched place to ash.

Good riddance, as far as Masahiro was concerned. If only he could convince Naoki and Seiji. Although the Dragon and Crab clans raised no opposition to Tokihito's ascension, neither had they endorsed the young prince. At least the Scorpion posed little threat. Like the falling of an ancient oak, Bayushi Terumoto's death had opened a patch of light in the thick canopy of Scorpion politics, ushering in a brutal struggle among those who had languished in the courtier's shade.

At least Tomiko seemed to have brought the Phoenix to heel. Her newfound heroic status rendered the young priest temporarily untouchable. Even the most poisonous mutters had quieted when Prince Tokihito himself deigned to visit her sickbed.

After the burning of Akifumi's lair, Masahiro had been feted not only by the Iuchi daimyō, Arban, but by the Old Stallion himself, Unicorn Clan Champion Shinjo Bataar. If Masahiro had been aware of Qadan's family connections, he might have made more of an effort to weather her stormy petulance back in Iuchiban's tomb. Fortunately, she seemed willing to let their past disagreements lie fallow – a sentiment Masahiro was happy to echo.

Which left only the Lion Clan.

Masahiro would have preferred to invite the Lion to a tea ceremony, or failing that, a mock duel. The Lion were usually more approachable once they had delivered a sweaty drubbing to a few mediocre Crane duelists. And yet all of Masahiro's invitations had been politely rebuffed, his artfully arranged "chance encounters" with Lion nobility met with scowls and cold courtesy. Normally he would have suspected the clan of pushing their own contender for the Emerald Throne, but despite a disconcerting buildup of soldiers in and around the Imperial City, the Lion Clan had thus far cultivated a sense of remove from the dynastic struggle.

So it was that Masahiro found himself in a rather drab practice field, breath steaming in the chill midwinter air as he waited for Lady Matsu Akoya to begin her daily exercises. Desperate, perhaps, but Akoya represented Masahiro's only connection, however tenuous.

He had called a meeting of Tokihito's supporters this very afternoon, and the Lion would be conspicuous by their absence – their massing army an unstated threat to any who would claim the Emerald Throne.

And so, Masahiro waited.

He had expected scowls and brusque antagonism as the retired Matsu lord made her way onto the practice field. Instead, he was astonished to see a smile crease her scarred face.

"Took you long enough."

"Apologies, lady." He bowed to hide his surprise. "I fear I do not follow your reasoning."

"To seek me out." Akoya undertook a variety of uncomfortable looking stretches. "I told the others to ignore you. Not a difficult request, given your... questionable history."

"I am the very model of courage." He waved the stump of his sword hand in mock outrage. "Lest you forget, I was there with you down in that horrid place – and with one hand, no less."

"Oh, I remember." Akoya's smile made Masahiro distinctly uncomfortable. He had expected a Matsu general, all brute and bluster. Instead he had found a canny strategist.

"They say you were once a passable duelist." She tossed him a practice sword, then helped herself to another from the rack.

"They?" He caught the wooden blade awkwardly. "Give me these rumormongers' names so I might have them beaten for slander."

That dragged a genuine smile from the old Lion lord. "I begin to see why she liked you. Then again, Chiaki was always captivated by broken things."

Masahiro frowned. "I was whole when she found me."

"Not that." Akoya's gaze flicked to his missing hand, then to the center of Masahiro's chest. "*That*."

"If you wished to reminisce about Chiaki, you could have asked." Masahiro shook his head, genuinely astonished.

"You talk too much, Crane."

"I have been accused of worse."

Rather than respond, Akoya hit him. Her strike came in high and to the right, almost too fast for Masahiro to see. The blow set Masahiro's wooden blade spinning across the frozen ground.

"Pick it up." She nodded at the sword.

"Are you going to hit me again?"

"I'm going to try."

"Then I would prefer to remain unarmed." He flexed his hand, still stinging from the fury of Akoya's lunge.

She bared her teeth, voice low and threatening. "Pick. It. Up."

He gave a helpless shrug. "If you're going to bludgeon me to death, I'd rather get it over with quickly."

She shoved him hard. Masahiro fell back, the shock of frozen ground driving the air from his lungs.

"How?" Akoya stood over him panting, her eyes bright with hurt and anger. "How is it she died for *you*?"

Masahiro drew in a rasping breath. "To be fair, Naoki and Qadan were there as well."

"Even now, you dissemble."

"What do you want from me?" He pushed to his elbows.

"The truth."

"I could say Chiaki and I bonded over shared loss, or that our alliance was born from vengeance, or a noble desire to bring Iuchiban and his followers to justice." Masahiro scrambled to his feet, incensed by the Lion's inquisition. "The truth is, we simply had nowhere else to go. Chiaki saved my life. She didn't have to, but she did. I tried to return the favor as best I could. Without my help, her head would be on some rebel's spear." Masahiro was almost face to face with the Matsu lord, his words quick and angry. "I took your master as far as I could, but in the end, she *chose* her time. Which is more freedom than most of us are accorded."

Akoya's sword clattered to the hard earth.

"Did Chiaki die well?"

"Better than any I have ever known." Masahiro felt the anger drain from him. "I would have composed a poem, but she threatened to haunt me forever if I did."

"A dire threat, to be sure. Although I might risk it just to hear her voice again." Akoya turned away, but not before Masahiro caught a glitter in her eyes. He considered offering some commiseration, but nothing seemed sufficient. Also, he very much did not want Akoya to hit him again.

"You came for the Lion's support." When the Matsu lord spoke again, her voice was hoarse. "You have it."

"Just like that?" Masahiro asked.

"Just like that." She nodded. "I needed to see what manner of man would advise our future emperor."

He bowed to her broad back. "I shall endeavor to be worthy of–"

Akoya gave a low hiss. "Don't push it, Crane."

"Understood." He took a quick step back. "So I can expect you at the meeting this afternoon?"

"I will be there," she said. "Now, get off my practice field." Akoya turned. Although her voice remained rough, mirth twinkled in her dark eyes. "Unless, that is, you fancy another duel?"

"Tokihito is still a child." Master of Rites Miya Katagiri helped himself to another rosewater cake from the small plate at his elbow. The confections were a gift from Masahiro, one he'd hoped would assuage the young minister's notorious sweet tooth; but while Katagiri seemed quite fond of Masahiro's cakes, he was proving less receptive to his arguments. Despite being only a month in his position as Master of Rites, the Miya lord haggled like a riverboat captain.

Masahiro glanced to Naoki for support. As a ranking member of the magistracy, a word from her would do much to assuage Katagiri's reservations. Unfortunately, the Dragon seemed lost in thought, one foot bouncing on the mat as she stared into the middle distance.

At least Naoki had come. Although he had responded to Masahiro's messenger, Kuni Seiji was notable by his absence. But such truculence was to be expected from the Crab.

"There have been younger emperors," Akoya said, the slightest hint of irritation bleeding through her stone-faced demeanor. Clearly she thought this meeting a waste of time.

If only she were right.

"In times of war or strife, perhaps." Katagiri bobbed his head, the beads dangling from his elaborate cap of office clicking together. "Are you implying the Empire is in danger?"

"It may well be if we equivocate long enough." Akoya crossed her arms, glancing to Masahiro.

He returned a helpless look. As Master of Rites, enthronement fell firmly within Katagiri's purview. Although he could not stop Tokihito's ascension, the Miya lord could problematize and postpone the ritual almost indefinitely, requiring that he be begged, bullied, or bribed into acquiescence.

There had been younger emperors – many, in fact. But history meant nothing to a self-important bureaucrat like Miya Katagiri. Like a gambler lucking into a big score, the man was drunk on his newfound bureaucratic position.

"Just the other day, Prince Tokihito and I attended the midwinter invocation," said Tomiko. Although the Phoenix priest had recovered from her wounds, a quaver in her voice spoke of less visible injuries. "A truly spectacular display. Lord Katagiri's incantations were reminiscent of the arias of Otomo Ranmaru." She gave a demure shake of her head. "If only the ritual chamber had been less shabby."

"Shabby?" The self-important smile drained from Miya Katagiri's face, his hand hovering above the sweets.

From the narrowing of eyes around the chamber, the insult had struck home. Even Naoki was roused from distracted contemplation, her gaze flicking to Masahiro.

He did not intervene. Knowing Lady Tomiko was no fool, he was curious to see what gambit she worked.

"Oh, yes," the Phoenix priest replied almost off-handedly. "There were holes in the screens, the gilding had peeled from several of the columns, not to mention the smoke stains on the eaves." She waved a hand as if parting smoke. "But one cannot expect exactness from a building so... ancient."

"There is beauty in imperfection." Masahiro restrained a grin as he realized Tomiko's ploy. "Then again, there is also beauty in beauty."

"One cannot be held responsible for the oversights of their predecessors." As usual, Tomiko was quick to grasp the thread of conversation.

"Quite so." Katagiri's smile returned. It was well known he had been a rival of the old Master of Rites, a bullish traditionalist who dispensed with pomp and gaudiness in favor of more ascetic pursuits. Fortunately, he and several other highly ranked ministers had expired of the same wasting disease that struck the previous emperor, contracted at a poetry reading some weeks ago.

"Such talent as yours deserves a place worthy of it," Tomiko continued.

"It is our duty to see the ritual chamber repaired and embellished," Masahiro said. "Especially if it is to host a new emperor."

"I am grateful for such consideration." Katagiri inclined his head. "But alas, repairs are already underway."

Although his face betrayed no outward sign of consternation, Masahiro's hand bunched in the folds of his robe. To refuse such a lavish bribe verged on incompetence. But Katagiri only sat, grinning like a fool holding a winning draw of hanafuda cards.

Which, figuratively, he did.

Masahiro could only stare at Katagiri, wondering how he had made an enemy of the man.

"We cannot enthrone a child." Iuchi Qadan spoke for the first time. Throughout the long discussion, the Unicorn had sat like a temple statue, far removed from the tawdry deliberations.

"Alas, yes." Although sorrow tinged Katagiri's tone, his frown was anything but apologetic.

"Then we shall have to name him an adult." Qadan shrugged, glancing to Masahiro.

"A naming ceremony?" Katagiri rocked back upon his heels, bemused. "Highly irregular for one so young."

"Irregular, but not unheard of." Masahiro took no small delight in watching the minister's face fall. Normally naming ceremonies were not undertaken before one's fourteenth winter, but exceptions had been made.

Katagiri's beads practically rattled, so vigorous was his

refusal. "As Master of Imperial Rites, I cannot conscience such a bending of custom and—"

"*Imperial* rites." Normally Masahiro would have let the lord finish, but they were far beyond such niceties. He looked to Tomiko. "Lady, correct me if I'm wrong, but naming ceremonies fall under the category of familial ceremonies?"

She tapped her chin as if considering. "Yes, I believe they do."

"In that case all we require is Prince Tokihito's guardian," Masahiro said. "And I think Lord Otomo Yasunori will be happy to oblige."

Katagiri's jovial demeanor fell away like a theater mask. "You would circumvent my authority?"

"I'm afraid you give us no choice." Masahiro pushed to his feet.

"You will not undertake this travesty within the Imperial Precincts," Katagiri responded.

"The Inner City boasts many fine pavilions – like mine, for instance." Turning away, Masahiro nodded for the others to follow. "We shall hold the naming there. It will let the people see their new emperor."

"It is not safe," Katagiri said.

"The Lion Clan guarantees Prince Tokihito's safety." Akoya rattled a fist on her breastplate.

"And the Unicorn," Qadan said.

"And the Phoenix," Tomiko added.

"And the Crane." Masahiro chuckled. "Although I hardly suspect our aid will be necessary given the prince has so many stalwart defenders."

He offered the Master of Rites a precise bow. "Once Tokihito is named, we shall proceed directly to the Imperial Precincts for his enthronement. I trust everything will be ready, Lord Miya?"

Although Katagiri offered little more than a glare in reply, Masahiro knew he would comply. The Master of Rites had tried his gambit, but ultimately he was as bound by propriety as all of them. To openly defy imperial precedent would risk censure, not only for Lord Katagiri, but the Miya family as a whole.

They left Katagiri fuming. Not really how Masahiro preferred to end a meeting, but the Miya lord had proven truly intractable.

"Bureaucrats." Akoya spoke the title like a curse. "I have fought duels less bloody."

"If not for our Unicorn friend, we might be in there still." Masahiro favored Qadan with a genuine bow, something he had never expected. "I shall inform Lord Yasunori of his new duties."

He grinned. Overseeing Tokihito's Coming-of-Age Ceremony to become the next Hantei emperor would be irresistible to an old fox like Otomo Yasunori.

"No doubt the Seppun will provide guards," Qadan said. "But Akoya and I shall assemble extra protection."

The Lion grunted in agreement. "It will do the people good to see our clans standing together."

"Lady Tomiko," Naoki called after the Phoenix priest. "Would you assist Seiji and I in our research? We rescued some papers from Akifumi's lair, but they contain spiritual references beyond our capability."

"Of course, magistrate." Tomiko slipped her hands into the

sleeves of her robes. "I must fetch a few warding scrolls from the Phoenix Embassy. One cannot be too careful when delving into the writings of so powerful a Bloodspeaker."

Naoki gave a sad shake of her head. "Unfortunately, I know that better than most."

Beyond the Ministry of Rites, they separated, each bound by their various tasks. Masahiro knew he should hurry to Lord Yasunori's manor, and yet he lingered.

It had been his and Hiroshige's dream to advise an emperor, but the prospect had always seemed impossible as the destiny of a pillow book hero. Now Masahiro stood ready to realize all their hopes.

It should have been exhilarating, yet try as he might, all Masahiro could summon was a vague sense of unease.

"You feel it too."

He let out a very indecorous yelp. Turning, Masahiro expected to see Seiji or Gensuke. But it was only Naoki.

"Something is wrong." The Dragon magistrate ran a nervous hand through her hair.

"You found something in Akifumi's notes?" he asked.

"Yes… no." She chewed her lip. "They're hard to decipher. I am hoping Tomiko will have more luck."

"Naoki. Look at me." He laid a hand upon her shoulder. "You're an Emerald Magistrate; it would be odd if you *weren't* suspicious. But take a moment and consider all we've accomplished. Iuchiban's physical form destroyed, Akifumi dead, his disciples scattered. In a few days we shall be able to call upon the emperor himself. What more is there to do?"

She drew in a slow breath, nodding. "You're right. I should be pleased. We should *all* be pleased."

Masahiro studied Naoki's face, her expression one of resignation rather than acceptance.

"And yet?" he asked.

"And yet I cannot believe Iuchiban truly beaten."

"If he rises, we shall face him." He gave Naoki a friendly shake. "*Together.*"

Her smile was tentative but genuine. "I'm sorry."

"For what?"

"For misjudging you." She glanced away, then back. "I thought you a selfish courtier blinded by ambition."

"You weren't wrong." Now he was the one who could not meet her eyes. "Being down there in the tomb… what we saw, what we did." He swallowed. "Everything is different."

She sagged in his grip. "I wish the burden had fallen on stronger shoulders."

"As do we all." His reply was almost a whisper.

"I should go assist Seiji." Naoki pulled away, scrubbing a fist across her eyes.

"If you discover something. *Anything.*" Masahiro fixed her with an earnest look. "Don't hesitate."

It was her turn to smile. "I never do."

He watched Naoki go, her shoulders straighter, the set of her jaw a bit less apprehensive. Masahiro was gratified to see some of his encouragement had apparently taken root. And yet as he turned away, Masahiro was less heartened by the formless storm of apprehension roiling in his own gut. Everything was *finally* working out, but Masahiro could not see Lady Sun for the pall Iuchiban had cast over all their lives.

He tossed his head, irritated to feel such unease even as victory approached.

Apparently Naoki was not the only one in need of reassurance.

CHAPTER TWENTY-SIX

Seiji had hoped Akifumi's death would muffle the bell. He did not expect a reprieve or reward. His ancestors were Kuni after all – once they had hold of something, they never let it go. But a moment of quiet would have been welcome.

If anything, the bell had grown louder.

"'*Onomastic rectification of hierarchically stratified cultures can be realized only through radical mis-denomination.*'" Seiji ground the heel of his palm into one eye. Akifumi wrote like a man waking from a dream, racing to scribble everything down before memory fled.

"There are references to at least a dozen cults, each with differing rituals and customs." Naoki searched among the piled books. They had gathered every mention of Iuchiban not only in the imperial records, but in the pillow books and the notes the magistrate had managed to snatch from Akifumi's burning workshop.

"It was the same with the High Histories." Naoki tapped one book, then another, frustration whetting every word. "The sources cannot even seem to agree on Iuchiban's actual name, let alone how to destroy him."

"There are references to terrible rites meant to draw the attention of beings outside even the sight of Heaven." Tomiko's brow furrowed in shared frustration. Although the Phoenix priest had been helpful in deciphering Akifumi's arcane ramblings, the thrust of the Bloodspeaker's work remained just out of reach.

"How do we fight a foe who deals with realms beyond comprehension?" Naoki massaged her temples.

"I am sorry." Tomiko's shoulders rounded. "Perhaps if we engage other scholars. There are many in my clan who–"

"No." Naoki shook her head. "If Qadan is correct about Akifumi's notes I will not risk corrupting others."

Seiji was forced to agree. They had considered handing the writings over to the Phoenix's Asako Inquisitors, but Naoki was loath to lose Akifumi's notes to the secretive clan. And the witch hunters in Seiji's own family would be more apt to destroy the records than read them.

"Is there not some imperial ministry tasked with such things?" he asked.

Naoki sighed. "The position of Jade Champion has stood empty for almost a century."

"Seems like an oversight," Seiji said.

"There were rumors of corruption. Infighting between Jade Magistrates and Asako Inquisitors," Tomiko replied. "It almost tore the court apart."

"What happened?" Seiji asked.

"Phoenix records speak of an unlawful inquest," Tomiko replied. "The Jade Magistracy had the temerity to investigate our Elemental Masters for corruption. As you can imagine, the Asako Inquisitors were furious at the transgression. The emperor wisely chose to allow the Jade Magistracy to wither rather than risk conflict with the Phoenix."

"So we have our ancestors to thank for this." Seiji could not hide the anger in his voice.

Rather than disdain, Tomiko cocked her head, brows knit in sympathy. "The past is ever a burden upon the present."

"For spirits of the departed, the ancestors' hand can be surprisingly heavy." Seiji could not but nod, surprised an Isawa elementalist would buck against her family's expectations.

"Mine yet live," Tomiko said. "I am not sure which is worse."

Seiji scowled. "At least the living can be reasoned with."

Tomiko reddened, looking away as she changed the subject. "A shame about the Jade Magistracy. It would be useful to have an expert or two close at hand."

"Unfortunately, I am as close to one as you are likely to find outside the ranks of the Bloodspeakers." Naoki gave a sad smile. "And I'm not even sure if Iuchiban is our foe's actual name."

"Does it matter what he is called?" Seiji asked.

"If this search has taught me anything, it is that names matter," Naoki replied.

"Is Iuchiban spirit or man?" Seiji asked.

"Both." Tomiko selected one of Akifumi's notebooks, running a finger along the page as she recited. "'…and so did the Carnival of Dusk surround a thrice-slain offering and exhort the Laughing Turtle. Then did the master deign to send the Oracle of Blood to deliver his wisdom unto them.'"

Seiji put his head in his hands, each insistent chime tugging at his thoughts. It wanted something from him, clearly. And yet short of wandering through the Imperial City in the hopes of stumbling upon a Bloodspeaker coven, Seiji had no ideas.

Naoki began to pace, fingers picking at the frayed sleeves of her robe. The magistrate's constant fidgeting might have irritated Seiji had he not been subject to his own spiritual aggravations. As it was, he sat back and tried to think not like a witch hunter, but an architect.

Seiji was reminded of the Disordered Stone Technique employed by Crab masons to erect walls without mortar. Large stones were piled atop one another, then smaller rocks inserted into the gaps to lock them in place. Rather than cut individual stones to fit, they worked with what was provided.

For the past weeks, he and Naoki had been trying to shape the evidence to fit their conception of who Iuchiban was, but perhaps the trick was to allow the sources to speak for themselves.

"What do we know of Iuchiban?" he asked Naoki.

She fixed him with an irritated look.

"Humor me, please."

Naoki drew in a long-suffering breath. "He is an ancient and corrupt name keeper who goes by many titles. He desires to conquer Rokugan, although by what means we have yet to determine."

"You and the others sought to destroy his heart." Seiji closed his eyes, sinking into the strange interplay of sense-memories his ancestors had branded into his mind. "The ancients in my memories attempted the same."

"The pillow books confirm as much," Naoki said.

Seiji frowned. "But there is no mention of a tomb, or even a heart. Not in the pillow books, not anywhere."

"Iuchiban must have bid his followers destroy all record of it," Tomiko said. "To ensure his weakness was impossible to find."

Seiji shook his head. That stone did not fit. "Bloodspeaker cults are small, disconnected. It seems unlikely they would have the power to remove so many records."

"Who else could have done it?" Tomiko sniffed. "Are you implying the emperor and his court were corrupted as well?"

"Not corrupted, but they did possess knowledge we do not." Seiji opened his eyes. "If we assume the emperor acted in Rokugan's defense, then the records must have been destroyed for a reason."

"But why expunge knowledge of Iuchiban?" Naoki asked.

"To erase him." Seiji smiled, stones slotting into place for the first time in weeks. "All this time we thought his heart was a physical object, something to be burnt or crushed, but what if it is like Iuchiban himself? Neither flesh nor spirit, but idea."

"Or perhaps a *name*," Tomiko said.

Naoki stopped pacing.

"And how do you destroy a name?" Seiji asked.

"You *erase* it." Naoki spun, excitement etched into every plane of her narrow face. "But Iuchiban must have collected scores."

"At least we know where to begin looking," Seiji replied. "And what we face."

"Names." Naoki's eyes widened. "Qadan! If any know how to battle such a foe it will be the Unicorn."

"She will be with her clan." Tomiko stood. "Preparing for Prince Tokihito's Coming-of-Age."

Naoki clapped her hands. "Then we must hurry."

Seiji followed them from the archives and into the choked streets beyond. News that Prince Tokihito's Coming-of-Age would occur outside the Imperial Precincts had filled the

Inner City almost to bursting. Fortunately, Naoki's magisterial credentials were enough to secure a small detail of overworked guards to clear their path.

For the first time since Razor of Dawn, Seiji was filled with genuine excitement. So intent was he on navigating the loud streets of the Inner City, he did not immediately notice the silence in his own thoughts.

The bell had stopped.

Only for a moment. Even so, he managed to pause, drawing in a deep breath of the cold winter air.

Not a reward. Never. But a moment of quiet.

And that would have to be enough.

CHAPTER TWENTY-SEVEN

Few people were pleased to see an Emerald Magistrate. The diffused, hierarchical nature of Rokugani politics meant that even those with nothing to hide did not enjoy imperial authorities prying into their affairs. During her tenure in the magistracy, Naoki had grown used to belligerence, suspicion, even outright defiance, but little in her experience had prepared her for the enthusiastic greeting she received at the Unicorn Embassy.

The guards recognized Naoki and her companions, waving them through without asking for her magisterial seal. A grinning majordomo in silver-trimmed furs led them to one of the many wooden pavilions that ringed the courtyard. Although clearly a permanent structure, the walls were layered with swatches of colored felt, no doubt meant to evoke the yurts the Unicorn favored when roaming across the wide grasslands of their fief.

Without being asked, the Unicorn majordomo departed to seek out Qadan, but not before ensuring Naoki and her companions were comfortable on the piled pillows and had been plied with rice cakes, roasted meats, and pitchers of warmed mare's milk to ward the afternoon chill. Although guards took up position at the pavilion entrance, their manner was jovial. Beyond, the courtyard was quiet but for the occasional group of riders, laughing as they cantered through the wide gate. If anything, the embassy had an air of celebration, unsurprising given that a new emperor was about to be enthroned with Unicorn support.

The thunder of hooves caused Naoki to glance up from her food. Instead of Qadan, she was surprised to see the name keeper's cousin, Arban. The Iuchi daimyō dismounted in one smooth motion, seeming almost to glide to the ground. Tossing his riding gloves to a nearby aide, Arban strode toward the pavilion.

"Apologies for the wait, my friends." The Iuchi daimyō's tone was warm as his grin. "I would have come sooner, but we are tangled in preparations for the coming enthronement. Qadan will be along shortly."

"It is we who should apologize for imposing on your time, daimyō." Naoki began a bow only to check herself as Arban collapsed onto one of the nearby piles of pillows, waving a hand to dispense with any formality.

"To what do I owe this visit?" He selected a skewer of roasted meat from one of the silver trays, chewing with gusto.

"There are some matters we wish to discuss with your cousin," Seiji answered.

"A few questions regarding name magic," Tomiko added. "And blood sorcery."

Arban straightened, demeanor turning serious. "We do not

like to discuss such things any more than your Kuni friend would care to expound upon the Shadowlands."

"We mean no insult to name magic, daimyō." Naoki raised a calming hand. "We only seek to understand how to destroy Iuchiban and believe your practices may hold the key."

He relaxed a bit, although the air of welcome had dispersed. "In that case, you may put your questions to me."

Naoki regarded the Iuchi daimyō. Although she had met Arban but once, and under distressing circumstances, the fact that Qadan trusted her cousin to battle Akifumi spoke well of the man's character.

She glanced to Seiji, then Tomiko. When neither raised any concerns, Naoki turned back to Arban with a nod.

"We believe Iuchiban to be a living name." She tilted her head. "More precisely, a collection of names, his power growing as knowledge of them spreads. Is such a thing even possible?"

"Not for any mortal or spirit I am aware of." Arban narrowed his eyes, considering. "Even the most powerful demons possess but one true name. Taking more would be anathema to their very existence. It could divide or even destroy them."

"But if a mortal sorcerer *were* to control such power?" Tomiko asked.

"They would be formless, bodiless," Arban replied. "A being of pure intellect able to affect the world only through the cruelest sorceries."

"It is as I feared." Another voice spoke from outside the pavilion.

Naoki turned to see Qadan. Jaw tight, eyes cold, she ducked

beneath the hanging curtain. "Cousin, beware. They have been corrupted."

The Iuchi daimyō looked to Qadan with surprise. "I don't understand."

"This is a misunderstanding. We–" Naoki started to rise only to drop back as Qadan raised a warning hand.

"You took books from Akifumi's lair." The Unicorn flung the accusation like a spear.

Naoki flushed, anger and shame coloring her cheeks. "We only meant to–"

"Tainted works brimming with dark knowledge and Bloodspeaker sorceries." Qadan spoke over her. "They have infected your minds."

"I am Kuni." Seiji's voice came level, uninflected like Tetsuo's had been. "I would sense if the corruption had spread."

"What would an architect know of corruption?" Qadan replied. "Tell me, Kuni. What would *your* family have done with Akifumi's notes?"

Seiji's troubled expression was answer enough.

"But we have finally discovered Iuchiban's true nature," Tomiko said.

"And what is that?" Qadan cocked her head. "A name? A rumor? I saw his body destroyed back at the tomb, felt his spirit flee. While you were steeping yourself in dark knowledge, my cousin and I were hunting down Bloodspeaker cults."

"My cousin speaks true. We have slain many dark sorcerers." At last, Arban stood. There was a wariness in the Iuchi daimyō's tone that Naoki misliked.

"Qadan, please," Naoki said. "We fought through Iuchiban's tomb together, destroyed the Monk, battled Akifumi."

"When my warriors and I arrived, it did not appear like you were battling Akifumi." Qadan spoke cautiously, as if testing each word. "What lies did he tell you?"

"Please, you must listen," Naoki said.

"I *have* been listening." Qadan turned, signaling to the guards outside.

"No." Seiji was on his feet in a moment, blade drawn. Naoki looked to Tomiko, but the Phoenix priest only watched the display like an oncoming wildfire, eyes wide and surprised.

"It does not have to be like this, Naoki," Qadan said, voice softening. "You are a good magistrate, wise and just. Can you not at least admit the possibility the Bloodspeakers have lied to you?"

It was as if Naoki were wrapped in heavy blankets, the air in the pavilion seeming close and hot despite the winter chill.

"Corruption corrupts," Qadan continued. "I do not wish violence, but I also cannot let you leave, not until we are sure you and your companions are untainted."

Naoki glanced about. Alone, outnumbered, in the heart of the Unicorn Embassy, there was little they could do. "What do you intend?" she asked.

Seiji gave a threatening growl, but Naoki waved him to silence. "It does not hurt to listen."

"You will remain in the embassy as guests of the Unicorn Clan," Qadan said. "There is no time now, but once Hantei XXVII is enthroned, we shall put this matter before the emperor and his high priests. If all is as you believe, you will have my aid and my sincerest apologies." She tilted her head. "But if you have been… misled."

Naoki's legs trembled, hands clammy in the folds of her

robes. For the first time it had felt as if they were beginning to understand Iuchiban – but what if Qadan was right? What if Naoki's mind had been clouded? She had read the confessions of many who had fallen to darkness. If there was one truth running through that litany of cruelties, it was that even the worst did not believe themselves corrupt.

"I have waited long to bring Iuchiban to justice." A few deep breaths and the tension seemed to flow from Naoki. "Another day hardly matters."

"I know it is little solace, Naoki. But I am sorry it has come to this." Qadan looked to Arban, who raised a hand for the guards to advance.

"Imprisoning two clan nobles and an Emerald Magistrate on the eve of the emperor's enthronement?" Tomiko spoke for the first time since Qadan had entered. "A dangerous gambit."

"These are dangerous times." Qadan nodded as if to acknowledge the priest's point.

"I give my word you will come to no harm," Arban said. "We shall treat you as visiting dignitaries."

"Is it common practice among the Unicorn to imprison your guests?" Although Tomiko spoke sweetly, there were knives in her smile.

The two Unicorn nobles looked troubled, but it was clear to Naoki that neither blades nor words would set them free. If all went as planned, Hantei XXVII would ascend the Emerald Throne with Doji Masahiro as one of his closest advisors. Naoki was confident the Crane would intervene on her behalf.

Carefully, she reached out a hand, gently pressing Seiji's blade toward the floor. "We shall do as you ask."

"Thank you, magistrate." Despite Arban's obvious

consternation, there was no regret in the Unicorn guards that led them across the courtyard toward one of the few stone buildings in the embassy. A rather imposing structure, it looked out of place amidst the brightly colored pavilions, but the few windows and stoutly barred gate made the building's purpose abundantly clear.

The prison was clean, if cold. Naoki and the others were divested of their weapons and taken to three of the higher rooms, reasonably spacious cells complete with sitting pillows, desks, and various amenities. Still, the walls were thick and the cells spaced far enough apart to make conversation impossible. From the furnishings, it was clear they were not the only noble "guests" the Unicorn had ever hosted. Not a surprise, many clans found it expedient to detain undesirable individuals rather than more affect more permanent solutions. Such tactics were often employed to maintain the veneer of propriety.

More food and drink was brought, but Naoki did not feel like eating. To have come so close only to be stymied by misplaced suspicion was galling. Patience had never been one of Naoki's stronger qualities, and now she felt fit to climb the very walls.

So she paced – ten steps forward, ten steps back; again and again and again – muscles so tight Naoki felt she might burst her own skin. It seemed impossible they had been corrupted, and yet Qadan's words had undermined the foundations of Naoki's confidence. The Unicorn had always been suspicious, it seemed their time in Iuchiban's tomb had only sharpened Qadan's doubting nature. Still, she knew name magic better than any. Could Qadan be right? Had Naoki been corrupted?

No matter, soon Naoki would bring her concerns before the emperor. She could wait that long, especially since she had little choice.

Naoki was starting perhaps her hundredth circumnavigation of the cell when a thud from outside the door gave her pause. Head cocked, she heard the bolt draw back. Slowly, almost tentatively, the door creaked open.

Of all the people Naoki expected to see, Shosuro Gensuke was perhaps the last.

The undead assassin was attired as a Unicorn guard, his face concealed by a full war mask, but Naoki would never forget his eyes, cold and precise as he glided into the room, closing the door behind.

Startled, she took a step back, expecting an envenomed knife.

Instead, Gensuke made shields of his empty hands.

"You must come with me." His words were soft but urgent. "If we do not act quickly, Rokugan is doomed."

CHAPTER TWENTY-EIGHT

Prince Tokihito's ceremony was going well. Far *too* well for Masahiro's liking. He felt like the arrogant minister in some old court fable, about to have his wealth and power stripped away by some cruel quirk of fortune. Even as he knelt upon the high dais – part of the presumptive emperor's attendants – Masahiro could not focus his attention upon the matter at hand.

It was not that he feared attack. Although the ceremony was being held beyond the arcane and physical wards of the Forbidden City, the District of Sagacity was one of the safest in the capital. Six layers of guards defended Otose's manor, a mix of imperial and clan samurai selected for their expertise and loyalty, patrols fortified by elementalists skilled in the spiritual arts. Out of respect to Tokihito, the champions of all seven clans were in attendance, each accompanied by a small pack of high nobles. Masahiro had spoken of allowing the new emperor to be witnessed by the people of Rokugan, but in truth, even the onlookers who lined the wide streets outside the imperial procession had been vetted by the Imperial Guard.

He sat within the safest place in Rokugan. And yet Masahiro's heart seemed to flutter each time one of the many attendants shifted position, every clack of the woodblock almost sending him to his feet.

Prince Tokihito looked resplendent in his ritual garb – a set of robes in imperial green, embroidered with elemental dragons, the Hantei crest picked out in gold thread upon the back. The very image of a young emperor, he made his way along the central aisle, treading upon a carpet of chrysanthemum petals cultivated in defiance of the season.

A light dusting of snow covered the courtyard – a nod toward the Winter Court over which the new emperor would soon preside. The soft flurries lent the proceedings an air of refinement, accenting the pale-white hair of Masahiro and his clan. What better way to signal an era of Crane courtly dominance?

Tokihito ascended the eight wide stairs leading to the dais. Each broad step bore the crest and color of a Great Clan, along with seats for the Champion and their entourage. Though Tokihito had not been enthroned, the champions offered respectful bows as he passed, symbolically acknowledging their support of the emperor to be. The eighth step was inset with three jade seals – one for each imperial family. Traditionally, only those with Otomo, Seppun, or Miya blood were allowed to occupy the high dais, but in acknowledgment for their recent service, places had been set aside for Masahiro and his companions.

Unfortunately, only Akoya and Qadan had deigned to grace the ceremony with their presence, even though Qadan looked as wan as some specter in a peasant tale. The Unicorn had waved off Masahiro's concerned murmurs. There would be time enough for rest once Hantei XXVII was securely seated upon the Emerald Throne.

She had the right of it, Masahiro supposed. And yet he found himself wishing the others were here.

No doubt Naoki and Seiji were neck deep in some ancient tome, but Tomiko's absence was troubling, especially given her friendship with the prince. It would represent a final and lasting rebuke of her parents – both in attendance along with Isawa Anzan, the elderly Phoenix Champion. Quietly, Masahiro added one more mark to his growing list of concerns.

"Try to at least *seem* like you're enjoying yourself, Crane," Akoya whispered from Masahiro's left. "This is the beginning of your triumph."

Or the end.

Masahiro managed a smile, breathing deep and slow through his nose as Tokihito knelt before Lord Yasunori, the Otomo noble's diminutive frame awash in the multi-layered robes that marked his exalted status.

Despite his youth, the prince's recitation was perfect as his posture, every word, every move an echo of his imperial forebears. If this ceremony were any indication, Tokihito would make a fine emperor – with a bit of guidance, of course.

Lord Yasunori's high, quavery voice sang the ritual reply, echoed by the ranks of imperial courtiers arrayed around the dais. Masahiro lent his voice to the call and response, as if the act might dispel the chill that rimed his heart.

A noble's high cap was placed upon Tokihito's head, Lord Yasunori's hands firm despite the tremor in his voice. The young prince rose, drawing a folded paper from the sleeve of his robes. Turning, he displayed it to the noble attendees, the characters for "Tokihito" written in dark ink upon the pale page. With a breath, he cast it into a nearby brazier, watching ribbons of smoke curl heavenward.

For the briefest moment, the prince was without a name.

The thud of a body hitting wood snatched Masahiro's attention from the ceremony. By reflex he reached for his sword, but none save the guards had been allowed weapons. Even so, he was on his feet, already scanning the crowd for more Bloodspeaker wickedness.

"Qadan has fainted." Akoya's rough voice called his attention back to the dais.

Masahiro blinked, concern blossoming into genuine anxiety as he glanced around the courtyard half expecting a horde of dead to come spilling over the walls. But all remained as it should be.

In a flutter of robes, a priest in Seppun colors knelt next to the fallen Unicorn, whispering incantations even as she pressed two fingers to her neck.

"Her pulse is weak." The woman frowned, head cocked as if trying to peer through Qadan's flesh. "As is her spirit."

"What is it?" Masahiro asked.

"I sense no imbalance," the priest replied. "This seems little more than exhaustion."

"Will she recover?" Akoya asked.

"With rest and care." The priest looked to Otomo Yasunori.

Although clearly irritated by the interruption, the old noble hid it well. "Have her seen to."

Mutters spread through the assembly even as attendants hurried forward to bear Qadan away.

"Iuchi Qadan has placed service to the Empire above her

own health." The prince's voice rose above the murmur, strong and clear. "The Unicorn Clan should be doubly proud." He nodded to the attendants. "See she receives the best care the palace can provide."

This seemed to quiet the crowd. Masahiro nodded in appreciation of the prince's clever redirection. By framing Qadan's collapse as a result of her dedication, he turned the incident from unfortunate to auspicious.

A fine emperor indeed.

Lord Yasunori's raised hands beckoned all back to order. Expressions somber, they watched as brush and paper were brought. Holding back the sleeve of his robe, the prince inscribed his new name upon the sheet, but rather than raise the inevitable "Hantei XXVII," he slipped the paper into the breast of his robe.

"It is not right to display my reign name. For I do not yet sit upon the Emerald Throne." The prince addressed the gathered nobles. A minor breach of protocol, but understandable given emperors did not often have Coming-of-Age Ceremonies immediately before their enthronement.

"As you wish, my prince." Lord Yasunori's bow spread through the assembled nobility. After a long moment he straightened, turning to the clan nobles. "Make way for the imperial procession!"

And make way they did.

The assembled worthies lined up in order of rank and title – imperial families followed by the clan contingents in order of favor. Naturally, the Crane were foremost. Even so, Masahiro hung back. Catching Akoya's eye, he nodded toward one of the many alcoves surrounding the embassy courtyard.

"What troubles you?" To his relief, the Matsu did not question Masahiro's motives.

"The others should have been here."

"This is but a formality," she replied. "They will attend the enthronement."

"And if they do not?"

Akoya's frown was not one of suspicion, but concern. "You suspect Bloodspeakers?"

"I know as much as you." He shook his head. "Even so, I cannot help but feel something amiss."

Akoya crossed her arms, nodding. "Better to suffer the discomfort of armor than die for its lack."

"One of Akodo's maxims?"

"One of Chiaki's," she replied. "Your presence is required at the enthronement. I will search out our absent companions."

"And if you go missing as well?"

She grinned. "Call up the legions."

"Thank you." With a bow, Masahiro hurried toward his place of honor just behind the imperial palanquin.

"All is well?" Lord Yasunori asked.

"A scheduling difficulty, easily rectified."

"Good." He signaled for the procession to commence.

It took the better part of an hour for the procession of high nobles to navigate the half-mile between the Crane Embassy and the High Gate. Onlookers crowded the side streets and tributaries, the brightly colored flood of high-ranking clan samurai and lower imperials kept back by a dam of imperial guards.

A bead of sweat tickled between Masahiro's shoulders, his face hot and clammy despite the afternoon chill. He had been a fool to allow this. Despite the myriad precautions, it was dangerous for the presumptive emperor to venture beyond the safety of the Forbidden City.

He should never have allowed Gensuke to walk free. The assassin had disappeared after their encounter with Akifumi and Masahiro's inquiries, discreet and otherwise, had failed to unearth him. It was too much to hope Gensuke was actually dead. This would be the perfect opportunity for the assassin to cut the head from the Empire. All would fall back to bickering and bloodshed, alliances shifting like winter winds.

Only when they reached the safety of the High Gate did the tightness bleed from Masahiro's shoulders. Protected by layers of Seppun wards built up over centuries, the walls of the Forbidden City repelled corruption.

At the gate, the procession's tail dwindled as clan samurai stepped from the line to join the crowd of noble onlookers. Only those with Hantei blood could pass the High Gate without an imperial invitation, a privilege extended on this occasion only to Masahiro and his companions.

They were met by a dozen grim priests from the emperor's Hidden Guard. Although not yet sworn to the prince, the presence of so many skilled spiritualists was a comfort.

The much diminished procession was conveyed through the nested gardens and pavilions of the Forbidden City, the sweeping breadth of imperial architecture seeming to dwarf even the most famous among them.

Amidst the gold-trimmed beauty, the Imperial Palace rose like a gleaming spear, walls of pale stone brighter than even the fresh-fallen snow, the glazed green of its tiered roof capped with statues of purest jade. Carp, dragons, lion dogs, and other auspicious creatures seemed to silently await their approach. Although Masahiro had been to the palace on several occasions, it never failed to conjure a sense of awe.

Outside, Miya Katagiri awaited with a large contingent of ritual assistants. Despite the Master of Rites' earlier truculence, he greeted the imperial party with the proper obeisance, voice raised in chants of welcome as they ascended the carved stone steps. Incense hung heavy in the air, the peal of gongs marking the beginning of the ceremony.

The accretion of centuries of rite and ritual meant it would be hours before the actual enthronement took place. More time for Akoya to locate the others.

In the meantime, it would be easy for Masahiro to lose himself in the quiet comfort of age-old rituals, secure in the knowledge he was beyond even the reach of immortal sorcerers. Even so, he could not seem to keep his gaze from slipping toward the empty cushions in the throne room, his comrades' absence like a missing verse in an otherwise beautiful poem.

No matter. If anyone could find them, it was Matsu Akoya.

If not, in just a few hours' time, Masahiro would call out the legions.

CHAPTER TWENTY-NINE

Naoki took a step back, hands instinctively curling into fists.

"I mean you no harm." Although Gensuke spread his arms to show he held no weapons, Naoki knew better than to think the assassin unarmed. She glanced to the slumped body of the Unicorn guard, relieved to see the man's chest rise and fall.

"Unconscious." Gensuke stepped back into the hall to reveal three other fallen guards. "But it won't be long until they are missed."

"How do I know this isn't a Bloodspeaker trap?" Naoki asked. Although Gensuke no longer wore Akifumi's cursed artifact, the assassin's scarred, bloodless face was concealed behind a Unicorn war mask.

"Hear me out, then decide for yourself." He moved quickly down the hall.

Cursing herself for a fool Naoki stepped to the door, peering out as Gensuke threw the bolt on the other cells.

"Demon." Tomiko began a whispered chant even as Seiji stepped forward to grab Gensuke by the neck, lifting the assassin bodily from the floor.

Gensuke did not attempt to resist. He only hung limp, gaze fixed on Naoki.

"Wait." Her call brought a confused pause.

"This was one of Akifumi's creatures," Tomiko said.

"No longer." Gensuke's voice came as a choked rasp. "I am free."

"How do we know that?" Naoki shook her head. "How do *you* know that?"

"I don't." The genuine anguish in his reply took Naoki aback. "All I know is what I have done. Destroy me if you wish, but please listen first."

The others looked to Naoki. She chewed her lip, considering. If studying Akifumi's works *had* opened their minds to corruption, listening to Gensuke would allow the evil to take root. And yet, the assassin had risked everything to come here.

Naoki sighed. "Seiji, release him."

"This is an abomination, an accursed thing." Tomiko said. "I can almost feel the darkness surrounding him."

"It is there, yes." Seiji cocked his head, frowning. "But different than before. Distant, disjointed – a shadow puppet, its strings cut."

"Strings or no, a puppet is a puppet," Tomiko said.

Seiji seemed not to hear. Slowly, he released his grip on Gensuke's throat, allowing the assassin to slump back against the wall.

"Quickly." Naoki sought to imbue her voice with a confidence she did not feel.

"I killed many as Akifumi's slave." The words tumbled from Gensuke like a confession. "We disguised the murders as political infighting – courtiers, clan officials, even nobles, struck down seemingly without reason or pattern." He pushed slowly to his feet, taking care to keep his hands in view. "At first it made no sense. Only later did I realize that it was not the deaths that mattered, but the changes they wrought."

"Speak plainly, creature," Seiji said.

"Akifumi had me remove obstacles," Gensuke replied. "Not to sow chaos, but to ensure others would rise quickly. Because of my acts, many suddenly found themselves thrust into positions of power – overlooked officials, disgruntled bureaucrats, nobles with formerly no chance to inherit, individuals the Bloodspeakers could influence, groom."

"To what end?" Tomiko asked. "Akifumi was destroyed, his followers scattered."

"His true followers infiltrated the courts," Gensuke said. "And I helped them rise."

Naoki's stomach clenched. If what Gensuke said were true, there were Bloodspeakers in the palace even now, perhaps even within reach of the new emperor.

"The Hidden Guard would winnow them out," Tomiko said.

"These are mortal agents, not sorcerers, not demons," Gensuke said. "Even the Hidden Guard cannot read minds."

"You believe the Bloodspeakers wish to influence the new emperor?" Naoki asked, already dreading the response.

"I do." The sound of boots on the tower stairs caused Gensuke to tense. "If the alarm is raised, even I cannot help you."

Naoki looked to her companions, uncertain.

Calmly, Gensuke unwound a silken rope from around his waist, one end bearing a rag-padded grapnel. Moving below one of the high windows, he swung the rope twice, then threw it to hook the bars.

"I do not trust him," Seiji said. "But neither do I wish to remain a prisoner of the Unicorn."

Tomiko glanced toward the stairs, then the assassin, already scaling the rope. "There will be more time for questions when we are free."

It seemed a fair assertion. Without delay, Naoki followed the assassin up the rope, her companions close behind. By the time she reached the top, Gensuke had already removed several of the bars and climbed up onto the roof.

Naoki took his proffered hand, restraining a flinch as her fingers closed around cold flesh. Despite his corpselike pallor, Gensuke easily pulled her up onto the tiled roof. Once Seiji and Tomiko were present as well, he drew up the rope and carefully replaced the bars. Not a moment too soon, as Naoki heard cries from below.

They wobbled across the tiles, leaping to catch the eaves of a higher roof. The commotion below seemed enough to mask their progress as they peered over the dizzying drop. Perhaps thirty feet separated them from the outer wall of the Unicorn Embassy, too far even for Gensuke to leap.

"Summon the wind," he whispered to Tomiko.

She frowned. "I'm not sure if–"

"Either we jump or we fall," the assassin said.

Tomiko drew in a steadying breath, eyes squeezed shut as she began a whispered incantation. The wind picked up, stray gusts tugging at Naoki's robes. A moment, and the updraft seemed almost strong enough to peel them from their perch.

"Go." Tomiko spoke through gritted teeth.

"Hold this." Gensuke handed Seiji the rope.

Without hesitation Gensuke leapt, arms spread as if to

catch the wind. It was not a graceful glide, more the awkward twisting of a man buffeted by waves. Naoki gasped as the assassin struck the wall with bone-cracking force. Seemingly unconcerned, Gensuke hooked an arm over the top, tying off the rope with the other.

Seiji wrapped the cord around a protruding downspout, then gave it a tug.

Heart in her throat, Naoki removed her belt and looped it around the rope. The wind snatched the breath from her lips – a lucky thing, it turned out, as she would have certainly screamed during the descent.

Gensuke caught her, pushing her atop the wall. Tomiko came next, faced flushed with excitement, then Seiji, his expression grim as the scowl on Gensuke's Unicorn war mask. Fortunately, none of the Unicorn samurai below had thought to look up yet.

It was perhaps thirty feet to the street below, a descent made far less troubling as Gensuke removed another thin cord from his robes. A few moments and they were sprinting across the cobbled street.

The afternoon sun made long shadows. The District of Rectitude was remarkably empty given the masses who had descended upon the Imperial City. Naoki was surprised until she realized the crowd must be seeking to catch a glimpse of the imperial procession.

Gensuke led them along a shadowed alley. A few quick turns later they collapsed in the shade of a watchtower, several imperial guards quick to emerge from within.

"We require privacy." Naoki displayed her magisterial seal, grateful Gensuke had the forethought to hide his twisted features behind a mask. They were led inside. Only when the guards had vacated did Naoki turn back to the assassin. "Iuchiban's body was destroyed. Even if his spirit survives, it would be turned back by the Seppun wards upon the palace."

"Iuchiban was not destroyed, he was freed," the assassin replied. "He is a spirit of pure intellect, capable of possessing mortals, hiding his corruption deep within their minds."

"Impossible." The word slipped through lips gone numb, as if denial might dispel the chill that spread through Naoki's chest.

"Is it?" Gensuke asked.

Naoki gave a low hiss. "When Qadan and I battled the corrupted monk, he was able to possess my body for a short time. If one of Iuchiban's disciples had such an ability, surely his master himself must have perfected it."

"If that is true, the sorcerer could be anywhere," Tomiko whispered. "Anyone."

"Not *anyone*," Gensuke said. "Six of us entered Iuchiban's tomb, but only one reached the end, just as only one witnessed his supposed destruction."

"*Qadan*." Naoki whispered the name.

"Are we to believe the word of some Bloodspeaker abomination over a decorated noble?" Seiji scowled. "I am no friend of Iuchi Qadan, but I sensed no corruption in her. She saved us from Akifumi. Naoki, you and Masahiro watched her burn that withered creature to ash. How could she be corrupt?"

Tomiko thrust her chin at Gensuke. "We should take this creature to the palace, let the Hidden Guard determine the truth of its words."

Naoki hesitated. Qadan had always been suspicious, slow to trust and quick to act. And yet as much as Naoki wished to deny it, the assassin's logic made terrible sense.

"Qadan is a name keeper," Naoki said. "And Iuchiban is master of names."

"Who better to resist his corruption?" Seiji asked.

Naoki squeezed her eyes shut, massaging the back of her neck. If only there was a way to know for sure. As tightly as name keepers were bound to their spirits, Naoki could not imagine them serving a creature like Iuchiban. Naoki had seen Qadan call down her fire spirit to annihilate Akifumi.

If it *had* been her fire spirit.

And just like that, Naoki knew how to discover the truth.

She turned to the Phoenix priest. "Can you summon specific elemental spirits?"

"Without a name?" Tomiko frowned. "Only if they wish it."

"I believe they do." Naoki nodded.

The Phoenix looked confused. "What elementals would you have me call?"

"Qadan's," Naoki replied. "If the name keeper remains uncorrupted, they will be bound to her. But if not, I suspect her spiritual allies might be desperate to communicate."

"A good plan." Seiji crossed his arms, expression grim. "Let us hope you find nothing."

Understanding smoothed the worry lines on Tomiko's face. Without hesitation she sank to her knees, voice dropping to a low drone.

A breeze stirred the papers on a nearby desk, cool on Naoki's sweaty brow. Firelight filled the office, the floor vibrating as if something tunneled through the ground beneath.

"They came." Tomiko opened her eyes, expression unbelieving.

"Ask them of Qadan." Naoki's voice trembled with excitement.

Tomiko's chant slipped through the air like half-remembered song, beautiful but impossible to grasp.

"Their friend was swallowed by darkness." The Phoenix paled, one hand pressed to her chest as if to still the beating of her heart. "They seek to free her, but fear the render of names will destroy them."

"What of Akifumi?" Seiji asked, voice tight. "If Qadan has been corrupted, was he truly destroyed by her flames?"

Tomiko gave a soft moan. "They cannot say. It has taken all they have to remain near Qadan."

"Do they know Iuchiban's goal?" Naoki asked.

Tomiko's incantations took on new urgency. "He wishes to unweave everything that is."

"How?" Naoki asked.

"Spirits' minds do not walk the same paths as mortals.'" A pained expression flickered across the Phoenix's face. "Iuchiban desires a rectification of names. The end of the Hantei and the beginning of… something else."

Realization struck like a spear thrust to Naoki's chest. "Iuchiban does not wish to influence the emperor, he seeks to *replace* him."

She pressed one hand to her mouth, not wanting to be correct, but knowing she was. It had been Qadan who told them of Iuchiban's demise, just as it had been she who suggested the emperor's Coming-of-Age Ceremony be held outside the Forbidden City's wards.

Naoki looked around, seeing horrified comprehension mirrored in her companions' faces.

"Iuchiban is a name." Seiji shook his head, voice breathless.

"And until he takes the throne, poor Tokihito has none," Tomiko said. "The prince would be defenseless."

"Ancestors have mercy," Gensuke said. "How could I have been so blind?"

Naoki shot the bolt, already calling to the guards as she stepped into the cool afternoon light. "Horses. Now."

As mounts were brought, she turned to the watch commander. "We require an escort to the palace."

Before the woman could reply, the hammer of hooves caused all to turn. A formation of Unicorn samurai clattered up the street at a full gallop, Iuchi Arban at their head.

"Bloodspeakers!" The Unicorn Lord cast out a hand. "Apprehend them!"

The guard commander glanced back and forth, tanned face creased with confusion. There was no time for explanation. Naoki snatched the reins of the nearest mount and leapt into the saddle, kicking the horse into a gallop.

She did not dare look back. Leaning low over the horse's neck, Naoki pounded through the streets, onlookers craning their necks to follow the commotion. She could hear little over the rush of wind. Fortunately, the streets of the Inner Districts were straight and wide.

She made for the palace. Tokihito's Coming-of-Age was complete, but there might be time to stop the enthronement if she could just reach Masahiro.

Something struck Naoki's side, hard and sharp enough to make her gasp. Naoki glanced over to see a Unicorn rider, spear in hand. At first she thought the samurai had stabbed her, only to see the man hammer the butt against her ribs once more.

Naoki toppled from her mount. Acting on instinct alone, she tucked her head, turning what would have been a bone-snapping fall into an ugly roll. She flailed up only to stumble, her limbs loose and wooden.

Naoki blinked back stinging tears as Arban cantered up, her companions in tow. "Quite foolish. Attempting to outride the Unicorn."

"You don't understand." Naoki's words came as a pained gasp. "Iuchiban–"

"I doubted my cousin." Arban's eyes were flat as a winter sky. "But seeing you flee with this *thing…*" He thrust his chin at Gensuke. "I should never have questioned Qadan."

"If you stop us, Iuchiban will become the next emperor." One hand pressed to her aching ribs, Naoki stood only to pause as a dozen spears pointed in her direction.

"Take them." Arban turned away.

A deadly hedge of steel hemmed Naoki in from all sides.

"Stand aside." A new voice shouted from beyond the ring of riders.

Arban twisted in his saddle, eyes widening in surprise. "Lady Akoya?"

"I have come for Naoki and the others."

Horses parted like grass to reveal Matsu Akoya at the head of a wedge of Lion samurai. Although none had drawn their weapons, they had the wary aspect of warriors prepared for sudden violence. The flicker of relief Naoki felt at seeing Akoya quickly guttered as Arban called back to the Lion.

"Your companions have been corrupted."

"How do you know this?" Akoya asked.

"Lady Qadan grew concerned when they admitted to studying Akifumi's scrolls." The Unicorn lord handed his spear to a nearby rider, displaying open palms to Akoya. "We were going to turn them over to the Hidden Guard after the enthronement, but they escaped with the aid of this Bloodspeaker abomination."

Akoya crossed her arms, frowning at Naoki. "Is this true?"

She drew in a wincing breath. "We *did* escape, yes, but we have not been corrupted."

Akoya's scowl grew deeper. "Explain yourself, magistrate."

"I can do better than that." Naoki nodded to Tomiko. "Show them."

Arban hissed as the Phoenix began her chant, but Naoki raised a calming hand. "She only communes with the spirits."

"I shall be the judge of that." The Unicorn lord drew a talisman of braided tundra grass from his breastplate. Eyes hard, he watched Tomiko, ready for any hint of betrayal. The air seemed almost to buzz, sharp and acrid like after a lightning strike.

Arban gasped. "It cannot be."

"What is it?" Akoya leaned forward. "Out with it, Iuchi."

"I *recognize* them." His words were slow, unbelieving. "Phoenix, how is it you can summon my cousin's spirits?"

"They have been waiting for the call," Tomiko replied.

Arban dismounted, approaching the near-invisible swirl of spiritual energy with almost childlike awe. "I don't understand."

"Iuchiban possessed your cousin and now holds the prince. We must stop the enthronement. I shall explain on the way to the palace." Naoki strode past Arban. "But first we must speak with Qadan."

"The Unicorn is in the Imperial Palace," Akoya replied. "She fainted during the Prince's naming ceremony."

Cold realization worked icy fingers through Naoki's chest. Qadan's illness could only mean Iuchiban had already seized Prince Tokihito. It also meant the Unicorn was free of the sorcerer's clutches. Naoki did not know what remained of her former comrade, but if Qadan had managed to retain any shreds of her past self through the ordeal, she could possess valuable insights into Iuchiban.

"We seek Qadan." She took her horse's bridle from the stunned Unicorn samurai, swinging up into the saddle.

"I will not face the sorcerer blind again."

CHAPTER THIRTY

For the first time in months, Qadan was alone in her skull. How many times had she dreamed of breaking Iuchiban's grasp? Yet in the end, it had been neither will or guile that freed her.

Iuchiban could have scoured Qadan's soul, leaving behind little more than an empty husk. Instead he had left her unharmed. A few hours of care by the imperial physicians and Qadan's strength had begun to return. She suspected her mind would take longer to heal.

None could witness such truths and come away unchanged.

When she had first regained consciousness, Qadan had considered revealing the sorcerer's presence to all. They might think her addled or confused, but a full-throated confession might be enough to forestall the enthronement. Such hopes were winter shoots, greenery confused by a few warm days only to wither beneath a blanket of spiteful snow.

Iuchiban never did anything without a plan.

At best, this was a test. At worst, a trap. Iuchiban might even wish her to reveal his plans as part of some deeper gambit. After months of questioning her senses, her thoughts, even her own body – doubt bound Qadan more tightly than Iuchiban ever had.

If anything, he *wished* his disciple to witness their final triumph.

"Ah, excellent." A kind-eyed physician had leaned close, mere moments after Qadan regained consciousness. "He desired you awake."

The man had ignored Qadan's whispered questions, departing with a smile and a wink – as if they shared some secret joke.

Perhaps they did.

So she stayed silent, unsure if it was courage or cowardice that stilled her tongue. The palace was awash in cultists. Conspiracies cultivated over centuries, they worked to realize their master's goals, unaware who they truly served.

At first she did not notice the commotion – raised voices and thudding feet drowning the soft protestations of palace servants. Only when the door to her sickroom was thrust aside did Qadan turn to regard the interlopers.

"Tell me it isn't true." Arban strode into the room, his expression troubled. Judging by the familiar faces that followed, Qadan knew exactly what her cousin asked. Naoki and the others had always been too clever for their own good. The only shame was that it was far too late.

Qadan considered sparing her cousin, but after so many forced falsehoods, it did not seem right for her first words to be more lies.

"Iuchiban controlled my body these last months."

He pressed a hand to his mouth, eyes shining with tears. "How? When?"

"In the tomb." It was Naoki who answered. "You freed him."

"Not by choice." Qadan looked to her hands. "I thought we had destroyed him, truly, but Iuchiban is more than a body."

"You could have resisted," Akoya said, hands tightening into fists.

Qadan's laugh was almost a sob. "If you believe that, you know nothing of Iuchiban."

"How do we know your mind is free?" Seiji's eyes were like flecks of sharpened flint.

"Iuchiban left me at the Coming-of-Age," Qadan said.

The Crab stared at her as if she were a venomous insect.

"Even if we believe you," Tomiko said. "What of the prince?"

"Iuchiban shall be Emperor of Rokugan." Qadan shrugged. "If Rokugan remains. Either way, the Hantei line is broken."

"How can you sit here?" The pain in Arban's words almost pierced the helpless haze that snared Qadan.

"The plans were laid before our birth, every cruel step executed with meticulous precision," she replied softly. "Iuchiban wanted us to breach his tomb, just as he wanted us to discover his names and to strike at Akifumi. My soul may have been his prisoner, but none of you were free. There is nothing you can do to stop him. Not now, not ever."

"We can stop the enthronement." Naoki turned. "Masahiro will listen."

"He will die," Qadan said. "As will all of you. Iuchiban has agents within the palace. If you even reach the throne room, it is because he wishes it so."

Naoki met Qadan's gaze, her expression a mixture of pity and horror. "What has he done to you?"

"The same thing he will do to all who resist him." Qadan

found her feet, voice rising. "The emperor is not special, not wise, no more than the clans who rule through force of arms. For all our claims of duty and justice, we are slaves – souls bound to a broken wheel, doomed to act out millennia-old grudges again and again." She held them with her gaze, willing them to acknowledge the hard truth in her words. "I do not know if Iuchiban's world will be better or worse, but I *do* know resistance leads only to more pain, more suffering, more blood." She chopped a hand through the air. "And I have seen enough of that to last a dozen lifetimes."

Qadan's companions stared back at her, still trapped by their limited understanding. She had not reached them, *could* not reach them. Sorrow welled up within her, cold and choking. Qadan drifted back to her knees, head bowed.

"Do what you must."

"We shall." Akoya gave a disgusted grunt, striding from the room.

Seiji and Tomiko followed without a glance back. Naoki lingered, gaze flicking back and forth as she worried the sleeves of her robes. "Of all of us, I never thought he would break you."

Qadan did not reply. There was no point. After a moment, the doomed magistrate hurried after her comrades, leaving Qadan alone with Arban.

She could not bear to look at him. The shame of all she had done, all she *was* doing, pressed down upon her like an icy avalanche.

"It would have been better if I died in that horrible place."

"You do not deserve death." Arban might as well have kicked Qadan in the gut.

She folded forward, arms around her chest, eyes squeezed

shut against a flood of stinging tears. When her cousin stood, Qadan expected him to leave as well.

Instead, he bent forward to cup her cheek, lifting her as his voice slipped into the rhythms of invocation. Qadan gasped as a familiar presence tickled the edges of her perception.

"*Eruar.*" The name seemed dragged from deep within her, rising as a pained moan. "Kahenu, Gion…" Qadan spoke the names of her spirits, trembling before their ageless regard.

"No, please," she pleaded through cracked lips. Qadan's only solace had been knowing her spirits were free. She raised her hands as if to shield her face from the sun – a corrupt and broken thing forced to endure the sight of all she had once been. Qadan could feel her spirits' sorrow, their revulsion. Whatever bonds they had were broken, whatever relationship they shared irredeemably poisoned. Like the others, they would leave, and then Qadan truly would be alone.

Except they did not.

Qadan flinched as Eruar tousled her hair, Gion's subtle rumble vibrating through her knees and up her spine, Kahenu bright as a fresh torch. It was agony, but the pain was that of a knitting bone. The spirits reached for her, *into* her, gathering up the bits of Qadan's mind like shards of a shattered vase, binding them together not with glue or staples, but liquid gold, as if her failures were not something to disguise, but to wear like battle scars.

Arban lifted her tear-streaked face.

"Forgive me," she whispered.

"You have done nothing wrong." Arban's smile was the same as the boy she remembered, warmth spoiled by the glint of mischief in his eyes. "But you were about to."

Qadan drew in a shaky breath, grasping for her talisman

satchel – saved by Iuchiban to support his lies. She clutched it to her chest, unable to believe the swell of elemental energy as her spirits returned to their homes.

"They did not abandon you," Arban said.

Qadan gripped her cousin's forearms, pulling herself into his embrace, head pressed into his shoulder, body racked with sobs. Then she pushed away, sniffing.

"I failed to stop him once." She nodded to Arban. "I will not fail again."

"It's good to have you back." He clapped her on the shoulder. "Come, cousin. Time to help save the Empire."

Despite Arban's confidence, Qadan's heart still fluttered as they hurried down the palace corridor. If Iuchiban had meant this as a test, she had certainly failed. And if this was a trap, she was about to blunder right into its jaws. Still, the decision was hers.

Qadan's hand slipped into her talisman satchel, feeling not for the nest of fire-blackened camphor that housed Kahenu, nor the circle of banner ribbons that was Eruar's home, but the talisman she had found deep beneath the stone, in a very different tomb than the one that had claimed her soul.

She felt the prick of its blades, sharp and heartless as the power it held. In his arrogance, Iuchiban had left the talisman – a gift, or perhaps a test, Qadan was not sure. His motives did not matter. The sorcerer might have many names, but one of them still belonged to her.

And she would use it to reveal Iuchiban for the monster he was.

CHAPTER THIRTY-ONE

"I am forever grateful for your wisdom and guidance, Doji Masahiro." The prince paused his slow approach to the Emerald Throne.

Masahiro bowed deeply, conscious that all eyes were upon him – jealousy, contempt, even anger that a mere clan noble had been allowed to participate in such an important ritual. There would be a presentment later, a more elaborate service for clan and court, but this was a sacred ceremony usually attended only by those of imperial blood.

Normally the Imperial Champions would stand upon the dais, but with the Emerald position standing empty and the Jade unfilled for almost a century, Miya Katagiri and Otomo Yasunori waited upon the throne dais flanked by a veritable horde of ritual attendants. Their voices threaded the air, the low, thrumming chant seeming to slip among the curls of incense. In a few moments, the prince would ascend to receive the final blessing and assume his rightful place as Emperor Hantei XXVII.

But rather than move on, the prince leaned in. "Come, Masahiro. I would have you at my side."

It was a breach of custom, but also one Masahiro could not ignore. In inviting him onto the throne dais, the prince had as much as named Masahiro his first advisor. Although the move would ruffle many feathers in the higher courts, such was a concern for another day. For the moment, Masahiro allowed himself to bask in the reflected glow of imperial approval.

Despite the prince's confidence, Masahiro did not receive a warm welcome upon the dais. Otomo Yasunori's nod was curt, almost dismissive.

Masahiro did not mind. He was used to such disdain. What he did not expect was the hatred in Miya Katagiri's eyes as the Master of Rites began the ceremony. For his part, the prince seemed either unconcerned or unaware that he had just sown the seeds of a rift in court. Back straight, the man who would become Hantei XXVII removed a silk-bound name scroll from the folds of his robe, the slightest smile upon his lips as he handed it to the Master of Rites.

Only when the door to the throne room boomed open did the prince's composure flicker. Although he turned with all the rest, his expression showed neither surprise nor anger, but amused interest. There were shouts and scandalized gasps, although no rebuke sharper than the blades suddenly leveled at the door.

Even so, Masahiro could not quite muffle his relieved sigh as he recognized the newcomers.

"Stop the ceremony!" Naoki stormed into the throne room, Seiji, Tomiko, and Akoya close behind. Seemingly blind to the weapons pointed in her direction, she pointed an accusatory hand at the prince. "The dark sorcerer Iuchiban has possessed this man."

The assembly's confusion blossomed into a mix of reactions – disbelief, derision, even outrage.

"You dare!" Miya Katagiri's aggrieved howl rose above the tumult. The lord thrust a hand at Naoki and the others, face shaking with rage. "Seize them!"

The Hidden Guard moved quickly only to pause as Akoya stepped to the fore. "On my ancestors' souls, Magistrate Naoki speaks the truth."

"Quickly, finish the ceremony." The prince turned to Otomo and Katagiri. "Only an emperor can restore order."

The Miya lord nodded, tremulous chant almost lost amidst the cacophony. Pale-faced, Lord Yasunori followed along, casting nervous glances back at the chaos.

Naoki struggled in the grip of a pair of guards while Akoya, red-faced and shouting, tried to pull her free. Seiji bulled past the leveled spears, aided by a blast of wind from Tomiko. The guards were quick to react, however, armored bodies barring their path toward the dais.

"Release them immediately." Masahiro sought to imbue the command with a bit more conviction than he felt. Although the guards did not withdraw, a pronouncement from the high dais was enough to sow confusion among their ranks.

A shadow dodged through the chaos, ducking between a line of shouting nobles only to leap over the heads of the guards. Masahiro recognized Gensuke a moment before he landed on the imperial dais, daggers blurring toward the prince's throat.

Despite the assassin's supernatural speed, the Hidden Guard were quicker. A spear of flame struck Gensuke in the hip, spinning him around. He tumbled back, thrown bodily from the dais by a maelstrom of cutting stone.

"Assassins!" Lord Yasunori shrieked a moment too late.

"Don't harm them!" Masahiro looked from the dais to the conflict below, unsure. Naoki must be mistaken. Iuchiban was powerful, yes, but even he could not possess an emperor in the heart of the Imperial Palace. The Seppun wards would have stopped him.

It seemed impossible. Then again, in the last long months, Masahiro had come to believe many impossible things.

"We must postpone the ceremony until I can speak with my companions." He stepped toward the throne only to be stopped by one of the ritual attendants.

"Are you witless?" Lord Yasunori fixed him with a contemptuous glare. "We need *order*, not discord."

"Even so." Masahiro winced. "I'm afraid I must insist."

Neither the prince nor Lord Katagiri even glanced up – not a good sign. Expressions grim, they bulled through the ritual chants, attendants forming a living wall around the dais as Katagiri unrolled the scroll bearing the emperor's reign name.

Masahiro gripped Yasunori's arm. "If there is even a chance my companions are correct, we cannot–"

"Remove Lord Doji from the dais." Yasunori nodded toward nearby guards. "A few hours of quiet contemplation should cure this foolishness."

Hard hands gripped Masahiro's arms, irresistible as age. Against his better judgment, he struggled in their grasp, muttering vile imprecations concerning the parentage of guards who would blindly follow orders when there was clearly something questionable afoot.

A new voice rose above the clamor. Powerful yet incomprehensible, it struck Masahiro like a closed fist, rocking his head back with the force of its incantations. Gasping, he looked toward the gates half expecting the Shadowlands hordes to come pouring into the throne room.

Instead, Iuchi Qadan stood in a circle of relative calm, the thunderclap of her sorcerous cry seeming to momentarily suck the wind from the shouting, struggling mob. Something glittered in her upraised hand, a tangle of jagged edges whetted with blood. She spoke into the silence neither words nor chant, but a single name.

The prince reeled back. The shriek that clawed its way from his open mouth could have arisen from no mortal throat. His outline blurred, one moment seeming that of a young man, the next a twisting gyre of crimson-laced shadow.

A despairing moan slipped from Masahiro's lips, his captors gone suddenly rigid with shock. Although he believed Naoki and the others, in his heart of hearts Masahiro had continued to hope his companions were merely overreacting. Now, seeing their enemy revealed, he was struck by an almost overwhelming sense of doom.

Iuchiban stood on the cusp of claiming the Emerald Throne.

And Masahiro had aided him every step of the way.

"Traitor." The possessed prince hooked a hand at Qadan and the name keeper fell like scythe-cut grass. She was caught by the Iuchi daimyō, Arban, who shouted incantations even as blood poured from her mouth and ears.

"It seems my companions were correct after all." Swallowing against the upswell of fear and remorse, Masahiro glanced to the guards holding his arms, then nodded toward the corrupted prince. "Far be it from me to tell the Hidden Guard how to do their job, but…"

To their credit, the guards acted quickly. Unfortunately, Iuchiban's servants were quicker.

Daggers flashed in blood-streaked hands as ritual attendants swarmed the nearest guards, bearing them to the ground through sheer weight of numbers. The two guards who had held Masahiro fell back as a fork of scarlet lightning crackled from the dais. Iuchiban cast a glance at the throne room doors and they slammed shut, a webwork of crimson capillaries crisscrossing the wood to bar the portal.

Masahiro was not surprised when Lord Yasunori fled the conflict, robes bunched in clenched fists as he all but tumbled from the dais. What *did* surprise Masahiro was when Miya Katagiri stabbed him in the stomach.

"Insolent upstart, you thought to replace *me* in Iuchiban's favor?" The Master of Rites bared his teeth. Masahiro tried to pull away only to earn a punch to the head for his trouble. They tumbled from the dais in a tangle of robes, Katagiri on top.

"Now, Crane, your much-deserved reward."

Metal glinted in the corner of Masahiro's vision. He flinched back, surprised as Katagiri's weight was lifted from his chest.

Shosuro Gensuke helped him to his feet. Blackened flesh showed through the holes in the assassin's clothes, one arm bent at an unnatural angle. Even so, a smile tugged at the scars upon his cheeks.

"Three."

"What?" Masahiro pressed a hand to his bleeding scalp, gaze crawling to where Katagiri lay in a spreading pool of blood.

"That's three times I've saved your life."

"Fortunes be praised." Masahiro snorted. "I'll raise a temple in your honor."

Chuckling, the assassin limped toward their companions. Outnumbered, the Hidden Guard held back the flood of concealed cultists, their struggle to reach Iuchiban further hindered by the panicked court nobles darting about the chamber. They could not unleash their more powerful elemental rituals for fear of annihilating some high minister or majordomo.

Fortunately, Masahiro's companions were less circumspect.

Seiji backhanded one of the cultists aside, smashing another to the ground with the butt of the broken spear in his other hand. Akoya fought at his side, a katana in each fist, her lined face lit by blasts of scouring flame unleashed by Tomiko. Naoki skirted the edge of the conflict as if searching for an opening. A mass of ritual attendants barred their path. Armed with daggers and stolen blades, the Bloodspeaker cultists would not hold long against the onslaught, but they only needed to defend their master for a few moments longer.

Masahiro flexed his hand, chest so tight it seemed a struggle to breathe. Soon Iuchiban would sit upon the throne and pronounce his reign name, sealing dominion over Rokugan.

But the ceremony was not finished, not yet.

Masahiro's gaze flicked to Katagiri's body, the emperor's new name writ upon the scroll clutched in the Minister of Rites' bloody hand.

Ears ringing, Masahiro hurried to the fallen minister, pried the scroll from his deathly grip and thrust it into the front of his robes. He also relieved Katagiri of his dagger, a paltry weapon, but better than nothing. Up on the dais, Iuchiban had returned to the Enthronement Ceremony. All that separated the dark sorcerer from the Emperorship of Rokugan was a few dozen lines of ritual and the recitation of his reign name.

"We need to reach the prince!" Naoki shouted as Masahiro rushed up – as if he could possibly be of assistance. Better to stay behind and out of the way of slashing blades.

Seiji and Akoya bulled through the mass of cultists like a runaway wagon, opening a path to the dais. Gensuke darted up the stairs to lunge at Iuchiban.

Only to crumple at his feet.

"Did you think Akifumi would fashion a weapon that could harm me?" Iuchiban glanced down at the fallen assassin. Although Gensuke seemed to have lost control of his limbs, Masahiro could see his mouth working, eyes furious.

With a shout, Akoya and Seiji broke through the ring of cultists. Despite her age, the Lion was quick, swords arcing toward Iuchiban's throat.

The sorcerer caught them, almost casual in his movements. With a twist he snapped both blades, then spat a word of power that wreathed Akoya in bruised flame.

Snarling, the Matsu general drove a shoulder into Iuchiban's chest. A flash of rage flitted across his calm expression and he brought a fist down on Akoya's armored back. It was as if a tree had fallen upon the Lion. She fell, unmoving, still smoking from the sorcerous fire. Masahiro gave a helpless cry, images of Chiaki falling to the Shrike's sorcery rising through his thoughts. He had not been able to aid Akoya's master and was even less capable now – one-handed with only a small dagger, but that did not mean he should stand idly by.

Not knowing what else to do, he hurried up the stairs, careful to avoid the struggle between the guards and cultists.

Seiji was but a step behind Akoya. Rather than aim for Iuchiban, he slipped past the sorcerer. Masahiro thought the

Crab had missed his charge until Seiji struck the Emerald Throne. War sandals scraping across the lacquered wood, he threw his weight into the ancient imperial relic. Seiji's plan became obvious as it began to grind toward the edge of the dais – what use was enthronement without a throne?

Masahiro scrambled to help the Crab, but before he had taken a step Iuchiban let out an inhuman shriek. Turning, he clawed at the air, fingers hooked like talons even as his words blistered Masahiro's ears.

Seiji coughed, streamers of crimson mist slipping from his mouth, his eyes, his ears. He gave one final heave, as if in defiance of Iuchiban's cruel sorcery, then slumped to the ground, the throne mere inches from a drop to the hard stone below.

Masahiro stood.

"Far too late, I'm afraid." Iuchiban stepped over Seiji's body to sit upon the Emerald Throne, his expression of ageless malice strange upon so youthful a face.

Masahiro raised Katagiri's dagger.

Iuchiban's gaze flicked to his hand and Masahiro dropped the blade with a hiss, the hilt painfully cold in his grip.

"Worry not." The sorcerer favored him with a benevolent smile. "I shan't hold that against you."

A jitte spun through the air, rebounding from Iuchiban's head. He turned to regard Naoki. Panting, she raised her other weapon as Tomiko unleashed a shrieking blast of wind at the ancient sorcerer.

Iuchiban gripped the arms of the Imperial Throne, emerald darkening at his touch. "*That*, however. Inexcusable."

A wave of billowing shadow swept down from the dais,

sweeping Tomiko and Naoki from their feet. Masahiro could see them struggling against the darkness, faces strained as if they sought to throw off a heavy weight.

"Resist him, Tokihito!" Tomiko's cry was strained. "I know part of you remains."

"Tokihito?" Iuchiban laughed. "That name is gone. All that remains is the one I have chosen – for me and for this Empire. I usher in a new era, an empire free of the shackles of cruel divinity." Iuchiban's voice boomed like thunder, filling the throne room. "The Hantei line has ended."

"No, it has not." Masahiro unrolled the scroll. The name upon it scorched his eyes, a blot of darkness somehow as bright as Lady Sun. It was agony to look upon, twisting deep into Masahiro's thoughts like the thorns of some burrowing vine. He staggered under the horrible promise hidden behind the burning sigils, teeth chattering, arms burning with the urge to cast the hideous thing away.

Instead, he raised the scroll high. Masahiro may not possess a surfeit or spiritual ability, but he understood the Enthronement Ceremony and all the fastidious ritual it entailed. It did not matter what was writ upon that terrible page, only what was uttered.

"I name you Hantei XXVII, Emperor of Rokugan, Descendant of the Divine Siblings and Lord of the Seven Clans!" Masahiro bowed to the new emperor, who writhed upon his Emerald Throne, body convulsing as if in the throes of a terrible plague.

Shadow boiled away like morning mist, Tomiko and Naoki surging to their feet. Behind, Qadan limped forward, supported by a man Masahiro now recognized as Lord Iuchi Arban.

"Begone, sorcerer!" Her voice slipped into arcane rhythms, strengthened by Arban's. A moment, and Tomiko's joined the rising chorus, as did the surviving Hidden Guard.

The air shimmered around Hantei XXVII in a gyre of formless energy. It tugged at Masahiro's vision, pain lancing through his skull as he raised a hand to blot out the arcane struggle. Light flashed around his fingers, bright enough to illuminate the bones in his hand.

Then all was silence.

Slowly, Masahiro lowered his arm, almost too afraid to see what sat upon the Emerald Throne.

It was a boy – small, scared, and altogether mortal. Gone were the twisting eddies of shadow, the gnarled purple flames. There was no anger, no malice, no arrogance in the new emperor's face, only the expression of a young man grappling with a truly terrifying set of circumstances.

Masahiro let out the breath he had been holding, a grin on his face as he turned to the assembled heroes and traitors.

"I present our new emperor," he shouted. "All hail Hantei XXVII!"

EPILOGUE

The throne room was silent but for the soft crackle of braziers. The bodies had been hauled away, the tatami replaced, every spot of blood laboriously scoured from wall and pillar before an army of imperial priests ceremonially cleansed every inch of the chamber. Seeing the gold, jade, and polished wood gleaming in the winter sunlight, Naoki could hardly believe it was the same place where she and her comrades had almost died a few days ago.

Although none had emerged from the confrontation unscathed, Naoki had fared better than the others. Despite the ministrations of the finest imperial healers, both Qadan and Akoya had limped to the throne room. Fortunately, Seiji's unnatural constitution apparently was sufficient to shake off the worst of Iuchiban's curses.

Seated on the imperial dais, Masahiro's self-important smile was spoiled by the occasional flicker of pain, hand drifting to his side as if to ensure the wound had not reopened. Tomiko knelt to the left of the throne next to Lord Yasunori, seemingly ill at ease in a position usually reserved for the emperor's chief advisor.

Her discomfort was eclipsed by Gensuke, who stood at the rear of the chamber, a member of the Hidden Guard gripping each elbow. After the battle in the throne room, Naoki and her comrades had been subjected to intense scrutiny – both arcane and mundane. Although Gensuke seemed free of Akifumi's taint, from their grim expressions, Naoki guessed the Hidden Guard had objected quite vigorously to the inclusion of the undead assassin in this private council, but the emperor's will could not be contravened.

"Thank you for coming." Hantei XXVII glanced to Masahiro, who returned an encouraging nod.

"You seven know Iuchiban." The emperor's high voice seemed at odds with the gravity of his speech. "We thought it wise to consult with you before issuing a formal response to recent… events."

"We are at your service, emperor." Naoki's words echoed through the cavernous hall.

"How was Iuchiban able to circumvent the Seppun wards?" asked Lord Yasunori.

Tomiko leaned forward. "Bloodspeakers are adept at disguising corruption, shifting it to others through ritual and sacrifice. The Coming-of-Age Ceremony removed the protection of Tokihito's name. Once Iuchiban possessed the prince's body, he would have been impossible to detect."

"The sorcerer held me in thrall," Qadan added, voice somber. "Even my own family could not pierce the deception."

"And now?" The emperor glanced to his guards.

"We shall work tirelessly to develop additional wards," Lord Yasunori replied.

"Excellent." The emperor nodded. "And what of Iuchiban?"

"We cannot be sure," Naoki replied. "His spirit was driven away, but it was not destroyed."

"I shall devote the Empire's resources to seeing this vile creature annihilated." The emperor stiffened. "Legions, priests, magistrates, once the word has spread there will be no place in Rokugan for Iuchiban to hide."

They were the words Naoki had been waiting months to hear. Now they filled her with dread. "That may not be wise, emperor."

Hantei XXVII cocked his head, frowning.

"Iuchiban gains power as his names spread," she continued. "I do not believe he can be defeated so long as memory of him remains."

"Then I shall have him stricken from every record." Points of color appeared on the emperor's cheeks. "None shall speak *any* of his names on pain of death."

"And the Bloodspeakers?" Akoya asked. "Will they be bound by such a pronouncement?"

The emperor reddened, but did not reply in haste. A good sign for Rokugan's future. In many youths, temper often struck before wisdom.

"The sharper our blades, the stronger our opponent becomes." He looked to Masahiro and Tomiko in turn. "How are we to battle such an abomination?"

"Your ancestors purged all mention of Iuchiban from the records," Gensuke said. "They locked his tomb away behind a mighty jade seal and still he broke free."

"Iuchiban has risen before," Seiji said. "And been defeated. My order was founded to guard against his return."

"And how many of you remain?" asked the emperor.

"Only myself." Seiji gave an awkward tilt of his head. "But there are many among the Kuni who would join."

Masahiro cleared his throat. "Tension among the Great Clans led to the imperial expedition's demise. If the conflict surrounding Emperor Hantei XXVII's ascension is any indication, it does not seem wise to gift more authority to the clans."

Akoya chuckled. "Odd advice from a Crane."

"I may have a solution that benefits us all," he continued.

"Now *that* sounds more like Masahiro." The Matsu general's laughter dissolved into coughing.

"Let him speak," Naoki said. Although she had harbored doubts concerning the Crane's motives, he had never let her down.

"In ancient times the office of the Jade Champion was responsible for protecting the Empire from supernatural threats." Masahiro looked to the emperor. "And yet the position has remained unfilled for a century."

The others shared doubting glances, but Naoki leaned in, excited by the prospect. "A secret order within the Jade Magistracy – answerable only to the emperor and the champion themselves. It could keep Iuchiban's existence from becoming common knowledge while working to eradicate Bloodspeaker cults."

The emperor frowned, considering. "I had intended to reward you all with court positions, but perhaps your talents might better serve the Empire elsewhere."

Masahiro shifted uncomfortably. "I would much prefer the court posting if it's all the same to you."

"The same court Iuchiban's agents infiltrated?" Gensuke's grin was positively venomous.

"It seems he has you there, Crane," Akoya said.

Naoki could barely restrain her own smile. "If these long months have taught me anything, it is that Bloodspeakers come from all classes. We will need courtiers as well as priests and warriors."

Masahiro seemed about to argue only to give a rueful shake of his head. "The ancestors must have a truly wicked streak to burden their most-beloved descendant with such desirable talents."

Masahiro frowned, as if considering his next question. "And what of the position of Jade Champion?"

"The Asako will not be pleased," Tomiko said. "Since they had a hand in removing the last one."

The emperor tapped his chin. After a moment of reflection, a wide grin spread over his youthful features. "Even they could not object to another Phoenix holding the position."

Tomiko eyes widened in shock. "Emperor, my arcane abilities–"

"Were sufficient to defeat Iuchiban." The emperor nodded. "I can think of no one better."

"As my emperor commands." Although Tomiko's tone was modest, there was a glimmer of quiet delight in her eyes.

"Kitsuki Naoki, Kuni Seiji, Doji Masahiro, Shosuro Gensuke." Hantei XXVII turned to each of them in turn. "Will you aid my champion in the fulfillment of her duties?"

Although the emperor's tone brooked no refusals, this was one command Naoki was happy to obey. Unlike the others, she was already a magistrate. A shift from Emerald to Jade would only formalize duties she had already undertaken.

"And what of me, emperor?" Akoya asked.

"You would be an asset to the Jade Magistracy, General Matsu Akoya." The emperor touched his throat. "But then the Empire would be robbed of an Emerald Champion."

Akoya's mouth fell open. In all their time together, Naoki realized she had never seen the old Matsu lord surprised.

"The emperor has been *very* generous." Otomo Yasunori's smile was not at all pleased. "There will be questions."

"These seven are heroes of Rokugan. It is right they be rewarded." Hantei XXVII leaned back in his throne, voice dropping. "Also, they are the only ones in the Empire I trust."

Although Yasunori's face darkened, he wisely held his tongue.

And with that, the matter was settled. After several rounds of obeisance, Naoki and the others departed the throne room. They lingered just beyond the palace gate, as if unsure how to proceed.

Akoya gave a brusque nod. "I must review the legions."

"And I must consult with my clan." Tomiko nodded to Naoki and the others. "If only to quiet any misgivings."

"Champions." Naoki bowed low.

"Rise." Akoya slapped her lightly on the shoulder. "None of you need ever bow to me."

"Nor to me." Tomiko grinned.

"Good." Masahiro turned up his nose, expression playful. "I hadn't planned on it."

Tomiko smiled sweetly, talking as if the Crane were not around. "You would think so many humiliations would have tempered our Doji friend's pride."

Masahiro straightened in mock outrage. "Alas, it is all I have left."

Sunlight sparkled on snow-covered roofs, somehow brighter than the gilded eaves beneath. Naoki and Masahiro's breath steamed like dragon smoke in the chill morning air. Gensuke's exhalations left no trace, much like the assassin himself.

They stood for a long moment, silence edging in around them, cold but not uncomfortable.

"What if I am still Akifumi's blade?" Strangely, it was Gensuke who spoke first.

Qadan crossed her arms over her chest. "What if this is yet another of Iuchiban's tests?"

"How can we defeat something that cannot die?" Naoki added her own concern to the growing constellation of anxiety.

Masahiro wrinkled his nose. "How am I ever going to rid myself of you accursed fools?"

A giggle bubbled up from inside Naoki, bright and manic. Qadan snorted, amusement adding color to her haggard face. Even Gensuke managed a smile. Soon they were all laughing, eyes watering as the tension and loss of the last months came pouring out – much to the consternation of several passing imperial nobles.

Blinking back tears, Naoki regarded her companions. Like kintsugi pottery, they had all been shattered and repaired – the cracks between them filled with glittering gold.

Naoki wished to stay in this moment, basking in the illusion of safety, of victory. But there were yet Bloodspeakers in Rokugan, cults that would name their dark master over and over and over. The return of the Jade Magistracy was a step toward eradicating such corruption, but the road was long, perhaps even endless.

Still, Naoki had faith – in herself, in her comrades, and in Rokugan.

Iuchiban may live, but he would never triumph.

ABOUT THE AUTHOR

By day, EVAN DICKEN studies old Japanese maps and crunches numbers for all manner of fascinating research at the Ohio State University. By night, he does neither of these things. His work has most recently appeared in *Analog*, *Beneath Ceaseless Skies*, and *Strange Horizons*, and he has stories forthcoming from Black Library and Rampant Loon Press.

evandicken.com // twitter.com/evandicken

NOW IT'S
YOUR TURN
TO FACE IUCHIBAN

Adventures in Rokugan
TOMB OF IUCHIBAN
A ROLEPLAYING ADVENTURE

COMING SOON

© Edge Studio 2023 © Fantasy Flight Games 2023. All rights reserved.

Legend of the Five Rings

The titles you *LOVE* from Aconyte brought to life in audio!

EVAN DICKEN'S

The Soul of Iuchiban

A LEGEND OF THE FIVE RINGS NOVEL

READ BY KAIPO SCHWAB

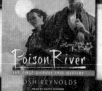

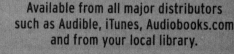

Available from all major distributors such as Audible, iTunes, Audiobooks.com and from your local library.

@TANTORAUDIO | TANTOR.COM

GO DEEPER INTO THE EMERALD EMPIRE IN EPIC NEW NOVELS!

Supernatural adventure – to the Spirit Realms and beyond.

Rokugan comes to life in this lavish full color art book.

Follow dilettante detective Daidoji Shin as he solves murders & mysteries amid the machinations of the clans.

AVAILABLE NOW IN PAPERBACK, EBOOK & AUDIOBOOK WHEREVER GOOD BOOKS ARE SOLD

ACONYTEBOOKS.COM // @ACONYTEBOOKS

© 2023 Fantasy Flight Games